AN ENTRY FOR THE

Stephen Leacock Award

FOR HUMOUR FOR

3 - 2013

Dating

Dating

Dave Williamson

TURNSTONE PRESS

Turnstone Press
Artspace Building
206-100 Arthur Street
Winnipeg, MB
R3B 1H3 Canada
www.TurnstonePress.com

Turnstone Press gratefully acknowledges the assistance of the Canada Council for the Arts, the Manitoba Arts Council, the Government of Canada through the Canada Book Fund, and the Province of Manitoba through the Book Publishing Tax Credit and the Book Publisher Marketing Assistance Program.

Printed and bound in Canada by Friesens for Turnstone Press.

Library and Archives Canada Cataloguing in Publication

Williamson, Dave, 1934–
Dating : a novel / Dave Williamson.

ISBN 978-0-88801-390-3

I. Title.

PS8595.I564D38 2012 C813'.54 C2012-901579-2

for Laura

Dating

Liz

It's New Year's Eve, 2007, and most of us are struggling to make it to midnight. Bea Branwell promised we would finish dinner before twelve, but at 9:30 she hasn't yet summoned us to the table. I'm in the Branwell living room with Cliff Knowles, half-listening to Darcy Jephson telling us about his daughter's intelligent ferret. I recall a New Year's Eve maybe forty or fifty years ago when, at midnight, someone's wife or girlfriend filled my mouth with her tongue. Tonight's New Year's wishes will be less dramatic: perhaps a brief hug, or a touch of cheeks, a squeeze of hand.

"Jenkins, you're a dog person," Darcy says.

I missed something; I have no idea how he segued from ferrets.

"Yes, I was once," I say. "Um, please excuse me while I refresh my drink."

As I turn away, I see the look of panic on Cliff's face. I'm abandoning him to garrulous Darcy.

On the way to the kitchen, I notice that the chairs in Bea's dining room aren't as close together this year. Of course. There are fewer of us. Our group has shrunk by two more.

In the kitchen, Betty Whatever-her-name-is pours herself some white wine. The tallest and trimmest of the women, Betty has been divorced twice and I don't know which surname she's using these days.

"Oh, Jenkins," she says, "I haven't told *you* yet." She flashes a disarming smile—perfect teeth, moist lips. "I should've told you earlier. I want people to call me 'Liz.' No more Betty. *Liz.* I know it's going to improve my social life."

I try it out. "Liz." It suits her face and her brunette bangs. It suits her black dress better than Betty. "*Liz.* All *right.*" I reach for the Scotch.

"Jenkins." Donald Branwell comes into the kitchen. "Haven't we got you weaned from that stuff yet? Come on, I'll pour you a rumsy-cokesy."

"No, I—oh, all right. Sure."

While I watch Donald open a new bottle of Appleton's, Betty/Liz leaves the kitchen. I want to catch up with her; she is suddenly the person I most want to chat with, but I have to humour Donald. It is, after all, his house and his booze.

This gathering is what's left of a rambunctious bunch who for years spent every winter weekend at Mount Agassiz. In the 1980s and '90s, Barb and I would start out on a cold Friday evening—even if the temperature was minus 30° and snow was threatening—and we'd drive northwest, eating sandwiches as we drove, or stopping in Neepawa for a snack and a pee break, eager to reach our cozy destination: a converted eighty-year-old railway car with a former construction shack attached as a sunken living room. The coach had bedrooms at either end and a washroom, shower and kitchen in the middle; the adjoining shack was cleverly disguised by wall-to-wall carpeting, upholstered furniture, a fireplace and a picture window that faced Nate Hirschfield's log cabin. Ours was part of a rag-tag scattering of dwellings that had been dubbed Nathanville after Nate, the ski-hill proprietor. The folks who owned places in Nathanville spent all day Saturday skiing, and every Saturday night would be party-time at somebody's place. Barb and one or both of our kids—and maybe one or more of their friends—would head off to the ski-hill on Saturday morning, leaving me in the secluded settlement. I'd achieved a certain notoriety—and an Honourable Mention in the *Winnipeg Free Press*'s non-fiction contest—with a little essay called "The Joy of Not Skiing." In it, I rhapsodized about the solitude of a winter day in Nathanville, the utter quiet conducive to reading, meditating, snoozing, occasionally writing or making preparations for dinner and pre-dinner cocktails. Come evening, when the skiers returned, pink-cheeked and exhausted, *I* was the one eager to get the party started.

Those days ended in 1999 when Agassiz closed down. We—the Nathanville Night Owls, as we called ourselves—had tried to recapture the old camaraderie every New Year's Eve since then, but in the city. We spent a portion of the evening outdoors, at Jack Hogue's house on the Red River. We didn't ski down the bank or cross-country along the frozen Red. We competed in a beanbag-tossing tournament. Jack had all the equipment we needed: two sets of four cloth beanbags; two slanted plywood sheets set up the regulation number of metres apart, with a circular hole cut out of each; a fired-up barbecue for warming our hands and keeping the hors-d'oeuvres hot. Betty and I were partners this year and we won. I attributed my success to bowling experience; Betty insisted that the key was the several highballs we'd drunk. While others huddled around Jack's barbecue or went inside between games, Betty (now Liz) and I ate and drank while we watched the others play. We eliminated every duo we faced and, in the final, we walloped Cliff Knowles and Melissa Hogue, 21–6. And now, for the last half of the evening, we are ensconced in the Branwells' River Heights home, the men in the sport shirts and jeans they wore under sweaters and parkas, the women in party clothes they changed to in Branwell bedrooms.

There's a palpable sense of anti-climax about this part of the evening, as the clock ticks far too slowly down to midnight. I make my way back into the living room after assuring Donald that his rumsy-cokesy is sheer nirvana. There is an absence of the kind of raucous laughter that used to characterize our après-ski parties. Oh, for the days when Doll Maynard would emerge topless from her sauna and make an angel in the fresh snow! Now there are no après-beanbag-toss hijinks. We're perhaps all too conscious of those no longer with us. In the past three years alone, we've lost six of our group, including Barb. You try not to think about that Agatha Christie movie, *And Then There Were None.*

"Are you going away anywhere this winter, Jenkins?"

Rosalind Sherman, who's never been part of our ski group but is a good friend of the Branwells, has turned away from the Sproxtons and, seeing me, asked her favourite question. Knowing she means *Are you going south?* I say the first thing that jumps into my head:

"Thought I'd go to Churchill this year, Rosalind. Love to get a good look at the polar bears."

"What a great idea, Jenkins! Would you have room in your suitcase for me?"

The vision of roly-poly Rosalind fitting herself into my suitcase makes me chuckle.

"Roz, you'll be basking in the Florida sun all winter, won't you?"

"Hardly *basking*. Don't you know direct sunlight is bad

for you? When I'm not golfing in appropriate attire and sunscreen, I'll be supervising the renovations on the condo."

"I thought you renovated last summer."

"That was the kitchen. Harry and I found it was too nerve-wracking to be here while tradespeople were tearing things apart down there. I had to fly down five times and even then they got the island wrong. So now we're closing in the balcony and extending the living room. You wouldn't believe the trouble the condo association gave us. Threatened to take us to court. Well, you don't threaten Harry, as you probably know."

It seems that Rosalind is always renovating *something*. Barb used to call her Rozzie the Renovator. I want to remove myself from her clutches, but I realize that, from this particular corner of the living room, I have a good view of Liz. She and Harry Sherman—Rosalind's Harry—are chatting with Darcy, who has Liz holding his drink while he makes elaborate gestures; he might be demonstrating how a factory robot moves, or perhaps he's acting out a scene from an old *Frankenstein* movie. From my vantage point, I think Liz looks quite lovely. She *does* seem more attractive as Liz than she looked earlier as Betty. I see her take a sip of what I'm sure is Darcy's drink, but she and Harry and Darcy are too wrapped up in Darcy's story to notice. Meanwhile, I try to toss comments into my own conversation with Rosalind: "Are you moving the furniture out while they work or just covering it?" and "What did the condo association object to?" and "Remember when Barb and I went down to visit and you took us to that restaurant where a magician performed at our table?" And Rosalind gives me long answers that I barely hear. Liz catches me watching her and she rolls her eyes and smiles.

It's close to eleven o'clock when Bea calls us for dinner. We file into the kitchen, pick up plates and serve ourselves from the platters assembled where earlier the booze and soft drinks had been. Being trapped with Rosalind would normally have intensified my weariness, but Liz's smile has given me new incentive to see the evening through. And when I enter the dining room, Liz waves at me. By some magical coincidence, or Bea's astute planning, my place at the table is next to Liz.

"Jenkins, how *are* you?" she says as I sit down.

I think she's drunk. Before I can answer, she leans so close that her breath tickles my ear and she whispers, "Brave of you to listen to Roz so long. I'd die."

I glance at Rosalind's husband, who's sitting on the other side of Liz. He's busy talking to Amy Jephson. The chairs on the other side of the table are only now being filled.

"What exactly was Darcy going on about?" I ask.

"Who the hell knows?" She *is* drunk, or feeling no pain, as they say.

"I saw you take a sip of his drink."

"Damn lot better than mine."

"So you knew it was his."

"Not really, but who's keeping track? Besides you, I mean. Wine?"

"Yes, please."

She pours pinot noir into my glass. "Guard it with your life," she says, and we both laugh.

We eat and banter and drink. Others speak to us, Bea makes a couple of toasts, Harry toasts Bea and Donald, and I comment, loudly enough for everyone to hear, on how marvellous the meat is. I'm grateful, in these days of vegetarianism and dieting and animal rights and having to cook for myself, to be able to enjoy a fine slab of medium-rare roast beef.

I fetch dessert—apple pie à la mode—for Liz and myself, and, when I sit down again, she quietly says, "Is it going to be another year until we see each other again?"

It could've been a harmless question, mere speculation about whether we might see each other by chance somewhere before next New Year's. But it strikes me as forward, suggestive, even sensual. Maybe the booze has helped her scale the wall of my bereavement. *It's nearly two years now, isn't it?* she might be thinking. Before I can give her some kind of encouraging reply, Donald is on his feet, pointing at his wristwatch.

"My god, you people," he says, "it's two minutes to twelve! Get yourselves into the living room! Bea, turn on the radio! Or the TV!"

All of us scramble into the living room and form a circle, crossing our arms to hold hands with our neighbours. Liz doesn't end up beside me. She isn't even looking at me as she grabs the hands of Cliff Knowles and Melissa Hogue. Bea puts the television on loud enough that we don't have to watch it; we just count down with the announcer.

"*Four ... three ... two ... one ... HAPPY NEW YEAR!*"

We raise our clasped hands and move toward each other in the circle and we repeat, "*HAPPY NEW YEAR!*"

We sing "Auld Lang Syne," most of us making noises that sound like the words because we don't know them. After that, we yell "*HAPPY NEW YEAR!*" again and cheer, and then we break from the circle to give our individual greetings—our handshakes, our brief hugs, our touches of cheeks. And suddenly there's Liz in front of me saying, "Happy New Year, Jenkins," and she takes my face in her two hands as if she needs to line me up to make sure her aim is true, and she kisses me on the lips, lingering there for at least two or three heartbeats.

When she lets go of me, I blurt out, "Let's *not* let a year go by ..." but she's turning away from me because Darcy tapped her on the shoulder, and he takes her and bends her back in a Great-Lover pose, and I don't know if she's heard me or not.

As the New Year greetings wind down, someone turns off the TV and Jack calls for our attention. He's holding a clipboard and the scoresheet he efficiently keeps every year. It's time for him to give out the beanbag competition prizes.

"I know it's well past bedtime for most of you," he says.

A couple of the guys heckle him and we laugh.

"All right, all right," Jack says, "I know most of you want to clear out of here. And you know you'll get out of here a lot sooner if you what?"

"Sneak out now," someone says.

Laughter.

Jack scowls.

"*Shut up and listen to you*," someone else says.

"*Correct*," Jack says. "All right, where is my lovely assistant?"

Bea steps forward carrying two or three bulging bags. "Vanna White at your service," she says.

We all know the bags contain prizes, mostly items like pens and coffee mugs bearing the logo of Jack's son's computer business, Hogue's Digital Solutions. There's a prize for everyone. Jack keeps the presentation to the champs until the end, and he comes up with new categories for everyone else. The first two prizes are for "The Best-Dressed Team," awarded to Cliff and Elaine; and that's followed by "The Most Serious Team" and "The Team with the Most Original Toss," and others I lose track of in the laughter and the cheering. At last he calls out, "And now, a fine example for us all, handily knocking down every obstacle that came their way, this year's undisputed champions, *Betty and Jenkins!*" He is immediately jeered, the group roaring more or less in unison, "Not Betty, LIZ!"

"What?" Jack says, bewildered.

"Betty wants to be called Liz," Bea explains.

"Nobody told me," says Jack. "Why didn't anybody tell me?"

Liz and I step forward and Bea presents us with our prizes: red polo shirts with the words *Champion Tosser* printed in bold Gothic capitals across the back. It's a shirt you wouldn't want to wear in England.

The festivities are over. The gang heads upstairs for their coats. I feel I have to speak with Liz before she leaves, even though I'm not at all sure whether I want to see anyone socially. To go out somewhere with a woman, I mean—just the two of us. But I'd left her question hanging. *Is it going to be another year before we see each other again?* That requires an answer. I attempted one, but she didn't hear it. At the same time, I don't want to turn this into *a big deal*. She was maybe just being friendly. She's drunk. She's probably forgotten she even said it. I follow her upstairs anyway. At the door of the bedroom where others are picking up their coats, I tap Liz on the shoulder.

"Do you want to go to a … a movie or something sometime?" I say.

She smiles, even chuckles, as if that's the craziest suggestion she's heard in a while.

"See?" She laughs. "My social life is getting better already!" She keeps laughing. Finally, she takes a deep breath and says, "Listen, I'm going to my daughter's for a few weeks. Why don't you call me when I get back?"

"Maybe February first?"

"Sure. I'm in the book."

She goes into the bedroom for her coat. It isn't until she's left that I realize I don't know what last name she's using these days.

Seeing Eye-to-Eye

"You're going on a day-ate, you're going on a day-ate!"

It's Bea Branwell on the phone, taunting me in a childlike, singsongy voice.

"Hello, Bea. What—"

"News travels fast, Jenkins. Liz e-mailed me. She has a date with you on Tuesday night."

"Well, I don't think you can call it a date. In fact, people don't date anymore, do they? We're just going to see a movie—*Juno*, with that young Canadian woman everybody's talking about."

"Ellen Page, yes. Jenkins, a date is a *date*. And I'm glad you're going out. It's time you did. And Betty—well, Liz—is a hoot. You'll have fun. Let me know how it goes—if you don't, Liz will."

The call bothers me. I hope this isn't going to be a gossip item. *Jenkins is taking Liz Oliver out on a date.* (Yes, I did find out what surname she's going by—her maiden name.) I realize how uncomfortable I am with the concept of *dating*. I think it's a term that, like *courting*, is passé, partly because the practice has fallen into disfavour. In recent years, *date rape* and the drugs associated with it have cast a bad light on dating. *Internet dating* seems to lead more often to women being victimized by perverts than to nice wholesome relationships. And they tell me kids don't go out on formal dates—they meet in casual groups. But another more personal reason for my discomfort is my status as a widower. How long is bereavement supposed to last? Will a date officially end it? Barb died less than two years ago, but I don't think it's indiscreet of me to go to a movie with a woman. Yet can I look Barb's portrait in the eye, knowing I'm going out on a date? Is there going to be a time when I have to assign her portrait to a drawer? It sits in a place of honour in the dining room and, now that I'm going to a movie with Liz, I feel sheepish every time I pass it on my way to the front door.

People will tell you that, as you get older, you forget close friends' names and what you ate for dinner yesterday, but you recall in detail events from your youth. As I anticipate this, this *date*, I have a vivid recollection, not of one of the countless times Barb and I went to see a film, but of *the very first time I took a girl to a movie.*

I was in Grade Eleven. The dating picture for me hadn't been encouraging. Our high school was a power in boys' basketball and most of the pretty girls went out with members of the team. I wasn't a member. I didn't play inter-room hockey either—I couldn't skate. Those were my excuses for not going out very much. But a pleasant new girl had moved into our neighbourhood and she appeared in my class, at the desk right next to mine. Her name was Shirley Kernigan. I

thought I might ask her out before the other girls got to her with a resumé of my defects.

A few minutes before class one day, I waited in the hall and saw her approaching our room alone. She was about medium height with dark hair cut just above shoulder length and pulled back from her pretty face. Her clear forehead and her wide-open brown eyes seemed to be somehow *right out there* in front of her—or *in your face,* as the kids say today. She smiled all the time and was always ready to give you her bubbly laugh. Her demeanour encouraged you to *make* her laugh. She had a rather thick waist and her modest bosom seemed to sit up higher on her torso than it did on most girls.

"Shirley," I said, and she gave me her beaming smile, "would you like to go to a movie this Saturday?"

There was a cardinal rule in those days: *When you ask a girl out on a date, especially if it's the first time, it must take place on a Saturday night.*

"Oh, Jenkins, I'd love to!" she said, and she laughed. It wasn't a derisive laugh, the kind a girl today might use to cut you down, accompanying a sarcastic "Yeah, right!" No, it was a genuine show of pleasure.

I suggested we go to see the double-bill at the Windsor Theatre and she said that sounded super. I said it was close enough to walk to.

I was sixteen but I didn't yet have my driver's licence. My older brother Allan had that past summer given me a few lessons in his company car. I may not have been athletic, but I'd gotten the message that *You need a car to get a girl*, so I was trying to learn. However, something happened on one of my practice runs that aborted the lessons for a time. I was driving south on St. Mary's Road with Allan beside me. The street had two lanes of concrete going south and two going north and in between was a grassy, muddy median with two sets of streetcar tracks. Somehow I wandered far enough to the left to have the driver's-side wheels slip off the pavement down onto the median. When I jerked the steering wheel to get back into my lane, the left-front wheel was several inches below the top of the concrete and too close to get purchase on the slab. By some law of physics, the car was wrenched sideways and since I, stunned, still had my foot on the accelerator, we bounced over both sets of streetcar tracks, across the two north-bound lanes and directly toward the plate-glass display window of Swanson's Drug Store. Luckily, there were no streetcars going in either direction at the time and no immediate traffic headed north. Allan was able to get one foot past my accelerator-foot onto the brake. We came to rest on the boulevard a few feet from Swanson's. As tolerant and even-tempered as Allan was, he didn't plan to take me out for another lesson anytime soon.

So Shirley and I would walk to the Windsor. When we spoke after classes on the Friday before our date, she told me she welcomed the walk.

"I walk as much as I can," she said. "People don't walk enough, do they? If they keep driving everywhere all the time, the human species is going to evolve into—I don't know—maybe seals or something?"

She laughed, and I thought, *Not me, I can't swim either.*

I called for her at 6:30 on Saturday evening. She lived two streets from mine. It was warm, one of those gorgeous windless September evenings that often followed a cold and windy preview of winter. Shirley came to the door in what I can only describe as an old-fashioned dress—what people used to call a frock. Her dark hair was arranged the same way she always wore it, pulled back from her forehead and held there by blue barrettes that matched her dress. Her gaze was so direct, her wide eyes so unblinking, I thought she'd be incapable of anything devious. There was no sign of any other family member.

"Let's go," she said. She stepped outside and closed the door. She wasn't carrying anything—coat, purse or wallet. This gave her a carefree air, a hint of recklessness that wasn't evident in her face. "I'm looking forward to this."

As we started down the sidewalk, I took her hand. She chuckled, but it seemed the natural thing to do, if only to prevent our hands from banging into each other as we walked.

After a minute or two of silence, she said, "Can you type?"

"Yes," I said, "I took Typing in Grade Ten as an extra option."

"They wouldn't let you do that at the school I went to in Regina. Not if you were in the matriculation program."

"I didn't take it for very long. About a month—just long enough to learn where to put my fingers."

She laughed and I blushed, as if I'd said something dirty.

I felt a need to explain. "When I found out we'd be tested for accuracy and speed, I dropped the course."

"I know what you mean. It's okay to be under pressure to answer a theory test, but having someone standing over you with a stopwatch—I wouldn't like that, either. I found out I can take a class during my spares. Maybe I'll do what you did, just learn the basics."

"Who's the teacher?"

"Mrs. Smithers."

"Oh, that's who I had. You'll like her." We walked past Martha's, a local hangout, and I didn't see anyone I knew. There were people here and there, cars going by, a streetcar—and I found it so natural to be with Shirley, I felt my usual inhibitions dropping away. "She's a bit of a character. When she's giving you a drill, she stands up on a chair and claps her hands to the rhythm of the keystrokes." I stopped walking, held my hands up ready to clap and did my Mrs. Smithers impersonation: 'Hands in home position! Altogether now! A-semi-S-L-D-K-F-J-G-H!'"

Shirley laughed and clapped her own hands, applauding.

The ice, it seemed to me, was broken. We were getting along well. I recalled my good friend Claude's edict: *You impress beautiful girls with your brains. You impress bright girls with your sense of humour.* Shirley was pretty enough but, based on what I'd seen of her performance in class, she definitely fit into the *bright* category. And I was definitely amusing her.

We crossed to the river side of St. Mary's Road just before The Junction—where St. Anne's Road began. I told her more about Mrs. Smithers's foibles as we approached the Windsor.

I don't remember what was playing that night. I do know the program consisted of an animated cartoon, a newsreel, a preview or two, a so-called B-movie, and a feature movie that had run in one of the larger theatres downtown some weeks before. Almost four hours for thirty-five cents.

I do remember feeling nervous as we walked up to the theatre. I wondered if I'd see kids I knew, couples who'd be in the back rows getting set for their long bout of necking. Where were we going to sit? I couldn't expect Shirley to sit at the back among the neckers. Or could I?

There was no-one I recognized going in at the same time as we were. I paid at the box office. In the lobby, Shirley declined my offer of popcorn, saying it was too soon after dinner. We entered the theatre, where low-wattage lights were still on. Shirley hesitated.

"Where would you like to sit?" she asked.

I glanced at the back row and recognized only one person, a guy named Merlin from our class. He was with a girl I didn't know but she was wearing a tight, light-coloured sweater that showed off her bosom. I doubt if Merlin and I had ever exchanged more than two words, but he looked surprised to see Shirley and me together on a *date*.

"I don't know," I said, "somewhere in the middle?"

"Sure," Shirley said.

There was no sign of relief or disappointment in her voice as we moved down the aisle to a row almost exactly in the middle. Two old couples stood to let us in. We sat. I remembered the Life Savers I'd brought from home.

"Candy?" I asked.

"Oh! Thank you."

I peeled back the wrapping. "If you don't like lime—"

"I love lime. Thanks."

And that was the end of our conversation because the lights went down and the first short came on. I have no recollection of what we watched over the next four hours. My head was full of what we must look like to the people behind us. I was overly conscious of not only Shirley on my right but also the person on my left, a middle-aged woman who smelled vaguely of mothballs and whisky and had the habit of uttering little grunts in reaction to each scene. I stole glances at Shirley, her pretty profile half-smiling and illuminated by the light from the screen. She kept her hands in her lap, away from my right hand which I sort of dangled off the end of the armrest, ready in case she wanted to seize it in a burst of emotion. At some point, I thought of touching her to offer her another candy but I didn't want to startle her, so I kind of waved the package in front of her face, and she cleverly took one without making any contact with my fingers. I thought of Merlin and the other guys in the back row, shoving their tongues down their dates' throats and doing terrible things with their hands, and I glanced at Shirley's mouth, which was looking more enticing by the minute, and I could hardly wait to get her home for what would surely be an amazing good-night kiss. She might even invite me in and let me mimic Merlin on her chesterfield.

The movies seemed interminable and yet, when I reminded myself that this was the first time I'd ever been to the pictures with a girl, I wanted to savour the experience. I glanced at Shirley innumerable times—trying to glance without turning my head so that I wouldn't annoy the person behind me—and she maintained that half-smile, as if she too was imagining something nice that would happen later.

As the lights came up and Shirley and I exchanged innocuous comments on the films, I tried not to look toward the back of the theatre. I didn't want to see girls hastily rearranging their sweaters and blouses and guys wiping off their mouths. Envious as I might've been, I tried to tell myself that such behaviour was juvenile and unseemly. We proceeded slowly to the exit and, when we reached the back rows, all the kids who'd been sitting there were gone.

Outside, Shirley said, "I liked both movies a lot."

"Yes, I did, too," I said. "Do you want to go to Martha's for a snack or something?"

"Oh, thank you, but no, I should go straight home, if that's okay."

"Sure," I said, relieved because I didn't relish the thought of running into the characters who frequented Martha's.

I don't remember what we talked about on the way home—maybe the films, or maybe we returned to Mrs. Smithers's typing class. All I know is, I was nervous. There was, after all, no guarantee that we were going to kiss. My wanting to kiss, my anticipating a kiss, my *expecting* that Shirley would want to kiss—those feelings had no basis in reality. Though all boys believed a kiss was the natural ending to a pleasant date, I knew there were girls who didn't believe in kissing on a *first* date.

When we reached Shirley's house, the lights inside appeared to be off, but the front outside light was on. I walked up the steps with Shirley, hoping she'd ask me in. She turned to me, still with that little smile on her face.

"I had a lovely time," she said. "Thank you, that was fun."

"Maybe we could go out again sometime?"

"Yes, I'd like that." There was an awkward but poignant moment, she looking at me with that smile, her face so open and guileless and trustworthy and fresh and happy. "Well, it's late. I'd better go in."

I had a sudden sinking feeling—maybe that moment, that awkward and poignant moment when I just looked at her, had been the time for me to make a move … and it had gone. Still looking at me, there under that beacon, she turned toward the door.

"Good night, then," she said, but before she turned her face away I put my arms around her and I didn't care who could see us, standing on the concrete stoop bathed in million-watt incandescent light.

I kissed her earnestly yet as tenderly as I could.

How long should a good-night kiss last? I think I was determined to make this one go on as long as Shirley let it. Imagine my delight when she allowed me to hold her and kiss her for—oh—seconds and *seconds*; she even *participated*, gently pushing back.

I made only one mistake.

My curiosity got the better of me. I wanted to see how Shirley looked with those big eyes of hers closed in rapture. I opened one eye—a slit, really—I just wanted a peek.

I'll never forget what I saw.

The one eye I could see was *wide open*. While we were kissing! Like the eye of a child's doll. So huge, so close, so *eerie*.

The sight shook me. "Oh!" I cried.

Shirley gave me the smile that up to that moment had seemed beatific. Now it seemed diabolical.

I said, "Good night!" and, trying not to appear scared or in a hurry, I left.

"Good night!" she called after me. "I had a great time!"

Juno and After

I haven't told my daughter Tracy that I'm going out to a movie with a woman. I heard from her two days ago—reports on how her husband Clay's business is progressing and how their daughter Mason is doing in school and in her gymnastics career. I chose not to tell her about this date. But what if I run into one of Tracy's friends—or Tracy herself—at the cinema?

I find what I think must be Liz's place; I can't see the number anywhere. There is no driveway; most people in her district have garages you reach by a back lane. A Lexus sits parked directly in front of her house, and beyond that is a fire hydrant. I decide to back up and park behind the Lexus. I put the gearshift in reverse, only to be jolted by a loud honk. A car comes out of nowhere and passes me. The driver gives me the finger.

Rattled now, I do an exaggerated shoulder check, see no-one coming up behind me, yet expecting another car to appear and bear down on me—no, not a car but a menacing Hummer, or maybe even a *tank*. Unconvinced that the street is clear, or even that I have the right of way, I park behind the Lexus. I feel as unsure of myself as a student driver on his first lesson, not the best way to arrive at Liz Oliver's. The prospect of walking her to the car, installing her in the passenger seat, starting the car and moving it away from the curb and around the Lexus, driving down streets, stopping at stop signs and red lights, squeezing into the hell-bent traffic on St. James Bridge, making the correct turns, and finding a parking spot at the Silver City Cinemas at Polo Park seems exhausting, even foolhardy.

I check behind me again before I open my door. It will not surprise me if a goddam cyclist appears at the moment I get out and crashes into me. Seeing no-one, I step out and close the door. I walk to the rear of the car and see that it's at a slight angle to the snowplowed curb—but it will do. I aim the key-fob at the car and press the lock button twice and the little honk reassures me the way it always does.

There is no shovelled path across the boulevard but there are enough footprints in the snow to make the approach to the hedged yard easy. Metal numbers on one gatepost tell me this is indeed the address I'm looking for. Beyond the gate, a sidewalk cleared of snow leads up to some steps and a front door sheltered by an eave. As I walk through the gate, a robust-looking man dressed in an overcoat and white scarf comes out of the front door and down the steps. I'm surprised. I think Betty's social life has not only improved since she became Liz, it's *crowded*, so much so that this fellow is barely getting out before the next shift arrives.

I feel as if I'm in a Monty Python sketch; we need only bowler hats so that we can tip them and say in that semi-bored but infinitely polite English manner, "Good evening." "Good evening." We converge. We can't ignore one another.

The porch light illuminates me but his face is in shadow, though I can tell he's handsome in a pudgy way, with a full head of grey hair. There is nothing I can think to say but:

"Good evening."

"It *is* a *very* good evening," he says, and, as he passes me, he uses his remote start to activate the Lexus. That gesture and his comment do nothing to comfort me.

I walk up the steps and ring the bell. I try to compose myself, show Liz the cheery face she last saw on New Year's Eve. If this fellow has left her in a dishevelled state, I'll do my best to ignore it. It occurs to me that I have no idea what her relationship is with her ex-husbands. Perhaps still chummy. Oh, I have no experience with this sort of complication.

Liz opens the door.

"Hello, Jenkins. How are you? Come in for a sec and I'll fetch my coat."

For the moment that I see her before she turns away, she looks absolutely ready to go out: makeup in place and not too much of it, an immaculate teal sweater and matching skirt, knee-high medium-heeled boots, auburn hair falling in a well-brushed way to her shoulders. She returns with a hip-length brown leather jacket, arranging a light scarf at her neck.

"You probably saw my brother on your way up the walk," she says, donning the jacket. "Did you see him? You've likely met him before, have you?"

"Your *brother*." I break into a smile. "No, I don't know him. You mean the fellow with the Lexus. We did say hello."

"Why didn't he introduce himself? I told him you were coming here. Honestly. That man has his head in the clouds sometimes."

"Are we off, then?"

"Yes. I'll just set the alarm."

I wait outside on the steps. She comes out, locks the door

and looks at me in the porch light as if verifying who I am, or as if she can't quite believe we're doing this.

"Jenkins," she says. "It's good to see you."

"Good to see *you*, Bet—I mean, *Liz*. Did you have a good visit with your daughter?"

"My daughter? Oh, yes, yes, I did."

"Where does she live?"

"Oh, Jenkins, is that your car? Do you want to—no, it's all right, I can get in okay."

We cross the snowy boulevard and I open the passenger door for her. She sits down bum-first and shifts her legs into the car and I close the door. The night is pleasant—very little wind. Still, I'm on edge. I hurry around to the other side. No cars are coming from either direction. I get in, start the car and fasten my seat belt.

"Oakville," Liz says.

"Sorry?"

"My daughter lives in Oakville. You know—near Toronto?"

We talk about Oakville, I telling her about an old friend who lives there and is an accomplished singer and hiker; I often think of him striding out along the Bruce Trail belting out hymns to the wildlife. Liz tells me about her daughter's husband, who's an instructor of Animation at Sheridan College. Her story of students who'd worked on some well-known animated Hollywood films makes the drive through River Heights and over the St. James Bridge go quickly. We're soon parked and headed into the noisy, glittery arcade atmosphere of Silver City. Despite the youthful surroundings, Liz makes sure I pay senior rates.

"I'll buy the popcorn and the drinks," she says. "What kind of drink do you want?"

I don't want popcorn because I'm watching my daily sodium intake—and besides, popcorn dries out my throat and makes me cough—and I don't want a drink because

I'm already worried that I'm going to have to urinate halfway through the movie, and a drink will bring it on even sooner. Yet, because this is a first outing with a woman I don't know that well, politeness and *wanting to seem like a nice guy who understands the contemporary woman's desire to share expenses* wins out over pragmatism, and I let her buy me as big a Diet Coke and bag of popcorn as she buys for herself. I tell myself that maybe the popcorn will sop up the drink. And I do manage to manoeuvre us into seats on an aisle without having to say that I might have to make a dash for the can midway through *Juno*.

Each seat has a receptacle for a drink and we take turns holding the bags of popcorn while we shed our jackets. We have to stand up a few times to let people into our row. Liz eats and drinks and I pretend to as the lights dim. I worry about having to cough or pee or both and, sure enough, the urge to do one alternates with the urge to do the other by the second preview. I'm about to excuse myself or—better—slink out so unobtrusively that Liz might not notice that I'm gone, when I realize that I have nowhere to put my popcorn. I think, *What the hell, I'll take it with me and I'll chuck it out in the men's room*, but on comes the announcement of the feature presentation. I tell myself I can hack it, at least for a reel or two.

Suddenly there's a teenaged girl's bare legs and her panties dropping down and there's a boy's knobby knees—he's sitting in a large easy chair—and she's climbing into his naked lap.

It's all tastefully done, but it seems as graphic as a porn flick. I'm embarrassed. I hope the boy isn't going to start moaning, the girl squealing or crying out. There's none of that, thank goodness. The scene does go on longer than I wish it would. I'm relieved when it ends, but I'm worried about how explicit this movie is going to be, and only a minute or so elapses before Juno is in a drugstore washroom, peeing onto a pregnancy stick … and that brings my previous urge back as forcefully as a running faucet would—or a sudden downpour of rain.

"Be back in a sec," I whisper.

"What?" Liz whispers back, but I'm already headed out.

Common as such fare might be in these explicitly enlightened times, I hadn't expected an opening sequence like that in *Juno*. Friends who'd seen the movie called it "cute" and "hilarious." Of course, my discomfort has little to do with *what* I've been watching and everything to do with *who*'s watching it with me. Not because I think Liz is straitlaced but because I don't know what she thinks of movies like this. Or because I know she doesn't know what *I* think about movies like this. Maybe she thinks I *expected* to see what we saw in the opening sequence, that I get *off* on shots of teenaged girls peeing and having sex in easy chairs.

I finish, wash my hands, throw away my popcorn, take a deep breath, and return to my seat. Liz takes the first opportunity to fill me in on the bit I've missed, and she doesn't question what happened to my popcorn.

When the movie ends, we do what people do only occasionally in a cinema: we applaud. Other people join in.

"Nice uplifting movie, wasn't it?" the woman on the other side of Liz says.

"Yes, it was," Liz says. "Nice to see a movie without violence."

I'm glad to hear her say that. "And none of those frantic cuts and crazy car chases," I say.

"You really believed Jennifer Garner—Vanessa—was going to be a perfect mother for the baby, didn't you?" the woman says.

"If not perfect, at least loving," says Liz.

Outside, on the way to the car, Liz says, "I liked Juno's line, 'We should let it get a little cuter.' That cracked me up."

Liz laughs as she gets into the car. We're getting along well.

"Want to go somewhere for a drink?" I ask, as I get in and buckle up.

"Oh. I suppose we could … or why don't we go to my place? I think I can find something—I know I have beer."

This is unexpected. I tell myself I'm not the gangly boy from the movie and Liz isn't Juno. And yet my mind is leaping ahead to a tastefully lighted scene in Liz's sitting room and she's making it obvious that she wants to be kissed. Or …

As we talk more about the movie, we head for her place. I'm feeling nervous now, wondering what Liz expects. But it's a good feeling. I like her looks, I like the fragrance she's wearing, and we agree on how we feel about the movie. It was after all a *feel good* movie, the perfect prelude to a compatible *tête-à-tête*. There is no need to rush anything; simply enjoy the conversation, enjoy the drink, enjoy the first embrace …

I do have qualms. I don't want to spoil the evening in any way, either by expecting too much or making an unwanted move or being oafish because I'm so out of practice. And I'm feeling some guilt—this might after all be *too soon* … I look forward to the drink. That will relax me.

I park in front of her house and we go inside. I take off my leather jacket while she de-activates the alarm, turns on lamps and scoops up errant magazines. She comes back to take my jacket.

"Thanks," I say. "Um—my shoes. I should …" I wiped them at the door but I think I should take them off. I dislike being shoeless, especially when I'm unsure whether or not one of my big toes is poking through a sock. I lean against the wall and lift one foot.

"Oh, you don't have to," she says, "or you can if—oh, *would* you?" She stands there, watching me put my foot down then raise it again.

"Sure, why don't I," I say, undoing a lace.

She turns away as if not wanting to see what I uncover—no, she's going on with the business of hanging up my jacket. My shoes off and set to one side, I enter the living room, relieved that both my socks are intact but wishing they were a better match for my olive trousers, not that insipid grey.

There's a silence and I realize that *Juno* has been the sole topic of conversation for the past half hour or so. I look at a bookshelf, hoping to see a title that might trigger a comment or an anecdote.

"Sit where you like," she says, waving at the sofa. "I'll get that beer. Does it matter what kind?"

"Not at all."

She goes out to what I assume is the kitchen. I hear a refrigerator door close. I hear a cupboard door squeak shut. I look around at the furnishings. They seem rather old-fashioned, or traditional, but they aren't worn-looking. Perhaps they had belonged to someone else. Perhaps Liz can't afford new things—I have no idea how financially well-fixed her husbands left her. It's a big enough house. Of course, *I* don't have new furniture. You reach an age when you *make do*.

She brings in two Bud Lights with glass tumblers perched on them. She sits beside me on the sofa and we both pour beer into our glasses.

"Jenkins, it's good to see you," she says. "Cheers."

"Cheers."

I take a sip. She takes a swig, and another.

"Ahhh," she says.

"That hits the spot," I say.

There's a lull. She takes a third swig.

"Your place is very nice," I say.

"Oh, no, it isn't. Needs new drapes, new carpet, new furniture, new interior paint job. But I'm procrastinating. I might sell the place in the spring."

"And go into a condo?"

"Move to Australia."

"Really?"

"Or Arizona. I don't know. Give me a better idea." She downs another mouthful as if she's parched.

"I thought you liked it in Winnipeg. But I guess if there's nothing keeping you here ..."

"Is there something keeping you here?"

"My daughter—and my granddaughter."

"Jenkins, it's *really* good to see you." She leans forward and, just like that, there's her face coming closer, her eyelids fluttering, her lips pursing—

The telephone rings.

"Shit," she says.

She surprised me by making a move and she surprises me again by letting a ringing phone interfere. She sets down her glass on an end table and goes to an alcove just off the dining room. She faces me as she picks up a walk-about receiver.

"Hello," she says in a cool voice, as if she wants to convey annoyance. But then: "Oh. Hello." Her voice softens. She turns away from me. She goes somewhere where I can't see her. She might've closed a door, too, because I can't hear her. Or maybe the caller is doing all the talking.

I curse the phone call. Everything was happening too fast but, at the moment of the ring, there was nothing I wanted to do more than kiss Liz Oliver. It's so long since I kissed a woman the way she seemed to want to be kissed. And there she was—so ready. Surely she'll deal with the call and come back and want to get right back *at it*. But what if the call is bad news? What if she still has a parent alive somewhere and that parent has taken a bad turn? What if her daughter has been in an accident? Or her daughter's in a bad marriage—the guy has threatened her, or hit her, or walked out on her? Doe she have any other kids? Does her daughter have kids? I know almost nothing about Liz. Is she still on speaking terms with her ex-husbands? Does one of them call every so often to give her a hard time? *To stop her from getting up-close and personal with her new friend?*

I drink more of my beer. I fidget. The longer she's gone from the room, the more I worry. How can she keep me waiting so long?

At last, she reappears. She stands in the archway between the dining room and the living room. She looks agitated, her face flushed. She smiles, and then she doesn't smile.

"Is everything all right?" I say. I stand up.

"No, no, sit, please," she says, "I mean, yes—oh, please sit and let me … let me explain."

I sit on the edge of the sofa. She comes in a few steps and sits, not on the sofa beside me but on a chair facing me.

"I'm sorry," she says, "I—I've been misleading you. What I told you earlier …"

"That wasn't your brother."

She gives a nervous chuckle. "Oh, yes, of course it was my brother—the man you saw leaving here—he was my brother. I meant … about visiting my daughter. I *did* visit my daughter, in Oakville, but I was in Toronto, too, meeting someone … someone you know. Oh, this is so difficult …"

"There's another man in your life."

"Darcy Jephson."

"I see. And Amy doesn't know."

"Let me finish. This thing with Darcy is on and off. I didn't want it to go on, this sneaking around. I told him that in Toronto. I looked forward to going out with you. Everything out in the open, everything above board."

"And now … ?"

"Well, now—I—I'm sorry, this is so awkward—that was him on the phone. He's told Amy. About me. And he's told her he's leaving her."

"I see. Wow. And … and you're happy about this."

"I think so—Jenkins, *I don't know!* I never thought he'd—he was always saying he was going to, but ..."

"Do you ... do you want to talk about it?"

"Oh, Jenkins, I can't. I mean, *you* can't! You can't stay, I mean."

"What—"

"Jenkins, I'm so sorry. I had a nice time with you, really I did—but I have to ask you to leave. He—he doesn't know you're here. And he's coming over here right now!"

Serene Doreen

Disappointment is no stranger to me. Especially where getting to know girls and women is concerned. As I leave Liz's house, I glance back at her and think she looks more attractive than ever. Hearing the door close behind me takes me way way back to another evening, another closing door.

It was my very first date. I think about it until I reach my house, where I pour myself a Scotch and soda and sit down and think about it some more.

It was morning, maybe twenty minutes before I had to line up with the rest of the junior-high kids. I was watching for Sylvia.

Sylvia had been in my class from Grade One and I noticed changes in her body before I noticed them in any other girl's. Sylvia had breasts in Grade Six.

I was fourteen, the age when boys today start stealing cars

and smoking dope. The year was 1949 and I was in Grade Nine. It was June, near the end of my last year of junior high.

I was about to graduate from Johnstone School, where I'd spent nine years—the first nine years of my education—no kindergarten or pre-school or nursery school back then. Because you had to move to Yarwood High School for Grade Ten, they had a graduation ceremony at the end of Grade Nine. There was a party planned for after the ceremony, a kind of dinner party at a restaurant called The Chocolate Shop. Some of the boys had decided they'd take dates.

Sylvia and I were good friends. We'd competed for top marks in most grades but it was good-natured competition. She was kind of like an older sister; she had a confidence that enabled her to be sociable with anybody, including the teachers. She had an aura of sophistication that told you she possessed worldly knowledge. I could talk on the same level with her about homework and world news, but we never talked about what she liked in boys or whether she was going out with anyone. My friend Claude said he'd seen her downtown with an older guy who drove a car. It was out of the question, then, that I would ask *her* for a date, but I felt comfortable asking her who she thought might be available.

There she was, coming down Blenheim Avenue—still a long way off but I could tell it was her because the sun was glinting off her long blonde hair. I dodged a couple of grappling second-graders and moved closer to the steel-bar fence, close to the spot where Sharky Stevens got his tongue stuck on the steel one winter. Sylvia carried a three-ring binder and maybe a couple of books in front of her chest—in those days there were no back-breaking backpacks.

"Hi, Sylvia!" I called, waving as she drew closer.

"Jenkins, you're never here this early. What's up?"

That was the year the kids started calling me Jenkins. I didn't like it at first, being called by my surname. My full name is Robert Henry Jenkins and my parents called me *Bobby* but, as Claude said, that was too "sucky." Claude hated his own real name, Reginald, and managed to get kids to call him by his uncle's. I'm left-handed and my friend Bud tried to get *Lefty* going, but nobody bit. Claude was the one who started *Jenkins* and it stuck, which disappointed me at first, but I soon saw I was getting off easy. Consider Donny, who was called *Bamboo* because he was so thin. Or Louise, whose large behind got her *Tremendous Bum*—TB for short. And then there was Bert, whose parents couldn't afford to install hot water—he was called *One Tap*. Kids could be cruel.

"I was thinking I'd like to take a date to graduation," I said.

"Jenkins, if you're asking *me*, I'm flattered, but you know I—"

I blushed. "Yes, I know you have a boyfriend—I just thought you might know who in our class doesn't have a date."

"You are a bit late. Some girls were asked weeks ago … but, listen. I know a girl who would be happy to go with you. Do you know Doreen Holden?"

For a moment I'd thought Sylvia was either going to tell me I was out of luck or suggest one of the plain girls in our class. The mention of Doreen Holden astounded me. She was in Grade Eight and she was *beautiful*. You know the kind of thirteen-year-old girl who has a grown-up face? Who already has a grown-up *shape*? Whose way of walking delivers a clear message that *I am not a boy*? That was Doreen. A lot like Sylvia herself, you could say, except brunette, and maybe not as outgoing.

I tried to keep my composure. "We—we sort of walk the same way to school every day," I said.

In those days, there was no cafeteria in the school, no vending machines. I think there was a room you could go to at noon if you took your lunch, but most of the kids went home. I always went home for lunch and so did Doreen, so I saw her four times each day. I kept my distance. The way she walked so regally and the way her friends walked on either side of her, looking at her, deferring to her, she looked as if she were being escorted. You had the feeling that, if you wanted to speak with Doreen, you'd have to go through her guards. The walk from my street, Vivian Avenue, to the school took me four blocks along Rue Des Meurons. I walked past Essex, Ellesmere and Harrowby Avenues before cutting through the infamous Frog Pond to get to Johnstone School. For much of the year, the Frog Pond was impossible to navigate. It was mostly ditches and bushes, and in spring the ditches filled with murky water; in summer the bushes were a mass of leafy branches and ugly thorns. Some kids were afraid to cut through the Frog Pond at the best of times, believing that evil creatures—or at least bullies—were waiting there ready to pounce. Doreen lived on Ellesmere. If I timed leaving home right, I could arrive at Ellesmere just after she and her acolytes had turned onto Des Meurons. I could walk behind them and watch her, appreciate how lovely and feminine her shoulder-length brown hair was, how serenely she floated over the tarmac road. Serene Doreen. They never ventured into Frog Pond territory, they went around it. Some days when I found myself ahead of them, I'd plunge into the Frog Pond thicket, trying to appear nonchalant. It was an attempt to show Doreen and company that I was fearless. I'd get badly scratched by thorns, or I'd leap and land just short of the other side of a ditch and get wet feet or stained trousers. And Doreen would never even know.

"She likes you," said Sylvia.

I blushed. Had Doreen and I ever spoken? Did she even know who I was? Sylvia had me believing that Doreen might be just as shy as I was, that she'd been *admiring me from afar.*

"How do you know her?" I asked.

"Our parents are good friends. We get together for family meals. If you like, I'll ask her if she wants to go to grad with you."

At first, I wondered about the wisdom of having a go-between, but I liked the idea of being spared the anxiety of approaching Doreen, or going through her bodyguards on the street, or worse, going through her parents on the phone.

"Would you?" I said.

"Sure," said Sylvia.

And together we walked to the junior-high side of the school just as the bell rang.

After school that day, I went a different way home—over to St. Mary's Road and past Page's Department Store and the Beehive Grocery—so that I wouldn't have to see Doreen. Next morning, I went a few minutes early so that again I wouldn't see her and look for *signs*.

That morning, Sylvia saw me on the way into our classroom and said, "It's settled. She'd *love* to go with you."

Just like that! I had a date. My first. With a beautiful girl! I wanted to know exactly what she'd said and how she looked when she said it, but I mentioned none of this, trying not to show excitement. It was my first attempt at guile.

Speaking quietly so that other kids couldn't overhear, Sylvia said, "I told her you'd call her to confirm all the arrangements."

In my giddy but fragile state, I was alarmed. Did she mean it *wasn't* settled? I said, "Arrangements?"

"You know, what time you're going to pick her up, *how* you're going to pick her up, who else you're going with, that type of thing."

I hadn't thought about any of those things. The logistics.

All I'd thought about was going somewhere accompanied by Doreen, having the other kids see me with Doreen. And when the evening was over, *kissing Doreen good night.* I hadn't given one second of thought to the logistics.

When I went home for lunch that day, and back to school and home again after four, there was no difference in Doreen's demeanour. If she looked at me, I didn't see it. Each time, she had two or three of her friends with her and once I thought I saw one of them look at me and snicker, but otherwise there was no change. I wondered if Sylvia actually *had* spoken to her. But, as the next couple of days passed, I supposed that Doreen's aloofness was part of her mystique.

Meanwhile, I worked on the logistics. My older brother Allan said he would be happy to drive my date and me to the Chocolate Shop. We would take Bud and his date Vera with us. We'd pick up Doreen at 6:30 and swing by Vera's, where Bud would be waiting. We'd arrive at the Chocolate Shop downtown by seven. At the end of the evening, Bud and I would split the cost of a taxi to take the girls home.

The night I phoned Doreen with this information, I made sure my mom and dad were both busy. She was sewing and he was at his basement workbench building a new platform for her to stand on when she put the wash on the clothesline. The telephone was mounted on the wall in the hall that went to the bedrooms. I closed the door to the living/dining room and dialled the number I'd memorized.

"Hello?"

"Hello," I said, my heart racing. "Could I speak with Doreen, please?"

"This is Doreen."

"Oh, hi. I wanted—oh, sorry, this is Bob Jenkins—well, Jenkins. I thought I'd better—I mean, thank you for saying you'd go to grad with me."

"It's okay."

It's okay? Not *You're welcome*? "I thought I'd better—I should—call you to tell you what time I'll pick you up and all that."

"Sylvia said you would."

I barged ahead, telling her all the arrangements. As I told her, I thought, *Gosh, I'm going to have to get her a corsage.*

She didn't comment, so I said, "How does that sound?"

"Fine," she said.

Fine? I thought. Just *fine*?

There was a silence. "Okay, then," I said. "I'll see you on Thursday, June 24, at 6:30."

"Okay."

"Well, I'll see you lots of times before that, won't I? On the way to school and on the way home."

"I guess so."

There was another silence.

"Good, then. Thanks again, Doreen. Good night."

"'Night."

I was disappointed that she hadn't been more expressive, but I wasn't disappointed for long. Now that I didn't have to converse, I could enjoy the euphoria of having my first date all planned, and I was anticipating *my first kiss.* I was imagining the softness of her lips and the sweet taste of her lipstick. I couldn't concentrate on my homework that night and I barely slept.

Next day, when our paths converged en route to school, I was with Jack, another buddy of mine, and she was with two of her girlfriends. She and I barely made eye contact. But, before the day was over, the word was out. *Jenkins is taking Doreen Holden to grad.* Guys kidded me about it. Girls whispered to each other behind their hands and pointed at me. It was the highlight of the schoolyard gossip for at least a day, and then it was old news, but I could sense an improvement in my status.

The day arrived all too swiftly. The graduation ceremony took place in the afternoon in the school gymnasium, and I sat through it with a smile on my face. My parents were both there, beaming. Afterward, my mother asked me which girl was the one I was *stepping out* with. I explained that Doreen wasn't there because she wasn't in Grade Nine.

"Aww, that's a shame," Mom said. "I wanted to meet her."

At 6:15, Allan picked up the keys from my father's dresser and he and I headed for the garage. Dad still drove the two-door '38 Ford he'd had since before the War, and Allan was proficient at operating the standard gearshift. Each of us opened one of the two garage doors that swung out to the left and right. Despite the warm night, I felt comfortable in my very first sport jacket, worn with tie, white shirt, dress trousers and oxford shoes. Dad had shined my shoes to his First-World-War-cavalry standard. And Mom had bought the boxed corsage. This first date of mine had become a family project. I carried the corsage in front of me as if it were a newly baked chocolate cake.

"If you like," Allan said, as he drove up the back lane, "I'll come for you when the party's over." At twenty-one, he drove the car every chance he got.

"No, it's okay," I said. "Bud and I want to take a cab. Thanks, anyway."

"Impressing the ladies."

"Something like that."

We were on Ellesmere in no time, approaching the Holden house too early.

"Want to drive around the block?" I said. "We've got ten minutes yet."

"What if she sees us drive by?" said Allan as he slowed down. "Don't worry. Girls like it when you're early."

We stopped in front of her house. Doreen's house was newer than ours, a storey-and-a-half with no verandah but concrete steps leading up to the front door. I noticed that the back door wasn't at the back but at the side, at ground level.

"Aren't you going in?" Allan asked.

"I'm waiting another minute."

"I thought maybe you wanted me to honk."

"No!"

He chuckled. He was being good about this. Even though he'd been dating for a few years, he didn't lord it over me.

"Okay," I said, opening the door. "See you in a minute."

"Take your time. She'll want to put the corsage on before she leaves."

"Right."

I stepped out and closed the door quietly. I started up the sidewalk and headed for the side door.

"*Jenkins!*"

I stopped and looked back. Allan was outside the car.

"The front door," he said.

Now I was embarrassed, hoping no-one had seen me or heard him. I always went to the back door when I visited a friend, but this was different. I should've known that. I waved to Allan and went to the front door, nearly tripping on the top step.

There was a doorbell. We didn't have a doorbell at our house. My dad had talked about having one installed, but it seemed silly when everyone used the back door and you could hear anyone coming through the gate, and a knock on the storm door in winter or the screen door in summer resounded through the house. A doorbell seemed impertinent; you could adjust a knock to the situation or to your personality, but all doorbell rings were alike: insistent, brash, startling. At the same time, a doorbell was modern, a sign of progress, so I thought I'd better use the Holdens' to show that I too was modern and progressive.

I pressed the doorbell button. The inside door was open and I heard the *ding dong* inside. Through the window in the outside door I saw a woman appear. She opened the door and gave me a welcoming smile.

"Hello!" she said. "You must be Jenkins. Come in. I'm Doreen's mom. She'll be down in a minute."

"Hi," I said.

"Is that your brother in the car? Does he want to come in?"

"No, no, he'll be all right."

"It's nice of him to drive you, isn't it? You must be good friends, you and your brother."

"Yes, we are," I said, entering and closing the door behind me.

Mrs. Holden was much younger than my parents, maybe forty. She was about Doreen's height, but chubby and not quite as pretty. She had brown hair that was lighter than Doreen's and eyes that I thought of as merry.

"Do you want to come in and sit down?" she asked.

"I—thank you—I'll wait here, if it's all right."

"I should get back to the dinner—Doreen's dad and her brother are waiting at the table with their tongues hanging out. Oh, is that for Doreen?"

She gestured at the box I was carrying.

"Yes—"

"Why don't I give it to her? She'll want to put it on in front of a mirror." Mrs. Holden took the box and opened it. "Oh! Isn't it lovely!" She disappeared from the vestibule.

I heard her speaking with someone—Doreen's dad—but I couldn't tell what either of them said. I heard a boy—Doreen's brother—laugh. I was a neophyte in these kinds of social matters, and I was sure that any comments or chuckles were derisive and focused on me. I thought at any moment the boy and his father would poke their heads around the corner, point at me and jeer. I'm sure Doreen's parents saw this whole situation—this *date*—as *cute*. For all I knew, this was *Doreen*'s first date, or at least her first formal date. Maybe there was something wrong with the corsage. Maybe it was too skimpy, or too *fussy* for a thirteen-year-old girl's first date.

As I stood there, quaking, I heard more muffled comments. I heard cutlery on china—the male Holdens were being fed. Minutes passed, but I reminded myself of what I'd heard about girls of good breeding: they must never appear to be too anxious to go out on a date—keep the boy waiting. Of course, it was taking extra time to put on the corsage. I imagined her mother helping her, the two of them standing in front of a mirror, admiring the effect.

Mrs. Holden reappeared. She stood there like a page announcing a princess, pointing with both hands to the doorway she'd just come through.

"Here she is!" she said, and she made a fanfare noise like one of those trumpets used in King Arthur's time.

"Oh, Mother." Doreen stepped through the doorway, sounding annoyed but looking unruffled. Indeed, she looked as serene and wonderful as a thirteen-year-old girl with a beautiful woman's face could look. She was wearing a gold dress that seemed perfect for the white-carnation corsage. She was carrying a handbag and a raincoat.

When you are fourteen and your date's mother is standing there, you don't say, "You look beautiful!" I was dazzled by her, overwhelmed, and even if I'd known what to say, I couldn't have spoken.

Mrs. Holden filled the silence. "Now, you two have a great time. Remember, Doreen, Jenkins is graduating from Grade *Nine*. This is an important event and a cause for celebration."

"Mother, I *know*," said Doreen.

It struck me later that Mrs. Holden saw in Doreen an indifference she didn't expect in a child of hers and she was doing her best to get her daughter into the spirit of the occasion. I would observe over the years that mothers and daughters seldom agreed in their opinions of the daughters' young men. But that evening, all I thought about were Doreen's luscious-looking red lips and how much time we had to fill before I could get at them. Mrs. Holden was, none too subtly, reminding Doreen that she had some responsibility in making this *a great time*, and surely it included a lingering goodnight kiss.

"Good night, Mrs. Holden, we won't be late," I said, as Doreen preceded me out the door.

"Good night, Jenkins. Do have a wonderful time. Good night, dear."

"'Night," Doreen said, without turning her head.

She walked rather stiffly down the steps. I thought she was worried about falling—perhaps she wasn't used to high heels, though hers weren't very high. Maybe I should've taken her arm, but I wasn't sure how. As she reached the sidewalk, I started to hurry past her to open the car door, but I saw that Allan was holding it open as if he were a chauffeur, and he had the front passenger seat tipped forward, expecting Doreen and me to ride in the back.

"Doreen, this is my brother Allan," I said, proud of myself for remembering to introduce him to her and not the other way around.

"Hi," she said.

"Hi, Doreen. Wow, you look terrific."

"Thank you."

She sounded pleased. Why hadn't I said something like that? Well, I was glad Allan had said it. He was like an extension of me, wasn't he? He was family.

"Here, let me hold those," I said.

"Thanks," she said, giving me her coat and her handbag.

She ducked her head and stepped into the back seat, taking care not to let the corsage or her hair touch the car. I got in beside her and sat back, still holding her coat and handbag.

"I'll take them now," she said.

I laughed nervously and gave them to her. As Allan drove, Doreen, sitting behind him, leaned forward as if she might be checking the speedometer or was about to whisper in his ear. There were no seat belts in those days. I tried to think of something to say, but the sight of her, the smell of her perfume, the very presence of her, daunted me. The silence lengthened. It was Allan who eventually spoke.

"How was school this past year, Doreen?"

"Oh, fine, thanks."

"Who was your home-room teacher?"

"Mr. Feeney."

"Big Al! How is he?"

"All right, I guess."

"People used to say he favoured the girls, but I liked him. Had a pretty good sense of humour. Does he still sit on kids' desks?"

"Yes."

"He sat right on my notebook once. Smudged the ink. Let's see—forty-five. Is this it?"

Allan stopped the car in front of Vera's and, as I was saying, "Yup, this is it," as jauntily as I could, Vera and Bud burst out of the little white frame bungalow. They ran toward us holding hands. Vera's mother stood in the front doorway, waving.

I stepped out of the car.

"Bud asked me to go steady!" Vera announced.

"Just tonight," said Bud. "Just two minutes ago."

"And of course I said yes. Isn't that exciting, Jenkins?"

"Congratulations," I said, not sure if that was the right word.

Their new status made it mandatory that Bud and Vera sit together, so I let them get into the back beside Doreen.

"Hi, I'm Vera. You must be Doreen. I'm sure I've seen you at school."

"Pleased to meet you," said Doreen, not sounding pleased at all.

"And I'm Bud. Oh, Vera, that's Allan, Jenkins's brother."

"Your driver for the first half-hour," said Allan.

"Did you hear our news?" said Vera.

"Yes," said Allan. "That's terrific."

I got into the front beside Allan, and we were on our way downtown.

"Took me completely by surprise," said Vera, "and I don't know who was more excited, me or my mom. I don't know if you saw her there at the door, big grin on her face. She just about squeezed the stuffing out of old Kolotylo here. 'Course, he's not complaining—if you saw my mom, you know why ..."

Vera jabbered on and on and Bud threw in a few snickers. I glanced at Doreen, who was sitting back now that Vera was beside her. Vera was leaning forward and punctuating everything she said with her hands, hitting Bud on the knee every time she mentioned him. Doreen had a grin on her face as if she found Vera entertaining. I resented Vera's monologue at first, but, as we approached the Norwood Bridge and she showed no sign of winding down—she was telling us about a girl named Jackie who'd wrecked her parents' living room by letting kids dance in it—I thought at least Vera was filling the void.

As we arrived at the Chocolate Shop on Portage Avenue, Vera was still talking, and she was still talking as I stepped out onto the curb and tipped the seat back. Bud jumped out and turned to help Vera, kissing her on the lips as she emerged; she managed a noise of appreciation. They headed for the restaurant, Bud's arm around Vera, his hand encroaching on her hip. They made me feel how much of a couple Doreen and I *weren't*. Yet I still had expectations as I offered Doreen a helping hand.

"Have a good time," Allan said.

"Thanks," Doreen said—to him, not to me. She got out of the car carrying her coat and her bag and ignoring my hand.

I told myself this wasn't being mean-spirited on her part; she didn't need help.

"Thanks, Allan," I said, and I closed the car door.

He drove slowly away, moving expertly into the flow of evening traffic. Doreen headed for the restaurant and I kept up with her, my hand behind her but not touching her. Bud and Vera held the door open for us.

Up the street, Claude, Gerry and Jack were walking toward us—without dates. "Anybody who takes a gash to Grade Nine grad is a suckhole," Claude had told me. The word was that he was going to smuggle a mickey of rye whisky into the Chocolate Shop. In those days, even if you were old enough—twenty-one—you couldn't get alcoholic beverages in a restaurant, nor could you take your own. The law allowed adults to purchase booze only at a government-controlled liquor outlet, and you had to take it directly home. The only public place in which you could consume anything alcoholic was a beer parlour, a barren, soulless place with a concrete floor, usually connected with a hotel. In Manitoba, only men were allowed into such places, only beer was served—not even soft drinks or food—and the beer came only in draught glasses, and you could buy only two glasses at a time.

"Wait up, Jenkins!" Gerry called.

Much as I wanted to ignore them, I couldn't. They were friends of mine. I felt out of sync—as people would say now—being with a girl when the likes of Gerry and Claude were not. They were the guys who constantly regaled me with stories of their girl exploits, the things they did *to* girls, never *with* them.

"Are you going to introduce us?" said Gerry.

"Okay," I said. Doreen was already inside.

"Did you buy her that corsage?" said Claude. "I bet you did, you suckhole, Jenkins."

Claude would say things like that, usually just out of earshot of girls, and I hoped Doreen hadn't heard him. Inside, I introduced the three of them to Doreen, and Gerry started right in talking with her about school, especially Home Ec, so that he could tell her about the neat stuff he'd made in Shops. Doreen didn't exactly become animated, but she did answer his questions, and she showed interest in the nutcrackers he'd knurled. Claude was only half-listening, but when Gerry mentioned nutcrackers, Claude stifled a guffaw and, walking away, he exploded. Gerry was such a smoothie, he kept right on talking, ignoring Claude's antics, and I didn't think Doreen knew what Claude was laughing at. Embarrassed by Claude and feeling as if Gerry had stolen my date, I noticed Bud waving from a booth.

I interrupted Gerry. "Uh, we're sitting with Bud and Vera. We'd better—"

"Okay, I'll see you later," Gerry said. "Nice to meet you, Doreen—and that's a beautiful corsage, Jenkins. Well done."

That was the kind of guy Gerry was, great at chatting up the girls, and able to make you feel good even while he was charming your date. Most of the kids were seated at booths and I nodded to the ones we passed on the way to ours. Doreen and I sat facing Vera and Bud, pretending to ignore Vera's smudged lipstick and Bud's hands roaming to various places on Vera's torso. Vera's agreeing to go steady apparently gave Bud certain liberties he'd never taken in public before, though Vera good-naturedly swatted him every so often. She talked and talked. A waitress came and we all ordered hot turkey sandwiches. Doreen smiled a lot and didn't say much. She didn't direct a single comment at me, but I didn't mind because I couldn't think of much to say, either. We were all glad to see Gerry when, between the main course and dessert, he came to visit us, squeezing in beside Bud. I sort of basked in Gerry's aura, telling myself that Doreen would like me just because Gerry was a good friend of mine.

Claude and Jack didn't come to visit. Claude told me the next day that he tried to get my attention a couple of times but "you were hooked on that ginch." He said he'd been giving guys snorts of rye in the men's can. Later, when I mentioned this to Jack, he said it was a load of BS.

I had hoped we'd see Sylvia, but the word was she'd gone somewhere else—likely with her mysterious car-driving boyfriend.

Some people were going to Marjorie's house to play records and the four of us were invited, but Bud was anxious to be alone with Vera, and Doreen said she wasn't allowed to go anywhere else. I was glad. All I could think about was the good-night kiss that my warped mind figured had been guaranteed by Mrs. Holden.

Bud arranged for the taxi. When we went outside, I was alarmed to see that it was still daylight. It was 9:30, but this was June. How could we kiss at a back door that wasn't at the back when the sun wasn't even down? I held the cab door open for Doreen and Bud and Vera, telling myself we'd find a way.

"Do you two want to come in?" Vera asked as we drove up to her place.

"No, they don't," Bud said.

"Bu-ud!" Vera said.

"It's okay, we'd really better go," I said, chivalrously, not blaming Doreen.

"I'll settle up the fare with you tomorrow, Jenk," said Bud.

On the short drive from Vera's to Doreen's, I cursed myself for not getting into the back with Doreen once we'd dropped off the others. Nobody spoke. When we arrived at the Holdens', the whole neighbourhood seemed floodlit. I paid the cabbie, giving him a ridiculously high tip that brought forth only a grunt from him, and Doreen waited in the back until I was out and opening her door. In the moment it took for her to gracefully step out, she seemed to me to be the most beautiful person I'd ever seen. I was astounded that I was with her, that this girl who represented everything feminine and untarnished had spent the evening as my date.

I followed her up the sidewalk, not daring to look at the front window in case her brother and father were there watching us and smirking. Surely her mother, the romantic, would've sent them somewhere out of the way. As we walked around to the side of the house, and Doreen still didn't speak, I thought, *Even if she doesn't want to kiss me, she'll feel she owes me a kiss after all the money I spent on her.*

Doreen tried the door. It was open.

"I had a nice time," she said, turning to me, looking right at me. I couldn't believe how beautiful her eyes were, how perfect her lips looked in the daylight.

"So did I," I said.

"Good night," she said, smiling.

"Good night," I said. There was a moment of hesitation. When I played that moment back in my mind, I saw *that* was when I should've kissed her.

She must've thought I didn't *want* to kiss her!

She turned and went inside, unkissed.

My Old Buddy, Claude

Claude's wife Gillian sits me down in a firm love seat, one that's kinder to old folks than those you sink into, and, sitting beside me, she slaps my thigh and says:

"All right, Jenkins. When are you moving out of that house?"

We've just finished a delicious roast beef dinner prepared by their part-time maid Lydia, who is now clearing the table, after which she'll carve some slices of meat and package them with leftover asparagus and potatoes and gravy for me to take home. Claude and his wife are one of a small number of couples who regularly invite me for dinner, never expecting me to return the favour. I always bring a good bottle of wine. At Claude's, no matter how expensive my bottle is, it disappears into the unknown—perhaps his cellar but more likely one of Gillian's charities. At table, we drink his wine. As Gillian speaks, Claude's off somewhere, supposedly opening one of his most expensive bottles of port. I know he's likely enjoying a smoke outside first. Claude still smokes in 2008, the only man I know who started smoking *after* doctors confirmed that cigarettes could kill you.

"I don't know," I say. "My daughter Tracy tells me there's a new condo development near her place. She thinks it'd be fun if I could walk over to visit her and Clay and my granddaughter. But the cost of a condo—and the condo fee—I think I can live more cheaply where I am. The house is paid for."

Besides that, I've grown used to living alone in the house. The thought of downsizing furniture, books and clothing to fit into a condo scares me. I've *expanded* to use every room. Besides the bedroom where I sleep and the bedroom I use as an office-cum-library, there's the bedroom where I keep my summer clothes and stacks of photo albums and videotapes, and the bedroom where I keep my blood pressure monitor. I read in the living room and watch TV in the basement family room, where I also keep my stationary bike.

"But surely that's not the *point*," says Gillian. "All right, I know there's a period when—it's been how long now?"

"Since …?"

"Barb passed away?"

Passed away. I'm not a fan of that euphemism. I don't know why people are afraid to say *died*—is it too harsh? Too final? Death is harsh and final. And it happens to all of us.

"A little over two years," I say.

"Yes, and I know it takes people a while to adjust, and it's good to stay in the house where everything is familiar and you're surrounded by memories and you can pretend Barb is just away somewhere—"

"Gillian, I'm not pretending. I *know* Barb is gone. We had a cremation and a funeral. Remember, Barb was sick for a long time, and one day at home, I was broiling steaks for us and she came into the kitchen and said, 'I think you're ready to carry on without me.'"

"Oh, that's so *sad*! But so sweet in a way, so brave, as if she was passing the torch. So then there's no reason for you to stay in that house. Surely it's a burden. To clean it, to maintain it—touching up the paint, taking care of things that go on the fritz—shovelling the snow, mowing the lawn ..."

"I have two women who come in and clean once a month—and I'd still need them if I was in a condo—"

"I wasn't thinking of a condo. No, the best thing for you is one of those assisted-living places—one of the nice new ones—where your meals and the cleaning and everything else are done for you."

Claude rejoins us. He's taller than I by about two inches and still quite lean. Unlike me, Claude still has a thatch of dusty grey hair. He comes in carrying a tray that holds two glasses of port and a tumbler of Perrier water accented by a wedge of lime. Since Claude's wet bar is fully equipped, the port is in short, heavy-based glasses meant especially for that particular liquor. As he approaches me to give me mine, I smell tobacco smoke.

"You'll love that," he says. "Nectar of the gods."

"Thank you," I say, though I'm certain my taste buds are numb from the wine and manhattans we'd had earlier. "Mmm. Beautiful."

He hands the tumbler to Gillian.

"Ta," she says. "Claude, I think Jenkins is aghast that I'd suggest he move into that new assisted-living place."

"Jeez, Jenkins," Claude says, "haven't you heard? Since the invention of Viagra, those places are hotbeds of fornication."

"Oh, *Claude*," says Gillian. "Jenkins, let me explain that I've done considerable research on Assiniboine Park Gardens and I highly recommend it. In fact, I've invested in it."

"Ah, the man hears the truth at last," says Claude.

Gillian ignores him. "Jenkins, if I give you a brochure, will you at least consider it?"

As I mumble a reply, she's already headed out of the room, presumably to fetch the brochure. Gillian is exactly the kind of wife Claude talked about in his youth: stylish, active on boards of cultural organizations, independently wealthy—her grandfather was a grain baron. She is also weird: loves snakes, plays the clarinet, and wears her dyed brunette bangs long enough to cover her eyes; you have the feeling she's looking at you through a grass curtain. Claude told me years ago that she'd had her heart broken by their only child, a daughter who called herself Che (after Guevara) and ran off to California with a rock musician.

The instant Gillian leaves the room, Claude produces a framed photograph.

"Look what I came across the other day," he says.

He holds it in front of me. It's a wedding photo: Barb and I flanked by our attendants.

"Good-looking bunch, weren't we?" I say.

"What was the name of the plump little wench beside your bride?"

"You know—that's Barb's old friend Gloria."

"Of course! Do you remember, at your twenty-fifth anniversary, how she'd been on a fitness kick and she showed up all slim and trim?"

"It was just after her husband left her ..."

"And guess who had his way with her."

"I know, you devil! You lived in Toronto then and you'd left Gillian at home—"

"Shhh!"

We both laugh raucously. It makes me recall the way Claude used to rate girls when we were in high school, how we'd cackle every time he made his judgment. For girls he disliked: "I wouldn't piss on the best part of her." For girls he liked: "I wouldn't kick her out of bed." When the newly sleek Gloria appeared at our party, he upgraded her from the ranking he'd given her at the wedding.

"All right, what's so funny?" Gillian says as she comes back into the room. "There, Jenkins," she says, handing me a glossy pamphlet, "there's a phone number on there, but, if you want to go and look around, let me know and I'll be glad to arrange it."

"I found this old photo," Claude explains. He hands it to Gillian.

"Who—oh, Jenkins, this is your wedding! Aww—look at the dresses—when was this again?"

"Fifty years ago."

"Fifty years! Exactly fifty?"

"Fifty years ago last June."

"Doesn't Barb look outstanding!"

"She was a gorgeous bride," says Claude.

For all Claude's lascivious banter when we were young, he was always respectful of Barbara. When he first met her, he told me afterward that she was "very tasty." The few times we double-dated, he brought respectable girls, most often a minister's daughter I thought he might be serious about. I was always glad that Barb had Claude's approval.

"See what a fine best man I was?" says Claude.

"The two of you look so thin!" says Gillian. "Didn't anyone ever feed you? The girl next to Barb looks well-fed, though."

Claude guffaws at that.

"Who are they all?" says Gillian.

I say, "The maid of honour is Gloria Steenson, Barb's best friend from childhood." The names of the others trip off my tongue, including that of Don Stanhope, a fellow I worked with at Radisson's.

"You worked at Radisson's?" says Gillian.

"Yes, in Advertising, for nearly twelve years, before I went into teaching."

"*I* worked at Radisson's in the summers and on Saturdays while I was at university. I was even part of their young executive program until my father talked me out of it. He said he didn't want me to be a *shopgirl*."

"And then I came along," said Claude, "and swept you off your feet."

"*Kidnapped me* is a better description."

I stand up and indicate it's probably time for me to go. Gillian gives me what she calls my "care package" and says:

"Jenkins, you know the Jephsons, don't you?"

"Yes, they used to be part of our group that skied at Agassiz every winter."

"Then you've heard about Darcy leaving poor Amy. It's probably old news by now but my *god*, Jenkins, what was the man *thinking*? I see Amy at the golf club—she's only just started playing again. I gather it happened way back in February. I said to Claude, Darcy's too old for a mid-life crisis, isn't he?"

"And *dumb*," says Claude. "She'll sue the ass off him."

"I don't know about that," says Gillian. "Amy's still quite willing to take him back, or so she says."

"Do we know who the broad is that led Darcy astray?"

"I don't know her," says Gillian. "Liz somebody, I think."

I shrug, visualizing Liz's lips descending on me that night. I feign not only ignorance but disinterest as I turn to the door.

It's 10:30 when I leave Claude's mansion on Lamont Boulevard, north of Corydon. I've drunk too much; my daughter Tracy would be livid if she knew I was driving after an evening at Claude's. Many times, she's told me, "If you have to drink, *take a cab*. Or call me and I'll come and get you. *God*, Dad." Her generation is far more responsible in matters like driving under the influence. I drive just under the 80-k.p.h. speed limit south on Route 90, which is relatively free of traffic, this being a Thursday night in August. I'm headed for my home in Fort Richmond, where I've lived for the last forty-one years. While concentrating on my driving—and sucking away on Halls cherry-flavoured Mentho-Lyptus candies—I think about Claude's photo. And that reminds me of the missive Tracy gave me less than two weeks ago. It's something Barb wrote on our honeymoon. We refer to it as *Barbara's Time Capsule*, because it's addressed *To the daughter I hope to have someday*, and she put it in a sealed envelope right after she wrote it. She saved it, intending to give it to Tracy when she reached a certain age and when she fell in love. I never read the piece, and I've resisted looking at it since Tracy gave it to me. I thought it might be painful to read, but the wedding photograph has piqued my curiosity.

I pull up to my single-car garage with the adjacent concrete slab that was once used for a second car. I get out to open the garage door; I still have a manual one in these days of electronic openers. (I still use cheques to pay my utility bills, I still go to my bank to get spending money from a live teller, and I never take my cell phone with me when I go out.) The inside of the garage is uncluttered, except for my bike and my electric mower.

I go into the house and look over at the portrait sitting in a place of honour on the buffet. It's my favourite photograph of Barb.

"Gillian was just as nutty as ever," I say aloud. "Pushing me into an old folks' home. Claude plied me with liquor as usual—but he showed a bit of his sentimental side. Still had the framed photo you gave to every member of the wedding party. I was impressed."

In the kitchen, I take a cereal bowl, a juice glass and a tablespoon and set them on the table for morning. I pour myself half a glass of skim milk, turn out the lights and head upstairs into my book-lined office.

I turn on my computer. One of the rituals of my quiet, solitary widower's life is to check my e-mail before bedtime. I may not do my banking on-line, and I might do all I can for the preservation of books, but the electronic era hasn't completely passed me by. There's one new message, from Patsy Glover.

Gerry died back in 1999 and his widow, Patsy, keeps in touch; she used to phone me once in a while, but now she e-mails me. Lately, she's been inviting me to her dinner group, which meets every two months. I went once—to have dim sum in a popular place in Chinatown—and the food was fine; it was Vera Kolotylo I couldn't stand. Since Bud died, she talks more than ever.

I open Patsy's message:

> Subject: Old Familiar Face
>
> Dear Jenkins:
>
> You will be interested to hear that Janie Hunter (née Sinclair) is moving back to Winnipeg. Her son Jason lives here with his family and I guess he's doing well. They have a big place in Linden Woods. I think Janie may have already moved in with them.
>
> Isn't she the one who named you The Kissing Bandit?
>
> Maybe we should all get together for a few laughs. You, me, Vera, maybe Fred? Let me know what you think.
>
> Cheers, Patsy.

The Kissing Bandit

So Janie Sinclair is back in town after all these years. Janie Sinclair—my high-school graduation date. But it wasn't Janie who named me The Kissing Bandit.

Back in those often heartbreaking, often exciting days, for guys like me, kissing wasn't a prelude to something else, it was *everything*. And when the kiss didn't happen on Doreen's doorstep, after days of imagining what it might be like, I despaired of ever having another chance to kiss anyone.

And then, *there* was this girl in the shadows of her unlighted back door, *wanting me to kiss her.*

It wasn't Janie Sinclair. That was years later at the end of Grade Twelve.

It was a girl I ended up with at a church-club dance, just two weeks after Grade Nine grad. I wasn't in a partying mood. I couldn't dance very well then, and I was preoccupied with what I'd done and not done on my date with Doreen. I was standing on the sidelines when Louise came over and selected me for a Ladies' Choice. Yes, Louise, the girl the guys in our club called TB—for Tremendous Bum. I was embarrassed at first, but the church hall was quite dark, and she was wearing a flared skirt that hid her proportions. She was a pretty girl with bobbed dark-brown hair and a slim body. It was only her behind that didn't seem to fit her but, if she knew people called her TB, she didn't seem to let it bother her.

The music was slow and Louise moved in close. Some girls just did that naturally, as if being close was essential to slow dancing. She felt good and she smelled good, and she followed whatever step I was making up as I went along. The chaperones, Mr. and Mrs. Swandell, were in the brightly lighted kitchen talking, oblivious to how dark the kids had made the hall.

As the record came to an end, Louise was in no hurry to break from me and, when she did, I asked her if she wanted to try the next one, and she said, "Sure."

We stayed together for a third slow tune. She held her body closer to mine each time and I could feel her face hot against my cheek. At some point I stopped thinking about Doreen and became fully aware of the female presence right there in my arms.

No one seemed to take much notice that I was dancing every dance with Louise. Most of the other kids were doing some pairing off of their own. Louise and I stuck to the slow dances; when a polka or a schottische came on, we sipped Cokes together.

I knew that dancing with the same girl many times led to certain expectations. When the last record ended, I asked Louise if I could walk her home and she said, "Sure."

We both lived a long way from the church—in opposite directions. She went to a different school in the southern part of St. Vital. It was a lovely summer night and I could've walked miles, I was so optimistic about the way the night was progressing. She didn't say much as we walked, hand in hand, but I was giddy, and that made me blather on, and she chuckled at my corny comments, even squeezing my arm.

Her house was a modest bungalow. She led me through the gate and around to the back. There was no outside light on. My eyes had adjusted to the night and I could see a look on Louise's face, one I'd hoped to see on Doreen's and hadn't. Expectant. Louise looked at my mouth and moved close to me as if we might be going to dance.

The kiss was as natural as our first dance had been. Just as she had placed her arms and her body and her feet in the right place for me on the dance floor, she now placed her lips perfectly. Everything seemed right about her lips: the warmth, the softness, the taste, the malleability, the scent. There was this complete willingness on her part to be close, closer than any girl had ever been to me. That in itself was exciting, never mind all the new and pleasant sensations.

I wanted to say something. I broke from her to say, "I had a terrific—" but she interrupted me with her mouth. She wanted to keep on kissing.

And so I kissed her and kissed her and I didn't care if her bum was bigger than it should've been because, up to then, I'd never had such a good time.

Most of the summer lay ahead of us and, without discussing it, we seemed to know we both wanted more kissing. There was something mysterious about Louise; she didn't say much, but I sensed that she knew a lot about intimacy. I'm sure she could tell I was inexperienced and that wasn't putting her off—in fact, she seemed delighted to be the one who was *breaking me in*. What we needed was a *place*. I came up with the idea of meeting at the church. I helped out at the Sunday services that summer and I had a key to the room where the choir members and I kept our vestments. There was a risk that Reverend Halliday or our janitor or someone else might show up, but that made it all the more thrilling. Louise and I met among the surplices, and we'd kiss our faces off in the dark. We didn't go about it the way couples do in movies these days, chewing each other's lower lip like cannibals. Louise was good at applying the right amount of pressure, so that my lips could sense the texture of hers. She'd use her tongue—barely the tip of it—as kind of a tantalizing surprise. We'd get feverish, and I suspected that Louise wanted to do more, but I was happy to kiss. And kiss.

We'd meet for an hour or less, and I didn't walk her home afterward—at least, not all the way—because I didn't want to get home later than expected. My parents knew nothing about Louise.

I didn't tell my friends about her, either, not because she had a large behind but because she had a *reputation*. For the same reason, I didn't want to go out on a formal date with her and be seen in public with her. We met on those nights after the choir had practised and left, and she seemed happy with that. Maybe she was meeting another guy on other nights, a guy who was "putting the blocks to her," as Claude would say. I was so wrapped up in the intrigue of our clandestine meetings, I didn't worry too much about anything else. And Louise was always at the church when I wanted her to be, ready to kiss.

But she wasn't the one who named me The Kissing Bandit.

We stopped seeing each other when fall came. I think it was because we were back at school. Or maybe she lost interest in me because all I wanted to do was kiss. Or maybe I was scared away by her wanting more.

And then there was Trudy. Trudy the tease. Anytime anyone mentioned the Winnipeg Flood of 1950, I thought of her.

When the flood came in the spring of 1950, we—my parents, my brother and I—had to move out of our house. Those were the days before the floodway. The government relied on dikes, and some suburbs were sacrificed to save downtown. St. Vital, where I lived, was one of those suburbs.

We were lucky to have a place to go to. The Mooneys, friends of my parents, were headed to Kansas City for a few weeks and they offered us their three-bedroom apartment downtown. There was a condition: We'd have to look after their sixteen-year-old daughter Trudy, who couldn't miss the rest of Grade Eleven. To enable Trudy to keep her own room, Allan and I had to squeeze into Mrs. Mooney's sewing room.

I hadn't met Trudy before. George Mooney, Trudy's father, and my dad both belonged to the same veterans' club, and our mothers had met at the club's social functions. Trudy hit it off with my mother, mostly because of the meals my mom made. Mom whomped up eggs and sausages and pancakes for breakfast, where Trudy never expected more than a piece of toast with cinnamon sprinkled on it from her own mom.

It bothered me to be suddenly in a household with a *girl*. For a boy whose Grade Ten peers talked endlessly about *boobs*, it was distracting to have a pair only a few feet away—on the other side of the wall—when I was lying on my cot. Based on my limited knowledge of what constituted nice boobs, Trudy's were quite lovely. I couldn't wait for a chance to tell Claude what a *well-stacked clootch* I was billeted with. I hoped for a glimpse of her in something less than the clothes she wore to school, but she was fully dressed whenever I saw her, even first thing in the morning when she was headed for the bathroom.

Trudy had beautifully plump Cupid's-bow lips. I wanted

to kiss them, sure that, if she'd let me, she'd be impressed with the technique I'd learned from Louise.

Little was said about Trudy's dating. I think she'd been given rules by her parents, but I didn't know what they were. Her getting along well with my mother was likely a factor in her sticking close to the apartment when she wasn't at school. I heard somewhere that a guy she really liked had knocked up a girl and that put a damper on Trudy's love life. She openly flirted with Allan, who'd already graduated from university with an Engineering degree, but she barely spoke to me.

Evacuees were encouraged to attend the school nearest where they were staying and, for me, that was Gordon Bell High, Trudy's school. Mom asked her to walk me there the first day and she did, reluctantly. After that, we tended to avoid each other—until one afternoon.

I arrived home later than usual and found her in the apartment alone. Dressed in her usual sweater and slacks, she stopped me on my way to my room by waving something in front of my face. It was one of the comic books I'd drawn. That was my favourite hobby in those days, drawing my own comics in scribbler-size books of blank paper called Jumbo scrapbooks. Influenced by Milton Caniff's *Terry and the Pirates*, I was fond of spicing up my comic-book adventures with statuesque women, who wore sweaters stretched tight across their bosoms. I was becoming adept at shading that made the fabric look taut in the right places. Trudy held the book open at one of the pages in which my character Robin Hawk first meets the luscious but sinister Leda.

"Is this supposed to be me?" Trudy asked.

"You took that out of my room," I said.

"Correction. I took it out of my mother's sewing room. This is me, isn't it?"

"Of course not. It's a character in my comic strip. Could I have it back, please? It *is* mine."

"If you want to draw me so badly, you just need to ask."

"Could I have it back?" I persisted.

"Come and get it," she said, and she held it on the other side of her, away from me.

"Can't you just give it to me?"

"Just try and take it."

"No."

"Chicken."

I lunged. Trudy laughed and held the book behind her back. I reached again. This time, I grazed her breast.

"I—I'm sorry," I said.

"I'm not," she said.

For a moment, I was confused. She was holding her lovely chest up to me, daring me. I bent to kiss her and at the same time put my left hand on her right breast.

"No!" she cried, twisting her face away.

Baffled and embarrassed, I said, "I'm sorry, I thought—"

"It's all right," she said, "I just don't want you to kiss me."

At last, I grasped her meaning, and I grasped her boob. I didn't know where to look. The good thing about kissing was, you could close your eyes, but Trudy was forcing me to look at her. I tried to put a serious expression on my face while I fondled her breast, using a motion similar to turning the dial on a console radio. I tried to concentrate on what it felt like, but her eyes and her grin were unnerving.

"That's—that's nice," I said, not even sure if I was doing what I was doing correctly.

"Hey, you've got *two* hands, haven't you?"

Unfamiliar as I was with this kind of situation, I again knew what she meant, and I placed my right hand on her left breast. It was a bizarre turn of events, and as far from intimacy as you could imagine, but it was a milestone, I had to admit that.

No more than thirty seconds after I'd first touched her, she bolted to her room and slammed the door, leaving my comic book on the rug.

If I thought Trudy and I had a new relationship, I was wrong. She barely spoke to me again, except at dinner when we were with the rest of my family—and once when my dad took the two of us to see our flooded house. In the boat in which we rowed up our inundated street, Trudy sat behind my dad and, whenever I looked back at her, she stuck out her chest, taunting me.

It was an odd experience to tie the boat at our front door and, in rubber boots, step onto the third of our three steps and into the verandah. Dad was relieved to see that the flood water, while filling our basement, hadn't risen to the main floor, and radio reports assured us that the level had reached its peak and was about to drop.

Trudy took little interest in the state of the house. She hid in a bedroom and, when I walked into it, she stuck out her chest again and gave me a saucy smile, even though my father was not far away. But that was the extent of her playfulness.

Some days later, when the water had receded and the Mooneys were due back and we prepared to return to our home, I came upon a basket of laundry and in it was a brassiere that I knew wasn't my mother's. No one was around, so I picked it up. I felt the cloth cups—the same contours I remembered from that afternoon, the same pliability. It dawned on me that it was the bra that Trudy had let me feel. I hadn't felt an honest-to-goodness *boob* at all.

Grade Eleven came, and my movie date with Shirley Kernigan, and, after it, we still got along fine at school. She was the same smiley person every day, and she never questioned why I didn't ask her out again. At times, when I was going weeks without a date, I'd think, *Why not give Shirley another try?* And then the image of her open eye would come back to me like a Cyclops in a horror movie.

I guess I didn't kiss another girl until Alice. She was about as pleasant and friendly as you'd want, and she had a trim figure. But her upper row of teeth protruded—it wasn't obvious until she gave you a broad smile. Her face was pretty when she grinned or looked serious, but the big smile gave the show away, causing guys to rate her low on the date chart.

One night, in the middle of Grade Twelve, the Yarwood High School basketball team, accompanied by thirty or forty loyal fans, was returning from an exhibition game against a North Dakota school. On the way down, I'd sat beside Gerry and the busload of us had raucously sung "Ninety-Nine Bottles of Beer on a Wall" and a bunch of other sing-along songs, but on the trip home, Gerry sat with his girlfriend Patsy and I just happened to find an empty seat beside Alice. Because I didn't think of her as a girl I'd like to go out with, I felt relaxed with her. She liked to paint in water colours, so we talked about her painting and my cartooning and the game, which our team had narrowly won. The bus grew pretty quiet, except for the sound of the bus engine and a whisper here and a suggestive chuckle there, and some kids settled into some serious necking. I don't know how it happened that Alice and I started kissing. I guess she thought, as I did, that it was the thing to do, in the dark, in a moving bus, when a lot of the kids around us were paired off and twisted into clinches. Given how well we were getting along and the lack of bright light, I didn't worry about what her mouth looked like. I was curious about what it felt like. She didn't flinch when I leaned over to her. Her lips felt warmer and softer and fuller than I expected. Her teeth were definitely *there*, but I kissed her as if I didn't give a damn. She turned her face to lessen the effect of the overbite and, before I knew it, she was fitting the oval of her open mouth to mine at a ninety-degree angle. It was a marvellous way to spend the two-and-a-half-hour bus ride.

But did I ask Alice out on a date? No.

Anyway, it wasn't Alice who called me The Kissing Bandit. Or Shirley. And it certainly wasn't Trudy.

Well, then there was Dianne, who would've been highly rated if it hadn't been for her thick glasses. One night, Gerry took me over to his girlfriend's. Patsy, who was in my room at school, lived way out by the sanitarium, and we went in Gerry's dad's car. The plan was that Patsy was going to teach me how to do Arthur Murray's Magic Step, a way of dancing that could be adapted to almost any tune. It turned out that Patsy thought she'd invite her friend Dianne to even things up, and then she invited four other kids to make it into a party. Since the four others were two couples, it was pretty evident that I was meant to be with Dianne. There was smoking but no drinking—no booze drinking, that is, just Cokes. Patsy and Dianne took turns showing me the step. When I'd perfected it, Dianne and I did some slow dancing together, all eight of us dancing to records in Patsy's rec room. Dianne and I were still dancing as the others found soft places to sit and start necking. Dianne gave me a look and took me to a corner where we could pretend we had privacy. She was a delicate girl with black curly hair and a clear white complexion—and the thick glasses that got in the way when we were dancing and would surely be a problem in kissing. What I didn't expect, since the glasses seemed so essential to her, was her taking them off. Removal of the glasses was as sensual to me as removal of her blouse might've been, her bare eyelids as sultry as the bare bosoms in Jack's *Sunbathing* magazines. The gesture made Dianne seem so submissive, she might as well have said, "Take me, I'm yours." Funny how easily you can fall into intense kissing when everyone around you is doing the same. We necked and necked and, when we broke for air, she whispered:

"Whew! You're a regular kissing bandit!"

For a long while after that evening, that's the way I liked to think of myself: *The Kissing Bandit.* It gave me new confidence; I thought it might even cause my own rating to improve if Dianne got the word out. It led me to make a date with Dianne—but since she lived out by Patsy's, it depended on Gerry's willingness to double-date with us and his ability to get his dad's car. The four of us went to a movie downtown one Saturday night in January. It was blustery—blowing snow—and Dianne worried the whole evening that we might have a problem getting the two of them home, out there in the country. After the movie, in the car, Gerry expected Dianne and me to neck in the back seat, but Dianne sat up, staring out the windshield, chewing her fingernails. It did look scary out there. Patsy kept saying, "Gerry, careful," and "Gerry, slow down, will you?"

Gerry dropped Dianne and me at her house. I thought it meant The Kissing Bandit would have some time to indulge himself, but both girls insisted that Gerry and I get back on the road quickly because the storm was getting worse. In fact, if Gerry hadn't argued that "the poor guy" needed some time alone with Dianne, we would've dropped the girls off at their respective houses and headed back, kiss or no kiss. Dianne and I sort of lingered on the landing just inside her back door. She went up the steps and shut the door to the kitchen—I think some member of her family was in there having a snack or something. When we kissed, Dianne didn't take her glasses off. She didn't even take off her coat. Though I tried to go about my *Kissing Bandit* business despite the obtrusive glasses, she showed little of the eagerness or enthusiasm so evident at Patsy's party. When I thought about it later, I worried that I'd done something wrong. I decided that, for Dianne at least—maybe for all girls—kissing at a necking party surrounded by your peers and kissing good night after a date were two distinctly different activities.

Two things conspired to prevent me from seeing Dianne again. One, Gerry wasn't keen on double-dating anymore because he said it was only a matter of time until he'd be climbing into Patsy's pants. Two, Dianne had another admirer. He was a broad-shouldered guy everybody called Bron and he was spending a second year in Grade Eleven. When I asked Claude why he thought a girl would date a guy who'd flunked, he said, "I hear he has a large wang." Well, one thing we did know: Bron had his own car.

As winter thawed into spring, it was time to give serious thought to finding a date for high school graduation. As far as grad dates were concerned, rating was a huge factor. Appearance was everything, and so the likes of Alice and Dianne were eliminated.

I had my sights set on Jennifer Jordan, runner-up in the Yarwood beauty pageant. She had honey-blonde hair and a gorgeous face and figure. I hardly knew her, but I'd seen how popular she was at school dances. During a Bingo dance, guys nearly stampeded to get to her first. (There was a symbol of high school: *the Bingo dance.* Two big wheels started it off—just the two of them on the floor—and the rest of the crowd stood on the sidelines, watching and waiting. The emcee or the music man called out "Bingo!" and that was the signal for the two to separate and go over to the crowd and pick a partner. Usually, the most popular kids were picked first. Now there were two couples on the floor and, at the next *Bingo!*, the four went and found four more partners. This process continued, often through more than one song, until everyone was dancing. The Bingo dance never worked perfectly, because there were always those steady couples who refused to separate. And there were those who were picky and looked for someone in particular and waited too long, until they found all their possible choices taken, as in a game of musical chairs. And there were those who withdrew early and headed for the sidelines or the washroom or home. After virtually everyone was dancing, the emcee or the music man would continue calling "Bingo!" just to mix things up. To me, the Bingo dance was a popularity contest, like so many things in high school. I was never asked to start one. I was one of the guys on the sidelines waiting to be picked. Once, I had the rare good fortune to be close to Jennifer just as "Bingo!" was shouted, and she turned to me from the guy she was leaving and slipped into my arms with all the mature confidence of a girl who knew how irresistible she was.)

Jennifer didn't appear to have a steady boyfriend—there was no pin on her sweater. On a scale of 1 to 10, she'd rank at least 9+, but since she was in Grade Ten, I was sure she'd be thrilled to go to an important function like graduation with a Grade Twelve graduate. All I had to do, I thought, was work up the courage to phone her.

I picked a time when my parents were watching something on their new black-and-white television set and I dialled Jennifer's number. My heart pounded as I listened to the ring. The phone at the other end was lifted. Sweat sprang from my brow.

"Hello?" came the female voice.

I asked the question I'd rehearsed. "May I speak with Jennifer, please?"

"Speaking," the female voice said.

"Hi, Jennifer, this is Bob Jenkins—you know, from Grade Twelve?" The similarity of our names sounded funny. My mouth turned dry.

"Oh, hi."

There was a pause—no more than two thumps of my heart but it seemed forever—as I decided whether to continue with pleasantries or to cut to the chase. It seemed wrong to cut to the chase, as if I were so unskilled at talking with girls like her that I didn't know what to say next, but the fact was, *I didn't know what to say next*, and so I said:

"Would you like to go to graduation with me?"

The question sounded so hollow, so devoid of feeling, so mechanical, so lifeless—in no way did it convey how badly I wanted her to be my date on this most important occasion of my life so far. *All because she was a beautiful girl.*

She said, "Oh, gee, no, I'm sorry, I can't," and, as my heart sank, and I tried to figure out what to say to salvage *something* from this ordeal, she added, "It's nice of you to ask me, though."

It was Gerry who came up with Janie Sinclair. She was a Grade Eleven girl I didn't know at all but I'd seen her on the basketball court, playing guard for the Yarwood girls' team that Gerry helped coach. Her arms seemed long and she was slightly round-shouldered, but she was pretty in an athletic way and she had a nice move when she dribbled. Gerry said she was a lot of fun and, since graduation was drawing mighty close, I thought I'd better phone her.

"Hello?" It was a raspy female voice.

"Hello," I said. "May I speak with Janie Sin—with Janie, please?"

"Oh, just a minute." The person sounded annoyed. "*Janie!*" I heard her yell. "Another goddam *boy*."

"Mom, put a sock in it, would you?" I heard someone else say. There was muffled noise—the receiver changing hands—and then: "Hello?"

"Janie?"

"That's me. Who's this?"

"Bob Jenkins."

"Well, hello there. Gerry said you might call. We had a bet on it. I guess I lose."

"You didn't think I would."

"You know how kids talk. The word is you don't—*Mom, would you mind? I won't be more than a couple of minutes.* Sorry, where were we?"

"You were saying the word is I don't call people much."

"Right. So, I guess that means I'm privileged. What's on your mind?"

"I—I wondered if you'd like to go to grad with me."

"God, yes. I'd be honoured."

"You would?"

"Yes, yes. Look, my mother's going *ape*. I'd better get off the line. Call me tomorrow, okay?"

And it was Claude who put the whole *Kissing Bandit* thing into its proper perspective.

He, Gerry and I were having milkshakes in Colwell's Dairy Inn when I announced that I was taking Janie Sinclair to grad.

"So," said Gerry, "the old Kissing Bandit strikes again."

"I guess so," I chuckled.

"What's with this Kissing Bandit bullshit?" said Claude.

"That's what the girls call Jenkins," Gerry said.

"I'm not surprised," Claude said. "Jenkins, you're the *Kissing* Bandit, all right. All you ever do on a date is *kiss*."

Gerry rented a new Ford for grad. Before we picked up the girls, he and Bud and I took it out St. Anne's Road to see how fast it would go. Gerry couldn't get it past forty-nine miles per hour.

"Shit!" he said, punching the steering wheel. "They said this thing had a governor on it but I didn't believe them."

"What's the problem?" I said. "Who wants to go more than fifty?"

"Listen to this shithead," Gerry grumbled. "Do we have to spend all *night* with him?"

Sometimes Gerry could be a jerk. I figured it might be because he was two years behind us—and Patsy—in school. He'd failed a couple of grades. He tended to make up for his academic deficiencies by smoking two packs of cigarettes a day, driving cars fast, and bragging about the things he did to Patsy. On the upholstery of Gerry's dad's car—the fabric on the inside of the left rear door, just below the window—there was a smudge where Gerry swore he'd wiped his fingers after they'd been inside Patsy. The smudge had become legendary. So many guys wanted to see the spot that Gerry could've sold tickets. I was glad we were using a clean rental car for grad.

As we drove back into town at forty-nine m.p.h., Bud and I got Gerry into a better mood by singing one of our Tit Parade songs. We had a repertoire of popular hits that we'd given dirty lyrics. We sang, loud:

I love whacking,
I love suck,
And then again I think I'd like to fuck....

It didn't matter that the lines were ungrammatical and nonsensical, the fun was in fitting the vile words to the tune. Just one verse was all it took to make Gerry fall into one of his laughing fits. He'd laugh so uncontrollably, he'd weep and have a hard time seeing the road. He'd stop to catch his breath, say, "*And then again I ...*" and off he'd go again, laughing like a crazy man.

We headed for Janie's house. I was thinking less about the

song and Gerry and more about the night ahead. This formal date with a girl everyone said was fun-loving raised my level of expectation; I imagined something along the lines of that Montgomery Clift–Elizabeth Taylor clinch in *A Place in the Sun*. When Claude and I saw it a few months earlier, I nearly tumbled out of the Capitol Theatre balcony. Clift and Taylor meet at a ritzy upper-class party, he in a tux, she in a strapless gown. They hit it off. They can't wait to be alone and, when their passion gets the better of them, they rush out onto a terrace for what must be the most sensual screen kiss of all time. The camera moves in for a close-up: their faces, full of ardour, fill the screen. I pictured myself in my new dark blue suit and Janie in a gown, dancing the night away, becoming just as caught up in the romance of it all as Taylor and Clift.

We pulled up to Janie's house, a modest two-storey on Kingston Crescent. I jumped out of the Ford and hurried up the driveway. The side door opened.

"I said I don't know *when* I'll be home—maybe *never*!" With that, Janie slammed the door. "*Bitch*," she mumbled. "Hey, Jenkins, how're we doing?"

She was wearing a white gown with a white sequined jacket. Her hair was wind-blown-looking, not much different from the way she wore it on the basketball court, bangs covering her forehead. Her face brightened as she came up to me and put her gloved hand under my arm.

Janie talked mostly with Gerry since she knew him better than Bud or me, but she had a knack of letting me know she wasn't ignoring me, hugging my arm and glancing at me while she talked. We drove over to Vera's. Bud went in to fetch her and they took longer than we expected. I had a fleeting remembrance of waiting for them exactly three years before, the night we were graduating from Grade Nine.

It was a different scene this time. Where three years ago they'd come rushing out together, bursting to tell us Bud had just asked her to go steady, Vera came out ahead of Bud looking as if she were on the verge of tears. Her gown was made of a shiny material, mostly brown-coloured, with short sleeves and a profusion of fake flowers on the bodice.

"He hates my dress, I know he does," Vera said as I held the door for her and she got into the back seat beside Janie. "I mean, I can't change it now. What am I supposed to do, stay home? God, is it that bad, Gerry? Tell me, Jenkins, if you think it's bad. I'm sorry, you're Janie, aren't you? What would you do, Janie, if your boyfriend didn't like the dress you were wearing to grad?"

We were all trying to answer her when Bud came up. Vera's mother stood at the door of the house looking concerned. She may have been crying.

"Hey, listen," said Bud, "I did not say I didn't like the dress. Vera, listen to me, would you? I did not say—"

"Bud, you don't have to say anything," said Vera. "It's written all over your face. As soon as you came in and took one look at me, I could tell. I know you, Bud Kolotylo, and the look on your face always gives you away and you do not like my dress and what am I supposed to do about it?"

The conversation went more or less like that all the way out to Patsy's place. Gerry went in to fetch Patsy and, when she got into the car, she said, "Oh, Vera, I love your dress!"

Good old Patsy. I guess Gerry had told her what was going on. She knew what to say.

"Thank you, Patsy," said Vera, and she began to cry. "Jeez, Bud, why couldn't you say something like that? Don't think I don't know what it is, Bud Kolotylo. I know you wish I was showing more skin, I know. If you could get your mind out of the gutter for once, you might think twice about ruining the evening for everybody ..."

"Vera, I never said—"

"Bud, you'd be better off to stop whining because

everybody in this car knows that you hate my dress and it's really pathetic that you'd even ..."

Bud rode in the front beside Patsy and Vera was in the back beside Janie and me. Vera sniffled and complained and argued and the rest of us couldn't say much. Without letting Vera see, Janie nudged me in the ribs as we drove and I nudged her back. Somehow I knew Janie's nudges were code telling me she thought Vera's dress was the worst-looking damned concoction she'd ever seen.

On the dance floor—the school gymnasium—Janie moved in close to me, closer than anyone since Louise. She had a natural way of tucking her head between my head and my shoulder; in her medium-high heels, she was just the right height for me. Her hair smelled lovely, like nutmeg. The first three or four steps, we bumped knees and my foot came down on her shoe, but we adjusted, she moving slightly to her left so that, when I took a step forward, my right leg was almost between her legs.

By the last dance—"Perfidia," always the evening-ending song in those days—Janie had taken off her jacket and her shoulders were bare except for the spaghetti straps of her gown, meaning she must be wearing a *strapless* bra. As we danced, I could feel, with two fingers of my right hand, the bare flesh of her back above the gown. She brought my left hand from out there at shoulder level into a clasp between us, so that my forearm was almost but not quite touching her bosom. Throughout the evening, she'd been attentive, welcoming me back after my jive with Patsy or my butterfly with Dianne and Vera, welcoming me back with her gorgeous smile. When Gerry or Bud or someone else danced with Janie, she maintained a discreet distance and, even if she was talking with her partner, she looked around until she spotted me and she nodded at me and arched her eyebrows.

The six of us left for the Highwayman nightclub. Vera had

reached a silent phase, Bud still sat in the front, and Janie quietly hummed "Perfidia." Gerry broke the stillness with a loud "AND THEN AGAIN I ..." and we guys burst out laughing, and the girls didn't know what in blazes we were laughing at, and Patsy said, "And then again you *what*?" and Gerry and Bud and I roared, and the girls knew it must be a reference to something dirty.

Because nightclubs at the time couldn't serve liquor, we—despite being underage—did what all the other customers did: ordered Cokes and poured rye whisky into them from the brown-bagged bottles we'd brought with us. Gerry and Patsy and Janie and I danced, leaving Bud to plead with Vera and plead with Vera and beg Vera to accept his apology. Janie and I picked up where we'd left off, jammed against each other, moving to the music, following the beat, except that now the lower part of her seemed closer to me than it had been before. I happened to prod her abdomen with an erection that wouldn't go away and I backed off—or at least that part of me backed off—partly out of embarrassment and partly because I didn't think she'd like to be prodded. But, at the fourth or fifth contact, mostly caused by another couple bumping into the back of me, Janie didn't snicker or move herself out of range, she just got warmer, and her nutmeg fragrance intensified, and I let myself push against her and she pushed back. During one slow dance, she somehow lifted herself so that the crotch of what must have been her girdle was sort of hooked over my hard-on. What was crazy and at the same time wonderful was that we didn't acknowledge those things that were going on below our waists—we were just *dancing*.

Well after midnight, we went back to the table to find Vera and Bud gone. I thought she might've insisted he take her home, but Gerry let us know he'd given the car key to Bud so that they could make up in the car. We thought it was time to get on to our next stop; when we got to the car, Vera was in Bud's lap.

"I'm not forgiving him," Vera said, "not for a minute, but I'll be damned if I'm going to let him spoil my graduation—I mean, this is my graduation, too, you know."

We headed for Lockport, north of the city. Skinner's hot-dog place was open till two or three in the morning and you could feed nickels into the jukebox and get in some more dancing. When we drove onto the gravel parking lot, a floodlight lit up those of us who were sitting in the back seat.

"Hey, Jenk," Gerry said. He was looking at me in the rear-view mirror. "What's happened to The Bandit? Not a bit of candy on your face."

"It's not my fault," Janie said.

Laughing, Gerry, Patsy, Bud and Vera stepped out of the car and Janie bent forward to follow them. In what was a rare impetuous move for me, I reached out and grabbed her around the waist and pulled her back into the car.

"Ohhh!" Janie cried, half-chuckling, as she fell back across my lap.

I bent to kiss her, but it wasn't the best of positions.

"Hold that thought," Janie said, sitting up to close the door, and she pivoted to face me, her torso against mine.

My lips missed the mark at first, but she made an adjustment and I felt her mouth squarely on mine, and I applied the technique I'd learned from Louise, and Janie's arms went around my neck and, a moment later, her fingers were in my hair and I wished I hadn't put on so much Brylcreem. She moaned a little and I felt her mouth open a little and I thought maybe I was losing my mind the way Montgomery Clift lost his in *A Place in the Sun*. And just like that, I was Montgomery Clift, out on the balcony, kissing Elizabeth Taylor's hot mouth at last after an evening of torment. And her tongue was darting in and out of my mouth and she was going, "Mmm, mmm!"

"Wow," she said, "you *are* a kissing bandit!"

She went back at it, and now she ran her hand over my hot face and slipped two fingers inside my shirt—in, out, in, out—with the same rhythm she'd got going with her tongue, and I cursed myself for wearing an undershirt, even as I took my turn sending my tongue into *her* mouth.

"Oh, God," she said, taking a deep breath, "we'd better go inside before ..."

She turned, took another deep breath and opened the door.

"Come on," she said, taking my hand.

Before ... ? Before what? Did she mean we'd better go inside before someone came out and saw us, or did she mean we'd better go inside *before she lost control of herself?* I'd heard of girls becoming so passionate, *so hot and bothered,* that they wanted or *needed* to go all the way. Is that what had happened to Janie? Had she reached a stage, dangerously close to a point of no return, the point where she'd expect me or *beg* me to unzip her dress and unhook her strapless bra and pull off her girdle and her stockings and her panties or maybe *rip* everything off? Did she recognize the stage because she'd been there before with other boys or did hot-blooded girls just know instinctively? These questions crowded my head as I shuddered, relieved that I hadn't been expected to fulfill her need but in a way disappointed that my first venture into the unknown had been denied. As I followed her across the gravel lot, her still-warm hand in mine, I thought, *Wait. The night is young. Maybe my first venture into the unknown has only been postponed.* The moment we reached the door, Janie turned to me and French kissed me so thoroughly, I felt as if I was on the brink of losing my own self-control.

Gerry was the first one we saw when we entered the

building and he took one look at my face and said, "Now, *that*'s a whole lot better."

We danced in the dimly lighted hall. I remember other kids being there, kids from other high-school graduations and kids who were just there to prolong late-night dancing to music from a jukebox that we all took turns feeding. Patsy danced with both her arms around Gerry's neck, his hands almost but not quite on her bum. Vera and Bud were dancing more or less the same way. A handsome black couple found a song they wanted and we all watched them do the dirty boogie, which did nothing to cool Janie and me off. While whatever was left of our rational selves might've chided the couple for exhibitionism, our bodies couldn't wait to press against one another during the next slow dance.

I don't know what time it was when we left Skinner's, but Gerry and Bud wanted to go and park on the bank of the Red River to watch the sun come up. Gerry parked on a grassy area well worn by past vehicles. Gerry and Patsy kind of stretched out in the front seat. I tried to ignore them, thinking that they might be going to *do it*, but they were pretty quiet. Squashed against me, Bud and Vera fell asleep. Somehow, Janie and I had enough room to continue kissing, though she refrained from making any of her little moans. This was now Hour Eight or Nine or Ten of our date and her mouth miraculously stayed fresh and moist and tireless. I hoped mine felt the same way to her.

In an hour or two of necking in a confined space, adjusting your posture this way and that can put considerable stress and strain on your clothing, especially formal wear, and, as the eastern sky grew pink, one of Janie's straps broke. She giggled quietly about it.

Soon after that, we were starting back to the city. We were all invited to Dianne's house for breakfast. Mercifully, Vera was still conked out.

"Patsy, do you have a safety pin?" Janie asked.

"Gosh, I don't," said Patsy, who was now sitting up. "Why, what ..." She glanced over her shoulder.

Janie held up the broken end of the spaghetti strap.

"*Jenk!*" Gerry cried out. He was checking his rear-view mirror. "What have you been doing? Bud—look what's been going on while you've been sawing logs."

Bud snapped out of his doze and sat up. Janie waved the strap at him.

"Jenkins!" he said. "Shame, shame!"

I was going to object but then I saw that Janie *wanted* them to think I'd been feeling her up. Still, I blushed.

"Wha—what have I missed?" Vera said in a sleepy voice. She leaned forward and saw Janie's strap. "Oh, Jenkins, you sly devil!"

"You never know about these quiet guys," said Patsy.

They all laughed.

"Still waters run *deep*," said Janie, kissing my cheek, and they all roared.

I smiled, trying to look smug. What I didn't understand was whether Janie wished I *had* felt her up or whether she saw the broken strap as a chance to enhance my image. Perhaps both. All of them made such a big deal out of it that I began to feel as if I *had* felt her up, even got my hand inside the dress, and they laughed and kidded me for the whole hour or so it took to drive to Dianne's, and it was inevitable that, before we got there, Gerry was calling me *The Copping Bandit.*

There was a crowd of kids at Dianne's—maybe twenty or so. Dianne was friendly to both me and Janie, even after the others razzed me about Janie's strap. She offered to sew the strap, but Janie said a safety pin would do just fine. She and Dianne went to a bedroom to make the repair, and Janie came out wearing the matching jacket over the dress.

Dianne's mother helped with the breakfast. I wondered where Dianne's date, Bron, was and heard someone mention that he was passed out in a bedroom.

When Gerry and Patsy drove Janie and me home, Janie said she didn't want me to walk her to the door. She wanted to slip inside as quietly as she could in case her parents were still sleeping.

"I had a fabulous time," she whispered, her warm breath tickling my ear. "Call me in a day or so."

Reluctantly, I watched her walk alone to her back door.

All that day, I relived every moment of the night before. I lay on my bed until Claude called and asked me to come over to his house. He said he wanted to reminisce about high school—after all, our school days were over forever.

I might've known that Claude's first question, when we were ensconced in his room with both his parents out, would be, "Did you get much last night?" I knew he was anxious to tell me what *he* got, he whose grad date everybody called Hot Pants, or HP for short. I thought about laughing off his question, but I knew he'd sooner or later hear from Bud or Gerry, so I lied.

"I copped some bare boob," I said.

Claude didn't seem the least bit impressed or surprised. He said, "Shit, is that *all*?"

The Lower Class

For a couple of days, I thought about what I might *get* on a second date with Janie.

But there wasn't to be a second date.

Before I called Janie, she called me. As soon as I heard her voice, I knew there must be something wrong, because in those days girls rarely phoned boys. It just wasn't *done*. On the pretense of visiting a sick friend, Janie had gone to a phone booth; she wanted to get hold of me before I tried calling her because her mother wouldn't let her receive any more phone calls from boys. Janie sounded upset.

"My mother was *livid* when I got home," she said. "She and I argued all morning. She told me she'd been worried sick all night—"

"But …" I interjected, "she knew we were going to be out all night, didn't she?"

"Sure she did. I *know* I told her. She said I didn't tell her. She said if I'd told her I was going to be out all night she would've demanded that she meet you and she would've talked to your mother. She said she was going to call your parents right then while she was talking to me and I begged her not to. We argued some more and, when I turned to walk away from her, she grabbed at me and the jacket came off and she saw the safety pin and she said you must've been groping me and she wanted to know where you'd touched me and by then she was screaming and accusing me of having no self-respect, going out with such terrible boys, and she accused me of sleeping with you and she went to the phone and I thought she was going to phone your parents so I tried to take the phone away from her, but she screamed that she was calling my dad, and she did, and he came home from work…." Janie sobbed.

"Janie," I said, hardly believing what our lovely night had turned into, "that's really awful. Shouldn't I speak with her? Wouldn't it be better if she met me—"

"No, no. My dad took me out in the car and told me this was a bad time for my mother—she's going through the change of life and we've got to be patient with her. He told me something I didn't know before, that most of our money is *her* money, the money her father left her, and if I wanted to go to university it was *her* money that was going to pay for it. And he told me I shouldn't have slept with you and I told him I hadn't and I pleaded with him to believe me and I told him what a nice guy you are and I think he started to believe me …"

"Should I see your dad? Couldn't I meet—"

"Jenkins, he made me promise not to see you again."

"Janie, that's nuts! Didn't you tell him we were with other kids the whole time? Surely he knows it's the thing to do—to stay out all night after high-school grad—"

"I'm sorry, Jenkins. Don't you think this is hard for me?"

"Of course, of course, Janie, but there's got to be a way—"

"Jenkins, I have to go, okay? I'm sorry. I *did* have a lovely time, and I'll always remember it."

"Janie—"

The line went dead.

For days after that, I wallowed in the depths of despair, depression, deprivation. Some nights, I told myself I should fight back—I was Romeo and Janie was Juliet and our love would find a way. I thought I should phone Janie's mother or her father—but Janie didn't want me to—and I thought of talking to Gerry about intervening on my behalf. Surely Janie's parents knew of Gerry's connection with the girls' basketball team and would respect his word if he vouched for my innocence—but then I remembered that Gerry believed I'd been feeling up Janie for hours in the back seat of the car.

Gerry told me in August that Janie was dating someone—a basketball player from Norwood—and the next thing I heard, she was moving with her parents to Alberta. All I could think about was the irony: being accused of untold atrocities when, in reality, I hadn't done anything but kiss her. Was this my reward for being a gentleman?

After a summer of working in my father's surgical factory, I started university. Keeping up with my studies took nearly all my time. I thought of calling Dianne or Alice, but neither was going to university; they were in a different world from mine and besides, they both had boyfriends. I eyed the girls in my classes, but they all seemed too sophisticated for me—too beautiful, too rich, too *busy*.

I went to a Christmas party given by one of the women who worked in my father's factory. It was a Friday night and I'd studied at the university library until it was time to go. The house was in a working-class part of south Winnipeg. June, the woman hosting the party, joked that she lived "on the other side of the tracks" and the fact was she *did*, on one of those streets off Pembina Highway that crossed the railway line to the United States. I took the bus to her street and walked the rest of the way. I wasn't looking forward to the party, but my dad, who had gracefully declined an invitation because he thought his presence might spoil some people's fun, had said I should go as a goodwill gesture.

I figured it would be like most house parties that working-class folks went to in the 1950s: everybody smoking unfiltered cigarettes and sitting around in a basement recreation room, the guys drinking rye and ginger ale, the girls drinking lemon gin and 7UP, the guys in sport shirts with the sleeves rolled up and grey or brown straight-legged trousers (as opposed to the "drapes" of their high-school days), the girls in tight skirts and tight sweaters that showed off the shape of their pointy bras.

"Jenkins!" June said when she opened the door. "We started to think you weren't comin'." She took me to the basement stairs and shouted, "Hey, gang, look who's here!"

There were about seventeen people in the rec room, mostly young women from the factory and their boyfriends or husbands. The men applauded my arrival. Someone fetched a drink for me. They weren't dancing or playing games; they sat in groups talking, some on the floor, some on the furniture. Before long, I was on the floor, listening to one of the boyfriends talk about hunting in the Netley marshes:

"… you know what I seen last time? This cotton-pickin' duck, eh? This duck, for cripe's sake, had three legs! I'm not BSin' here …"

I suddenly noticed Mary. I didn't know why I hadn't seen her earlier—maybe the smoke in the room or my own self-consciousness. Quiet, unobtrusive Mary, at seventeen or eighteen the youngest in the factory. She'd been working there for about a year; she hadn't finished high school because her parents needed her to bring money home. She had a cute face, except when she smiled and showed the two or three teeth that had gone bad. She was about five-foot-two with dark brown shoulder-length hair and a nice full bosom. She wore a purple velvet dress that de-emphasized her bust, setting her apart from the other girls in their sweaters and skirts. She seemed to be the only one without an escort. While the hunter talked, I moved into a space on the floor beside Mary, who was sitting primly on a hassock.

"Hi," I said.

She smiled without parting her lips. Dimples appeared in her cheeks.

"How are things at work?" I asked. "You still on the clicker?"

"No, no," Mary said. "I'm learnin' da cuttin'."

"Good for you."

"You know da cuttin' table?"

"Yes?" It was the broad, long table where bolts of material were laid out for the women who'd cut them into various shapes and sizes for surgical corsets.

"I'm a bit too short, so your fodder built a step for me."

"Hey, I knew that! At least, I knew he built a platform in his basement workshop. He loves making things like that."

"Yes. He's a nice man, your fodder."

I told her about his taking apart, piece by piece, the power frame, a machine that could knit four elastic stockings at a time. He'd done that in the spring of 1950, when there was a distinct possibility of the flood inundating the factory. The frame would've been ruined by a flood.

I got up to fetch new drinks for the two of us. June winked at me—she apparently was glad to see me taking an interest in Mary.

Later, after more drinks and some salami and rye bread and cheese and pickles, and after we'd all opened crackers and put on the paper hats and read the corny jokes, somebody held mistletoe over Mary and me and I kissed her and everybody cheered. Mary blushed but I'd had too many drinks to care what anyone thought.

The party broke up and Allie's husband Ed offered to drive Mary and me home. Ed did the driving with Allie beside him, cautioning him to be careful after all the booze. In the back seat, Mary snuggled against me as if it were expected of her. Made bold by the drinks and Mary's compliance, I took off one glove and slipped my hand inside Mary's coat. She didn't budge.

As Ed headed north up Pembina Highway, I inched my hand further until it covered one velvet breast. I was amazed at how easily my first-ever move of this kind was happening, and Mary accepted it without a twitch.

"I didn't believe that crap about the three-legged duck," Ed was saying.

"Sounds pretty far-fetched, all right," said Allie. "I mean, if there was such a thing, wouldn't it get in the papers?"

"Or the *Guinness Book of World Records*," I said, as I played with the buttons on Mary's dress.

I discovered they weren't decorative; they did undo. As best I could with the hand that was inside her coat, I undid a button and ventured inside the bodice.

"If you shoot a duck with three legs, you take a goddam picture of it, don't you?" Ed said.

Through fingers that seemed to me to be unbelievably more sensitive than normal, I determined that Mary wasn't wearing one of those bras shaped into twin nosecones by padding and stitching, the kind Trudy Mooney wore. Rather, it was, as far as I could tell, a simple cotton bra and what was inside it was *all Mary.*

"Down Marion, isn't it, Mar'?" Allie said, without looking back at us. She knew there was something going on.

"Yes," said Mary in a clear voice, even as I felt a nipple

through the cotton and caressed it into an erect state that mimicked my own. "You turn left on Kenny."

"Oh, yah, that's right."

"Next time he'll tell us he shot a duck with two beaks," said Ed. "Or a moose with two dongs."

"Edward!" Allie laughed. "Really!"

When we reached Mary's house, a two-storey clapboard that looked battered by weather and years, Ed pulled up to a path that led to the front door. I withdrew my hand and put my glove back on.

"Want us to wait?" Ed asked.

"No, no," I said. "I can walk from here."

Mary didn't object, nor did she offer any opinion.

"G'night, then, you two," said Allie.

"Good night," Mary said. "T'ank you for da ride."

"Yes," I said. "Thanks, Allie. Thanks, Ed."

As Ed drove away, I didn't think for a second about how far it was from Mary's house to mine. I thought only about returning my hand to where it had been. I took Mary's arm and gave her support because she was wearing high-heeled party shoes, not boots, and I let her have the narrow path while I walked through the snow in my overshoes.

"Nice house," I said.

"We live upstairs," said Mary. "Dere's anudder fam'ly on da main floor."

I looked at the wooden structure, what some people called a saltbox. "You live with your parents, right?"

"Yes. And my two li'l sisters."

I was only temporarily daunted by the prospect of trying to fool around with Mary in a crowded walk-up. In my liquored state, I reasoned that, if she told her parents the boss's son had brought her home, they'd be sure to give us privacy.

"Do you wanna come in?" Mary asked.

I disregarded the lack of feeling in the question. "If you think it's all right."

She opened the door, which hadn't been locked. I followed her into a tiny vestibule. The door to the main floor was closed. To the right of it was a wooden staircase. Mary led me up; about halfway, one step gave a loud creak. The door at the top wasn't locked and, when she opened it, it also creaked.

"I'll go an' tell dem I'm home," Mary said, stepping out of her high heels.

Inside was a small kitchen and beside that a living room with an Arborite side table and a sofa and three chairs. On one of the chairs lay some girls' clothing and a few school books. The lamp on the table was on; the floor lamp beside the sofa wasn't. Mary hung up her coat, did up the button I'd undone and went through a door off the kitchen.

I took off my coat and my overshoes and I waited. I checked my watch: 1:30 a.m. Mary came back and quietly closed the door.

"Were they asleep?" I asked.

"Ever'body but my mudder. She'll go ta sleep now I'm home."

"Good," I said, a little too quickly.

"Do you wanna drink?"

"No, thanks. Come here."

I took her into my arms, nearly lifting her off the floor, and I kissed her more tenderly and more meaningfully than I had under the mistletoe. *The Kissing Bandit strikes again.*

"I wanted to do that all summer," I lied.

I took her by the hand and led her to the sofa. She arranged herself in one corner and smiled up at me, again without parting her lips. I sat down beside her, one arm along the top of the sofa behind her, the other at her waist. She didn't say anything. She didn't look expectant or ardent or frightened. I might've described her expression as benign but, in my new rather aggressive state, I thought I detected encouragement.

I kissed her again and this time I sent my tongue into her yielding mouth. I thought I could feel one of her cavities. But, if her teeth had a rough edge or two, they were the only parts of her that did. While still kissing her, I moved my hand up from her waist and into the v of the velvet neckline. My fingers caressed the smooth flesh above her bosom. I returned to the curve I'd felt in the car, the round plumpness of one breast in its thin cotton sling.

"You feel so nice," I whispered, and I meant it.

Though she wasn't expressive, I thought she must be enjoying this, if only because I was enjoying it so much, and she'd become so warm. Still, I thought I shouldn't expect too much too soon. I desperately wanted to feel her bare breast—the first bare breast I'd ever felt—but I thought she might balk at any advance into the bra. I'd heard enough stories from Claude and Gerry to make me believe that girls saw it as their duty to resist—whether they sincerely disliked being fondled on first dates, or they viewed the mating ritual as a progressive activity broken into incremental steps, or they simply liked playing the role of elusive prey. Wasn't the girl supposed to give you a fight at every stage, push your hand away, then let you advance a little, then push your hand away again, then let you go further, but only after you'd coaxed her with caresses and compliments?

Mary said nothing. We kissed more feverishly—or at least *I* did—and I undid the top two buttons of her dress. It was time to venture inside the bra. I thought I'd do it slowly and gently and, at the first sign—a hand on my wrist, a sound of annoyance, a slight move away from me—I'd pull back.

I pushed my fingers under the cotton. I marvelled not only at the smooth fullness of the breast but also at my own restraint, the fact that I could be so patient despite the raging booze-soaked excitement I felt. And she let me go ahead.

It might've made good sense for me to ask her to undo the bra—I certainly couldn't undo it from the position I was in and with her wearing a dress, and even if I could reach around and get my fingers on the hooks, I had no idea how to undo them—but for her to do it, she'd have to take off the dress and I couldn't expect her to with the family in the vicinity; she could go into the bathroom and take the dress off and take off the bra and put the dress back on but that would destroy the moment and, besides, it was a lot to ask her to do and it seemed mechanical and unromantic.

The main problem was, there was no room inside the bra for my hand and her breast. I wasn't sure how possible it was to push the cup off the breast without hurting her, but I tried. She didn't complain. And—ahhh, *there*—for the first time in my life I held an honest-to-goodness bare breast in my hand.

There was a loud thump.

Jolted, I sat up and said, "What was *that*?"

"Jus' da house," Mary said. "It does dat in winner."

I resumed my happy exploring, gently tweaking her erect nipple.

We were half-leaning, half-lying on the sofa now. I was on the outside, figuring I was blocking any view of what I was doing. As we kissed, a wild idea popped into my head. While caressing a girl's shapely breast should've given me all the thrills I needed for one night, the idea of touching her somewhere else jumped to the front of my frazzled brain. There was no doubt she was happy to have her chest fondled, but what about her thighs? I might reach a point that she considered off limits but, since everywhere was new territory for me, shouldn't I at least see how far I could go?

I took my hand out of her bodice and moved it to her leg. She was wearing stockings. The smoothness and the curve of her leg just above the knee were almost as lovely as the smoothness and the curve of her bosom.

I kissed her neck, finding she wasn't the least bit ticklish there, as I moved my hand ever so slowly under the hem of her dress and up her thigh. I felt the top of her stocking and, beyond that, her bare flesh. Surely she was going to stop me! But she didn't. I was so overwhelmed by the feel and thought of what I was touching—*her upper thigh!*—that I had to kiss her even more passionately.

My fingers inched up to the edge of her undergarment and I nearly cried out when I realized she wasn't wearing a girdle, only what felt like cotton panties. Some other contraption with garters was holding up her stockings. My heart raced as I moved my fingers slowly sideways, and I discovered that her legs were slightly parted and I was easily able to move my anxious middle finger onto the band of cotton between her thighs. I stifled a moan of surprise and appreciation and pleasure. I was sure I could feel *hair* under the cotton. I was astonished at the heat there and at the same time I was amazed at how far I'd progressed and how close I now was to the ultimate goal of every heterosexual young man.

But wait. What was going on here? This wasn't supposed to happen on the first date. This wasn't even a date—I'd taken her home from a party. Well, it wasn't as if she was a pick-up I'd just met; I'd known her at the factory, and I'd often smiled at her and kidded with her. But why was she giving me so little resistance? Especially with her parents maybe twenty-five feet away, probably listening to every muffled movement, every whisper, every sound of clothing being lifted, adjusted, pushed up or pulled down. Was this some kind of *trap*? I thought of Shelley Winters in *A Place in the Sun,* the factory girl connecting with the up-and-coming Montgomery Clift, letting him have his way with her, dragging him down …

I moved my hand back to her thigh, congratulating myself

on being able to stop short of—of what? Feeling her bare naked crotch or *going all the way*? Surely she didn't expect or want me to go all the way, here on this narrow sofa, a few feet away from her parents and her sisters—I didn't even have a prophylactic! Well, maybe that was part of the plan, all part of the trap; maybe her parents were in on it, maybe their plan was to trap the boss's son—if we went all the way and Mary got pregnant, I'd have to marry her and that would better the family's economic situation. Or maybe everyone at the party was in cahoots with Mary—they were all plotting to bring the high-flying university boy down to earth.

No. I couldn't believe that of Mary. She was so innocent and likable.

And so *hot* down there.

I returned there, this time with two fingers—it just seemed to be the place for them.

I opened my eyes and for the first time I saw the crucifix on the opposite wall.

My god, I thought, *divine intervention!*

I pulled my fingers back from her thinly covered inferno. Only a week before, as a member of the Canterbury Club for Anglican university students, I'd gone to a retreat at St. John's College. It was a Saturday, the idea being that the experience would be more meaningful if you sacrificed the one day in the week most people devoted to frivolity. Reverend Merrihew led us in prayers, he discussed moral and ethical issues with us, and he left us alone for periods of meditating and reading. As the day passed, I began to feel the presence of something or Someone. A spiritual presence. Merrihew had succeeded in calling a spiritual power into our midst. Was it possible that this divine presence was watching over me and had intervened at the perfect time *to deliver me from temptation*?

If so, then what about Mary? If she was religious, why had she led me on?

That was unfair. She hadn't done much leading. She'd simply gone along with what I wanted to do. It was likely her sweet nature that was dictating her compliance.

But if I stayed a moment longer, I didn't know if I could continue to deny myself the pleasure of—

"I'd better be going," I whispered.

"All right," she said.

I hated to release her, but I peeked at the crucifix again and sat up. I slowly got to my feet.

As I put on my coat and overshoes, Mary stood there, looking forlorn and, I thought, sad, as if she was never going to see me again. She did nothing to put herself back in order; her hair was flattened in one place and sticking out in another, her dress was unbuttoned to the waist and her bra was still awry. It was as if she wanted to stay that way, letting me leave with this image of what I'd done to her. In these rude surroundings—worn carpet, cheap furniture, lamp with a torn shade—she looked like a typical representative of the Lower Class, as described in my Sociology textbook. Her willingness to be groped was a symptom of her station in life—the textbook said Lower Class people had lax morals.

"Thank you for the nice time," I said.

"I had a nice time, too," she said.

I leaned forward and kissed her lightly on the lips. I turned and she closed the door behind me as I started down the stairs, the image of her messed-up appearance imprinted on my brain. The step halfway down shrieked. I felt suffocated in the narrow stairway. I hurried to get out of there.

I walked to Rue Des Meurons, the street I could follow all the way to Vivian, perhaps two miles away. Few cars went by—it was three in the morning. I rubbed my ears with my scarf. Like young people everywhere, I didn't wear a hat in winter.

What an incredible texture her breast had! What an incredible shape! Classic!

I should've been nicer to her. I *attacked* her.

Oh, the *heat* of her down there … !

Thank God I'd stopped when I did. A less rational fellow with that many drinks under his belt would've ripped off her pants. She got me so worked up …

Why didn't I go back to the boobs? I didn't get enough of her boobs!

What was the matter with me? I took advantage of her. The way I left her!

I could see her again. Why not? What a little treat she was!

I shouldn't.

I should.

That's what was going on in my head as I walked and I got home in what seemed like five seconds flat. I let myself in through the back door.

"Where have you *been*?" My father jumped up from his kitchen chair.

"Sorry, Pop. The party *did* go on."

"People stayed at June's till *this* hour?"

"Well, 1:30 or so. Then Allie and her husband drove me home—well, Mary and me."

"You and *Mary*?"

"I went into her place."

"You went into Mary's blooming *house*?"

"Yes."

"What did her parents say?"

"They were asleep. It was just to unwind, Pop. No harm done."

"I blinking well hope not."

My father went to bed. He seemed disappointed that I'd

taken one of the factory girls home and unconvinced that *no harm* was done.

I went to my room, shut the door and switched on the desk lamp. In the middle of my desk blotter was a letter for me, and the return address said it was from Janie Sinclair.

My God! I thought, *this is my reward for resisting temptation!*

The Return of Janie

I turn off the computer and get ready for bed. I floss my teeth, doing a more thorough job than I ever did when I was young. It's essential if I'm going to avoid any more exorbitant dental bills. I brush. I swallow the little blue Aspirin that is supposed to keep your arteries unclogged. I wash my hands, using antibacterial liquid soap. I pull back the covers on my king-size bed and glance at the manila envelope on my night table. *Damn.* I'm in no mood now to read *Barbara's Time Capsule.* I put it away in a night-table drawer.

I go back to my computer. I *do* want to see Janie again. I switch on my computer and send Patsy a message telling her so.

"Hello?"

"Hello. Could I speak with Bob Jenkins, please?"

"This is Bob Jenkins."

"Jenkins. Jeez, it's been a long time."

"Who—"

"Janie Hunter. Janie Sinclair. Patsy gave me your e-mail address, but I said, heck, give me his phone number. I'm not big on all the new gizmos. I can't stand them, to tell you the God's truth."

Her voice sounds almost the same, if it's possible to say that about a voice you haven't heard for more than fifty years. There's a slight suggestion of Granny Clampett—a twang—reminding me that Janie, like all of us, has aged.

"Nice to hear from you, Janie."

"Jenkins, I'm sorry about your loss. I never knew your wife—was it Belinda?"

"Barbara."

"I didn't know her, did I?"

"I don't think so."

"But you can be grateful for the long time you had together, can't you? It's twelve years since my Harry went to meet his Maker. That's too soon, Jenkins. He didn't deserve to go so young."

"No."

"Listen, I've been here six weeks and I've still got bags that aren't unpacked. It's been a nightmare moving—half my stuff's in Calgary—have you ever moved?"

"Not for a long while. We lived in Saskatoon way back in the Sixties."

"A lifetime ago! Harry and I had a few places—well, you have to upsize when you keep having kids. Did you know we had six?"

"I think I knew that, yes—"

"Then we found out what was causing it. Old joke. Now, I'm downsizing. Big time. Maybe Laura told you—"

"Who?"

"Gerry's wife?"

"Patsy."

"Yes, sorry—what did I say? Laura! That's my son Patrick's wife—sorry. Patsy might've told you my son Jason and his wife Krista live here. They aren't nuts like Harry and me—they have only three kids. Well, two of them have left home—I can't believe how those kids have grown and matured—one's still at home—Krista—no, I mean Deirdre—she's the youngest and she's at university—well, I tell you, Jason and Krista have set things up for me pretty nice. My own everything. Still, you know, you have to get rid of stuff. I've got this curio cabinet—who needs it? Listen to me going on."

Her "going on" is making me weary. I begin to wonder if I really do want to see her again. Since Barb died, the number of my friends has shrunk to a few I see every so often. I golf with a group of guys about once a week, and I see people like Claude and Gillian, Charlie and Gwen, and my neighbours, Mark and Hildy, for meals maybe once a month. And Donald and Bea—what—once a year? I like my solitude.

"We've got lots to talk about," I say.

"Lot of water under the bridge," she says. "Might take at least two coffee breaks."

"Should we maybe go for dinner one evening?"

That's out of my mouth before I decide what I want to suggest. It seems to be the direction we're headed, but a part of me thinks it isn't at all necessary. The conversation has taken on its own momentum.

"You mean, without Patsy or … or whoever? The two of us?"

"Keep it simple."

"Hey, if you're game for dinner, I'm all for it."

Her voice is full of enthusiasm. My mind conjures up an image of the teenaged Janie—on the basketball court, in my arms on the dance floor—and I have to remind myself that she's a senior citizen, just like me.

I say, "There's a Keg on McGillivray—how about going there Monday night? It shouldn't be so busy and we can take our time. I'll pick you up."

"That'd be terrific."

"Just tell me where you live and I'll find it."

"Oh … just a minute … I'll get my son Jason to tell you how to get here. Just a minute."

I hear them talking to one another.

"Hello, Mr. Jenkins?" It's a strong, corporate voice.

"Yes, hi."

"This is Jason Hunter, sir." I like the way the younger generation calls me *sir*. "Where will you be coming from?"

I tell him where I live in Fort Richmond and he gives me directions to his home in Linden Woods. I scribble them on my desk calendar.

"Thank you, Jason," I say. "Uh—could I speak with your mother again?"

"Oh … I think she's gone somewhere. Could I … ?"

"If you wouldn't mind, please tell her I'll call for her at six o'clock. That's this coming Monday."

"Right. Thank you, sir. I'll make sure she's ready."

It's Sunday afternoon, three days after my evening with Claude and Gillian, and a day after Janie's call. Tracy is coming over to my place with her daughter Mason. I love their visits. I'm grateful that Tracy and her husband Clay choose to live and work here—unlike my son Brian, who's struggling to make it as an actor in Toronto.

I hear them drive up into my driveway.

"Hi, Papa!" comes Mason's voice from the front door.

Mason is now thirteen, already developing womanly curves. She has none of the gawkiness associated with her age, perhaps because, after dabbling in soccer, skating and ballet, she's followed her mother into rhythmic gymnastics, and all the rigorous training that's required if you're going to be competitive. She has naturally curly dark hair like Clay's, but her mother works at straightening the curls and keeping the hair pulled back in a bun or a ponytail—a requirement of the sport. She has Clay's eyes, nose and mouth, as well as Tracy's kind of beauty—that grace of movement, erect posture, and an open-faced confidence that tells you *Mason Heller matters*. She's dressed in shorts and a T-shirt bearing the St. Boniface Leopards logo, and she's carrying a set of rhythmic-gymnastics clubs.

"Hi, Mason," I say. "Nice out there, I gather."

Tracy comes in. "Dad," she says. "What were you *thinking*?" The look on her face is serious, with a suggestion of a scowl.

Sensing unpleasantness, Mason says, "I'll just be in the back yard practising."

"What now?" I say, as if Tracy is always taking me to task about something.

"You were going to do me a favour on Monday night—take Mason to gym and bring her back here to stay overnight because Clay and I are going to Minneapolis on business."

"Right. So?"

"So I was just in Sobey's picking up your perogies and I ran into Mrs. Kolotylo. And she says, 'Isn't that *something*—your dad going out on a *date* on Monday.'"

I'm stunned. As is my habit, I go into the kitchen and look at the wall calendar, where I record my appointments and commitments. I know I agreed to take Mason; I don't need to look it up—it's written down all right—I just need the moment to consider my stupidity. I have to believe that my *date* is so much in the realm of fantasy, I haven't gone to the calendar to record it.

"I guess I had a mental lapse," I say. "But it's easily remedied. I can change it to another day."

"I'm thinking you must be pretty excited about it to forget Mason. You always say you love watching her at the gym and having her sleep over."

"It was a mistake, all right? You *know* how much fun Mason and I have together."

"Who's the woman you're dating?"

"I'm surprised Vera didn't tell you."

"I didn't *let* her tell me. I pretended I knew—I didn't want her to think my dad wouldn't tell me. Besides, you know how that woman can *talk*. I wanted to get out of her clutches fast, so I told her I was in a hurry, Mason was in the car, which was true. So are you going to tell me about your date?"

"It's nothing. An old, old friend from school has moved back here. I haven't seen her in—would you believe—over *fifty* years. It's just sort of a courtesy on my part to welcome her back."

"For some reason, you're not telling me everything. What's her name?"

"Janie Sinclair—well, that was her maiden name. Janie Hunter."

"I gather she's a widow now."

"Yes."

"Did you date her back in school?"

"Only once."

"Wow! Must've been some hot date for you to get so worked up about her now!"

"I'm not worked up!"

"Worked up enough that you forgot about your granddaughter!"

"Okay! I admit I was preoccupied. But not by *her* necessarily. The whole idea of going out to dinner with another woman is pretty foreign to me."

"Dad. You're not telling me why she's so special. Did you take her to graduation or something?"

"You should be a lawyer. Yes, my high-school graduation."

"Aha! I'll bet you spent the night with her!"

"Come on, Trace, it was completely innocent. We stayed out all night with two other couples—one of them was Mr. and Mrs. Kolotylo, for God's sake. Hey, did I grill you like this about your graduation?"

"*Touché!* No, thank God."

"Right. Anyway, this new *date*, as you call it, will be just as innocent as the first one. More so, in fact. Do you want a drink or something?"

"Do you have any Limonata?"

"I think so."

Before opening the fridge, I look out the window into the spacious back yard. Mason is doing her club routine on the lawn. I watch her run, throw the clubs high into the air, do a somersault and catch the clubs. Tracy comes up behind me and watches with me.

"She *nailed* it," I say. "She's going to be as good as you."

"Better," says Tracy.

"Is *she* dating yet?"

"Are you out of your *mind*? There's a boy keeps hassling her, e-mailing, leaving cell phone messages. Thank God she's too busy for boys."

"Tracy, the day is rapidly approaching when she will want to encourage them."

"I know. It's scary. I look at her and think I'll *kill* anyone who tries to lay a hand on her."

"Oh oh. You don't want to be guilty of over-protecting her."

"Dad, she's *thirteen*. Give me a break here."

"It's a crazy world we're in now. I don't know what the rules are anymore—if there are any. When you were growing up, your mother hoped you and she could have a relationship that was different from the one she had with *her* mother—"

"I know, I know. I cried when I read that part in her *Time Capsule*."

"I haven't read it yet."

We watch Mason nail another perfect club routine.

Tracy puts her arms around my waist and her head on my shoulder. "Now I'm trying to interfere with *your* social life," she says. "Sorry I got on your case, Daddy."

"Hey, it was stupid of me to forget I had a commitment."

"Not that. It's just ..."

"You think it's too soon after."

"No, no. I guess I'm too sentimental. I thought of you and Mom as partners for life."

"We were."

"I just can't imagine you, my father, with another woman. I know it's crazy."

"I should've told you before you heard it from old Vera. Who would've thought—Jeez, gossip travels with the speed of *light*. Anyway, it's not a big deal."

"I know. I'll get over it." She opens the fridge. "Good, you do have Limonata. Do you want something?"

"I'll have one of those Mooseheads, please. Let me go upstairs right now and phone Janie and change the date."

"Wait, no. You don't have to. I was going to tell you—Clay had to cancel Minneapolis."

Secrets

That night, all those years ago, I tore open the envelope. It was a one-page letter, written in clear, almost child-like handwriting.

> *Dear Jenkins:*
>
> *How are you?*
>
> *I've been wanting to write to you for a long time. I need to apologize.*
>
> *I'm not much of a letter-writer but here goes.*
>
> *I've thought about you a lot. Grad was fun. You were fun.*
>
> *I was honoured to be your date. Did I tell you that? Well, I was. It was the best date I ever had.*
>
> *I wish we could of gone out again. I was dumb*

to let stuff get out of control. None of it was your fault.

But here's what I want to apologize for. I blamed stuff on my mom. The thing is I used her. Cuz I wanted to go out with another guy. He turned out to be a jerk.

I'm here in Lethbridge now and missing you.

I shouldn't tell you this. Oh well. It'll be our secret. I'm touching my bubbies right now, wishing it was you touching them.

I know. I'm terrible. I shouldn't of told you that. But there.

I hope we can be penpals.

If you'll forgive me, that is.

Hope you're liking university.

Sincerely,

Janie.

XXX

P.S. Say hello to Gerry.

J.

I stared at the letter, wondering how to feel about it. I reread it and reread it and I got undressed and put on my pyjamas and turned off the light and climbed into bed and I thought about the letter and I turned the light on and read the letter again. By then it was after four in the morning. It was the first letter I'd ever received from a girl and I was astounded by Janie's candour. I kept going back to the part about her *bubbies*. I tried to visualize Janie sitting on her bed with her door shut, a pad of paper in her lap, one hand going up under her T-shirt or her pyjama top, fondling her own *bubbies*, first one and then the other, or maybe squatting there topless and tossing the pen down and using both hands in a rush of autoerotic ecstasy. How I wished I could've done that on grad night! But then I reread the part about her mother and that bothered me. Had Janie actually *lied* about her mother being mad at me? Did she write the letter because she liked me or was she just easing her conscience? And then I thought about Mary's lovely plump right breast that I had held in my hand less than two hours ago, and I wanted desperately to hold it again, and I finally went to sleep thinking, A *boob in the hand is worth two in Alberta.*

And so the next day I phoned Mary, not from home but from the hotel two blocks away; I didn't want my dad to know I was calling her. A girl I assumed was one of her younger sisters answered and I told her who it was, hoping it would excite the household. I heard muffled conversation in the background—it sounded like French—and at last Mary came to the phone. I told her I'd like to see her again, *that night* if it was okay with her. I imagined an exact re-enactment of our session on the sofa, but it dawned on me that I couldn't expect to start necking until the family was tucked away in bed, so I quickly blurted:

"I thought we could go bowling."

"All right," she said.

I agreed to pick her up at eight, believing I could borrow my dad's car since I now had my driver's licence. The car could be an alternate site for smooching if the coast wasn't clear at Mary's.

Since Christmas was only a few days away, I thought I'd

buy Mary a gift. That would help put her in the right mood. I walked from the hotel to the drugstore nearest our house. The gift had to be something nice but not too expensive, since this was technically our first date. It had to be small, too, small enough to fit into my parka pocket where I could hide it from my parents. I settled on a small bottle of toilet water and Mrs. Baker, wife of the druggist, gift-wrapped it for me, assuming it was for my mother.

When I casually asked my dad for the car, acting as if I was going out with the guys and it was my turn to drive, he reminded me that it was the night of his veterans' club's annual dinner and dance. I reverted to Plan B.

I took the streetcar into Norwood and walked to Mary's, figuring we could walk from her place to Coronation Lanes. Mary came to the door in a red cardigan over a matching pullover. Her bust looked like Leda's in my "Robin Hawk" comic book. She led me into the living room to meet her mother and her two sisters.

The tableau I came upon was touching. Sitting in the very spot where I had fondled Mary were a pretty girl of maybe fourteen, a cute girl of no more than six, and a middle-aged woman who was smaller than the fourteen-year-old. The six-year-old was sitting between the others, slowly reading a children's book aloud—in French. The prospect of plundering Mary's pullover in this place suddenly seemed sacrilegious if not downright dirty.

Mary introduced her mother and Julie and little Lorenza. I noticed the Christmas tree that'd been put up that day—it was surprisingly lush, decorated with what seemed to be home-made ornaments, mostly Roman Catholic—and I commented on it in French: "*Quel bel arbre de Noel.*" Mary's mother beamed and Lorenza answered me, speaking so quickly that I had no idea what she said. Mary translated and Julie said something in French as she boldly looked me over.

I said to Mary, "*Où est votre père?*" and she explained in English that he was out working an evening shift.

Mary and I walked to the bowling alley. I had brought my own bowling shoes and I had the gift hidden in the shoe bag, keeping it for a strategic time later. I rented shoes for Mary. Since this was a Saturday night, there were no leagues filling the alleys—only two other couples like ourselves and a group of kids who were celebrating a birthday. Mary threw her first three balls down the gutter; I started off with a strike. She claimed to have bowled before, but I saw a need to help her, and I explained how to roll the ball over a spot on the alley instead of aiming at the pins. We played two games, I scoring a 274 and a 252, Mary seeming to try but managing only 50 and 71. I felt as if I could bowl all night—or at least until they closed the place.

"You go ahead and play anudder and I'll watch," Mary said.

"No, it's all right," I said. "Let's go somewhere for coffee."

Not much more than an hour had elapsed. We went to a café. Mary had a glass of milk and nothing to eat while I drank coffee, ate a toasted pecan bun and talked about bowling. I fought to keep my eyes off her sweater. She laughed at some of the inane things I said as I kept up a patter, trying to make the time go faster. I found myself running out of things to say when it was barely ten o'clock, much too early to take her home. But I was so restless and Mary was looking so tired, I *did* take her home. Her mother was in the kitchen baking, and Lorenza was in bed, but Julie had a friend over and they talked Mary and me into playing a card game—*Go Fish.*

And that's the way the evening ended, with a ripsnorting game of Fish, and me losing, and Julie laughing at everything I said and sitting close enough to me to nudge my leg repeatedly with hers, and Mary seeming content to go through an evening unmolested. At the door when I left, teetering at the top of the stairs, I gave her the gift, and she thanked me with a kiss, and I pulled the door shut so that I might at least put my hand on her chest—when the door at the bottom of the stairs opened and there was her dad, home from his shift.

Dear Janie:

It was good to hear from you after so long.

When I look back on grad, I don't see how it could've been better. You were the perfect date.

I don't quite understand what you mean about using your mother. If you mean she wasn't really mad at me and you just said she was, I can see why you'd want to apologize.

In any event, I accept your apology. I just wish we could've gone out again, but maybe it wasn't meant to be. Who knows, maybe a second date wouldn't have been as good as the first. This way, we'll never know, and grad will always stand out as perfection.

I have some great memories of you, Janie.

Are you in Grade 12 in Lethbridge? How's that going? Still playing basketball?

If you get back to Winnipeg, I hope you'll let me know.

And I'm happy to be your penpal.

All the best in the New Year.

Jenkins.

Shortly after Christmas, I was invited over to Mary's house on a Saturday afternoon. I found Julie there babysitting Lorenza. Mary had phoned to tell Julie that she and her mother were going to be late and Julie should invite me in. Lorenza had fallen asleep in a bedroom and Julie, taking her assignment seriously, hung up my coat and sat me down on the sofa. The infamous sofa. She fetched me a Coke and sat beside me.

"Do you like my sister?" Julie asked.

"Yes, I do," I said.

"Do you like me?"

"I certainly do."

"Would you like to kiss me?"

I was alarmed. She put her hand on my arm and her face close to mine, her eyes trained on my lips.

"Oh, now, Julie, I can't," I said.

"Sure you can. I want you to."

I felt trapped. I didn't want to tell her she was too young. I thought I'd appeal to her sense of fair play.

"Julie, you know I'm a good friend of your sister—I guess you'd say I'm her boyfriend—and she wouldn't like it if I kissed other girls."

"She doesn't need to know."

Julie pushed herself closer. Her not inconsiderable bosom pressed against my arm. She was giving off an almost irresistible fragrance, and she was breathing heavily. *Why can't Mary be this passionate?* I wondered, instantly hating myself for thinking that way.

"I'm not going to keep any secrets from Mary," I said. "Want to play some cards?"

I stood up and kept my distance until the rest of the family arrived home. Julie pouted but not enough to cause anyone to question her. Everyone got into a game of Monopoly, and after that, it was time to prepare dinner.

When I went home, after a lovely lingering kiss—but only

a kiss—from Mary at the door, I found my father waiting for me.

"You've been at Mary's, haven't you?" he said.

"Yes, Pop," I said.

"You know I don't think it's a good idea for you to fraternize with the factory staff, don't you?"

"Yes, Pop."

"I know she's a nice girl but I'm afraid there can't be any exceptions. Besides, there must be lots of university girls who'd like to go out with a bright young chap like you."

Dear Jenkins:

I'm so glad you forgive me!

Boy, does that take a load off my mind!

I hate to have anyone mad at me, especially you.

You know you're someone special to me, don't you? You are. I know I'm a klutz for treating you so badly. Maybe I was just afraid of getting too close or something.

I'd never tell Harry this. Harry's the guy I'm going out with here. I might tell him someday. Maybe not.

I just think you and I have a special bond or something. Do you think that could be?

Yes, I'm in Grade 12 here and I play basketball. I think I have the most points on the team.

I know I told you how much I liked your kisses. You bandit, you! But your eyes, Jenkins, I love your eyes.

I'm writing this in English class. I'm supposed to be writing an essay. I'd better get on with that.

Write again when you have a chance, won't you?

I absolutely <u>adore</u> your handwriting!!!

Affectionately,

Janie.

Marcia Pentland and I met in the Canterbury Club. She was what people today call petite and she had dark brown eyes and bobbed brunette hair. Marcia talked me into being on the club executive, which meant more meetings as well as the bi-weekly services at St. George's Church. Partly motivated by my father's urgings and partly by Marcia's hints that she didn't have a steady boyfriend, I asked her for a date. I suggested a movie, but she wondered if we could go to the symphony instead. Now, as a guy who knew the William Tell Overture only as the theme music for *The Lone Ranger* radio serial, I might've balked, but, in the interest of self-improvement, I told her I'd get tickets.

I felt pretty smug when I asked my father if I could have the car to take a university girl to the symphony. He patted me on the back as I went out the door in my blazer, grey slacks, white shirt and tie. There were tears of happiness in my mother's eyes.

Marcia's parents were out of the country for a year and she was living with her aunt in a fashionable apartment building on Hugo Street. She was ready to go as soon as I got to the door.

"What kind of car is this?" she asked.

"An Austin," I said, feeling self-conscious.

"It's cute," she said. "My aunt drives a blunderbuss, a Caddy. Hard to park."

I began to feel better when Marcia complimented me on the Auditorium seats.

We both enjoyed the program and, over coffee afterward, I tried to carry on an intelligent conversation about it. The only flaw in the discourse, from my point of view, was Marcia's over-use of the word *exquisite*, as in "Wasn't Walter Kaufmann's conducting exquisite?" and "I thought the string section was absolutely exquisite."

When we got back to the car, she said, "Oh, that concerto was so exquisite, it gave me goosebumps!"

I was experiencing goosebumps for another reason. Marcia seemed so happy with the evening, I anticipated an oscular reward of appropriate intensity. *The Kissing Bandit enters high society*, I told myself.

We parked and I accompanied Marcia through the crisp winter air to the building and up the flight of wide stairs. The hallway was too well-lighted for what I was expecting, but I thought she would surely ask me in.

She didn't.

"That was *exquisite*," she said, turning to me. "Thank you, Jenkins."

I didn't say anything—maybe that was stupid of me—and I bent to kiss her.

"Whoa, just a minute," she said, ducking away from me. "Let's not rush things, maestro. We'll see you in church on Sunday. Good night."

I could only assume that sophisticated symphony-attending girls didn't kiss on the first date.

Dear Janie:

Thanks for putting me ahead of your English essay, but you shouldn't do that too often.

I don't think I was ever mad at you. I don't think I could be mad at you, Janie.

You know, you might be onto something when you mention "a special bond." I feel a connection, too.

A few weeks after the last time we spoke, no, it was a few weeks after I'd heard you'd left town, I woke up one morning and I had the feeling you were in the room. I could smell your perfume. It was strongest near my wardrobe cabinet and, for a weird minute, I thought you were hiding in there.

I opened the door and traced the scent to my suit, the suit I wore to graduation. Of course! That sexy nutmeg fragrance was imbedded in my suit.

I was ecstatic. All I had to do to conjure you up was sniff my suit.

Janie, I've spent a lot of time in the past few months sniffing my suit. Beware, any mother who tries to send that outfit off to the dry cleaners!

Glad you're doing well at basketball.

Say, it won't be long until you graduate. Do you think there's a chance you might go to university in Manitoba?

Ah—just took another whiff of the suit. Now I can get by until I hear from you again.

Thanks again for being my grad date, and thank you for writing.

Happy Valentine's Day!

Jenkins.

Marcia and I saw each other in Economics class three times a week and at Canterbury Club meetings and at church, and, on our second date, we went to see the movie *High Noon,* which was being touted for an Academy Award (Gary Cooper was *exquisite*). Marcia's seeming enjoyment of my company, her laughter, the way she'd touch my shoulder or my arm with delight—these things led me to believe that we'd go home to her aunt's apartment and—if the aunt, whom I hadn't yet met, had retired for the night—neck till the cows came home.

Once again, I didn't get past the door.

Marcia reached up and gave me a quick hug and softly said, "I know a little smooch is probably important to you, Jenkins. But the feeling has to be mutual, and you and I just aren't on the same page right now."

I left the apartment building disappointed. Though there was a chance she might be building up suspense for something spectacular, I was getting frustrated.

So one night, I arranged a date with Mary. It was weeks since I'd seen her last and I told her, in my phone call from the local hotel, that I'd been ridiculously busy with my studies. I told my dad I was going out with Marcia but I felt bad about lying, so, on the way over to Mary's, I resolved to tell Mary I couldn't see her anymore. We'd neck first and then I'd make my dramatic announcement and then we'd do some more necking because it was going to be the last time.

But when I saw her before she put on her coat, in a powder-blue sweater and dark blue slacks, looking so feminine and cuddly and enticing, my resolve melted away and I could barely wait till we'd driven out to Lockport and parked on the riverbank just above the locks—a good distance from where Janie et al. had parked on grad night. How marvellous it was to taste Mary's mouth again! My tongue eagerly explored the cavity in her tooth as if it were a gold mine. And she unhooked her bra for me and, with her coat covering us and the Austin windshield steaming up, I found one of her perfectly formed handfuls of flesh and squeezed it the way today's corporate executive might squeeze a stress ball—not as hard, of course, but enough to give me instant comfort and relief. *This is where I was meant to be*, I told myself.

On the way home, my arm around Mary, who was snuggled against me, I said, "Just one minor little problem. My father doesn't think the staff should fraternize—you know, date one another. And since I'm going to be working there again this summer, it'll be best if nobody knows we're dating. Okay? Just a nice little secret for you and me to keep."

Janie's next letter came liberally doused in nutmeg. My mother brought it to me in my room but, being the least nosy person I ever met, she didn't say a word.

> *Dear Jenkins:*
>
> *That was the best letter!*
>
> *So funny! So touching!*
>
> *You had me laughing and then crying.*

But I've got something to tell you.

God, you've got to promise to burn this right after you've read it. I mean it!

When we were dancing? You remember how close we were? I felt you against me. I know you know that. And we fit together so perfectly, I wanted you, Jenkins.

I mean it.

I wanted you and we hadn't even kissed!

Then when we did kiss, I couldn't stand it. Everything felt so good! I wanted you right there in that stupid rented car.

I got scared. I thought I was losing my mind. I had to get out of there. I thought, what are you going to think of me? You were going to think you were with a crazy girl.

It wasn't the booze. I know it was just us. Being just right.

God, you see what I mean? You HAVE to destroy this.

But I'm glad I told you.

Luv,

Janie.

I'm sure I wasn't the first guy receiving letters from one girl who fantasized about his touching her, was officially dating another girl who wouldn't let him touch her, and was secretly dating a third girl who would—all at the same time. Still, I guess I should've realized I'd never had it so good. I should've savoured it.

My fourth date with Marcia was the symphony again and somewhere in the evening she let me know that her aunt was away. *This is the night,* I told myself. *This is what she's been waiting for.*

On the way out of the Auditorium, she said, "Want to come to my aunt's for a snack?"

My ont's. Lovely. *A snack.* Yum. "Yes, I'd like that," I said.

Marcia showed me into a sitting room or den. There was a wall of books, floor to ceiling, and a desk with a covered typewriter, and a sofa with a coffee table in front of it. On one of the walls was an original oil painting of what was perhaps a Paris street scene.

"Do you want some wine?" she said. "Maybe some chardonnay?"

I was glancing at some of the books. "Oh, please," I said.

"And why don't you give me that?" she said, gesturing toward my blazer.

"Yes, thank you," I said, taking the jacket off and looking into her eyes for some sign of longing. I didn't see any, but perhaps she was a little nervous.

She took my jacket and headed out of the room. "Make yourself comfy," she said.

I sat down on the sofa, thinking this was the kind of date I'd always dreamed about. This was classy. I loosened my tie and wondered if she'd return in *something more comfortable.* She was gone for a while and I began to think she'd come back in something sheer, maybe a negligee. She came back in the same thing she'd worn to the symphony, a high-necked, long-sleeved black and grey dress. She was carrying a plate of crackers with something pink on them as well as two stemmed glasses of chardonnay.

"That's salmon," she said. She pulled up an upholstered dining-room chair and sat across from me.

"Lovely," I said, thinking, *Seafood—good for lovemaking.*

I took a cracker and ate it in a well-mannered way. I took a glass and raised it.

"Cheers," I said.

"Yes," she said. "Oh, Jenkins, excuse me for saying this, but it's best to hold the glass by the stem only."

"Of course," I said, adjusting my hand.

"Look, Jenkins, I wanted to talk with you and I thought now was a good time."

I looked at her apprehensively.

She said, "We've had—what is it now—four dates?"

"Yes, four, yes."

"It's been exquisite. We've had a lot of fun, I think, and one thing I like, we leave the Canterbury stuff in the meetings. I'm going to level with you, though, Jenkins. I've noticed that at the end of every one of our dates, you have this look of utter disappointment on your face, like a child that's been denied dessert. You obviously think it's your God-given right to kiss me and touch me in some sexual way."

"I thought it was natural for a couple who—"

"Let me finish, please. I like being with you. And Jenkins, what I'm going to say has nothing to do with our coming from different social stations or with anything the Church has to say in these matters. You and I are young, but we are, I think, using dating as a prelude to mate selection. We want the usual things, like emotional security and appreciation of personal worth and companionship and fulfillment of physiosexual need. As I said, Jenkins, we have fun together, but there isn't any spark. There has to be fireworks, Jenkins—"

"We haven't even *kissed*—how do you know—"

"Jenkins, I'm sorry, I just don't have any desire to kiss you. That doesn't mean you're a bad person. I'll repeat. We have a lot of *exquisite fun* together. And since we know that, I'm asking you, do we have to spoil what we have? Can't we just be *good friends*?"

It was the end of April, a lovely spring day, and I was celebrating the end of exams. We were parked at sundown a few feet from the beach at Matlock on the west side of Lake Winnipeg, and my hot left hand was for the very first time inside Mary's panties, venturing into her slippery-wet warmth, when I felt her shudder and, although in those days we knew nothing about female orgasms, I thought maybe I was arousing her in some way, but I stopped kissing her because she seemed to be gasping or choking, and I tasted a salty tear that had run down her cheek onto my lips and I still thought it might be arousal affecting her, even as I said, "Are you okay?"

She took a few moments to calm herself and then, her voice breaking on every few words, she said, "I'm sorry, I'm sorry … it jus' doesn' seem right … we … we shouldn' be doin' dis … behind yer fodder's back … it jus' isn' right, Jenkins … I'm sorry … oh, I'm so, so sorry …"

That autumn, I went to a press night of *The Manitoban*—the university student newspaper—to see if they needed a cartoonist. The editor gave me an assignment to try me out: do something on the theme of freshmen adapting to campus life. At home, I worked on "A study on the evolution of frosh" in two panels: the first showed a typical beanie-topped young man crazily roaring around campus, tearing the sweater off a co-ed; the second depicted the same guy in cramming mode days before the December exams. The editor liked it and ran it in the next issue, and it was closely followed by "What every male student wants for Christmas," which gave me a chance to draw Marilyn Monroe. Such a hit was my rendering of Monroe in a bathing suit, I was asked to do a cartoon every second issue, one cartoon a week.

I drew the panel at home every Sunday and drove to the editorial offices to hand it in to the editor Sunday night. The staff worked till all hours, often not finishing up till morning. The offices didn't belong to the university; by day, they housed a local printing company, so the *Manitoban* staff had to confine their in-office work to evenings, every Sunday and Wednesday, publishing the paper Tuesday and Friday. Some days, the cartoon ideas wouldn't come, and I'd stare at my blank sheet of art paper until it was late and I started to panic. Sometimes, I'd deliver the finished product at two in the morning. There would always be some staff members there and often the editor's door would be closed. Legend had it that the closed door meant the editor was in there making love to one of his female reporters. I didn't believe it; even when I waited and the door opened and Shelley Kurtz or Lisa McMurtry came out, adjusting her clothing and looking flushed of face, I still didn't believe it. I'd go into the editor's office with my cartoon and look around—at the uncomfortable chairs and the cluttered desk and the bare hardwood floor—and conclude there simply wasn't anywhere to do it. The editor, a tall, well-built guy with a crew cut and a confident smile, loved every cartoon, usually laughing more heartily than the piece warranted. If it depicted a shapely co-ed, he'd light up a cigar and say, "Great tits, Jenkins."

My new-found notoriety as campus cartoonist failed to bring the girls frothing to *my* door. On press night, someone like Shelley Kurtz or Kitty Elliott might intercept me when I arrived and demand to see my latest creation, and she'd lean her boobs against me while she looked over my shoulder, but that was the extent of my thrills. At the staff Christmas party, Kitty caught me under the mistletoe and French kissed me, but I was only one of a series of guys she was accosting, and she left me with a taste of the editor's cigar.

It was a barren time. The past summer, I'd worked at my dad's factory, mostly in shipping, where I could keep to myself, but I did have daily glimpses of Mary, working at the cutting table. I respected her wishes—and therefore my father's edict—that we have no more surreptitious dates. I went out once with my *friend* Marcia, thinking the summer might've melted her resolve; we went to an outdoor concert and we sang some of the songs in the car afterward. "You've got an exquisite tenor voice, you know that?" she said, and she was out of the car and heading into her aunt's apartment building before I could suggest anything else.

In September, after I'd heard nothing from Janie Sinclair for weeks, there came this letter:

> *Dear Jenkins:*
>
> *How are you?*
>
> *I'm kind of giddy, I guess is the word. Excited! My feet haven't hit the ground yet.*
>
> *Harry proposed to me!!!*
>
> *Boy, did he take me by surprise! I said yes, and now my whole life has changed. I'm not going to university after all. We're thinking we'll have a mid-winter wedding and go somewhere warm for our honeymoon.*
>
> *Harry says he wants kids right away.*
>
> *My mom and dad are really happy. My mom and I haven't got along this well in years.*
>
> *I hope you'll come to the wedding. I'll send you an*

invitation. Only right that my favourite penpal comes to my wedding, isn't it?

I know you'll like Harry.

How's your love-life going? You haven't said much about it. I'll bet you have to beat the girls away with a stick.

Well, I wanted you to be one of the first to know my news.

Wish me luck!

Sincerely,

Janie.

Anticipation

I go out for a dry run—not all the way to Jason Hunter's house, but close. Linden Woods is a maze if you're going to someone's house for the first time. Guided by Jason's directions and my coil-bound *Sherlock's Map of Winnipeg*, I find the street and I'm in good shape for Monday night.

I go home and pour myself an Appleton's Rum and Diet Pepsi. Now that Tracy—and Vera's grapevine—know about my date, it seems real. Much more real than … whatever I had with Liz Oliver.

I sit in the living room and think, If this truly is a *date*, what should my expectations be? Is Janie now a feisty feminist? If so, what will *her* expectations be? How will I know what her expectations are? Will she revert to being a kid again the way I might, or will she be a mature woman who sees anything like holding hands or nuzzling each other or kissing as *juvenile*? Janie was so turned on by our kissing all those years ago, *so* turned on, she almost lost control of herself—what if she's still that way? Since she's been a widow for a number of years, might she be even more anxious for intimacy? Just after she moved away, she told me in a letter that she thought we had a bond—does she still feel that? Will she be inclined to finish what we started all those years ago?

I get up and put a frozen spinach pizza in the oven and pour a second drink. This one tastes better than the first and my thoughts grow more risqué. If we kiss—and I can't imagine our not kissing—will she expect to be groped? Will she grope me? Do people our age *neck*? Will I kiss her in the car, in the restaurant parking lot, or will she expect to go somewhere and then kiss? Where will she expect to go? A hotel? My house? If we go to my house, will she be freaked out by photos of Barb? Do I need to put the photos away in anticipation of our going back to my house? Will she want to see photos of Barb? What if she is so savvy about contemporary behaviour, she sees this date as a chance to *hook up*? Since neither of us has any commitment to anyone, will she expect to go to bed? If she does expect to go to bed, will she prefer to go to the guest room? I can't remember who last slept in the guest room—do I need to change the sheets in anticipation of our using it? If we *do* go to bed, will I remember what to do? Is it like riding a bicycle—you never forget—or is it so different with a different woman that it's like starting all over again? If we do go to bed, I'll have to use a condom—should I buy some so I'll be ready? What if, at her age, she needs vaginal cream and doesn't have any with her? Will we break from our clinch to make a run to the drugstore? Or will she expect me to be ready for any eventuality, *be prepared,* like a Boy Scout? Will she expect me to have taken a prescription drug to ward off any possible erectile dysfunction? Will someone like Janie be thrilled with these kinds of preparations or will she be totally turned off by sex that's so obviously premeditated?

I'm so full of anxiety, I can barely eat my pizza.

Next morning, after a troubled sleep, I think, that whole line of thinking last night was absurd. When it comes right down to it, how do you introduce the topic of sex in the first place? You might not even want to. People our age don't fall into an embrace and suddenly start ripping at each other's clothes. Besides, I have no desire to get in deep with Janie Hunter. I have no reason to believe that Janie wants anything more than a bit of chat, a bit of reminiscing.

Yet later, in the shower before I leave, my subconscious delivers to my brain the song "Perfidia"—what they played for the last dance at high-school graduation—and I sing it in my loudest tenor voice before my rational side reminds me once again that I'm a foolish old fart, and that the person I'm going out on a date with is no longer the girl I'd spent the night with fifty-six years ago.

On the way over to the Hunter residence, I have misgivings. All those years ago, after I found out how passionately Janie could kiss and I got razzed for doing things to her that I hadn't done, there was a mystique surrounding my memory of her, a strong sense of unfinished business. And there were those letters of hers that were probably intended to drive me crazy and did. But I was a kid then, with laughably little experience in matters of the opposite sex. And Janie knew it. If she'd stayed in Winnipeg, she never would've made herself accessible to me. For all I know, all these years later she's still toying with me, letting me buy her dinner, tolerating me for a couple of hours while maybe she quizzes me about how the old town has changed.

So why, despite that unfortunate evening with Liz a few months ago, am I feeling like a kid on a date? Why is an irrational part of me looking forward to a *good-night kiss*? Why do I feel a certain *swagger*, as if I'm going out to dinner with a lovely and wanton young woman? Why do I have an *erection*?

The house is a large, yellow two-storey with a broad driveway. Three late-model SUVs are parked there, but I have lots of room to pull up beside one of them. I take several deep breaths. In case there's a chance I can be seen from the house, I try to step out of the car with some remnant of agility. I feel a sharp pain in my left instep, the one I usually get from having the foot at a weird angle while driving. I fight to keep from hobbling, which brings a grimace to my face. Instead of keeping my head up to appear jaunty and devil-may-care, I frown down at the concrete in my path, watching for anything that might trip me. One of the SUVs is dirty, and that's the one I rub against, putting a grey smudge on my sport jacket which, fortunately, is grey. I look up at the front door just as I approach the first step; I don't quite get my foot all the way up to the step—I trip but keep my balance, half-running the rest of the way and stopping inches from the door. No sign of anyone there, thank God.

I ring the bell.

Except for the fact that the house is twice as large, this could be Doreen Holden's front door. Doreen, my very first date. I half-expect a smiling Mrs. Holden to appear. I have a momentary twinge of having forgotten something … *the corsage!*

The door opens. A handsome man with a receding hairline stands there looking at me as if I might be selling chocolate bars for my school. He's wearing a short-sleeved dress shirt open at the collar.

"Hi, I'm Jenkins," I say. I'm not sure what else to say. He knows why I'm here.

"Mr. Jenkins, come on in, sir. Mother should be down in a minute."

I enter. He closes the door and holds out his hand.

"I'm Jason Hunter," he says. "A word before she comes down. She cannot, I repeat, *cannot*, under any circumstances, have anything to drink of an alcoholic nature. Do you understand?"

"Yes—"

"Good. I'm holding you responsible. She'll tell you she can have a glass of wine. *She can't.* That's one of the reasons we moved her here. So we can keep an eye on her."

"I see."

"And if *you* drink?"

"I'll get a taxi to bring us home—but I likely won't drink—in fairness."

"Good. She has some pills. She'll have them with her, but you might have to remind her to take them. With water. Before dinner. Got it?"

"Got it." I no longer feel like a kid going out on a date. I'm a foot-soldier being sent into battle with life-or-death instructions from his sergeant.

"And I trust you'll bring her straight home after dinner. Oh, here she comes."

A shapeless woman appears; her torso in a rust-coloured pantsuit seems to be the same thickness from shoulders to hips. She has young Janie's face and hair, except the face is wrinkled and the hair is grey. She's carrying a large leather handbag and she's giving off a sharp fragrance.

"Gerry," she says. "It's been *so* long." She comes to me and gives me an aggressive hug.

"Mother, it's *Jenkins*," Jason says.

"Of course it is," says Janie. "What did *I* say, *Gerry*? Well, no harm done, right, Jenkins?"

"Right."

"How are you, Jenkins, after all these years?"
"I'm fine, Janie."
"Well, let's go, shall we? See you, Jason. Don't wait up."

Dating Then

I met Barbara at Grads' Farewell, the last university social event before I graduated. She was with Neil Charnetski, a guy I'd met in Money and Banking class. He and Gary Johnson and I decided to go together once I managed to get myself a date.

Here's how my date came about. I was studying and cartooning my way through my final year—another dateless winter. One day in February, walking from the Arts Building to the new library, I bumped into Jennifer Jordan, the gorgeous blonde who had turned me down for high-school grad.

"Jenkins!" she said. "I was hoping I'd see you one of these days. I love your cartoons!"

"Glad you like them."

I thought that would be the end of the conversation, but she was in no hurry. She told me which of my cartoons she'd liked best and she laughed about not knowing they were *my* cartoons until somebody told her. She said she was taking Science but wasn't doing well. Then I said, "Still going out with—?"

"Doug? No, we broke up ages ago. Say, I never apologized to you for turning you down that time. I was stupidly chasing Doug. I wish I'd gone to your grad with you."

"You don't have to say—"

"I mean it."

"Hey—um—listen. We have Grads' Farewell coming up and I haven't … well, do you think you might like to go with me?"

"Gee. I'm sort of going out with—when is it?"

"Middle of March."

"It wouldn't mean—you know—oh, you know what? I'll go."

"You will?"

"I'd like to go to Grads' Farewell with you. It doesn't mean we have to go out together between now and then, does it?"

"No!"

"Then you've got yourself a deal."

"A *deal*?"

"Well, a date."

"Jennifer, thank you."

"No, thank *you*."

Charnetski, Johnson and I took cabs because, as Charnetski put it, "This is a night when you want to get stinking drunk." I had a taxi pick me up and then Jennifer. She was so slender and beautiful in her gold-trimmed white strapless gown that I felt dazzled by her and, when the six of us met in the Marlborough Hotel lobby, I noticed that the others kept gazing at her. We went up to the room that Charnetski had rented for our coats and our stash of booze.

Johnson had curly red hair, wet lips and a slouchy posture, and his date Valerie had dark hair that was shorter and curlier than his. Her light green strapless gown exposed shapely shoulders and prominent collarbones. She stood ramrod straight in her high heels, making her a few inches taller than Johnson. Charnetski, wearing a rented tuxedo just like Johnson and me, was tallest of us all and had blond hair that was already receding from his broad forehead. His date, Barbara, was the nurse he'd been telling me about ("You know what they say about nurses"). She was pudgy with what guys called baby fat and her chubby cheeks made her eyes almost Asian. She wore a turquoise gown that matched her eyes and her hair was dark brown, done in a pageboy. The bodice gave her breasts a kind of understated prominence that allowed her to maintain a certain elegance.

We went up to the ballroom on the top floor, hid our bottles under the table and ordered soft drinks, as everyone did in those strange times before the liquor laws changed. There was a live band and some couples were already dancing. The roomful of young men in black and young women in bright colours radiated prosperity and promise for the future.

Barbara was anxious to dance. "Any takers?" she asked.

"I'll be ready in a minute," said Charnetski, sipping his drink in a mock-genteel way. "Someone warm her up for me."

"Go ahead, Jenkins," Jennifer said. "Get us started."

I jumped up and did an exaggerated bow in front of Barbara. The band was playing "String of Pearls."

Barbara was a good armful, taller than Jennifer, not as rigidly erect as Valerie. She adjusted immediately to my step, which meant I could hold her close, making conversation unnecessary. I liked her perfume and the texture of her gown, but most of all I liked how easily we danced together.

As we moved across the floor, I saw people I knew—Shelley Kurtz, who waved at me; the editor, who was squiring around a glitzily dressed girl he'd imported from Toronto; Charlotte, a pretty but enigmatic girl I hadn't seen since Grade Twelve.

When the music ended, Barbara said, "Thank you, that was very nice," and we walked back to our table.

Charnetski held a drink out to her. "He's a regular Mr. Twinkle Toes, right?"

"Absolutely," Barbara said, and she gave me a playful wink.

"You two looked good out there," Jennifer said to me.

"Your turn now?" I said.

"Why not?" she said.

I'd danced with Jennifer only once before—that brief segment of a Bingo dance back in high school. I walked with her onto the dance floor. The music began: a polka.

"Oh, no," I said.

"Don't like polkas?" said Jennifer.

"Can't do them."

"Come on. Let's give it a try."

The last thing I wanted was to do a polka as my first full-length dance with Jennifer. You couldn't adapt the Magic Step to a polka. I started, holding her at arm's length, bending my legs and trying to watch my own feet. I bumped into several other dancers. When I thought I'd figured out what to do, I collided with a girl and she fell.

"I'm sorry!" I said. I stopped dancing to help her up. "I'm terribly sorry."

"I should've seen you coming," the girl said.

"You should've honked," her dancing partner said to me.

"We'd better sit down before I do any more damage," I said to Jennifer.

The next dance was a slow one. Charnetski asked Jennifer and Johnson picked Barbara, leaving Valerie to me.

"Do you know anything about parrots?" Valerie asked me.

She was so stiff, I felt as if I were dancing with a plank. I remembered hearing that parrots lived as long as humans and I was about to tell Valerie that when I noticed Jennifer dancing close to Charnetski, her head on his shoulder.

"Why—why do you ask?" I said.

"A friend of mine wants me to babysit hers."

"Does it talk?"

"That's the problem. It says the worst swears."

The band took a break and I knocked back a couple of stiff drinks. I had a spirited conversation with Johnson about what we were going to do after graduation; Johnson liked the idea of teaching "except for the goddam students."

At last, I got a chance to do a slow dance with Jennifer. I wondered if her eyes were closed the way they were with Charnetski. Her head was tucked to one side of my jaw and I didn't disturb the arrangement to see her eyes. As we danced, she did a little clicking sound with her mouth. At first, it seemed cute. After a while, it got on my nerves. Twice I stepped on her feet.

I danced again with Barbara and preferred her humming to Jennifer's clicking, even though it seemed off-key. I thought Barbara was dancing more closely. Was I imagining it, or was her pelvis looking for mine? *You know what they say about nurses.* I gave her a squeeze at the end of the dance and she squeezed me back.

At one a.m., the evening was over. As we said our goodbyes in the hotel lobby, I swore that Barbara winked at me. But did Charnetski have to kiss Jennifer on the cheek?

In the cab, Jennifer didn't speak. We drove along Main Street, over the Main Street and Norwood Bridges. The cabbie, a swarthy guy in a golf cap, didn't speak either. I started to chuckle.

"What are you laughing at?" Jennifer asked.

"Nothing."

"Are you drunk?"

"No!"

"You are. That's why you're laughing at nothing."

"I'm laughing at the absurdity of life."

I let out a burst and held back any more. My shoulders shook. It was the kind of spasm that used to come over Gerry.

When the taxi pulled up to Jennifer's house, a bungalow on St. Elmo Road, I leaned forward to check the meter and dug into my pocket for money.

"You don't have to walk me to the door," Jennifer said.

I wasn't sure how to respond. I paid the cabbie and hurried to get out of the cab and around to Jennifer's side, but she was already out. She headed up the sidewalk.

"Hey, wait!" I called.

Rumour had it that Jennifer had slept with previous boyfriends. With confidence bred of booze, I thought the least I could expect was some heavy necking. This *cold shoulder* I was getting was probably part of a game she liked to play.

At her back door, where the light was off, she said, "I had a nice time. Thanks."

"I had nice time, too."

"Good night, then."

I laughed. I was in that kind of mood. "Don't you want me to come in?" I said.

"I told you I'd go to Grads' Farewell with you. I've kept my part of the bargain."

"*Bargain*?"

"I said I'd go because I hurt you when I turned you down before. That's all there is to it."

"I thought, if we had a good time, you might … or I might … or we might—"

"You want to kiss me, is that it?"

"Well, yes."

"Go ahead."

"*Go ahead*?"

"I'm going in."

"Okay! Okay!"

I lifted my arms to embrace her but, as she leaned forward with pursed lips, she held me back with both her hands on my chest.

In May, on the very day I started work as a merchandise trainee at Radisson's department store, I received a printed invitation to a nurses' dance. There was a handwritten name at the bottom: *Barbara Mason*.

The night of the dance fell during one of those cold snaps that make you think summer might never arrive. I wore a trench coat over my sport jacket, sport shirt and slacks. I parked my dad's car and followed the posters to a gymnasium that was part of the nurses' residence building near Redwood and Main. There were lots of guys in pairs and threesomes headed that way. At the gym entrance, I lined up to show my invitation and receive a name tag. Some guys were being met by their girlfriends. I tried to look nonchalant, the bon vivant who was invited to functions like this all the time.

"Oh, Jenkins, you *did* come."

It was Barbara, looking lovely in a pink sweater and grey skirt. She was one of the girls checking guys in. She winked at me.

"Wouldn't miss it," I said. "Thank you for the invitation."

I hadn't heard from Charnetski lately; I knew nothing about where he fit in this picture.

"I've got to stay here for a while," Barbara said. "Go in and relax, maybe have a pop or something, and I'll come and find you. I've told my roommate what a good dancer you are, so you might have a twirl or two with her. Okay?"

"Sounds fantastic."

The roommate was a redheaded girl named Melanie with hundreds of freckles on her face. She wore a plaid skirt and a green sweater with a little white collar. She led me into the low-lit gym, where a slow dance was in progress—Kitty Kallen's "Little Things Mean a Lot."

"Barbara couldn't say enough about your dancing," Melanie said. "I'm anxious for a sample."

I settled into the Magic Step. "Hardly any pressure at all," I said. "I'll likely step all over you."

Melanie seemed nervous, but she followed me, her head tilted forward so that I got a whiff of her shampoo. "Yikes," she said. "This is such a nice song."

"Do you know if Barbara is still going out with a fellow named Charnetski?"

"Oh, gosh, I don't think so. No, that's been over for a while. Well, I don't think it was ever very serious."

That wasn't the impression Charnetski had given me—but that was before Grads' Farewell.

I bought Cokes for Melanie and me and we talked about what kind of nursing Melanie wanted to do and what kind of training I was getting at Radisson's—selling books one week, towels and blankets another. I began to think I could get interested in Melanie; I wondered if freckles covered her whole body.

"There you are." It was Barbara. She looked slightly dishevelled, ruffled. Her forehead glowed. "The music man's been paid and a couple of problems taken care of. I guess I can relax now."

"Melanie's been a perfect hostess," I said.

"You were right," Melanie said. "He *can* dance."

"Ready, Jenkins?" said Barbara. "I know I am."

Barbara and I danced to the McGuire Sisters number, "Sincerely." She seemed sure of herself in my arms and we moved together like long-time dance partners. I felt her breasts touching my chest and all thoughts of Melanie's freckles vanished.

"I gather you aren't going out with Charnetski anymore," I said.

"That was over before your Grads' Farewell. I thought you might've been able to tell. I agreed to go just because it was a formal event and he promised to behave."

"Oh."

"I think we dated no more than three times. Once I found out all he wanted to do was *maul* me, that was it."

Almost involuntarily, I increased the distance between us so that our fronts didn't touch.

"You must've noticed how he was going after your date," Barbara said when the song ended.

"Now that you mention it, yes."

"I thought, What kind of friend is he? You must've heard what he did later that night."

"No, I haven't talked to him since then."

"He bragged about it when he took me home. He said he and—what was your date's name? Jennifer—he and Jennifer had a plan to get together after she—as he so nicely put it—'got rid of you.'"

"I'm not surprised," I said. "She went to Grads' Farewell with me as part of a—a bargain."

"I won't ask what the bargain was. Sounds like we're well rid of those two."

She laughed and so did I, and I noticed, as we jived to "Rock Around the Clock," that she could follow me as perfectly to fast music as she did to slow. As I twirled her, brought her in, spun her out, sent her under my arm and back, I thought, *She's enjoying this as much as I am.*

The last dance was Glenn Miller's "Moonlight Serenade." I felt her close to me again. She hummed.

"Can I walk you to your room after this?" I asked.

"Off limits. I'll walk you to your car, if you like."

The record ended. The lights went up too quickly and Barbara stepped back, adjusting her sweater and her hair. I glanced at her curves. *Once I found out all he wanted to do was maul me, that was it.*

I picked up my coat while she attended to some details with the girls responsible for clean-up. She and I headed down the hall to the main door.

"Too cold for you without a coat," I said.

She stepped outside and took a deep breath. "Ahh! It's invigorating. Come on, I said I'd walk you to your car." She pulled my arm.

"It's this way," I said.

Both of us ran. When we reached the car, she cried, "It's freezing!" and I did something so spontaneous, I surprised myself: I unbuttoned my coat and held it open wide. Without hesitation, she stepped into it and I wrapped my arms and the coat around her. I looked into her eyes. They were shining, reflecting the light from a street lamp. The night, the passing traffic, the guys leaving the dance, the buildings, the trees, the cold—everything dropped away and I was in a cocoon with this girl who seemed happy to be with me and was expecting me to do something. I knew what to do.

As I drove home, I went over and over the evening, recalling what Barbara said and how she looked and how she felt in my arms and what the kiss felt like. *The kiss.* It had come about so naturally. There was no desperation on my part—it was simply *the next thing to do*—and, by her response, she was in complete agreement. There was nothing tentative about the way we approached it; both applied pressure, but nothing that could be called aggressive. There seemed to be no need to embellish the kiss in any way; any attempt to bring my tongue into play would've tarnished the experience. As it was, without opening her mouth, she was able to convey the impression that she liked me, that she liked kissing, that she liked kissing *me*, that she liked being with me, that she felt enough at ease with me that she could let me take her into my coat and kiss her right out there on the street on a cold spring night, that she wouldn't mind seeing me again, and that she could deliver a just-right counter-kiss, just right for the moment, just right for the time of night, and just right for a guy who perhaps deserved some encouragement.

She explained before we parted that the best time to call her was on the one day a week she spent at home—Saturday. Since Saturday was the very next day, I took a break from selling men's hats—barely twelve hours after I'd left her—and, inside the tiny Men's Furnishings office, I dialled her number.

"Hello?"

I recognized her voice. "Hi, Barbara, it's Jenkins."

"Oh, hi! I just got here. Dad came and picked me up."

"I wanted you to know how much I liked the dance last night."

"Oh, good! Me too."

My impulse was to move straight to an invitation to go out, but, despite my lack of dating experience, I knew it was bad manners to appear too eager.

"You're a nurse," I said. "Maybe you've seen something like this. I was trying a hat—a fedora—on a man this morning and I was standing on one side of him and setting the fedora on his head just so, the way you're supposed to, and there on the side of his head facing me was this *hole* between his eye and his ear."

"A *hole*?"

"That's the only way to describe it—a hole in his skull,

around the temple, maybe an inch or so in diameter. I had to look away, I had this sick feeling, as if I was looking at the raw brain—"

"I've never heard of anything like that—what was the flesh like around it?"

"I'd say sort of *healed*, as if there wasn't going to be any attempt to fill it in or cover it, and he could go on living with this gaping hole in his head. You might say he was so optimistic, he was buying a new hat."

"Could you see what he was thinking?"

There was a moment of silence and then we both laughed.

"I'm awful," said Barbara.

"I guess the main thing is, from the point of view of a salesman, he did buy the hat. But listen … to change the subject to something more pleasant … I was wondering if you'd like to go to a movie."

"Sure, that'd be nice. When?"

I'd reached a critical point in the conversation. I knew a guy shouldn't presume that a girl was sitting around waiting for his call or that she didn't have any plans for the evening.

I said, "How about next Saturday?"

"That should be okay. Or it might have to be Friday. I'll have to check the schedule."

Time to say what I really wanted to say. "You know what?"

"What?"

"I'd rather see you tonight, if it's possible."

"I'd like that."

"You would?"

"Sure. I don't get out much. Sometimes it feels like I'm in a convent."

I drove my father's Chevrolet into the driveway on Kingston Row. The Mason home was about three miles from where I lived, a sprawling single-storey ranch-style house with a maple tree standing guard beside a driveway that led to a double garage. The house, in my sociological view, placed the Masons among the city's *nouveaux riches*—it had definitely been built since the war and the maple must've been transplanted.

I walked up the concrete steps to what was surely an oak front door. The coach lamps on either side were on. The shape of the doorbell reminded me of a woman's breast and I pressed the nipple. There was a small translucent window in the door and a blurred image appeared. The door opened and there was Barbara.

"You're right on time," she said. "Come in—I'll just be a minute."

As I stepped across the threshold, all my senses shouted at me that *this* was the classic date, the kind of date guys like me wished for.

Barbara wore a white sweater, a flared plaid skirt, bobby sox and saddle shoes. She gave off a piquant fragrance—perhaps something by Chanel—that lingered after she'd gone into another part of the house.

It's important to remind you that this was 1955, a time when perfume was used as much to hide body odour as anything. I myself had prepared for the date by having a bath and a shave just before leaving my house. Bath soaps like Lifebuoy were meant to combat body odour, not underarm smells specifically. There was no such thing as a spray deodorant then, and the best any young man like me did was wash well under the arms—and all over, if you had time for a bath. I knew that my mother owned a mysterious jar of cream called Odorono, but she kept it out of sight, leading me to believe it had something to do with *female hygiene*. I had no idea *where* she applied it, and I certainly wasn't going to ask. Before spray deodorants were marketed in the 1960s, under-arm odours were *never* spoken of. Some might say that under-arm deodorants were a triumph of the advertising industry, that we didn't even know our armpits smelled until arbiters of good manners allowed advertisers to tell us they did. (The first ads on the subject avoided that dastardly word *armpit*, referring instead to the *curve of a woman's arm*.) It was assumed that women might have to take some precaution when wearing a sleeveless blouse or dress in the summer; men kept their jackets on, especially at work, and if they gave off an odour, well, it was likely the masculine odour that was expected of them. As for me on this night, I had covered the lower part of my face with after-shave lotion. It could be that Barbara had applied the relatively new Ban roll-on deodorant, but most likely she relied on a good wash and perfume, since girls of a certain class believed they didn't give off any odour.

I stood in a vestibule that featured an oriental rug over cream-coloured broadloom, and an oak table with a lamp and an ornate dish that was likely intended for calling cards. Barbara came back with a woman who looked like an older version of her—just as erect in posture, hair the same shade of brown, just as tall, only slightly less shapely—except that she had a beauty spot on her upper lip where Barbara was blemish-free.

"Hello, I'm Barbara's mother," she said, smiling as brightly as Barbara, one eyelid fluttering in a potential wink. "You must be Jenkins."

"Hello, Mrs. Mason, yes, hi."

We didn't shake hands. Women seldom shook hands with men or other women in those days.

"I understand your Christian name is Robert," Mrs. Mason said.

"Yes, that's right."

"I like *Robert.* A shame it gets contracted to *Bob.* But in your case they call you neither. Why is that?"

"Oh, you know how kids can be. I'm glad I didn't get one of those crazy nicknames." I thought of a guy I knew named Bill Baxter whom everyone called La. The nickname had evolved from *Baxter* to *Backhouse* to *House* to *La Maison* to *La.* "I guess my friends thought I was more of a *Jenkins* than anything else."

There was no sign of Barbara's father. In Barbara's social class—Upper Middle, if not Lower Upper, using Burgess's six-class theory—fathers normally didn't make an appearance when a boy went to a girl's house for the first time. In the patriarchal, pre-feminist period that extended through the 1950s, meeting the father was a serious matter, reserved for a later date.

"We're off to a movie," Barbara said. "We won't be late."

"What one are you going to see?" her mother asked.

"*Marty,* with Ernest Borgnine," Barbara said.

"Oh, I've heard that's very good," her mother said. "Have a nice time."

Barbara took her raincoat from the front closet.

"Allow me," I said. I reached for her coat and she let me hold it open while she slipped her arms into the sleeves.

"Thank you," she said.

I saw her glance at her mother as if to say, *Big improvement over the louts who've come calling before, don't you think, Mom?* She kissed her mother on the cheek. I opened the door and stepped aside to let Barbara precede me out onto the landing. I closed the door.

"Your mother's very nice," I said.

"We get along," Barbara said. "It helps that I'm in residence and we don't get to see much of each other."

I walked her to the passenger side of the car and opened the door for her.

"Thank you," she said, and she eased herself into the seat. I made sure her coat was tucked inside before I closed the door.

So far, so good.

I didn't have a checklist of things you should do on a date, but I might as well have. My head was full of *dos* and *don'ts* accumulated from many sources. There were the things I'd seen my father do on social occasions: helping my mother with her coat, opening doors for her, helping her out of her coat, pulling a chair out from a table and slipping it under her as she sat down, walking beside her or behind her and never in front of her, fetching her drink before his own. There were things I'd seen my friends do: dropping off a girlfriend at the door before parking the car, letting her go first into a room, staying on the traffic side of her when walking together on a sidewalk, complimenting her at every opportunity, paying for her movie ticket and her popcorn and her post-movie snack. And there were things I'd seen in movies: lighting your girlfriend's cigarette, holding your umbrella over her even if you yourself got wet, summoning the waiter when her dinner wasn't quite right. I'd tried to abide by these guidelines as far back as on that first date with Doreen; I'd tried to be observant and attentive with Shirley, Janie, Mary, Marcia and Jennifer, but somehow it seemed more important to be observant and attentive with Barbara. She was more refined than the others, or *I saw* her as more refined. That could be because I'd seen the interior of her home—or at least the vestibule—and I'd met her mother. It could also be because of what she'd said about Charnetski—*Once I found out all he wanted to do was maul me, that was it.* I very much wanted to—well, let's not say *maul*—*touch* her, but I had to prove I was a considerate gentleman first.

Midway through the movie, I reached for Barbara's hand and held it loosely. It felt warm, soft, relaxed. I tried not to transmit my anxiety caused by keeping my hand in one place for such a long while—I turned any twitches into squeezes that she returned. I rejected the idea of playing with one of her fingers or slipping one of mine between two of hers—too phallic. My palm covered the back of her hand; her keeping her palm turned from mine was virginal—beautifully so. Somewhere near the end of the movie, she turned her hand over so that her palm faced mine, a gesture that seemed suddenly submissive, loving, trusting. It sent a wave of warmth throughout my body.

We went to a small restaurant on Portage Avenue called The Ivanhoe. Over coffee and toasted pecan buns, we talked about the movie. I didn't let on that *Marty* closely reflected the life I'd been leading ("*Whaddaya wanna do tonight, Marty?*" "*I dunno, whadda* you *wanna do?*"). We agreed on how likeable Borgnine's character and the others had been. After finishing her bun, Barbara excused herself and came back wearing fresh lipstick. I loved the happy red colour of it and the fragrance of it, and I couldn't wait for the moment when I'd be able to taste it.

That moment arrived in the breezeway of her parents' house—a latticed enclosure between the side door and the garage. Barbara went inside the house to turn off the light and take off her coat and she came back out and stepped into my open coat, which I closed around her. So much anticipation, so much pleasure, so much goodness was packed into that climactic event called *The Good-night Kiss*. Not only the luscious taste of the lipstick but the sensation of her pliant lips pressing on mine, the scent of her facial skin up close, the murmur from her as I pressed, the way our two mouths fit together. As I continued to hug her after the kiss, she reached her mouth to my ear and whispered:

"*I had a fabulous time.*"

"Wow, so did I. Can we do this again whenever you're free?"

"Oh, yes."

And that was the way things went for the next several months. Except for a three-week vacation Barbara spent with her parents, on a car trip to visit her married sister Sandra in Toronto, we went out on a weekly date. We'd hold hands and talk and laugh and I'd kiss her good night in the breezeway.

We went to a Halloween party at the home of Barbara's friend Gloria, I dressed as a graduate in gown and mortarboard, Barbara as my parchment, in a kind of wrap-around gown with a wide pink ribbon tied at the waist. Afterward, in the breezeway, Barbara did something that she'd never done before: she slid the tip of her tongue into my mouth. This new dimension ignited a flame that burned happily throughout November.

Only once did I think our level of intimacy was lacking something. That was the night Claude and I went out for a beer and Claude reacted to the news that I was dating someone with his customary "Getting much?" I coyly talked about where Barbara lived and how we liked doing some of the same things, only to have Claude report on the girl who'd sucked his cock in his car the night before. He made it clear there was a horde of girls out there that provided a vital service: giving guys experience. You shouldn't date girls you respected until you were ready to get married, and the girls you married *expected* you to bring experience with you. He said I was making a big mistake if I was getting serious about someone I respected before I'd rutted around with a few horny broads who were *good for only one thing*. After that evening, I went back to my weekly regimen, and it took only one bracing breezeway embrace to convince me that I was living a full life.

Many times that fall, Barbara and I double-dated. Parents liked their kids to double-date, the unspoken reason being that you were less likely to "get into trouble" if you were with two other people. Whenever I went out on a date, my mother—who was the least meddling mother one could imagine—would say, "Is anyone else going with you?" Even she implied that single-dating put you on the road to debauchery if not pregnancy.

There were reasons why kids themselves preferred double-dating, or even triple-dating. Some guys worried about their communication skills, and they thought that if they didn't know a girl well, it might be good to have somebody else along to help with the conversation. Some girls who were leery of what a guy might expect figured having another couple with them would inhibit the guy, prevent him from getting "fresh," as they used to say. Some kids just thought a date was *less serious* if you had another couple with you.

Barbara and I went out quite often with Gloria and Gloria's boyfriend Tony. Gloria was pretty, shorter than Barbara, and perpetually concerned that she was losing a battle to make her chunky body less chunky. Tony was my age, in his last year of Engineering, and if he saw Arts men as lesser beings, he didn't show it. He was nice enough, but he found endless excuses to pat Gloria's bum, which he referred to as her "caboose." At first, I thought that the liberties he took hinted at rampant sexual shenanigans when they were alone; after a few dates with them, I figured he took those liberties when he was with us because that was the only time he could get away with them. Whatever the truth was, his ass-grabbing embarrassed me, since it fell into the verboten *mauling* category.

Despite that, our double dates were fine, once I got used to the encoded banter that passed between Gloria and Barbara. A typical scene would find Tony driving his own Meteor, and Gloria half-turned in the passenger seat, so that she could look at Barbara, sitting behind Tony in the back seat beside me. Gloria said something like "... so Poodle went and did exactly what Nate didn't want—" and Barbara said, "Don't you mean Puddie?" and Gloria guffawed and Barbara laughed too and Gloria said, "Oh, Jeez, do you know why I said *Poodle*?" and Barbara stopped laughing just long enough to say, "Of course I do!" and I didn't have a clue what they were talking about. Neither did Tony, as far as I knew. If their banter went on too long, Tony would reach across and seize Gloria's hip or buttock and say, "Get your caboose over here, Babe."

Tony and I seldom spoke to each other, except maybe when the girls were in the ladies' room. He'd ask me about my job and, after I said how much I was liking it, he'd let me know that he'd never shopped at Radisson's in his whole life.

Sometimes Barbara and I went out with Don Stanhope, one of my colleagues at Radisson's, a likeable guy whose favourite expression was, "You don't have to be old to be a dirty old man." Don was dating a girl named Milly from the Controller's Office at Radisson's. She made up for an ordinary face with a good sense of humour and beautifully applied makeup, and, for rather obvious reasons, she was known among the guys as *Hilly Milly*. Wherever we went, Don liked me to drive, and, after the usual pleasantries when we picked them up, you wouldn't hear anything from the back seat except a moan or a snicker from Milly and maybe the odd "*Don, don't!*" It put the onus on Barbara and me to carry on a conversation and act as if there was nobody with us.

Hearing the other couple fooling around always made me remember that time with Mary, after the party at June's, when Ed and Allie drove us home. I had to admit I viewed it with a certain amount of nostalgia.

Then one night Bud took me out for a beer and told me he'd really like it if he and Vera could go out with us. I'd been avoiding a double date with Bud and Vera because she talked so damned much, so I tried to be vague, saying it was tricky to plan because Barbara's hours changed all the time. After three or four glasses, Bud told me what he really wanted.

"Jenkins, you're one of my best buddies, right?"

"Yes, I guess so."

"You and I have been friends just as long as I've been going out with Vera, and that's a long time."

"Yup."

"I'm going to level with you, Jenkins. Vera and I are going to get married someday, there's no two ways about that, but we want to wait till we've saved a bit more money, you know what I mean?"

"Sure."

"But this waiting can get to a guy. And to her, too. She has *needs*, Jenk, and God knows I do, too."

"Bud, are you sure you want to—"

"Jenk, I need you to do me a favour. We'll plan this date, okay? And you and Barbara will come over to Vera's and pick us up and we'll tell Vera's mom we're going out with you and you'll deliver us home again, but, in the meantime, you'll be taking us somewhere—I haven't got that part worked out yet—"

"Wait, wait. Hold it. You want Barbara and me to cover for you while you go somewhere and have sex with Vera?"

"Jenkins, listen. Vera's mom watches us like a hawk. We have to account for everything we do, and she's just about insisting that we go out with another couple or she won't let Vera out of the house. But, she *likes* you, Jenkins. She respects you."

"Bud, I hardly know her."

"Just do this little thing for me and—"

"Bud, no. I'm not going to lie to Vera's mother. And I

certainly don't expect Barbara to be a party to something like this."

"Christ, Jenk, I'm begging you—"

"No, Bud."

So, while other guys were grabbing their girlfriends' asses or feeling them up in the back seat or planning where they'd go to have a piece of tail, I was trying to be content with a hands-off policy. No matter how our double-dating went, the evening would be redeemed by Barbara's willingness to dally in the breezeway for some good old French kissing. But by December, I was thinking about *going further.*

I realized it was time I asked Barbara to go steady.

We'd been to a house party and I'd watched Tony dance with his hand more or less on Gloria's caboose most of the evening. In the breezeway, Barbara was out of her coat and inside mine and, just before I kissed her, I asked her.

She answered, "Oh, yes, of course, Jenkins, yes!"

In that instant I thought it might be the time, now that she had a commitment from me, to put my hand on her bosom. But it seemed all too mechanical, as if I thought her agreeing to go steady gave me a licence to *maul* her. Maybe I should tell her I loved her and then put my hand on her bosom.

"I love you, Barbara," I whispered.

Suddenly, there was *her* hand, taking mine and moving it up her cashmere sweater, placing it … placing it squarely on her left breast.

"I love *you,*" she whispered.

"Oh, *God!*" I gasped.

Moments later, she said, "I'd better go in now."

"Yes," I said, ungluing my hand from its new-found treasure.

When I left, the night shone in theatrical splendour; the city resounded with symphonic crescendos. I didn't need a car. I leaped from Barbara's house to mine in a single bound.

Old Flame

As soon as we're in my car, Janie says, "I think I made a big mistake, coming to live with Jason. He and Krista, his wife, keep me on a short leash and they're always telling me what I can't do."

"I'm sure they mean well," I say, backing the car out of the driveway.

"Yeah, well, I'm not sure how much more of it I can take. Hey, at least I'm out of there tonight, aren't I? Free! Free at last!" She pats my knee. "Sorry I called you Gerry—I'm just so excited about actually going out on a *date*. It's a million years since I went out on a date."

"Really?"

"I felt no need to, you know? Or … I don't think I've been out on any dates since Harry died—not lately, anyway. Maybe I did go out a bit in Calgary … cripes, it's awful, growing old, isn't it? Losing my memory, calling you Gerry—by the way, how *is* old Ger?"

"Janie," I say, feeling worse about this evening every minute. "You must know Gerry died in 1999."

"Of course. See? There I go again. I guess it's just hard for me to accept. I can still see him on the basketball court—a real smoothie but kind of sneaky, too. Were you on that team, Jenkins?"

"No, I wasn't."

"Funny, I thought you were. I wanted to look you up in one of the old Yarwood yearbooks after we talked on the phone, but I couldn't find them. I *know* I brought them from Calgary. I think Krista must've put them somewhere. She does that, you know. Takes my personal things and stashes them God knows where."

Minutes later, I drive into the restaurant parking lot.

"'The Keg,'" Janie says, reading the sign. "I've heard of that. I think we had a Keg in Calgary."

I park the car and turn off the engine. Janie unfastens her seat belt and puts her hand on the door handle.

"Janie, just a sec," I say. "I don't know any gentle way to tell you this, so I think I'll just come right out with it."

"Are you going to tell me you're gay?"

I'm too depressed by the situation to smile. "No, no, nothing like that. Janie, back there at your son's house, before you came down, he asked me to make sure you didn't drink any wine, beer or spirits."

"*Did* he?" She looks hurt but not surprised. "Isn't that lovely? You see how he's trying to ruin my life? Did he tell you I was an alcoholic?"

"No."

"Well, I am *not* an alcoholic. What did he say would happen to me if I drank?"

"He didn't—"

"Jenkins, I'm not going to have a seizure, I'm not going to

faint, I'm not going to drop dead on you. Don't worry about a thing. I'll be fine."

"Janie, I know this is bizarre—I should've discussed it further with Jason, but you appeared and there wasn't any chance—"

"I know. Wonderful. Don't discuss it with *me*. What kind of a *son* is that? I'm going to drink what I damn well please."

"Janie, it's just one evening. Let's have a nice evening without booze. I won't drink either. We don't need booze to have a good time. I don't know what Jason thinks the problem is, but we can have it out with him another day."

"You're going to kowtow to that *tyrant*."

"I gave him my word."

"Sure put you in a lousy position, didn't he? All right. I'll go along with you." She pats my knee again. "It's nice to see you. Let's make the best of it."

"Are you sure?"

"Yes. Let's go. I'm famished."

I feel so relieved that I want to hug her, perhaps catch a flicker of my old flame. But she lets herself out of the car.

Inside, we're shown to a booth. The low lighting and the deep wood tones of our surroundings make the restaurant conducive to nostalgia. I expect us to talk about *that night,* relive our slow-dancing and our necking, take our imaginations to the brink.

"What can I get you folks to start?" says our white-shirted waiter. "A beverage? We have a special tonight—"

Janie says, "I'll have … what's that water called again?"

"Perrier?"

"Yes, I'll have Perrier with a lemon twist."

"I'll have the same, except with a lime."

"I'll be right back with those."

Janie looks around. Her face in the subdued light looks almost young. "This is very nice, Ger—there I go again—*Jenkins*. Thank you for bringing me here. What's it called, again?"

"The Keg."

"Yes. I think we had a Keg in Calgary."

"I'm pretty sure there is one there. Probably more than one."

"It's a chain, then."

"Yes."

"Very nice."

The waiter brings our drinks. "Folks, would you like to order now? Perhaps an hors d'oeuvre to start?"

Janie and I exchange glances.

"You know, we haven't looked at the menu yet," Janie says. "And we haven't seen each other for—how long, Jenkins?"

"Over fifty years."

"Yes, so you see, we have a lot of catching up to do. We'll take our time, if that's all right?"

"That's excellent, ma'am. I'll just check on you from time to time, but the two of you just make yourselves at home."

"Having said that," says Janie, "I'm starved, so could we start with some—oh, I don't know ..."

"Some chicken fingers and, say, a honey dill sauce?" I say.

"Oh, yes!"

"Very good. I'll be back with that."

As the waiter goes away, I say, "Where should we begin?"

"Well, I'm dying to hear about your kids—and I want to tell you all about mine—they've been my life, after all. So why don't you start?"

It isn't where I wanted to start, but since she's been so co-operative about the booze question, I think I'll humour her. I tell her about Tracy's rhythmic gymnastics career, how she competed internationally, won medals. The waiter brings the chicken fingers and I explain how Tracy met an entrepreneurial guy, married him, and is now heavily involved in his sportswear company. Janie says she'd never heard of Clay Heller clothes and I'm sure she probably has, but I don't press it. I go on to tell her about Brian and his acting career, which hasn't exactly taken flight but is good enough to keep his CD and DVD collections growing to ridiculous proportions. When I tell her he's based in Toronto, she says:

"He probably knows my son Pat—no, *Matthew*. Is your son in movies?"

"He's been in a few. Small roles. He does commercials when he can—even does a bit of stand-up comedy now and then."

"Matthew provides those big white trucks they use in movie shoots."

"I'll ask Brian if he knows Matthew. What's his company called?"

"Oh, I don't know, Southern Signals or something. I can't keep track."

"Brian has never married, but he lives with a woman named Naomi who works in the movie business, too. If Brian doesn't know Matthew, she likely does—she works as a production assistant. They have a little girl named Kit."

"Is that your only grandchild?"

"No, sorry. Tracy and Clay have a daughter Mason who's a budding gymnast like her mother."

"I have—what is it—fifteen?—yes, *fifteen* grandchildren and three great-grandchildren."

"Wow!"

The waiter stops by. "How are you folks doing?"

"You know, I think I'd like to order," Janie says. "What were you going to have?"

"The prime rib is always good," I say.

We both order medium-rare roast beef with broccoli and a baked potato.

When the waiter has gone, I say, "Your turn."

"All right, but first, I'd better visit the washroom. Do you know where it is?"

I point it out and, as she leaves, I take a deep breath. I no longer want to discuss the past. I'm weary—and hungry—and I'm irritated by the orders Janie's son saw fit to give me, and by my own stupidity for initiating this so-called *date*. I'd be happy to eat and run. I look around at the other patrons. The place is about half full, and the six young people across from us are getting noisy.

"That's better," Janie says, returning in a cloud of newly sprayed perfume. It's too pungent for my liking, not the pleasant nutmeg scent of yesteryear. "All right, where were we?"

"You were going to tell me about your kids. But first—I believe you have some pills you're supposed to take?"

"Who told you that, Jason? He certainly gave you a crash course in minding Momma, didn't he?"

"Janie, I'm sure you need the pills."

"Okay, okay! Get me another water, would you?"

I find the waiter and he brings more Perrier. Janie takes out her plastic pill container—marked MONDAY P.M. She swallows several pills with several gulps of Perrier.

"And now," I say, "your kids?"

"Yes—hey, how about this for a handy-dandy little memory jogger?" She holds up the palm of her left hand. Printed in black ink across the lifeline are six letters: *G, J, P, M, L, S*. "Helps me remember the order—thank *Christ* they all have different initials."

"*J* is for Jason—so he isn't the eldest."

"No. My darling Gail came first. She was our love child. Poor Harry—rest his soul—was a stubborn cuss when he was young. I tried and tried to get him to wear a *French safe* but he wouldn't. So, naturally, we had to get married. We said

Gail was premature, but we weren't fooling *anybody*. She weighed damn near eight pounds."

Janie's voice is getting louder—I'm sure the kids across the way heard "French safe," but they probably don't know what it is.

To try subtly to get Janie to speak more softly, I use a quieter voice to say, "Where does Gail live now?" I want to speed up the process. If she dwells on Gail's conception, birth and childhood, we'll be in The Keg all week.

"She lives—what's that city in Georgia where—you know the guy who was kind of simple but did all these great things—where he sat in one of the town squares—he was played by that famous actor—"

"Savannah. Forrest Gump. Tom Hanks."

"Bingo! You win the jackpot. She married a retired American army officer and they live in Savannah. I love going there to visit. Poor Gail. Her eldest daughter was married to an absolute *shit*—"

"Okay, not so loud, Janie. We don't want to get thrown out before dinner."

"Gail has two other kids—I don't remember their names right now—but one of them has twins—the cutest little buggers."

"Your great-grandchildren."

"Yeah, well, two of them. I don't remember who has the third one, but it'll come to me."

"Let's move on to your other kids."

She looks at her palm. "Okay, we did Gail … oh, Jesus, *Jason*. Well, you already know enough about that bastard. Him and that wet noodle wife of his—but you'd like their kids—well, the one who's still at home. I should've written her name down—I think it starts with D."

"Deirdre?"

"That's it! You're good."

"You mentioned her when we talked on the phone."

"Did you meet her?"

"No, I saw only Jason."

"Lucky you. Did I tell you what he does? Big goddam wheel for some aerospace company. Christ. Okay, enough on him. P. Oh, you'd love Patrick! You have got to go down there and visit him. That's the cat's ass, where he lives."

The waiter brings our dinners. "Will there be any wine tonight?"

"I'd have a *vat* of pinot noir if you could get rid of my killjoy escort," says Janie.

"No, thanks," I say. The waiter looks perplexed. "Maybe more water."

"All this *water* is getting to my bladder," says Janie. "I'd better head for the pisser."

"Shall I keep your dinner warm, ma'am?"

"Sure, just sit on it while I'm gone, honey."

As she leaves, I say, "It'll be okay."

"I'd rather keep it hot," the waiter says. "I'll watch and bring it as soon as she comes back."

"Okay."

The evening is turning into an ordeal again. But maybe Janie has a legitimate problem: a weak bladder. Or an infection. Or diabetes.

She and the waiter come back simultaneously. She gives him a huge smile.

"Oh, if only I was about fifty years younger," she says, growling, as he withdraws. "Hey, this looks good, Gerrins." She cuts off a large chunk of meat and chews it. "Bloody good."

"Now, tell me about Patrick. Where does he live, somewhere south, you said?"

We gradually sort out that he's a hotel manager in Hobart, Tasmania. She's been to "Tassie" many times, says it's the prettiest place she's ever seen. Virgin beaches, rugged mountains, lush forests, caves full of glowworms. She was there once when an American aircraft carrier came into the Hobart Harbour. Thousands of American sailors swarmed the city, and the pub in Patrick's hotel advertised free beer for any girl accompanied by a sailor.

"The escort services advertised fresh part-time girls—*none of the tough-skinned old pros for the gobs*!"

She skips over Matthew, "the one with the Christly big trucks," because she's already talked about him, and she goes on to Lolita, who has "bubbies out to here—Jesus knows where she got those from!" She was in *Playboy* once—not a centrefold, but she should've been—and she's divorced and living with some "well-hung drug dealer" in Vancouver. And last of all is Janie's baby Samuel—"speaking of *well-hung*"—and he's a salesman for some damned company or other in Edmonton. Janie can't remember some of the names of the spouses and the kids. She's beginning to slur her words and, if I didn't know better, I would think she's getting drunk. Perhaps she's just getting tired.

As she finishes her main course, she says, "Sorry, I've got to do peepee again—and maybe a *big job*."

This time, I go too.

Over cherry cheesecake, Janie finally talks about the old days, but it comes out oddly: "How do you and I know each other again?"

I might've been crushed if we'd started that way, but Janie's memory is so erratic in regard to her own kids, I suspect she might be suffering from dementia or Alzheimer's.

"I took you to my high-school graduation," I say. "We had a terrific time. We stayed out all night and went to a classmate's house for breakfast."

"Did we fuck?"

The young people near us are leaving. I'm sure most of

them heard Janie. At least two of them laugh, but Janie is oblivious.

"Janie, we're going to have to leave if—"

"It's a simple fucking question, Ger-Jenkins. Did we or did we not have sex?"

"We did not. We had a lot of fun dancing. It was a different, more innocent time then."

"Jenkins, yer starting to piss me off. You don't have to come on all high and mighty just because I can't remember something that happened in the fucking Ice Age."

"Janie, please try not to speak so loud—"

"Oh, so now I'm loud. You want to hear loud? I'll show you fucking *loud*—"

"Let's go. I'll pay on the way out."

The waiter appears. "Sir, is there something—?"

"Just the check, please."

"Waiter," says Janie, suddenly all sweetness. "Would you call me loud?"

"Ma'am, I don't want to judge, but there's the odd word that could be said just a tad more softly …"

"A tad? Okay." Now she's almost whispering. "See, Gerry? There's a nice way to tell me."

The waiter leaves and Janie comes over and sits beside me. She leans close to kiss me and I know it's wrong to resist, even though we've become a spectacle for some of the folks still in the restaurant. One of her hands goes inside my jacket and grabs a handful of shirt at the same time that she kisses me hard. Embarrassed as I am, doing this in full view, I notice something.

Something on her breath.

Something subtly alcoholic.

Vodka.

It dawns on me what's going on. Those trips to the

washroom … I don't panic. The main objective is to get her out of the restaurant.

"That was lovely," I say. "Just like old times."

"That *was* nice, Jenkinsh," she says, so quietly that I can barely hear her. "And there'sh a lot more where that came from."

The waiter brings the check and this time Janie doesn't look at him. She's kissing my ear. I let her do that while I take out some money. Luckily, I have enough cash for the bill and a sizeable tip—I don't want to have to wait while he processes a credit card.

"Thank you, sir," the waiter says. "Have a good night, both of you."

Janie stands up and staggers. I have to support her, avoiding the looks of everybody we pass, as we head out to the car. She's laughing. I help her into the passenger seat and put the seat belt on for her.

"Thanksh, Ger," she says, "thash nice of you."

When I get in behind the wheel, she squeezes my thigh.

"Are you married?" she asks.

"Janie, come on. You *know* my wife died two years ago."

"Will you take me to your place?"

I'm horrified at the thought. "No, Janie, I'd better get you home."

"It'sh not even night yet, for fuck'sh shake."

"We're both tired."

"I don't *want* to go home. The last pershon I wanna shee is that bashtard Jashon."

She's right. How the hell can I deliver her home drunk?

"All right," I say. "I'll take you to my place."

"Thanksh, Ger. You're a fuckin' prinsh. I'll make it worth your while."

As soon as I start the car, she falls asleep. With my two

hands, I gently move her head to a more natural position and she doesn't wake up.

Petting and Popping

No sooner had I put my hand on Barbara's breast than I was being invited to meet her father. The occasion was dinner at the Masons' the very next day, one of those rare Sundays that Barbara could spend at home.

"Barbara tells me you've embarked on a career in retailing," Mr. Mason said, when we were settled in the living room with pre-dinner drinks.

"With Radisson's, yes, sir," I said.

"Grand old Canadian company. I'm told they like to move their young executives around to other cities. Are you prepared for that?"

"I think I'll be ready for whatever they want to suggest, sir," I said.

"Where would you like to be five years from now?"

"Oh, Rolph," Mrs. Mason said, "Jenkins is here for a relaxing meal, not the third degree. Why don't you tell him a little about *your* business?"

Mr. Mason took a deep breath and seemed to decide that he probably was rushing too soon into my ambitions and qualifications. He proceeded to explain that he was vice-president and general manager of Pine & Grundy Investment Dealers. (I made a mental note to pull out my Economics textbook—the one by Samuelson—as soon as I got home, because it was time to brush up on stocks and bonds.) Mr. Mason spoke about new issues of stocks as if he were giving hot tips. He had a full head of grey hair and black eyebrows that were so bushy, you felt you could see them growing as he talked.

When dinner was ready, Mrs. Mason assigned me to one side of the dining-room table, Barbara opposite me. Mrs. Mason sat at the end nearest the kitchen and Mr. Mason took his place at the other end in the captain's chair, the only chair that had arms. Barbara served the plates, which were already filled with roast beef and potatoes and beets and asparagus. Mr. Mason poured red wine. I was encouraged to begin eating first, and I hoped that my family's method—regarded as the *English* or *The Queen's* way—would be acceptable. By this method, you kept your fork in your left hand and your knife in your right at all times, lifting portions to your mouth with your left hand. The other method—labelled the *American* way by my parents—called for you to have your knife and fork in your two hands only while you were cutting your meat and to lay your knife down and move your fork to your right hand to convey food to your mouth. I was relieved to see that the Masons did indeed practise The Queen's method. I made sure my serviette was on my lap and I minded my table manners, even remembering to pick up my wine glass by the stem, as Marcia had taught me. I passed things before being asked to, I kept my mouth closed as I chewed, and I restricted the size of each mouthful.

While Mrs. Mason spoke about a fund-raising event she

was working on, Mr. Mason looked at me as if he were accusing me of something. I wondered if there was some nicety of dining that I was neglecting, and I glanced across the table to be sure there wasn't a tell-tale handprint on the front of Barbara's sweater. If Mr. Mason remembered being young and courting his future wife, and so could empathize with me, he didn't show it.

After dinner, I offered to help with the dishes, but I was urged to accompany Mr. Mason into the living room while Mrs. Mason and Barbara did their *women's work* in the kitchen. Mr. Mason indulged in a cigar and approved of my refusing one, as if cigars were something you couldn't handle until you were middle-aged and successful. He quizzed me about the Radisson training plan, looking not at me but at his cigar and his cigar smoke as I answered.

The women finished the dishes in time for *The Ed Sullivan Show* on TV. We all went into a separate sitting room where the sectional furniture faced a massive console. In this tight little foursome, sipping tea and watching television, I felt more or less at ease, yet I also felt emasculated, as if familial camaraderie were intended to take away my horniness.

Christmas came and went, and New Year's Eve, and Valentine's Day, and the anniversary of our first date, and I was reasonably content with my weekly outings with Barbara—movies, dances, house parties, double dates—ending each time in the breezeway. As the weather warmed up, our breezeway clinches warmed up, too. I found a spot on Barbara's neck that she loved to have kissed and she joked about the ingenious ways she'd cover up the hickey I'd created. And I was helping myself to a little feel, but still outside the clothing.

By the spring, on the basis of an aptitude test and a

discussion with Personnel, Radisson's had made me copy chief in the advertising department. I not only wrote the copy for the men's wear ads, I supervised three other copywriters, all female: Lasha, who forever looked busy, running around the selling departments collecting last-minute details for an ad that should've been finished days before, and complaining about breaking one of her long fingernails on a typewriter key; Melissa, who never looked busy, sat in her cubicle day-dreaming, yet produced copy that never needed to be edited and was completed on time; and Clarise, who was taller than I was and misty-eyed and who couldn't write her way out of a wet paper bag. I spent too much of my time editing Clarise's copy, but the assistant manager, Chet Bigley, thought she was too nice to fire. Chet was a diminutive fellow who was overworked, constantly covering for the manager, Maurice Fisher. Fisher's marcelled hair gave him the look of a movie producer; he had the air of a man who had bigger fish to fry—he was usually out of the office. Chet ran the day-to-day operation, which included, besides the writers and me, an office secretary, three artists, a production artist and Ricky Rhodes, our talented art director.

By mid-summer, the Masons were inviting me to their Victoria Beach cottage for the day, and Barbara and I frequently found ourselves necking in wet bathing suits while her parents were drinking cocktails next door. Resisting the impulse to yank Barbara's bathing suit down, I told myself that necking was important in its own right; you learned what you liked and didn't like about the other person's breath and skin and mouth up close.

Barbara promised after nearly every bout of necking that we'd go *further* soon. She said it might be fun to plan the occasion when we'd get more physical so that we could both look forward to it. Making do with the usual fumbling grope,

I waited and waited for the night when she said *everything would fall into place.*

Autumn came and went, and a new year, 1957, dawned, and I began to believe that *The Night* might never arrive. I wistfully considered trying to find out what Mary was doing these days—or her sister Julie, who would now be a nubile seventeen—when Barbara announced that Saturday, February 9, 1957, would be the date I was waiting for. The Masons were taking off that very day for a three-week vacation in Florida, leaving the house to Barbara.

Nearly insane with anticipation, I carefully drove my father's car over to Barbara's on the designated evening. There'd been a thaw and the streets between my place and hers were slushy and slippery. I worried that I might go through a red light or slide into a parked car or hit a pedestrian because my head was so full of—*what*? I had no idea what to expect. I was bathed and shaved and, under my overcoat, I was dressed in my terra-cotta trousers and what I called my *Italian* shirt—the one with the short sleeves, the high open collar and the wide tan and white stripes. I had called to my parents something vague like "Just going over to Barbara's"; I hadn't told them the Masons wouldn't be there.

Barbara greeted me at the front door. "Hi." That was all she said. I was disappointed by her choice of clothing: prim white blouse, pearl earrings, plaid skirt. I thought maybe she was emphasizing her youth.

"Mmm," I said, closing the door behind me. "What's that I smell?"

"Cinnamon buns. I thought we'd have them with tea while we watch Perry Como."

"You *baked* them?"

"Such as they are, yes."

"I *love* cinnamon buns."

"I know. I hope you like these."

I started to take off my coat.

"Hold me," she said.

I hesitated, then I realized what she wanted. I opened my coat—our old ritual—and she stepped inside and I wrapped the coat around her.

"You're shaking," I said.

"I'm nervous, I have to admit it."

"Why?"

"We're here in this big comfortable house with nobody to prevent us from doing whatever we want to do."

"You trust me, don't you?"

"I *do* trust you. I *love* you, Jenkins. It just doesn't feel right. I'm just wondering … if we—oh, God, the buns!"

She ran to the kitchen. I took off my coat and hung it up. I had to admit I felt different too, as if I'd left my adolescence behind, simply because my girlfriend and I didn't have to sneak off anywhere. I entered the kitchen, where I found Barbara wearing oven mitts and placing a pan of goodies on the stove.

"Saved them," she said. "Why don't you go in and turn on the TV? I think it's started. I'll just be a couple of minutes."

"I'll save you a seat," I said.

Perry Como was his usual self, singing "Round and Round." I felt uneasy and, as I sat down and watched his show, I thought a guy could learn a lot from Como on how to be unbothered—or at least look that way.

Barbara brought in a tray laden with buns that were smaller than what I was used to but still gave off that irresistible cinnamon aroma. She went back to the kitchen and returned with plates and butter and knives and spoons and sugar and milk and cups and saucers and a teapot.

I devoured one buttered bun and another. "These are terrific," I said, taking a third.

Sitting on separate sections of the sectional sofa, we

finished off the buns as if food was what we were hungry for. Barbara poured a second cup for both of us and, when the show ended, I collected the empty plates and things and carried them into the kitchen. Barbara followed. After I set the tray on the counter, I turned to find her *there*.

"That was so g—"

She gave me an open-mouthed kiss made up of a mixture of tastes—tea, cinnamon, lipstick. I held her tight, feeling wicked—we'd never kissed in the kitchen before.

"Let's not worry," she said. "Let's enjoy ourselves."

"I just don't want you to think—"

"Did you hear me? Let's not analyze and question and—well, you know how we carry on sometimes. Now, you go downstairs."

"I was going to help you wash up."

"We're going to leave everything. Go, and I'll be with you in a few minutes."

I went downstairs, not sure why we weren't going to neck in the TV room or the living room. Maybe she was respecting boundaries set by her parents: *If you must neck while we're away, please neck in the rec room.* That's where we'd been going lately—I'd begun to call it *The Neck Room.* Well, I wasn't complaining. We were going to fool around, that was the main thing. My heart was pounding.

I checked myself in the downstairs bathroom mirror: the shirt looked good, except I needed to undo the second button. There, that was better, with a suggestion of chest hair showing. I went into the rec room. It felt dank; I started the fake fire. I sat on the sofa, picked up a *Time* magazine and leafed through it without seeing a thing on the pages. I wondered what Barbara could be doing. Maybe she was having second thoughts. Cold feet. I stood up and walked around, peeking into the dark room where the furnace hummed. I looked into the Ping-Pong room and on the green table two bats embraced a ball. Suggestively.

I heard her footsteps on the stairs. I hurried back to the rec room and sat down on the sofa, hoping to look composed, as if I'd been relaxing. The *click click* of her footsteps told me she'd changed her shoes; it wasn't the sound of loafers, it was—yes, it was definitely the sound of high heels.

Now she entered the room, and she was wearing black pumps all right, and black slacks, and a patent leather belt, and a sleeveless black jersey with a rhinestone pin, and rhinestone earrings, and her lips were moist with brighter red lipstick, and her eyes seemed greener somehow, framed in mascara, and she'd changed her hair so that a lock fell over one side of her forehead. She seemed a little shy about the effect she was trying to create, but she held herself poised. She came to me and she bent over me and kissed me and kept kissing me as she knelt on the sofa beside me and ran her fingers over my face and inside my collar, and she touched her lips to my temple and my cheek and my earlobe and that place where the jaw meets the neck, and lower and lower.

"You wear a stiff white collar at work all day," she whispered. "When you're in the office on Monday, think of my lips being here … and here …"

"Oh, yeah," I said, and I moved my hands over her sweatered back.

I noticed something different. There was no bra strap.

"You took off your—"

"Shhh," she said, pushing her mouth hard against mine.

I didn't want to rush this—it was too much of a good thing—I wanted everything to last and last, and we did after all have lots of time, so, as she changed to a sitting position beside me, I moved my hand slowly until it came to where her right breast began and I was astounded by the softness that undergarments concealed. I moved my hand further but still ever so slowly, until the breast filled my hand and I could feel the nipple pushing through the jersey. As we continued to kiss, she tugged one side of the jersey out of her belt and I knew this was an invitation for me to send one hand under the jersey, and I moved my hand so slowly I couldn't believe my own patience, and I felt how smooth and feverish her flesh was, and there, *there*, was the curve of the lower part of her bare breast, and the mere touch of it against my fingers sent a hot tremor through me.

"I love you!" I shouted.

"You're boiling!" Barbara said. "Your face is on fire. Stay there." She got up.

"Where—"

"I'll get a cool wet face cloth. Doesn't that sound good?"

She went in bare feet to the basement bathroom. I heard water running. She was right, I'd never felt so hot. She returned with the wet cloth and a towel and she gently wiped my face and neck and under my chin and into the top of my shirt.

"Ohh, thank you," I said.

She stopped to dry my face and comb my hair. She said, "I'm so glad you aren't badgering me to take off my clothes and you aren't trying to touch me—you know—down there."

"Barbara, I'm happy just being here with you, you know that," I said, but I couldn't wait to get back to what I'd been doing.

"We should thank God for showing us how to respect each other and keeping us rational so that we aren't tempted to do something crazy."

I so much wanted to do something crazy or at the very least hold that breast again, but I said, "You're right."

"Let's get down on our knees."

"What?"

"That's the way you talk to God."

"Can't we—"

"Come on."

She knelt beside the sofa and bent her head and held her hands together under her chin like a praying little girl. I'd never seen this religious side of her, but I had to admit I wanted to thank *somebody* for letting me caress her bare boob after all these months. I knelt beside her.

She said, "Do you want to say it?"

"Oh … I …"

"Come on."

"Okay. Let's see—um—thank you, thank you, Lord, for giving us the desire we have for each other … and … and for giving us the wisdom to guide us and govern that desire."

"Amen," she said. "Oh, Jenkins, that was beautiful!" She turned to me and, with us still on our knees, she pulled me to her and whispered, "You touched one, and the other is jealous. Will you touch the other one, please? Please?"

In those days, petting—as the Sociology books called sexual touching—was not foreplay. Petting was an end in itself. By that summer, Barbara was a registered nurse, working full time and living back at home, and part of every date was devoted to petting in The Neck Room. Sometimes I was content to feel one breast from outside her sweater or blouse. Or I'd put my hand inside the sweater but outside the bra. If she was wearing a blouse, I might unbutton it enough to let me slip my hand onto the breast but again outside the bra. Often, if she was wearing a blouse, I'd kiss her throat and undo a couple of buttons so that I could kiss the skin above her cleavage, the place that blushed so tellingly in our petting sessions. Or she might do what she started to do back in February—disappear for a few minutes and take off the bra and leave the blouse or sweater on—and now she was bold enough to do that kind of thing when her parents were home, but usually after they'd gone to bed. Sometimes I wanted to feel the contour of the breast, the smooth curve below the nipple. Sometimes I wanted to hold the breast and marvel at its spongy malleability. I loved the feel of the bare breast in my hand, but I could get almost as great a kick out of feeling the breast in the bra, the fullness pushing out against the lacy fabric. Going into the blouse from the top and going into the blouse from the bottom seemed like two completely different experiences—and different again when I undid all the buttons and approached either breast sideways. It could be fun, too, to open the blouse when the bra was still on and reach around and unhook the bra and watch and feel the effect, how the bra kind of went limp and I felt like a liberator, releasing twin maidens from captivity. These moves required me to sit beside her—on one side or the other, it didn't much matter, as long as both of us were comfortable—and both of us would have to swivel from the waist to face each other, and, if I was on her right, I used my right hand and went into the blouse, if that was what she was wearing, and felt the breast furthest from me, the left one; and if I was on her left, I used my left hand and went into her blouse—a little more easily because women's blouses, the opposite of men's shirts, opened that way, the right side of the blouse overlapping the left—and I felt the right one, which might in fact be a little different in size and shape from the left one since most women's torsos weren't symmetrical, but it seemed to me that Barbara's right breast felt exactly the same in my left hand (which, come to think of it, wasn't an exact replica of my right) as her left breast did in my right hand, and one was just as sweet and lovable as the other. It was another matter if she was wearing a sweater or that slinky black jersey of hers, since the only way in was from the bottom—at her waist—which was awkward and not nearly as efficient for the task at hand (ironically, the prim blouse was thus more amenable to getting at her boobs than the slinky jersey). The process could've been simplified if Barbara had taken off whatever top she had on, but this was made impossible partly by the chance that her parents might come downstairs at any minute—though they almost never did—but mostly by Barbara's not being ready for that kind of intimacy. And all of these manoeuvres took place from sitting positions because *lying down together* was still out of the question, but I did sometimes fondle her when we were standing up, though that never seemed as satisfying for either of us. The only exception had come one night in April, after a party where we'd both had lots to drink. We were saying good night in the breezeway, and when Barbara turned to go in, I pulled her back to me from behind, my hands clasping her breasts and my mouth all over her neck, and I thought how naturally my hands fit her breasts in that position, as if men's hands were made to fit women's breasts that way, like a sort of human brassiere. Of course, on a given night I might skip the breasts entirely and feel the curves of her caboose, especially if she was wearing slacks. But that wasn't easy when we were sitting side by side. It worked best when we were in a standing position facing each other. On a night when Barbara didn't want me to leave and we stood at the door with our hot mouths and bodies jammed together, it felt good to hold the cheeks of her bum in my hands.

Part of the fascination with petting was curiosity. The first thirty-five times or so, I was finding out what *a girl*'s body felt like, and after that I was finding out what *Barbara*'s body felt like, and how it compared with the (precious few) others I'd touched. It eventually became clear that what was important to find out was how my touching her body made Barbara feel. This was contrary to the way Claude or Bud or Gerry talked; as far as they were concerned, a guy did things to a girl for his own gratification, no matter what they made *her* feel like. Though Barbara and I never discussed it, I thought it was good to try to figure out what method of touching I wanted to repeat and what method she wanted me to repeat. What I think excited Barbara as much as anything was *participating in something naughty.*

Since it wasn't always convenient for us to indulge in a petting session, when it *was* convenient, the progression of my moves could be almost the same each time, and the whole experience would seem wonderful all over again. (I'd often lie awake in my bed and marvel that there were many experiences you felt you only needed to have once—like seeing the Eiffel Tower or riding to the top of the Empire State Building—you could remember exactly what it looked like or felt like and you didn't care if you never experienced it again; while not only did you want to feel your girlfriend's breasts all the time, you forgot what they felt like the minute you weren't feeling them and you craved the sensation again as soon as possible.) Petting might've proven to be boring for Barbara if I didn't show some imagination, so I tried to vary my approach. Sometimes I'd skip the suspense altogether and grab her boobs before I did anything else, but I didn't think she was so keen on that. In summer at the beach, there was the added dimension of a romantic setting; we knew a secluded spot in the bushes where we could watch the sun go down on the lake and not be seen from any cottage, and there was something fabulous about sitting on a blanket, leaning against a tree, and feeling the breasts of the girl you loved while you both stared at the ruby-red sky and its reflection on the water. Just as amazing was to park in some lovers' lane during a summer storm, and turn her soft nipples into hard pellets while the rain pounded on the car.

Of course, there were occasions when Barbara wasn't in the mood. She'd let me know how she felt by pushing my hand away or turning from me or giving me a brief closed-mouth kiss. I'd be disappointed—after all, I was *always* in the mood!—but I'd chalk it up to the differences between men and women. Women were moody. What was more, women had their monthlies, and the word was that women didn't feel much like petting when they were menstruating. Not that Barbara ever discussed this condition with me.

Then came that night, taking us both by surprise, the night we came close to splitting up over some dumb argument or other. I was heading out the door when I thought I heard her voice, not the harsh voice that had been berating me but a soft voice, calling my name from downstairs. I went down to the Neck Room, where the tri-light had been turned down to low and I found Barbara on the sofa, semi-reclining, the hem of her sheath raised above her knees.

"You forgot to kiss me good night," she said.

I dropped my coat on the floor and rushed to her. So relieved was I that I knelt in front of her and kissed my way up one of her legs, pushing the hem further back and kissing past the top of her stocking, kissing up her warm bare thigh, finding the scent of perfume there, pushing my nose into the panel of girdle between her thighs, feeling her hand in my hair, hearing her softly saying, "Oh, Jenkins, I didn't mean any of it, oh, come here, ohh," and moving my face up to her bosom and kissing the dress material stretched across it and working my way up so that now I was kneeling beside her on the sofa, as I found her hot mouth at last and I tasted Wild Cherry Life Saver and at the same time I felt her hand on the front of my trousers where it had never been before, and the taste and the touch made me wild enough to reach down and rub her where my nose had been and she cried out, "*OHH!*"

"I love you, Barbara," I said.

"Oh, God, I hope my parents didn't hear me!"

She sat up and pulled down her hem and listened for

someone on the stairs or someone calling down to see if anything was wrong. When no-one did come down or call, we hugged chastely, letting our breathing settle down, realizing we'd transgressed into what the sociologists called *heavy* petting.

It was time to buy a ring.

At lunchtime the following Monday, I walked up Portage Avenue to Birk's, the store that had a reputation for the best jewellery in town. Before I found the ring section, I saw one of my copywriters, Lasha.

She said, "Jenkins, if I'd known you were coming here, I'd've got you to do Fisher's little chore for him." She gave the good-natured laugh she was known for.

"Fisher gets you to shop for him?"

"Something for his wife, he says. His wife, my foot. You know the girl modelling in the refrigerator ad? That's Fisher's latest little popsy. So guess who gets to find her a trinket."

"Why you?"

"He thinks he's giving me a perk. Take all the time you want, he says. Why are you here? Don't tell me. I'll bet you're making a major move on that sweetie of yours."

I blushed.

"I knew it!" Lasha said. "Hey, why don't you let me help you find something?"

Much about Lasha was a mystery—she was of undetermined age and, while I'd heard that her boyfriends were a series of married men, nobody knew for sure—but she had a reputation for excellent taste in clothing and accessories. That's why she wrote the copy for the fashion ads.

"I want to pick it," I said, "but I'd appreciate your opinion."

"Terrific! Okay if I try them on?"

Half an hour later, I had an engagement ring that was slightly more expensive than what I could afford, and I was headed to the phone booth at the back of the store. I took a deep breath and dialled.

The secretary put me through.

"Mason speaking."

It was customary in certain levels of society back in 1957 for a young man to ask his girlfriend's father for permission to marry his daughter. The young man was expected to seek the father's blessing before asking her, though many fellows I knew talked it over with their girlfriends first (to say nothing of guys like Gerry who *had* to get married). It was perhaps foolhardy for a young man to buy an engagement ring before either the father or the daughter had been consulted but, as far as I knew, the sequence of events was dictated by cultural tradition.

"Mr. Mason, it's Bob Jenkins," I said into the phone, trying to sound confident.

"Oh, yes, Jenkins, how are you?"

"Fine, sir. I—I was wondering if I could see you sometime this afternoon."

"I have a meeting in a few minutes. Maybe later—what's on your mind?"

I had a quick decision to make: Should I ask him over the phone or should I stew for a few more hours? "I'd like to discuss this face-to-face, sir."

"Then, by all means, come into the office. How is four o'clock?"

"If you don't mind, sir, I'm kind of anxious—well—I'd like to know if it's all right with you if I ask Barbara to marry me."

"Good for you, Jenkins, to get right to the point. I like that."

"Thank you, sir."

"So we don't need to meet at four."

"Very good, sir."

"You probably have work you have to do this afternoon."

"Well, yes. A flyer to edit, some copy to proofread …"

"Good talking with you, Jenkins. Now, I'd better get ready for my meeting."

"Sir?"

"Yes?"

"*Is* it all right if—"

"You ask Barbara to marry you? Absolutely. Didn't we establish that?"

"No, I don't think so."

"When would the wedding be?"

"Forgive me, sir, but I'd want to discuss that with you and Mrs. Mason and Barbara."

"Of course. Good for you. Well, thank you for the call, Jenkins."

"Oh, thank *you*, sir. And, sir?"

"Yes?"

"Would you mind not mentioning this to Barbara or Mrs. Mason until I've talked with Barbara?"

"My lips are sealed."

"Thank you, sir."

"What wedding?"

"Right, sir. Thank you."

"Jenkins?"

"Yes, sir?"

"You're a fine young man. I know you'll be good to her. She's our baby, you know."

"I'll look after her, sir, you can count on it."

"Get back to work, Jenkins."

The months and months of dating had unfolded as they should, and now I was on the brink of popping the question.

As I thought about when and where it should happen, I wondered where that turn of phrase had come from. *Pop the question.* Of the millions of questions people asked, why was it only one—"Will you marry me?"—that was ever *popped*? An absurd notion popped into my head: Since the guy who was going to ask the question was supposed to run it by her *pop* first, hadn't it already been *popped* before he asked it?

What the term implied was that the young man—*the popper* (I felt more like a pauper now that I'd spent so much on a ring)—would spring something on his girlfriend, something *from out of the blue* or *out of left field* (to use two more curious phrases). Yet when a couple had been going steady for as long as Barbara and I had, surely both had thought about marriage and both felt that engagement would be a logical next step. Though both of us had studiously avoided the M word, we were headed in the direction of M. In our most rational moments, we believed we were establishing ourselves in good jobs in preparation for the *future*, which in the case of couples like us always meant M, and, in heated petting sessions, our minds prevailed over our ripe young bodies, postponing *going all the way* till a future time that again meant M.

So I didn't see the question as one that I was going to *pop*, but rather as one that I had to recite as if it were the next line of a script.

But there was the *timing*. I thought Barbara was expecting me to raise the topic any day now, but she'd want the time and the place to be right. Since it was up to me when and where this would happen, and she had no idea when I'd be ready—that is, when I would've bought the ring and spoken to her dad—I suppose you could say that, *from her point of view*, the question would seem popped.

The evening after I'd called Mr. Mason, Barbara was working a late shift at St. Boniface Hospital and I'd agreed to pick her up just after eleven o'clock. It was a mild October night; by then, I had my own car, an Austin A55, and I waited at the hospital entrance, parked at the curb. Just knowing the ring was in the left pocket of my jacket made me excited—my buttocks were tingling. The moment I saw Barbara, I was struck by how gorgeous she was, and I suddenly wondered, *What if she says No*?

I jumped out, said "Hi," and ran around to the other side of the car to open the door.

"Thank you, kind sir," she said, giving me a quick kiss as she slid into the seat.

"How did it go tonight?" I said, pulling away and turning onto Tache Avenue.

"It was a bit slow. So I'm exhausted. I like it best when we're hopping."

Meanwhile, all I could think about was *popping*. I chuckled.

"What's so funny?" she asked.

"The thought of you hopping."

"You know what I mean."

"So there were no elderly guys trying to pinch you?"

"Oh, Jenkins, you have such a warped idea of a nurse's life." There was an edge to her voice.

"Tell me what you did do, then."

"I'm really beat, honestly. You tell me about *your* day."

She leaned her head on the back of the seat and I talked about McKenzie wanting to change his whole sport jacket ad in the flyer we were trying to finish up; I gave all the innocuous details while my head raged with the question I had to pop. As we approached the junction of St. Anne's and St. Mary's Roads, I noticed she wasn't commenting on anything I said. Was she falling asleep? I couldn't wait any longer. I pulled over into the Safeway parking lot next to Regent Park United Church and I stopped the car.

"Are we home al—Jenkins, why are you stopping here?"

"I've got something to ask you."

"Can't you ask me at home?"

"Barbara … you know how much I love you."

"Of course I do, Jenkins. Can't we go home? I'm really not in the mood for—oh oh, what's this?"

A car pulled up beside us on my side. A police car. I rolled down my window.

One of the two cops had his window down and was looking me in the eye. "Move along, buddy," he said.

I was agitated. "Officer, could I just have a minute?"

"You hear me? I said, 'Move along.'"

"I'm just about to pop the question!"

"What?" said the policeman. And then he grinned.

"*What*?" said Barbara.

I pulled the jewel box out of my pocket. I opened it and showed it to the cops.

"Have a good night!" the guy said, and, laughing, they pulled away.

"Jenkins, for God's sake, it's beautiful!" She took the open box and leaned close and kissed me. And she took the ring from the box and tried it on and it fit and she cried.

"I take it the answer is Yes," I said.

"Oh, yes, Jenkins, *yes*!"

"And I haven't even popped the question yet."

"Does Daddy know?"

"I spoke to him this afternoon. He gave us his blessing."

"Thank you, Jenkins. Thank you for calling him." She looked at the ring from every angle. "I love it, Jenkins. I absolutely love it." I gave her some Kleenex and she wiped her tears and blew her nose. "Just one thing, Jenkins. You know how important it is to my mother—well, and to me, too—that we don't *do it* before we're married. That's all right with you, isn't it?"

I'd waited this long; I could certainly wait a little longer. "Of course, it is," I said.

"I know it's going to be a little nerve-wracking, but I think it's good to keep *a little mystery* in our lives, don't you?"

"Certainly," I said.

"Good!" she said, kissing my cheek. "Oh, Jenkins, what a lovely ring!"

"Uh, when do you think we should have the wedding?"

"Maybe a year from now. I think we need a year."

A year! a voice inside me screamed. "Sounds good," I said, rather mournfully.

"Oh, Jenkins, can we go and tell Mother now? *She* doesn't know yet, does she?"

Manhattan Mood

Janie's handbag is on the floor between her left leg and the gear shift. I reach down and ease it up into my lap and open it. Despite all the paraphernalia, there is room for a mickey of vodka. But there is no actual mickey.

She must've finished it off and thrown it away. I consider going back into the restaurant to have somebody look in the washroom garbage. I decide not to—I feel sorry for Janie, the way you do for someone who passes out beside you—I'm in no mood to start playing private investigator. I'm also in no mood to take her to my place.

She's still sleeping—even snoring—when I pull up to Jason's house. Clouds cover the setting sun and it's darker but not quite dusk. I consider leaving the car running while I go inside to make my report to Jason—the purr of the engine would keep Janie undisturbed. I decide *not* to leave it running; I'm going to be subjected to enough wrath from Jason without risking his mother's driving away drunk. I turn off the car. Janie mumbles something but continues to sleep. I slip noiselessly out of the car, closing the door but not latching it.

Jason must've heard the car. He's at the door when I walk up the steps.

"Mr. Jenkins, what's wrong?" he says.

"Your mother is in the car, asleep. We didn't have a thing to drink—I can show you the bill—but she must've had a bottle with her."

"What the bloody hell!"

"I checked her handbag—nothing. I'm sure, if you phone the restaurant, they'll find an empty in the women's washroom. She went there a few times."

"*Krista!*" Jason yells.

His wife comes out of a room looking scared.

"Krista, didn't you check her bloody handbag?"

"Dear, I thought *you* did."

"We'd better go and get her," I say. "She's going to be shocked when she wakes up and sees where she is."

"Did she get rowdy?"

"No," I say. I'm not going to give Jason a detailed account. Let poor Janie have *some* dignity. "She started slurring her words—and they say you can't smell vodka, but when you're not drinking anything yourself, you can."

"Usually she gets loud and lewd," says Jason, as we step outside. "Sometimes, I think if we left her to it, she'd drink herself to death."

I open the passenger door quietly—I don't want to startle her—but Jason steps in front of me.

"Come on, Mom," he says, shaking her shoulder. "You'll feel a whole lot better in your bed."

"What? Jason?" Janie sits up as he undoes the seat belt. "Where's Gerry?"

"Mr. Jenkins is right here. Come on. I'll help you up."

I don't know what to say. Janie looks at me, bewildered, and then with an angry scowl as if I've double-crossed her. Jason shows his strength by virtually lifting her onto her feet and he guides her to the house.

"I'll get you for this," she says to me, her eyes slits, as she passes me. "Jason, I can *walk*."

I follow them with her handbag. Jason delivers Janie into the hands of Krista, takes the handbag and deposits it inside. He closes the door. The two of us stand on his front step, I feeling like an adolescent who's violated my girlfriend's father's dating rules.

"I'm sorry you had to see her like that," he says.

"Will she be all right?"

"She'll sleep it off. Did she take her pills?"

"Before dinner, yes."

"She'll get back to sleep fast enough."

"Could I maybe see her before—"

"She's mad at you for bringing her home—but you did the right thing. I'd leave it at that."

I turn to leave, but it feels wrong. I turn back to him.

"Jason … I know you're trying your best … but she seems scared of you. Is there any way you could show her … you know, a little more love?"

He glowers at me. "I don't believe this. You waltz into her life from out of the dim dark past and dare to give *me*, her *son*, your crumby *advice*? Who the fuck do you think you are?"

"Take a good look at yourself in the mirror, Jason. I'll be running along."

"Don't you *ever* try to contact her again!"

"Good night."

I sit in my living room in the dark, feeling anything but tired. I'm angry at Jason Hunter for being so cold-blooded, but maybe he was embarrassed. People don't like strangers to see their parents the way I saw Janie. I'm angry at myself for thinking I could help the situation by spouting platitudes. I'm saddened by the sight of Janie deteriorating before my eyes. I'm angry at myself for being disappointed that Janie couldn't remember our date—the close dancing, the heated necking, the broken strap on her dress. Still, wasn't that the whole reason for getting in touch with her? So that we could relive our memory of a golden night when we were young? What I *should* be angry at isn't Jason or myself but the whole scary process of *growing old.*

I succumb to the urge for a drink. When something bugs me, I find it helpful to make not just a drink, but my all-time favourite, a manhattan. I go to the kitchen and assemble the necessary ingredients on the counter: Jack Daniels Tennessee whisky, Cinzano sweet vermouth, Angostura bitters, maraschino cherries with stems. And ice. And my cocktail shaker that's shaped like a penguin. I place three cherries along with a dollop of syrup from the cherry jar into a manhattan glass. I remove the penguin's upper body and toss in about ten ice cubes. I pour in four ounces of Jack Daniels and two ounces of Cinzano. Then the all-important couple of dashes of Angostura. I put the penguin back together and shake it, holding it above one shoulder and then the other, the way the best bartenders do. After about thirty seconds of shaking, I take off the penguin's head and pour the concoction into the glass through the sieve in its neck. Ah. The deep red colour makes the manhattan the best-looking drink, bar none.

I carry the drink back into the living room, sit down and take a sip. What a marvellous taste! A man could do a lot worse than settle down in the late evening with a manhattan.

It becomes clear to me how ridiculous it is for me to start

dating again. Tracy is right. I had a life-partner, and *her* life by mere chance ended before mine. Now I'm alone. I've adapted to the solitary life and I'm reasonably happy with it.

I stand up with my drink and go to the dining room.

"I guess you heard all about my Big Date," I say to Barb's portrait. "I don't think you ever knew Janie. Kind of sad, really, what happens to people. Well, you and I had some good times, right?" I lift my glass to her. "Here's to you. It's time I read your *Time Capsule*."

I go upstairs, take the manila envelope from the night table and go back to the living room. I savour a sip of the manhattan, open the envelope and take out the handwritten pages.

To the daughter I hope to have someday:

As I write this, I'm sitting on a deck chair in front of a log cabin. With the view I have, I feel like I'm on top of the world. I'm on a mountain, but not on a peak, more like a long ridge. I guess that's why they call it Tunnel Mountain. It's not far from the town of Banff in the province of Alberta.

Tunnel Mountain is part of the famous Rocky Mountains. You'll learn about them in school. I hope you come here one day. We might even bring you here.

I'm writing this just six days after an event that's supposed to be the greatest in the life of a girl. I'm going to tell you about it and about the days that led up to it. My hope is that I'll be able to explain everything in a truthful way.

I want you to hear about it from the young woman who just experienced it. Before I get older and become a mother. Your mother. I think a woman's way of looking at things changes when she becomes a mother, and it changes even more as her children grow up.

What I want to tell you about is my wedding.

Your father and I are on our honeymoon. It took us three days to drive here, and now we're relaxing and pampering ourselves. They say that kind of honeymoon is best, the kind where you relax with each other instead of sightseeing. He's in a chair beside me, reading. At the moment, he's stopped reading and closed his eyes.

When you meet a boy and fall in love, you'll want to get married. You'll have your own ideas about the kind of wedding you want.

From a very young age, you'll be bombarded by other people's ideas, in magazines, movies and store displays. You may go to other people's weddings and see things you like and things you don't like. You'll come up with a bunch of definite ideas on what you want.

What I want you to know is, your wedding will be exactly that: <u>your</u> wedding.

If you want to ask us, your father and me, for advice, we will give it. Only if you ask. And the final decision on everything will be yours.

Many of the decisions will be hard to make. Expect that. If you go into your wedding with a good attitude and our assurance that we won't interfere, it can be as wonderful as it's supposed to be.

Your father and I got angry and frustrated with the planning of our wedding. You will, too, with yours.

In our case, my mother wanted to dictate every detail. I fought with her on just about every single thing. It was the last straw when she accused me of seducing your father a few weeks before the wedding. Such a thing never happened.

I was so mad, I talked your father into eloping.

We got into his car one night, about three weeks before the wedding, and we took off. It felt so good to just chuck away all our responsibilities.

I went without any clothes, only the summer things I was wearing!

We liked the idea of eloping but we didn't have a clue how to go about it. All we knew was the old story about the boy putting a ladder up to the girl's window, but I was already out of the house when we decided to go, and besides, I lived in a bungalow.

We started out for Ontario. We got no further than Beausejour. That's a town a few miles east of Winnipeg.

You might chalk it up to excitement that we had to stop so soon. I think we had to test our nerve. If we'd driven further, we would've gotten tired and moody. We probably would've started to fight.

The place we stopped at was old and quaint. Not a seedy motel but two rows of old-fashioned cabins. The proprietor was a nice old geezer who gave us cake to help us celebrate and ginger ale to go with our rye.

When we settled down for the night, we finally faced the reality of what we were doing. I didn't like to face it. So I drank.

Your father wanted to see me with no clothes on but I hid under the bedcovers. I didn't want to tell him how bad I felt.

It wasn't anything like the dreams I'd had. There was a squeaky bed and a mattress that sagged in the middle. The stuffiness of the place nearly made me gag. The paint was chipped. There was a shower but no bath. I saw spiders in the corners.

But I knew why we were there. We were rebelling against my mother, and besides that, we were putting an end to our virginity. I pretended to be happy.

I stop reading. I take another sip and look up at the framed photograph on the living-room wall, one taken of the two of us at the lake, some months after we were engaged.

A Little Mystery

It was all right for me to sleep overnight at the Masons' Victoria Beach cottage once Barbara and I were engaged. With spring, the Masons decided we'd all take a break from the wedding preparations, as soon as the weather was decent. We went, even though the municipality hadn't yet turned on the water system.

During the preceding week, Barbara and her mother had barely spoken to each other. Over the months, they'd argued about every single detail of the wedding, from who the attendants should be to what kind of reception they should have. Barbara wanted Gloria to be maid of honour, but Mrs. Mason insisted that Barbara's sister Sandra *had* to be—and, since she was married, she'd be the *matron* of honour. Barbara argued that Sandra hadn't been around for years, and, because she lived in Toronto, she'd be no help with the preparations and therefore she should be a bridesmaid and nothing more (I wondered why a married bridesmaid wasn't a *bridesmatron*). Mrs. Mason questioned why Gloria should be included at all: "She's a dear girl, but don't you find she's much too *short*? When you're all standing up at the altar, she'll look like the runt of the litter. It will look as if we don't think these kinds of things matter." "But, Mother," Barbara cried, "they *don't* matter!" Mrs. Mason refused to talk about it after that. As far as the reception was concerned, Barbara wanted a sit-down dinner and a dance afterward with a live orchestra. Mrs. Mason said it sounded as if Barbara wanted a *Ukrainian* wedding. "Next, you'll want the caterers to make *cabbage rolls* and you'll expect the guests to bring envelopes full of *money*," Mrs. Mason snarled. "But Jenkins and I love to dance!" Barbara cried. "It's always been my dream that he and I would start a bingo dance at my wedding." "A *what*?" Mrs. Mason shrieked, as if Barbara had said she wanted a *belly* dance. "You know very well what a bingo dance is," Barbara said. "Dear," said Mrs. Mason, in her most condescending tone, "this is the social event of the summer. We don't want our guests to perspire. This will be a tasteful, late-afternoon do where good friends can mingle and be able to hear themselves converse—none of your loud band music. I thought perhaps a harp in the background—" "A *harp*?" said Barbara, aghast. "Mother, you're making this sound like a goddam *funeral*!" "What did you say?" Mrs. Mason fired back. "Who taught you to speak like that? Does your father know you speak like that?" "Mother," said Barbara, immediately contrite, "I'm sorry, I'm really sorry ..." Mrs. Mason said, "You are going to regret you ever spoke like that to your mother." Well, those were two examples. I wasn't sure what the disagreement was about this time—the bridesmaids' dresses, maybe, something about the size of the bow on the back or whether there should be a bow at all. I thought it was a bad idea to go to the lake under these conditions, but Barbara assured me that her mother would be nice to me because she wasn't mad at *me*, and besides, Barbara's father was refusing to take sides and he could use some male companionship. The four of us had driven out on Friday evening in Mr. Mason's Buick Roadmaster, and Mrs. Mason, sitting in the passenger seat up front, had directed most of her conversation to me, sitting in the back seat behind Mr. Mason. Barbara sat behind her mother. This seating arrangement worked well because Mrs. Mason could ignore Barbara and didn't have to look at her, while Mr. Mason could see Barbara in his rear-view mirror and the two of them carried on wordless communication that involved surreptitious winking and smiling and grimacing. The topic of the wedding was avoided. Most of the two-hour trip was taken up with Mrs. Mason's commenting on fashions and fashion advertising—she hoped that the sheath dress would never go out of style—and asking me all about how ads were produced and what procedures were followed in our department, as if she were deeply interested. I knew I was being patronized. I knew she was trying to get Barbara's goat, as the saying went. In reaction, Barbara flashed exaggerated looks at her father—the worst involved her facial muscles pulling down the corners of her mouth and her eyes bulging. When we arrived at the cottage, Mrs. Mason and Barbara put out some pre-made sandwiches and hors d'oeuvres without speaking to each other and Mr. Mason poured drinks. After the meal, Barbara and I went for a long walk to the pier and back. It was twilight when we left, dark when we returned. Barbara's mother and father were already in their bedroom with the door shut. I gave my fiancée a kiss at her bedroom door and we retired to our respective beds. Mine was in the little room off the kitchen, the furthest away from the Masons'.

I was close to dozing off when I heard my latch move. Startled, I turned to see the door slowly opening. In came Barbara, on tiptoe, in a wine-coloured robe that had once been her father's, one with a sash and satin lapels. Her movements were so stealthy that I wondered if she'd done this kind of thing before. I leaned up on one elbow to watch her; she put a finger to my lips—I wasn't to utter a sound.

I wished I could've expected her. If I had, I wouldn't have worn pyjamas to bed. Pyjamas weren't masculine. Any guy spending a weekend at the lake wore his undershorts to bed, with maybe a plain white T-shirt. Yet this *was* the Masons' cottage, and I was sure Mrs. Mason would expect me to wear pyjamas. At that moment, however, it wasn't Mrs. Mason I wanted to please.

Barbara closed the door, making sure the latch didn't make an audible click. She gestured for me to move over. The bed was no more than a cot, but I did make room by lying on my side, and I turned back the covers in a *Come on in* manner. I leaned my back against the bare-wood wall, where earlier I'd noticed a cobweb, but that didn't bother me now. She untied her sash, took off the robe and let it fall to the floor. She was wearing baby-doll pyjamas. I could smell her lovely mixture of hair fragrance, lipstick and body heat. The cot squeaked as she lay down beside me.

This was a first. In nearly three years of dating, we'd never been in bed together. We'd regarded *being in bed together* as synonymous with *sleeping together* which was a euphemism for *making love*, which in turn was a euphemism for *going all the way* (which of course was also a euphemism), and in accordance with our pact to keep *a little mystery* in our courtship, we'd vowed to avoid any situation where we'd be tempted to climb into bed.

Now, here we were, in this narrow cot in her parents' cottage, with her parents sleeping (or maybe not sleeping) only a few yards away. Under the covers, she sent one hand on an expedition inside my pyjamas.

"Oh, my!" she whispered, and she gave a throaty little chuckle.

I too went exploring.

"Why don't we do it?" she whispered.

"What!"

"You heard me."

"We made a vow."

"I don't care. I'm so *mad* at Mother."

"We shouldn't. Not here."

"Come on. It's more fun this way."

"Don't I need—you know—some protection?"

"I can't get pregnant at this time of the month. Besides, if I do, it'll serve her right."

"I don't think being mad at your mother is—"

We heard a noise. Footsteps. It sounded like her father. We froze (if it was possible to freeze when you had your hand in someone's warmest place). Mr. Mason passed through the kitchen, right by the door of the room we were in. We heard him unlock the back door and step outside.

"He's going to the outhouse," Barbara whispered.

"Would you stop doing that? I might—"

"Don't you dare!"

"Then stop! … What are you doing now?"

She'd let go of me and raised herself up to peek under the window blind.

"I didn't hear the outhouse door," she whispered. "I—oh, no!"

"What now?"

"He's peeing against a tree! In the moonlight!" She shook with muffled laughter.

"You're watching your *father*—"

"I can't actually see him. He has his back to us."

"Get down before he turns around and sees you!"

We heard his footsteps on the back steps. We heard him

open the door—too noisily, I thought. We heard him walking—and he stopped. For all we knew, he might've thought he heard something and was listening at our door. We held our breath. He continued on until a distant click told us he was back in the bedroom he shared with Mrs. Mason.

"I'd better go back," Barbara whispered. "If Mother gets up, she'll pick up my scent. She has the nose of a bloodhound." She got up and put the robe back on.

"Shouldn't you stay a bit longer? Your dad won't be back to sleep yet."

"If I stay, I'm going to rape you. G'night."

One night, three and a half weeks before the wedding, I received a frantic call from Barbara. She'd had another shouting match with her mother and she'd run from the house and was calling me from the pay phone in Murphy's Drug Store.

"She's accusing us of *doing it*," Barbara said. "That night at the lake. She said she heard me go to your room."

"But we didn't—"

"I can't take any more of this. I want to elope."

"Just a minute." I closed the door to the living room so that my parents couldn't overhear. "Okay, calm down, okay?"

"I mean it. Listen to me: *I want to elope*."

"Okay! How do we go about it—meet one day after work and get someone to marry us?"

"I'm talking about right *now*. You come and pick me up and we just *go*. Out of town somewhere. Anywhere!"

"You have to work tomorrow, don't you?"

"I'm not going to worry about that right now. Just come and get me."

"You could probably phone somebody to cover for you, couldn't you? I can call Chet and make arrangements to—"

"You don't make *arrangements*. The whole idea is to walk away from everything, isn't it? It's *arrangements* that're driving me crazy!"

"You want me to just walk out on my job?"

"I want to get away, that's all! I want you to be *spontaneous*!"

I had to admit that the idea of being reckless on a Tuesday night was thrilling. "Where do you want to go?"

"I don't know, we'll just drive. When it gets dark, we'll start looking."

"It might be hard to find someone to marry us at this time of night—"

"Oh, Jenkins, that can wait till tomorrow. Tonight, we'll just look for a motel."

A motel! The very thought of it aroused me.

I said, "You mean, pretend we're Mr. and Mrs. Smith or something?"

"We don't have to pretend anything. We're practically married now. I have a ring."

"An engagement ring."

"So what? Motels don't care, do they? Kids are always checking into Bobby Jo's on Pembina Highway. Would you hurry up and come and get me?"

She told me she'd be at the corner of Sherwood and St. Mary's and I said I'd be there right away.

Barbara had been distraught a lot lately, so much so that I'd refrained from touching her or even expecting to neck on our dates. I had blissfully believed that, once the wedding was out of the way, all the tension would disappear and we'd instantly become The World's Greatest Lovers. Now I found myself torn between humouring Barbara, which would move our long-postponed union up by a few weeks, or trying to talk her out of this sudden and irrational change of plans. I checked on my parents; my mother was watching television in the living room and my father was making a birdhouse at his basement workbench. Whatever I took with me tonight would have to be smuggled past them. I went to my room to figure out what to take. From my desk drawer I dug out the wedding ring and the box of condoms (necessary for birth control in those days) and a bottle of rye whisky. From my wardrobe cupboard I took the small suitcase I'd used for visits to the Mason cottage. I hesitated—Barbara wouldn't like my bringing a suitcase because it lacked spontaneity—but I needed *something*. I put the bottle and the box into the suitcase and, to prevent them from rattling around, I threw in a couple of pairs of underwear shorts and socks and a couple of shirts. I considered pyjamas and rejected them. I was wearing a red short-sleeved sport shirt and grey slacks; I put the ring box and a fresh hankie into one trouser pocket and my wallet into the other. I picked up my car key and went to my back window. My dad had removed the screen, intending to fix a warp in it, and he hadn't put it back. I opened the window and dropped the suitcase into the garden below. It was still light out, but any view from the neighbouring yards was obscured by the lilac bushes, my father's pride and joy.

Before the sight of all the familiar trappings—my desk, my lamp, my books, my framed university degree—dissuaded me, I left the room.

"Just going over to see Barbara, Mom," I said.

"Don't be late, now," my mother said. "You both need lots of rest for The Big Day."

I kept moving. I went out the back door, retrieved the suitcase from the garden, and scuttled out the back gate to the car. I put the suitcase into the trunk. It was nine o'clock, a few days after the longest day of the year, and the sun wouldn't be setting for at least an hour. I drove the several blocks to Sherwood and St. Mary's, where Barbara stood on the corner, looking impatient. She was dressed in beige cotton chinos, a white sleeveless blouse and brown and white saddle shoes. She wasn't carrying anything, not even a purse.

"What kept you?" she said, jumping in and slamming the door.

"Sorry—a few things I had to do."

"You packed a suitcase. I'll bet you packed a suitcase."

"No, I—all right, I did bring one."

"I *knew* it! How *could* you?"

"I didn't want to look too suspicious at the motel."

"I'm standing on a corner going out of my mind and you're packing a suitcase!"

"Not much—hardly anything. Which way do you want to go?"

"I don't care. Just *drive*!"

I drove, heading north on St. Mary's Road.

"We're going to save everybody a whole lot of bother by eloping," Barbara said. "I guess Daddy will lose his deposit on the banquet room, but there's still time to send out cancellation notices."

"I like that idea, sending out wedding *cancellations*."

Barbara clapped her hands. "Think of the excitement it'll cause! This was just another wedding everybody expected because we've been dating forever. Won't we shock them when we call the whole thing off?"

"The nice thing is, we call off the wedding but we still get married."

"You know who's going to be happiest? Gloria. She's been trying like mad to lose weight for the wedding. Now, she can stop. I should call her tonight and tell her she can go on a *binge*!"

"I brought a bottle of rye, in case we want to make a toast."

"You just want to get me drunk so you can ravage me."

"Isn't that what this is all about?"

"Oh, you *are* awful! I love you!"

As I drove through town, I thought about the work that was waiting to be completed in the morning. Someone had to take a final look at the ads that were running that day. Chet always gave the approval, but only after I'd done a last proofreading. Chet was a good guy. I could call him and say I was sick and Chet would look after things. No, I'd level with Chet. I'd tell him I was eloping. He'd be impressed.

"I'm going to call Chet and tell him we eloped," I said.

"I just *love* the sound of it, don't you? 'Guess what, Mom. Jenkins and I *eloped*.'"

"Don't you think you should call your parents tonight? They'll be worried sick."

"Good. Let them *stew*! Oh, I feel so *free*! To take off with nothing but the clothes I'm sitting here in!"

"You didn't even bring a purse."

"It's okay. I have everything I need in my pocket." She held up a lipstick and a roll of Wild Cherry Life Savers. "I knew *you'd* bring money."

"You might get cold. I have an extra shirt you can wear."

"Who needs a shirt? I've got *you*." She patted my thigh.

We drove up North Main and I began to catch some of Barbara's euphoria as we put the city behind us. I liked the feeling of pointing my car toward the wide open spaces and having no particular destination in mind. I checked the fuel level—half full.

"Penny for your thoughts," Barbara said.

"We'll have to stop for gas in a couple of hours or so and I don't know if there'll be anything open."

"Where are we headed?"

"I thought we'd go east."

"Not too far, I hope."

"I thought maybe Kenora. You know, across the border and into another province. Just like outlaws."

"I like that. How long will it take?"

"Three hours? Not much more than that."

"We won't get there until after midnight."

"The witching hour. If I don't get you there before then, you turn into a pumpkin."

Barbara giggled. "I can't remember when I've had so much fun. Isn't it great just to drive and not care about tomorrow?"

"I have to admit I've given *some* thought to tomorrow."

"Well, stop thinking! Savour the moment!" She rolled her window down. "Put yours down, too. Feel the fresh air! Let the fresh air get rid of all your worries."

I rolled my window down. The rush of cool air did feel good. Barbara held her face to the open window and let the wind blow her hair around. She'd been letting it grow longer so that it would fall below her shoulders on our wedding day. I hadn't seen the wedding dress her parents had bought for her; the groom wasn't supposed to see his bride in full regalia until the wedding ceremony when she came down the aisle. Now I would never see her in it. I felt a pang of regret that I wasn't going to experience the dramatic feeling when I came out of the vestry with Reverend McIntosh and Claude, my best man, while Mrs. Wilson played the organ and Melanie, Barbara's roommate from nursing school, started up the aisle with Sandra and Gloria and the bride behind her in procession. I'd been looking forward to that moment.

"Do you think your folks will be able to sell the wedding dress?" I asked.

"Who cares?"

"Right."

"You know, there's something about the dress I don't like. That's another reason I'm glad we're eloping. The dress doesn't look like me, somehow. Looks Elizabethan. It flattens me up front."

"That's the last thing we want."

"What?"

"You flattened up front."

"Oh, Jenkins, sometimes I think that's all you care about."

I tried to think of a rebuttal. It seemed prudent to let the comment go.

After a few beats of silence, Barbara said, "So you admit it."

"I'm not going to get into a debate about which part of you I like best."

"Speaking of parts ..." She walked her fingers down the front of my trousers. "Oh, my!"

"Everything present and accounted for?"

She laughed. "Maybe we'd better concentrate on the road," she said, taking her hand away.

"Maybe we'd better stop sooner than we said."

"Whatever you like, Captain. You're driving."

We commented on things we saw along the highway—cows, a well-kept farm with a newly painted red barn, a forlorn-looking hitchhiker, a smashed-up jalopy, two crows picking at a dead groundhog. The sun had gone down by the time we approached the town of Beausejour. Barbara hadn't spoken for a while. There was a row of cabins coming up on the right.

"What do you say we pull in here?" I said.

"What? Oh. I must've dozed off. The air—what did you say?"

"*Shady Nest Cabins.* Want to stop here?" I slowed down.

"And not go to Kenora?"

"No. We can find somebody to marry us in Beausejour."

"You wanted to cross the border."

"I'm getting a little tired."

"I could drive. That snooze did wonders for me."

"Let's pull in here."

"Looks a little run down."

"But better than a motel, don't you think?" I brought the car to a stop on the gravel shoulder of the highway.

"Okay."

"Are you sure?"

"I want to be spontaneous. This is spontaneous."

I drove in and stopped at a house that had a sign, *Office*, in the front window.

"Before we go in," I said, "would you mind putting this on?" I took the box out of my pocket and opened it.

"Jenkins! It's beautiful!"

"See how it matches the other?"

"Perfectly!" Barbara wiped tears from her eyes with the back of her hand. She took the ring out of the box and slid it onto her finger. She held her hand up. "Jenkins, they look *fantastic* together. God, I don't know … do you really want me to wear it?"

"Please."

"Before we're married?"

"Yes."

"This feels so *bad*!"

"Ready to go in?"

"I think so."

I put the box back in my pocket and stepped out of the car. I looked around, as if I expected some kind of authority to swoop down on us.

"Would it be better if I went in alone?" I said.

"No. I want to be with you. I want to hear what you say."

We walked up to the front door—the office door. I opened it and heard a bell ring inside. We entered. A tall, thin, bald man appeared. He wore glasses and one of those checked shirts that country folks seemed to prefer.

"Howdy," the man said.

"Hi," I said. "We wondered if you had a room—I mean, a cabin—available."

Barbara held her ring-hand to her face in an obvious way.

"You can have your choice," said the man. "They're all available."

"Do you have a Number Seven?" I asked.

"Yup. Would you like to see it?"

"That won't be nec—"

"Could we?" said Barbara.

The man turned to a rack of keys and took down Number Seven.

"I'll wait here," he said, handing the key to me.

Outside, in the dusk, the numbers were difficult to see. There were five cabins on the left side of the property and five on the right. *10* was the first cabin on the right. We counted our way down to *7*, the second from the end.

"Lucky Seven," I said, opening the screen door.

"I didn't think you were superstitious," said Barbara.

"I'm not, really. But a little good luck doesn't hurt."

I had trouble with the lock, likely because I was anxious. It took some manipulating but, on the third try, the door opened. We went inside.

Except for a closet that housed a sink, a toilet and a shower stall, what we entered was one not-so-big room. It contained a double bed with an iron-rung head and foot, a night table beside it with a lamp that had a dented shade, one upholstered chair, a wooden kitchen table and two wooden chairs, an ice-box and a kitchen sink. On the kitchen table were a water pitcher and two glasses. Inside a cupboard beneath the sink were a few unmatched dishes and cups, a kettle, a teapot, and some cutlery. Barbara crossed the linoleum floor to the bed and pulled back the covers.

"Looks clean enough," she said.

"Not exactly a honeymoon suite," I said.

"But this isn't a honeymoon."

"Hey, what about the honeymoon plans? The reservation in Banff?"

"The last thing we need to worry about right now."

"Okay. So. We'll take it?"

"I'd say so."

"Okay, I'll go and pay and get our stuff."

"What stuff?"

"Our pretend stuff."

I returned to the office.

"We'll take it," I said.

"For how long?" the man asked.

"Uh—tonight—one night."

"That'll be six dollars." He wrote a *7* on one page of a ledger and handed a pen to me. "Need yer name and address right there. Where ya from?"

"Winnipeg." I looked up and saw the man's stern face. "We just got married."

"I knew that," the man said without a hint of a smile. "I took one look at the two of yez and I said, 'Them's newlyweds.'"

I scribbled my name and address on the page, hoping they'd be too illegible to decipher. I took six dollars from my wallet and laid them on the page.

"Good night," I said.

"Don't let the bugs bite," the man said.

I went out, got into my car and drove it into the grassy space between Number Six and Number Seven. I tried to be conspicuous as I took my suitcase out of the trunk, but I didn't look back to see if the man was watching. I imagined him and his wife looking out at me and the wife saying, "There, you see? He *does* have a suitcase."

I hesitated at the cabin door. There was a strange cart-before-the-horse feeling about what we were doing. Going to bed together before we were married after all the plans and promises. It was as if I'd been progressing along a Monopoly board, doing all the right things—not buying property and paying rent, but dating, going steady, asking the father for her hand in marriage, popping the question, setting a wedding date, resisting temptation—when suddenly I'd landed on a square that changed my course: *Go to bed. Move directly to bed. Do not pass through the church. Do not collect wedding presents.*

I took a deep breath and entered the cabin. "We're registered," I said.

Barbara was sitting on the bed, still in her clothes. She stared at the suitcase and said: "Do you have pyjamas in there? I'll *bet* you have pyjamas in there."

I locked the door. Barbara had pulled down all the blinds. I placed the suitcase on the bed beside her and snapped it open.

"Shirts," said Barbara. "Underwear. Rye whisky. No pyjamas! Congratulations. What's in the box?"

I opened the box and showed her the contents: rows of little silver boxes. I took one of them out and opened it.

"Oh," she said.

"You've seen these before."

"At school, yes. In a clinical setting. How come you brought so many?"

"I just grabbed the box. You know I was in a hurry."

"You've got enough there for an *army*."

"Or a very active honeymoon."

"There's that word again."

"Sorry." I pocketed the silver box of three and put the rest back in the suitcase. "Do you want a drink?"

"Yes, please. I'm parched. You don't have any ginger ale, do you?"

"No. I thought we could get some at the motel … if we stopped at a motel."

"Do you think Mr. Nest has some?"

"Old Shady? I didn't notice any soft drinks in the office."

"I'll go and ask him."

"No, no, I will."

"And ice?"

"And ice."

I went back to the office. The bell brought the man to the counter, likely expecting new business. His expression said, *Not you again.*

"I wonder," I said, "do you happen to have any ginger ale?"

"We don't sell soft drinks."

"Do you know where I can get some?"

The man looked at me for a moment. "Wait," he said. "I'll see if I have any."

"And possibly some ice, please?"

The man scowled and went behind the scenes. I thought I could hear conversation. The man came back with an Eaton's shopping bag and he showed me the contents: two bottles of ginger ale and some ice wrapped in a towel.

"Thank you, this is wonderful," I said. "How much do I owe you?"

"Consider it a *wedding* present." As before, the man's expression was deadpan.

I returned to Number Seven. Barbara, *still* in her clothes, stood beside the table holding the bottle of rye. She'd poured liquor into the two glasses.

"Whoa, those are big drinks!" I said. "Hardly any room for the ice and the ginger."

"I don't know anything about pouring drinks. If these are stiff ones, that's good, isn't it? I feel like getting drunk. What's in the towel?"

"Ice. And he gave us the ginger ale on the house."

"Ahhh—wasn't that nice of him."

I found a bottle opener among the utensils and opened

one of the bottles. I put an ice cube in each glass and topped each up with ginger ale.

"Here's to a most beautiful blushing bride," I said.

We clinked glasses. With her free hand, Barbara wiped away a tear.

"Why'd you have to say that?" she said.

"Sorry. I thought I should say *some*thing."

She drank half her drink, gasped for breath and coughed. I drank slowly.

"I'm still glad we did this," Barbara said.

"So am I."

"My mother's going to be livid."

"*Hang* your mother."

"I'll drink to that!" She finished her drink. "Mm-mm good. Not too strong at all. Pour me another."

"Let's have the next one in bed."

"I wish I had a nightgown."

"You can wear one of my shirts."

"It's okay. I'll get under the covers. Would you turn away for a minute while I—"

"I thought you might do a striptease."

"Oh, sure. For you and Shady? As if this isn't nerve-wracking enough. Turn your back, okay? And could you improve the light? You know, the ambience?"

I poured a new drink for her and topped up my own. Keeping my back to her, I turned off the kitchen light, making the room dark. I went into the bathroom, turned on the light and positioned the door so that it was maybe three inches ajar.

"Pretty good," Barbara said. "Okay, I'm in bed. I just threw my clothes on that chair—I hope you don't mind."

"Of course not." My heartbeat accelerated. *We are really going to go through with this.*

I turned to see that she was lying in the bed with the covers pulled up to her chin. She had her pillow folded double to prop up her head so that she could sip her drink. I saw her clothes, not in a heap but folded. Her bra was lying on top, so white, so virginal, *so empty*.

There was a knock on the door.

"Oh, no!" I said. "We're being apprehended already!"

"Who—"

"The police!"

"It couldn't be. Go on, answer it. Whoever it is knows we're here."

I had the presence of mind to open the bathroom door so that the room was brighter. I opened the main door and through the screen I saw the man from the office, holding a tray.

"Hello there," I said.

"The wife sent over some baking," he said. "*Matrimonial* cake."

"Oh! That's very kind of you—and her. Thank you."

I opened the screen door. The man gave me a baking pan that contained the cake cut into squares.

"You can leave the pan in the sink," said the man. "'Night."

"Good night and thanks!" Barbara called from the bed.

The man didn't answer. He turned and walked off toward the house. I closed the door and locked it.

"Isn't that sweet!" said Barbara.

"Sweet? I think he expected to catch us doing it. The guy's a pervert."

"You're crazy."

"He knows we aren't married."

"Oh shush. Give me a date square—that's what I call it. Date square to celebrate our hundredth date."

"Is it?"

"Who's counting? Must be close, though."

I found a plate and took three pieces to her. She sat up, holding the covers over her chest.

"Thank you," she said, and she puckered her lips.

I kissed them lightly.

"Now, come to bed, would you?"

Taking her lead, I opted for modesty and went into the bathroom to undress. The whole escapade felt rather sordid, but I had to admit I had a fiancée who could surprise me. *To think that all the months and months of patient petting, of postponing the ultimate, are about to end!* I opened the door, stepped out and turned to adjust the ambience.

"I must be delirious," Barbara said. "I see a naked man in my room."

I pretended to strut, like a proud rooster, but she averted her eyes and took a long pull of her drink. I slipped into bed beside her.

"This bed is terrible," I said. "The mattress dips in the middle."

"Soundsh good to me."

"You're drunk."

"Jush feeling good."

She set the drink on the night table. Turning to me, she slid down into a lying position. I reached for her and, as best I could, executed a horizontal hug.

"Oh, ouch!" she said.

"What?"

"You squished my boob."

"I'm sorry."

"You can kish it better."

She pushed the covers down to her waist. I groaned with appreciation, seeing her this way for the very first time. I kissed one breast.

"Thash nice," she said, "but ish the wrong one."

I leaned over her to get at the other. For the very first time, I took her nipple into my mouth and gently sucked. It felt lovely.

She rearranged herself under me.

"Wait," I said. "I should put one of the things on."

"You didn't do that yet?"

"Couldn't you see I didn't?"

"I washn't looking."

"Why not?"

"I jush didn't want to shee it right now, okay?"

"I don't—okay. I'll just be a minute."

"I wish you'd done that before."

I got up, went into the bathroom and took the little silver box out of my trousers. I'd been planning to try a condom on before the wedding night but I hadn't done it yet. *Who would've dreamed I'd need one three weeks before the wedding?* To hear my buddies talk, it was a simple procedure; in fact, they never really talked about *putting one on,* so I assumed it was easy. I took one of the three out of the box and judged how best to start. Whoever designed them couldn't have factored in a young man's nerves. I took a deep breath and started.

"Jenkins?" It was Barbara. She thumped on the door. "*Jenkins*! Let me in!"

The condom half on, I opened the door. She pushed past me and sat on the toilet.

"Get out, would you?" she said in a frantic voice. "Out of the bathroom! Please! Quick!"

I did as I was told. She slammed the door and turned a tap on.

"Barbara?" I said. "Barbara, what's wrong?"

"My visitor!" she cried. "My monthly visitor! It's come *days early*!"

A Millionaire's Family

I make myself another large manhattan and return to *Barbara's Time Capsule:*

I should tell you that, although we were virgins, we had fooled around a lot. Not as much as some couples, but you know. We'd done our exploring. We knew we had the right equipment. Whenever we did fool around, it felt exciting and sexy. We could get pretty worked up. Feeling we were doing things we shouldn't be doing made it even more exciting.

But that night it didn't seem that way. It seemed mechanical. The whole idea of two people running away to a shack in the country and taking off their clothes and getting into a shabby bed together seemed absurd. The idea of him getting on top of me and pushing his thing into me seemed utterly ridiculous. We pretended it was romantic. We drank.

Your father was so earnest. I couldn't look at him or I would've laughed out loud.

I held so much back, the disappointment, the revulsion. I felt sick. I wanted him to get it over with.

He got into bed with me and then he had to get up again to put on his prophylactic.

It was when he was in the bathroom that I realized what was happening to me. I was feeling menstrual cramps! All the anxiety was bringing my period on early! I'd never even discussed menstruation with your father. And now it was coming on me full force and he was in the bathroom!

I'll spare you the details. You can imagine how embarrassed I was.

It certainly ended our night of romance.

I cried. I cried most about the awful look on your father's face, first shock, then disappointment. What a sad pair we were!

About fifteen minutes later, when we were both dressed again, he said, "Wait." He was actually grinning. "Maybe this is all to the good," he said.

Your father could be an optimist in the strangest situations. I liked that about him.

He said we should look at my period (what we called "my visitor") as an omen. We weren't meant to elope. And there was nothing to stop us from going ahead with the wedding as we'd originally planned.

At first, the thought of going home to my own bed

and having to face my mother horrified me. I had convinced myself that I never wanted to see her again.

I looked at the awful wallpaper. Somebody had played tic-tac-toe on it. I asked your father what we should do about this cabin we'd rented.

He said all we had to do was leave. He said he thought the old man expected us to. He figured the old man knew we weren't married.

We did leave. The funny thing is, we felt sneakier leaving the cabin before midnight than we had felt checking in.

We left the key in the cabin but we took the cake with us. We drove home, eating the cake and talking about what we had to do in the morning.

Suddenly, all the plans I'd hated seemed like fresh new ideas. Because we'd come so close to not having a wedding, I wanted one ten times more!

I still had disagreements with my mother. There were things that didn't go as well as they should have. But I did enjoy the day.

The wedding night was better than the night we tried to elope. But it still wasn't sensational. I talked too much, all about the day, and I got the giggles. I got so ticklish, I wouldn't let your father touch me for the longest time. When I wasn't laughing, I was crying. When we did get close, we were so clumsy!

But we did consummate the marriage, as they say.

Here we are now, on our honeymoon, surrounded by majestic mountains and lovely green forests. The air is beautifully clear. Every day has been sunny.

We think we're getting quite good at sex. It seems to make more sense now.

I don't know what I expect you to learn from these ramblings. I'm not for one minute recommending that you do anything the way we did!

What I think I'm trying to tell you is that the whole process of falling in love and wanting to get married and planning a wedding is never smooth sailing. I wanted you to know what I went through, but you'll have a whole different set of problems to solve and it won't be easy.

Your father and I will be ready to help whenever you want us to, but only if you want us to.

Love,

Mom.

I weep at the thought of the dear young woman who wrote those lines fifty years ago. How innocent we were! How naïve! How impossible it was for her or anyone else to imagine how times would change!

It's time for me to go upstairs. Some minutes later, as I lie there in the bed I shared with Barb for so many years, I think of a particular weekend back in the late 1980s. Barb was down in Grand Forks, North Dakota, shopping with some of her friends. It was her idea of a treat, to be away with other women, drinking Scotch, telling raunchy jokes, playing bridge in her nightie. And Tracy chose that occasion to seek me out—I was in the park walking our golden retriever Dave—to tell me that Bill, her boyfriend, wanted her to move out of the townhouse she shared with two other girls and move in with him. I balked because her strategy was so blatant: with Barb out of town, she saw me as a pushover and, if she got me onside, it'd be easier for her to convince her mother. I also balked because neither Barb nor I liked Bill.

Had Tracy and Bill ever gone out on a date? Had Bill ever come to our house to call for her? Had he ever stood in our vestibule, waiting for Tracy to get ready, and actually looked Barb or me in the eye? Or was dating passé by then? I didn't remember Tracy ever having a boy call for her. Was she that unattractive? Absolutely not. Had she sat at home wishing a boy would take her out or waiting for the telephone to ring? No. Tracy was never at home. From age ten to seventeen, her life was devoted to a gymnastics career, spending evening after evening in a gymnasium practising, most of the time having to be driven there by Barb or me. Shortly after she got her driver's licence, and because she'd shown such a practical and responsible side enhanced by a gymnast's regimen, we thought she deserved her own car. We bought her a second-hand Trans-Am and gave it to her as a Grade Twelve graduation present. (Brian, her older brother, showed no resentment—he hated driving.) Tracy's life had been so organized—so many hours for school, so many hours for gymnastics, every day—and her diet so dictated by the sport, that she'd had no sense of the luxury of spare time, or the frivolity of fast food. When she quit gymnastics—mostly because working out on the floor without a mat as they did then was crippling her back—it was as if she'd been released from solitary confinement. In her car, she bombed around town, flitting from place to place—her back seat littered with empty Slurpee cups and Big Mac wrappers—never lighting too long in one spot, rubbing it into her head that she was *free*, free of the cloistered existence imposed by a difficult sport. Where Barb and I had regarded her controlled, list-making life as wonderful preparation for young adulthood, it became something to rebel against when her career ended.

The boys in her life were met away from the house, in groups that congregated—where? Who knew? It appeared that *our house* was a meeting place when we were on vacation or at the lake for the weekend. There'd be a bash that attracted kids from all over, kids who brought booze and pot and cocaine, a party that required rearranging of the furniture, tough guys to act as bouncers, food and music brought in, a party that featured all manner of little atrocities that had to be covered up or cleaned up, like vomit on the broadloom, blood on the walls, urine in the bathtub, semen in the sheets. So boys—and certainly Bill—had been in our house when we weren't there, never when we *were* there. Barb told Tracy she wanted to *see* any boy that Tracy went out with but, as far as I knew, she didn't. At least, not before things turned serious with Bill.

There was a row—more than one, in fact—when Tracy wanted to move out of our house and live with her friends Carol and Dana. I saw it as another phase of Tracy's declaration of independence; Barb saw it as a declaration of *war*. I orchestrated something of a truce when I talked Barb into going over to Southdale to visit Tracy and her girlfriends—Tracy, I was sure, did a major clean-up before we arrived and all three girls made certain there'd be no casual visits from boys while we were there.

And within months, there she was, tracking me down in our local park—Dave so happy to see her and making a fuss—and she told me that Bill had this apartment he'd been sharing with some guy, and the guy was moving down east, and Bill wanted Tracy to take over the guy's share of the rent. And Tracy wanted to oblige. I tried to take a practical approach, tried to tell her now was the time to concentrate on furthering her education and she could do that best back at home. What I really wanted to say was, "Whatever happened to *dating*? What's wrong with seeing a guy two or three evenings a week? Why this great rush to *play house*?" Instead,

I stuck with the education argument and she didn't buy it. "Living with Bill won't stop me from going to university if I want to!" she cried. And then another dog came into the park, a German shepherd that was more obedient than Dave, on a leash administered by a guy in a cold-weather track suit, and Dave was (illegally) off his leash, bounding around, barking, wanting to play. I had to calm Dave down and get the leash back on, while the owner of the German shepherd paused, drew his dog into a sitting position and glared at me as if I was the most incompetent dog-walker on the planet. Impatient, Tracy took off.

Barb arrived home the next day in a good mood that vanished as soon as I gave her Tracy's news. Within minutes, she was phoning Tracy and we headed over to the place she shared with Dana and Carol. When we arrived, the other two girls weren't there but Bill was. Barb and Tracy argued as soon as they saw each other and Barb, ignoring Bill, said, "I gather you are already having sex."

The look on Tracy's face said, *Hel-lo! Where have you been? What century is this?* and, trying to stay calm but speaking more loudly than normal, Tracy said, "Mother, if this is a lesson, you're too late. Like, I know about HIV and I know about birth control. Okay? End of story."

"I see," said Barb. That was when she pulled the manila envelope out of her handbag. "I wrote this especially for you a long time ago, Tracy. I wrote it when I was your age. I wanted you to read it at a certain time of your life. And now, as you say, it's too late. But I'm going to leave it with you, anyway. Maybe someday you'll understand how I felt when I wrote it and how disappointed I feel now."

She put the envelope on the kitchen table and walked to the door.

"Mother," Tracy said, "I don't want *anything* from you." She threw the envelope at Barb and it landed on the floor.

Bill said, "*Trace*," and stepped between her and her mother. Barb walked out.

I bent over to pick up the envelope. I handed it to Tracy, saying, "Please read this. Not now. Sometime. When you have a quiet minute or two."

Tracy said, "She can't stop me from moving in with Bill!"

"She's not trying to," I said. "She just wants you to understand what it's like to be a mother."

Tracy sat down, crying, and said, "I'm sorry, Daddy. Will she be okay?"

And I said, "I think so."

The morning after reading *Barbara's Time Capsule*, I wake to a ringing phone. I pick up on the fourth ring.

"Hello?"

"Oh, Jenkins, dear, did I wake you?" It's Gwen Foster.

"It's all right, I was just having a little lie-in, as they say."

"Jenkins, I'm so, so sorry. Shall I call back?"

"No. Gwen, it's fine. Time I was up." It's after nine. I'm feeling those manhattans.

"Oh, look, I won't keep you. I'm wondering if you're free for dinner next Saturday. Charles and I are putting together a little dinner party, probably no more than six. Do you think you could make it, love?"

Dear Gwen. She and Charlie have been mighty good to me. Charlie taught English for me at Yarwood High, one of those guys a principal needs—always in sync with me on every issue. We've had some good times.

"Sounds terrific, Gwen," I say.

"Lovely! Oh, I'm so pleased. One thing, Jenkins—I'm thinking of inviting a friend of mine from tennis. She's younger than I am, divorced, but I want you to tell me if it's all right before I ask her. I don't want you to think I'm trying to set you up with her or anything, and I want to make absolutely sure you're comfortable with my asking her."

I think of the previous night's disaster with Janie. I think of the embarrassment with Liz back in the winter. Both times, I was alone with the woman. I see no problem in being part of a group of six.

"Gwen, I'm fine with whatever you're planning. I'd be happy at one of your dinner parties even if you invited Joan Rivers."

Besides, Gwen makes some delicious meals.

"You'll like Iris, Jenkins, but I want to emphasize that I'm not trying to be a match-maker."

"You've made that clear. May I ask who the other two are?"

"Of course—didn't I say? The Krugers—you know, Kathy and Hans."

"Good. What time should I arrive?"

"Oh, sixish. And Charles says you don't have to bring wine."

"Is that a reflection on my taste?"

"No! Of course it isn't."

"I'll bring my usual fine bottle of Wolf Blass Yellow Label pinot noir."

"All right, then, love. We'll see you Saturday at six. And Jenkins, it's casual."

If I don't have errands to run or doctors (foot, eye, GP, dentist) to see, mornings are my favourite time for reading. After breakfast, I take a second cup of coffee and a book into the living room. I usually have several books on the go. I'm nicely ensconced when the telephone rings. It's a long-distance ring. I have a walk-about phone and it would make sense to take it with me to the living room but, to be frank, I leave the phone in my office so that I'll get the exercise of hurrying upstairs to answer it. Despite this, I curse the interruption as I hit the stairs. I hope it isn't a telemarketer; I know I could get my name on a list to stop telemarketing calls, but again I do like the exercise. I grab the receiver after the third ring.

"Hello?" I say, between pants.

"Hi, Dad, it's Brian." My forty-four-year-old actor son.

"Hello, Brian, *you old loaf-ah,*" I say, quoting from a scene in *Billy Liar*—long ago picked by Brian and me as our favourite movie—the scene in which Billy fantasizes that his father is rich.

"*I've got that job,*" Brian says, switching the scene to the one where Billy tells his workmate Arthur Crabtree he's going to write scripts for a comedian named Danny Boone.

"*You haven't,*" I say in Arthur's voice.

"*I have!*"

"*Why, you jammy bugger!*"

Brian reverts to his own voice to tell me he's landed a part in the CBC series *The Border.* It'll bring in a good paycheque and he can continue with whatever commercials his agent finds for him.

"That's terrific," I say. "And how are Naomi and Kit?"

"Naomi might get a production assistant job on the same show, and Kit's going to audition for *Cinderella* when school starts."

"Wow! Good for all of you."

"*Aye,*" he says, back to Billy's voice, talking with old Councillor Duxbury, "*well, I'll be on me way, Councillor.*"

"*All right, then, lad,*" I say in Duxbury's voice. "*Think on't!*"

As we hang up, I recall that it was shortly after the first oral contraceptive—*The Pill*—had become widely marketed that Barb and I abandoned birth control. We wanted a baby. We were living in Saskatoon by then—I'd been transferred to that city's Radisson's store as the advertising manager. Barb said it was no surprise to her that Saskatchewan was a leader in agriculture—she felt so *fertile* once we moved there.

Pleased as I was about the promotion, I was glad to move out of the Winnipeg office for another reason. We had finally talked Clarise into leaving and we'd hired an experienced copywriter named Danielle Lacosse, who impressed me with both her ability and her Gallic sensuality. She was older than I, perhaps mid-thirties, fluently bilingual, and she had two distinctive features: shiny black hair, cut short, and bright green eyes. I knew nothing of her past, but her many nights of working late suggested a limited social life, and there was something about her that made you believe there was heartbreak in her past. We had her write institutional ads and she'd research them at night, and, when Barbara worked evenings, I'd stay late too and often drive Danielle home. When she was busy producing new ideas as well as writing her share of flyer copy and handling some of the more tedious chores, even through the day, she'd seem to be in the throes of passion. She'd sweat. Her nostrils flared, she breathed heavily. She cried out little French expletives. I loved the smell of her when she was working hard. I liked to talk with her about the style of ads we were switching to—using photographs instead of artwork. I found myself making opportunities to be alone with her. One night when I drove her home, she told me she was going to Paris for her vacation and I was envious. I had to ask her to do something for me over there—perhaps she could pick up two books, Henry Miller's *Tropics*, which were still banned in Canada. Without hesitation, she said she would. I didn't think she saw anything suggestive or forward about my request, but I worried that I might be capable of crossing a line, that propinquity with this hot-blooded woman was bringing me close to doing something silly.

There's nothing like a promotion and a move to another

city to focus you on your real purpose in life. I remember how thrilled we were when Brian was born, how healthy and chubby he was, but Barb had difficulty feeding him at first. She became so engorged with milk that her breasts ballooned and hardened and the nipples didn't protrude far enough for him to be able to latch on. Spending the better part of a week in hospital, as all new mothers did in those days, Barb wept with frustration. One afternoon, I dropped in to visit her just as a nurse was taking Brian away, saying they'd try again in an hour.

"Feel them!" Barb cried.

She was wearing a negligee and she thrust out her chest. I reached over and placed my hand on her left breast. That old Lucky Strike cigarette slogan jumped into my head: *So round, so firm, so fully-packed.*

"That's remarkable," I said, trying to put a frown of concern on my face while I secretly enjoyed the phenomenon. The breast, so soft and pliable before, was now as solid as a sculpture. What came to me like an epiphany was the realization of what breasts were really for. Yet here we had a baby that wasn't being gratified while I, veteran of countless Neck Room forays, was.

I moved my hand to the right breast, pretending to examine it with the objectivity of a scientist.

A nurse walked in. "Aren't they something?" she said.

Her own breasts were high and prominent and I thought her next comment might be *Want to try these now?* My face turned red—I'd been caught with my hand where it'd normally be only in private.

"I know you're not feeling good about this," the nurse said to Barbara, "but if he doesn't find a way when we try again, we'll express the milk and feed it to him. Can't let you keep all that good stuff to yourself."

"Aren't my nipples too small?" Barb said.

"They'll be fine," said the nurse. "The main thing is, try not to be upset. He'll feel your anxiety and that makes it tougher. Just remember that, with some mothers, it takes a couple of days."

"I'm a nurse and I can't nurse!" Barb said, weeping again.

"It might be best if we express a little anyway. But, in the long run, you're going to be fine."

"There, you see?" I said. "It's going to be okay."

"Oh, what do *you* know," said Barb.

Three years later, we were still in Saskatoon and now there was a new baby, Tracy. "You're so lucky to have one of each," Barb's mother told us. "A millionaire's family." She came up from Winnipeg to help out. By then, Barb's father had died, suddenly, one fall afternoon at the Winter Club. He'd been having chest pains and he'd been told to take it easy, but he wasn't the kind of man who knew *how* to take it easy.

Mrs. Mason—Eleanor—stayed on, making meals, playing with Brian, cleaning the house. One beautiful day, we went for a drive to talk about the possibility of my going back to university to take Education. Eleanor loved the idea, saying if we moved back to Winnipeg we could move in with her, save some money while I wasn't earning any.

She sat in the back seat of our Plymouth station wagon with three-year-old Brian on one side and Tracy in a car bed on the other. She read to Brian and taught him games like *I spy with my little eye.* At the least sound from the baby, Barb turned and knelt on the seat—still no seat belts then—and leaned over to adjust Tracy's blanket or to move the teddy bear to where Tracy could see it. As we drove out on the highway, Tracy whimpered and Barb lifted her into the front seat. Figuring Tracy wanted to be fed, she undid the front of her blouse and unsnapped the flap of her nursing bra. Where Brian had had difficulty, Tracy had taken hold right from the start.

I liked to believe I'd helped the nursing situation by doing some suckling of my own. I'd become quite fond of suckling Barb's breasts. I had told Barb more than once that there were times—like on a Monday before getting up to go to work—when I would be quite content to suckle for a minute or two and it didn't have to lead to intercourse. (She never believed me.) As we drove along, I smiled at the happy sound of Tracy slurping away. I thought about how welcome the nursing bra would've been, with its easy-opening flaps, if she'd worn one back in the days when we were dating.

And so I left Radisson's and we moved back to Winnipeg and I took Education and became a teacher and eventually a principal. I was busy with job and family and made no attempt to find out where Danielle was, though I heard all Radisson's advertising departments had been consolidated into one big one in Toronto. I never thought of her again until one day years later I received in the mail a literary magazine called *Blatz*. The envelope bore no return address and I assumed the publisher had sent it to me as a promotional gesture. But then I saw in the Table of Contents Danielle Lacosse's name. I happened to be in my office at home and I turned to the story. I read it quickly and found it, to say the least, unnerving. It was about a woman much like Danielle who goes to Paris and buys Henry Miller's *Tropics* for her boss, at his request. Written as a confession to a priest, the story tells how, on a rainy day in her Montmartre hotel, the woman reads a few pages of *Tropic of Cancer*:

> ... I have to say that, they were straightforward sexual passages, I have to admit, and I thought about my boss—yes, I have thought about him in that way—not in a bad way, but in the way that Henry Miller was describing, and I had the book in my left hand, Father, and I had no intention of reading, but

I imagined I was with my boss, who can be so very nice, Father, I have often wished that he would forget he is married—oh, I am sorry, Father, it is not right, I know, to have these thoughts about a married man, but I do not think it is harmful to anyone if I think these things and, anyway, I held the book in my left hand and, before I realized what I was doing, Father, my right hand was—well, I did not ever plan to do such a thing, but you must understand the effect that Mr. Miller's prose and my thoughts of my boss were having on me, and I cannot remember ever doing this kind of thing before, perhaps once when I was an adolescent experimenting, but, Father, there was my right hand down there, I do not want to say where, and I hope you will forgive me, Father, down there between my legs, touching myself, Father, and it felt so good, Father, you have no idea, Father, and I guess that is why I am here today, Father, because it felt so *good.*

At Gwen and Charlie's

Gwen and Charlie Foster live in a newish development in South Winnipeg. Gwen's good-natured mother, now ninety-two, helped with the 2004 purchase on the condition that she have a room there. Within the last few months, she'd made her own decision to move into a nearby old folks' home. Charlie, who is ten years younger than I and retired at age sixty just prior to moving into the new house, loves living among upwardly mobile young families. In summer, he potters around in his back yard, chatting up a young mother over the back fence and ogling shapely teenaged girls who sun themselves on raised decks nearby. Both Gwen and he rhapsodize about the camaraderie of the folks in their street. Charlie told me about one young couple who had a reputation for being swingers and, at a party at their place, while showing folks around, the host pointed out a shower stall that was big enough for six. The young husband across the street walks his dog at seven in the morning every day and then rides a bike to work. This admirable routine affected Charlie, who gets up early most mornings, not to emulate the fellow but to give him a thumbs-up from the living-room window. Gwen, no slouch herself when it comes to outdoor activity—she plays tennis and golf—often takes up a post at the end of the driveway to offer Gatorade to passing early-morning joggers.

I turn into Charlie's driveway and park my Pontiac G6 alongside Hans Kruger's Audi SUV. Charlie and I, both former English teachers, get a kick out of Hans's refusal to read books. Hans's wife Kathy is a faithful member of Gwen's book club, and Hans tends to view reading books as a women's thing. He claims he had to do enough reading in his work as an insurance executive, he's damned if he's going to read for *pleasure*. Kathy is his second wife; they met over the back fence years ago in another suburb and carried on an affair for a year before leaving their spouses. Though Gwen and Charlie are happily married, I can't help but think that Charlie has the Hans-Kathy model in mind whenever he tends his geraniums and waits for the yummy mummy to appear at his back fence.

I wave to Rudy, the guy next door, who is, on this August night, playing goal with a regulation-size net while drilling his five-year-old son in the fine art of slapping shots with a tennis ball. Motivated by visions of multi-million-dollar NHL contracts, Rudy put a hockey stick in his son's hands before the little fella could walk.

I lock my car. As congenial as the neighbourhood is, Charlie had a vehicle stolen right off his driveway the first year he lived here.

There's a new *Welcome* mat on the front step. I ring the bell and the door opens.

"Sorry, we don't want any," says Charlie, and he slams the door.

Every time I arrive at Charlie's house, he slams the door on me. He's been doing it for over thirty years. I open the door and there is Gwen.

"Poor Jenkins," she says, and she gives me the one-armed hug that so many women seem to favour in social situations these days. "I don't know why Charles still thinks that's so hilarious. How are you?"

She looks outside and closes the door behind me. Gwen is dressed in a lime-green sweater and skirt, with a beigy silk scarf arranged in what I consider a retro look—it's pinned to one side with a massive gold brooch. Her dyed brunette hair is cut short in the no-nonsense way of most busy wives.

"I'm great," I say. "Don't tell Charlie I gave you this." I hand her the bottle of Wolf Blass.

"Oh, Jenkins, thank you! You *know* it's my favourite."

"Tell me, Gwen, how is your mother?"

"Jenkins, thank you for asking. She is fine, absolutely fine. The old darling—she didn't have to go into that home, you know. Charles and I told her countless times that we loved having her here, she was no bother at all, but she insisted it was the right time for her, and, Jenkins, I have to say the place she's in is wonderful. One of those new assisted-living complexes."

"Well, guess what? You know my old friend Claude—he and his wife think it's time I went into one of those places. I could keep your mother company."

"Jenkins, love, that's preposterous! You're in your prime! A condo, maybe, but you're so comfortable in the house—no need at all for you to move. Look, come on in—the Krugers are here—and where did Charles get to? He should have your drink poured by now."

I go ahead of her down the hall to a point where the kitchen is on my right and what is now called *the great room* (formerly the family room) on my left. Hans and Kathy stand near the great-room fireplace, holding drinks in front of their matching bellies.

"Good evening, Mr. Jenkins," Hans says, raising his glass as if in a toast.

"Who let him in?" Charlie cries from the kitchen, where he has his bar set up on the centre island. He's wearing a grey sweatshirt that commemorates his favourite TV comedy series, *As Time Goes By*.

"Jenkins, how are you *do*ing?" Kathy says in that tone people reserve for addressing the bereaved. Kathy has spoken this way to me, her eyebrows arching, every time I've seen her since Barb died.

"I'm doing okay, Kath," I say, "but I'd be doing a whole lot better if I could get a drink around here."

"Did I hear you telling Gwenny you're moving into an old folks' home?" Charlie says in his loud, bantering voice. "About time, I'd say."

"Aww, Jenkins, you're no-ot!" Kathy says in her same tone.

"Kath, for God's sake, Charlie's *kidding*," says Hans. "But, Jenkins, the way the financial institutions are screwing up to the south of us, I hope you have a good pension."

Hans is wearing a powder-blue cardigan that might've once belonged to Perry Como, though on Hans, worn over a dark blue sport shirt and slacks, it looks stylish. He's retired but claims he still does consulting work for Great West Life.

"They say Bush is going to bomb somebody before he leaves office," says Hans. "His ratings are at an all-time low anyway, so he might as well do it to take people's mind off the lousy mortgage situation."

Kathy, whose dark brown turtleneck and brown, calf-length slacks strain to contain her, says, "Obama and McCain won't let Bush bomb anybody, will they?"

It's common in gatherings of this type across Canada for American politics to be a hot topic, especially with the 2008 presidential election approaching. A Canadian election is approaching, too, but nobody cares.

I turn to the host. "Do you have that Scotch and soda poured yet?"

"Scotch and soda?" Charlie says, feigning astonishment. "What happened to Planter's Punch and Lime Diet Coke? You mean I went to all the trouble to—"

"All right, Planter's Punch and Lime Diet Coke!"

Charlie opens the fridge. "Oops, sorry, no Lime Diet Coke. I could've sworn … okay, Scotch and tonic, you said?"

All this kibitzing is Charlie's way of setting the mood. He loves the fact that Kathy Kruger never knows when he's joking. He used to talk about a son who'd been kidnapped before Gwen finally made him confess to Kathy that the three daughters whose photos were on the mantel were the Fosters' only children. "Our Foster-children," Charlie called them, leaving Kathy bamboozled.

"Hans, Kathy, do sit down and make yourselves comfortable," Gwen says, coming into the great room.

"Where've *you* been?" Charlie asks her.

"I was watching for Iris," Gwen says. "It's not like her to be late."

"Did you try her cell?" says Charlie. "She's bound to have her cell with her."

"Oh, of course!" says Gwen. "Oh, Charles, why didn't I think of that? But first—Jenkins. Hasn't Charles poured you a drink yet?"

"Right here, right here!" Charlie says, handing me a drink. "The perfect rye and ginger."

"Charles, you *know*—"

I take a sip. It's good old Johnny Walker Red and soda. I pretend it isn't, grimacing, and Hans roars with laughter.

And so the Krugers and I settle into the upholstered furniture, while Gwen fusses with dinner preparation and Charlie circulates with a tray of hors d'oeuvres. Kathy gets talking to me about books—her book club is reading Elizabeth Hay's *Late Nights on Air* and she wonders what I think of it—and that sends Hans into the kitchen to look at the floor and the cupboards Charlie had the developer replace. After I've spoken about Hay's novel, Kathy admits she's read only a few pages and what she really wants is a quick summary.

The doorbell rings.

"Oh!" Gwen says from the kitchen. "That'll be Iris."

"Good of them to make all these adjustments," Hans is saying, opening cupboards and inspecting the woodwork and the hinges. "What, at no cost to you?"

"You're damned right, no cost to me," says Charlie. "Not a penny. Well, you saw how everything was. Did the company want me to advertise the kind of shoddy work they do? No bloody way."

"Sorry I'm late," comes a new voice. "The guy I told you about? We had this long phone conversation yesterday and I thought that was the end of it. So, five minutes before I wanted to leave tonight, he shows up at my condo. Of course, I don't buzz him in. So he keeps talking on the intercom. I finally say I have to go, he's made me late, and I hang up. Well, when I'm driving out of the underground garage, he's *there*! On the ramp just outside the door. Talk about creepy! I almost ran over him. I mean, come on, *get over it,* already!"

"Did you speak with him again?" says Gwen.

"No way," is the answer. "Well, I did open my window and tell him to *stop stalking me*, and I drove off."

"Iris, poor you! Come in and meet everybody."

I stand up and so does Kathy, and Charlie and Hans come out from behind the island. Into our midst walks a shapely woman, younger than all of us, perhaps late forties, in a black long-sleeved top, black jeans and black pumps. Her hair is shoulder-length, brownish blond in colour, a lock covering the left side of her forehead and her left eyebrow—a style similar to one popularized by Hollywood actress Veronica Lake in the 1940s and called a *peekaboo bang*. Iris's attractive face seems flushed—perhaps from her recent ordeal, or from telling about it, or perhaps it's her reaction to strangers whose attention is focused on her. There is no sign of any makeup; the colour in her full lips seems natural. A turquoise pendant at her v-neck tastefully draws your gaze to a hint of cleavage.

"Iris, you remember Charles … and this is Hans Kruger, and over there is his wife Kathy, and that's our old friend Bob Jenkins. Everybody, Iris Barstow."

"Just call me Jenkins," I say, reaching to shake her hand.

"Or anything you damn well please," says Charlie. "You know, Iris, I used to teach for this guy, and as my colleagues always said, 'It's not the kids in Yarwood High that are the problem, it's the principal of the thing.'"

Everybody groans. Charlie can be relentless in trying to emphasize that *God damn it, this is a party!*

"What can we get you to drink, Iris?" says Gwen.

"Do you have a martini of some sort?"

"Specialty of the house," says Charlie. "The classic dry martini, with lemon rind instead of an olive, as prescribed by Kingsley Amis. That sound all right?"

"Sounds lovely. Who's Kingsley Amis?"

"That's what I said, Iris," says Hans. "I thought maybe he was the bartender at Rae and Jerry's."

"He's one of Charles's favourite writers," says Gwen. "And I warn you—this martini is nearly all gin."

"It's excellent," says Hans. "It's what I'm drinking."

Charlie takes a pitcher out of the fridge and a glass out of the freezer. The martini really is one of his specialties.

Iris sits on a hassock next to Kathy.

"Tell me, Iris, what do you do?" says Kathy.

"Well." Iris seems unready for interrogation. "I co-manage a children's clothing store—The Lucky Elephant in Polo Park."

"Do you have children of your own?" Kathy asks.

"No, thank God. Oops, there's my bias showing. I never wanted to be a mother. I was in the birthing room when my sister had her daughter—that was fascinating—but I'm happy if I don't see kids till they're at least ten years old. My co-manager at the store, Margot, does the buying. I do most of the computer work and keep the books. We hire people to do the selling."

"Excuse me, everyone," says Gwen, standing at the great-room entrance, "dinner is just about ready. So, when Charles rings the bell, you'll please come and help yourselves in the kitchen and then go into the dining room and find your place card."

Charlie brings in Iris's martini. "Iris," he says, "why don't you tell them about your sky-diving?"

"You jumped out of a plane?" I say.

"Oh, that was a long time ago," says Iris, as the colour returns to her face. She takes a sip of martini. "That's very good, Charlie, thanks. Well, what can I say? I like to try *everything* and you know, in the free-fall part, you get an adrenaline rush like no other. But hey, that was years ago. I couldn't do it now."

"You jumped more than once?" says Hans.

Kathy is staring at Iris with a horrified look.

"Yes, lots of times," says Iris. "But the guys in the club gave you a terrible hazing when you reached one hundred jumps, so I kept pretty vague about the number I was at."

"How many jumps did you make?" says Hans.

Iris chuckles. "I'll never tell."

Charlie rings an authentic town-crier's bell. "Okay, folks, come and get it."

As we get up, Kathy, still aghast, says to Iris, "I don't know how you could do it. Standing at the open door of the plane? *That* would finish me."

Kathy goes first, then Hans, then Iris, and I follow her.

Iris turns to me as she picks up a dinner plate and says, "Gwen tells me you've written a book."

"Well, like your sky-diving, that was a long time ago."

"Oh, Gwen, this is lovely!" says Kathy.

"What a feast!" says Iris.

Before us are platters of ham slices, perogies, mashed turnips, green beans, mixed salad and sour cream. We fill our plates and go into the dining room. The seating plan puts the Fosters at either end of the table, Kathy and me on one side and Hans and Iris facing us on the other. Iris and I are at Gwen's end of the table.

"Charles, will you say grace?" Gwen asks.

"Good friends, good meat, good God, let's eat."

"Oh, Charles, that isn't what I had in mind, but please, everybody, go ahead. And there's lots left for seconds."

Iris says, "So, Jenkins, what's your book called?"

"*Never Too Early.*"

"What's it about, sex in the morning?"

Hans lets go one of his loud outbursts of laughter.

"You'd be surprised how many people have asked me that," I say.

"Seriously, I think it's a good topic, sex in the morning," says Iris. "Most women—no, I won't speak for other women—" looking over at Kathy, whose face is likely registering horror again "—I know *I* prefer sex in the morning. I think it's a guy thing, you know, taking a woman out for a lovely big dinner like this and then taking her home and expecting her to enjoy sex on a full stomach. That's why so many women order salads. The truth is, sex is much better in the morning when you're well rested and your stomach's empty and you can devote all your concentration and your energy to what you're doing."

Charlie chips in: "I was saying that to Gwenny just this morning, wasn't I, Precious?"

"Oh, Charles," says Gwen, "you were snoring away when I left for my walk. You didn't even know I was gone."

We all snicker, and Iris says, "*Seriously*, it's the nature of our bodies, isn't it, that makes men and women look at these things so differently …"

I catch Hans rolling his eyes at Kathy with an expression that says, *Where did Gwen find this bimbo?*

Gwen comes to the rescue: "Oh, Iris, I just noticed your fingernails!" Gwen reaches to take Iris's right hand in hers and Iris sets down her fork. "Kathy, Iris gets the most creative designs on her nails—little pictures done in acrylics. What are they this time?"

"Beach scenes—as sort of a last gasp of summer," says Iris.

Hans can't stand it any more. He asks Charlie where he got the ham and how he cooked it. Iris reaches her left hand across the table to Kathy, who says, "Oh, aren't they lovely?" I ask to see them and Iris gives me both hands. Her fingers in mine feel softer and smoother than I expected. The tiny pictures are remarkable: Each shows a sand-coloured beach with an azure sea or lake that matches Iris's pendant. On one nail there's a tiny white beach-house with a red roof; on another, a couple of starfish in the sand; on a third, a red and white blanket, and so on. While the miniscule designs are a visual treat, her touch is a sensual bonus.

"Very nice," I say.

"Thank you," says Iris. "Now, I'm sorry for the digression—what *is* your book about?" She looks directly into my eyes, as if she's not simply conversing—she's genuinely interested in my answer.

Hans and Charlie have heard my spiel a time or two, so

they continue their own conversation, now on the prospects of the Winnipeg Blue Bombers.

"It's about literacy," I say. "How to encourage kids to read. The title comes from the theory that it helps kids to become literate more quickly if you read to them even before they're born."

"Read to a *fetus*?" Iris says, sounding skeptical.

"That's what scientists tell us," I say.

"Oh, but your book is about so much more, Jenkins," Gwen says. "Iris, he wrote this, what, ten, no fourteen years ago, and it's as relevant today as it was then, maybe more so. Schools still find books are the best medium for learning to read. And Jenkins gives specific examples of what to read to kids early and what they should try reading on their own."

"I *love* to curl up with a book," Iris says. "Yes, the *feel* of it, the *smell* of it—there's no substitute."

"Iris, more wine?" says Charlie.

"No, thank you."

"Another classic dry martini?"

"No, no, it was wonderful, but one is enough. I'm driving."

"I'll have another, Chas," says Hans. "Kath's my D. D."

Over a dessert of strawberries and ice cream, the three of us at Gwen's end of the table continue to talk about books, Iris telling us she prefers true crime but might read any book if she likes the first page. As Gwen keeps deferring to me for titles and authors' names she can't remember, Iris grows weary of the topic and, hearing Charlie mention fishing, speaks about catching walleye in Rainy Lake. She engages Hans and Charlie in a discussion of the best fishing spots in Manitoba and what is the best bait to use to catch pickerel. Before long, she's telling all of us about prawning off the coast of Vancouver Island and skiing at Whistler. I'm beginning to feel terribly one-dimensional—*the guy who reads a lot of books and wrote one once*—so I mention golf, and Iris says she likes that too, and she suggests maybe a few of us could make up a foursome sometime.

With Kathy protesting that it's time to leave, Gwen talks us into moving back to the great room for a game of Trivial Pursuit, possibly hoping to show off the skills of her husband and me. Iris wins.

The hands of the Fosters' heirloom mantel-clock have inched close to 11:30 when we guests get up to depart. I realize that, since Kathy's empathetic greeting when I arrived, there's been no reference to my widower status, no discussion of *how I'm getting along.* I feel a twinge of disappointment, but mostly relief. With Iris to look at all evening, I got away from thinking about myself. I'm fascinated with her face, her hazel eyes—greenish with an inner circle of light brown around the pupils—and her mouth—the biting edges of her upper front teeth together form a convex curve that perfectly fits her smile. While we sat across from each other, I studied her as if I were cramming for an exam.

After we've said our goodbyes, I'm outside and in my car when Iris, on her way to her own vehicle, stops by my window.

"It was great to meet you," she says. "I wanted to tell you I'm interested in writing a book. Maybe you could help me get started."

"Gosh, I've written so little—"

"But you have written a whole book. And had it published. I'm not interested in publishing—I'd just like to do it for myself. And you've done it. And you've read so widely, and you're a teacher. I think you'd be a tremendous help."

"If—if you say so."

"Could we maybe go out for a drink some night to talk about it?"

"I guess so—if—"

"Here's my business card. You'll see my cell number on there. Why don't you give me a call when it's convenient?"

"Sure—okay."

"Thanks. I'll look forward to it. Good night."

"Good night."

She hurries off, the *tap tap tap* of her heels on the driveway echoing in the quiet neighbourhood.

Turning Out All Right

Dad?"

"Hi, Tracy."

"Sorry I haven't called you for days—we've been really busy. How did the date go with your old girlfriend?"

"It was nice to see her. We did some reminiscing, talked about our kids. We went to The Keg. Good dinner, and we didn't order a single drink."

"Not even a glass of wine?"

"No."

"Wow. I'm impressed. Are you going to see her again?"

"Oh, maybe. We'll see."

"I gather she wasn't as hot as she used to be."

"Trace, it was *high school*."

"Dad."

"What?"

"Why we've been so busy? Hank's found a business he thinks we should buy. Says we could get it cheap."

Hank is Tracy's father-in-law. He's always been ambitious for his son.

"What does Clay think?"

"He'd like to expand. This is a sportswear line that would complement ours. We've been doing a lot of homework."

"Good. Don't let Hank talk you into something you'll regret."

"Dad."

"You know Hank."

"Sure, but I know you, too, and you're too cautious. Sometimes you just have to go for it."

I don't see much of Clay's parents, Dot and Hank Heller, but whenever their names come up, I think about that day my first grandchild was born.

It was April 1, 1995. We had told Brian that his sister's baby was due that day and he flew in from Toronto. I went to pick him up and, in the Arrivals area A at Winnipeg International Airport, he appeared at the top of the escalator with a willowy black-haired woman. Was she someone he'd met on the plane, or ... ?

"You thought I was coming alone," he said. "April Fool! Dad, this is Naomi Lovett."

Naomi: the woman Brian had been seeing for nearly six months. I was struck by her gauntness and her sallow complexion. She looked much older than Brian.

He embraced me and then *she* embraced me.

"Good to finally meet you," she said.

I smelled tobacco smoke in her hair and in her dark blue cloth jacket. "Hi, Naomi," I said. "Welcome."

Brian said, "She didn't have the baby yet, did she, Dad?"

"No, she's under strict orders not to give birth until you get here."

Naomi looked slatternly, like one of the unstable female characters in a Tennessee Williams play. She was pretty in a Mia Farrow sort of way. She went into a coughing spasm and Brian put one arm around her, a package of menthol lozenges at the ready.

When she could speak, Naomi said, "I need a smoke," and I thought that was the last thing she needed.

"Any luggage?" I asked.

"Only these," Brian said, indicating his backpack and the small suitcase he was carrying.

"This way, then."

Once outside, Naomi lighted up a cigarette and took a long drag. "Ahh," she said, "I feel human again."

"We'll head home and check if there's any movement on the baby front," I said.

There was a note from Barb on the kitchen table:

> *Tracy's about to deliver. I've gone to the hospital. Maybe it's best if the two of you come right away.*
>
> *Isn't this exciting!*
>
> *Barb.*

"Can Naomi come?" said Brian.

"I don't see why not."

"Could I grab a shower first?" said Naomi. "I feel grubby."

"I'll stay here with Nome, Dad," said Brian. "We can go later."

"Good plan. For all we know, she won't deliver for hours."

And, I thought, this'll give me a chance to tip off Barb about Naomi.

On the way to St. Boniface Hospital, I found myself praying that Tracy would have an uncomplicated delivery. I'd heard of athletic women whose muscles fought against childbirth instead of easing it. With all the information young people had these days, though, surely Tracy would know what to do. She and Clay knew all kinds of things about the unborn baby at every stage of the pregnancy. At twelve weeks, it was the size of a lipstick tube and was growing toenails. At sixteen weeks, the eyebrows and eyelashes were emerging and all the limbs could move. At twenty weeks, the baby was eight inches in length, its hair was starting to grow and all five senses were developing. Tracy and Clay knew the gender of the baby, thanks to ultrasound, but they chose not to tell it to anyone.

I hadn't known a damned thing about either of my kids before they were born. I knew when Barb became pregnant—she told me—and I saw her figure grow more and more distended, and I knew at what point intercourse wasn't recommended. I knew nothing about what was going on inside Barb—she had morning sickness with Brian but not with Tracy; she gained almost no weight with Brian (except in the bosom), "tons" with Tracy—and I thought little about the approaching birth until the water broke, the sign it was time to head for the hospital. There was no question of my being present in the delivery room; it just wasn't done in the 1960s, at least not in our circle of friends. The hospital designated a space as The Fathers' Room and that's where I was expected to wait—I hadn't made it that far with Brian, but with Tracy I'd had time to read quite a bit of *Couples* by John Updike. With both babies, a doctor came looking for me to tell me whether it was a boy or a girl and to reassure me that mother and child were doing fine. I couldn't see Barb until she was good and ready to be seen—her hair brushed, lipstick applied, perfume on, her brow patted dry of perspiration. In 1995, a husband like Clay went into the delivery room and witnessed the whole process, seeing his wife in an unpretty and natural state performing the most miraculous of animal functions, and the doctor gave him things to do so that he could say he took part.

I found the room where Barb was waiting with Clay's parents, Dot and Hank. Hank was a sporting goods salesman and former linebacker about ten years younger than I. Dot was one of those tiny doll-like women with boundless energy, the kind that often married big ham-handed athletes like Hank. You could imagine him lifting her up and holding her overhead with one hand, the way I'd held Tracy when she was about five years old.

"Nothing yet, old buddy," Hank said.

"How's Brian?" Barb asked.

"Fine," I said. "Did you know he was bringing his girlfriend?"

"What! I certainly did not. What on earth does he think—"

Clay burst into the room wearing a green smock, green hat and white mask.

"It's an eight-pound baby girl!" he announced. "Mason Dorothy Heller."

Mason. I'd heard nothing of any plan to saddle the poor kid with a moniker like Mason. I disliked this fad of giving girls names that, in my experience, had always been surnames—Madison, McKenzie, Taylor, *Mason*. I was so confused by the name that, while Clay was embracing his parents, I whispered to Barb, "*Where did* Mason *come from?*"

She must've been pissed off about Brian's bringing a girlfriend without telling us, because she snipped at me: "*It's my maiden name, you asshole.*"

Of course, I thought, turning red as I watched Barb give

Clay a lavish hug. *Mason* for Barb's family, *Dorothy* for Dot, and Hank's surname, *Heller*. The Jenkins side was shut out.

"Congratulations, Clay," I said, shaking his hand.

Clay, ebullient as ever, threw his arms around me and slapped me on the back, saying, "Hey, Gramps, how does it feel?"

Hank laughed. He gave me a good slap as well. "We gotta decide what we're going to be called," he said. "We can't have two *Grampses*."

"Dot wants to be Gram," said Barb. "So I'm Nana. Jenkins, you can be Papa."

"They'll be taking Trace to recovery," said Clay. "You'll be able to come and see both my girls in a bit—but just two of you at a time."

Clay left and Hank suggested we all go for coffee while we waited. Barb and Dot said they wanted to stay put so they'd be right there when it was okay to visit.

"Why don't you boys go?" said Dot.

So *we boys* took the elevator down to the basement cafeteria and Hank treated me to coffee and a doughnut.

"Clay's got his head screwed on right, no doubt about that," Hank said. "Got everything in the right order—sports, career, wife, baby. I'm telling you, there's nothing wrong with the kids today. . . . Eh? Am I right?"

"You're right." I thought of Brian. Was *his* head screwed on right? Could you say that about a guy over thirty who was still trying to make it as an actor? Working as a waiter or a cook's helper between gigs? Coming home with this woman out of a Chas Addams cartoon?

"Oh, I know you see some hard cases at your school," Hank rambled on. "But, hey, did I ever tell you about the girl Clay dated before Tracy? Now, *there* was one screwed-up broad. Whacko. I mean, when I think he might've—Jeez, you wonder how your own flesh and blood could—what am I saying? It turned out all right, didn't it? That Tracy is a great kid ..."

It turned out all right. Hank spoke as if the story of his son had come to an end. He enumerated Clay's accomplishments, starting with the track and field ribbons in junior high, and I saw that Tracy was going to be an item on the list. Would there be a time in the near future when I'd talk that way about *my* son? "*Yeah, we thought she was one screwed-up broad when he first brought her home, and, son of a bitch, we were right.*" As Hank talked—he was up to Clay's learning the clothing business one summer at Holt Renfrew—I thought about Tracy and how she seemed to have *turned out all right.*

Agreeing that Clay and Tracy were the best and the brightest young people in the universe, Hank and I returned to the maternity ward. Dot and Barb had been in to see Tracy and Mason and come out cooing words like *adorable* and *sweet* and *What a little princess!* and *She's the image of Clay!* and *I saw a lot of Tracy in her.* Clay escorted his father and me into Tracy's room.

"Hey, Dads!" said Tracy.

She was lying in bed looking relieved. Beside her was the infant—*Mason*—resembling Mr. Magoo more than anyone. Yet she seemed magnificent and unique, a fresh new link in the chain of life, carrying my blood into the future, if not my name.

"She's a *doll,*" Hank said. "And why wouldn't she be, with parents like the two of you?" He kissed Tracy on the cheek.

"Good for you, Trace," I said. "She's a keeper." I kissed Tracy on the clear forehead I'd always thought was her best feature.

"We've been doing what you recommended in your book, you know, Daddy," said Tracy. "We've been, like, reading to her since the second trimester."

"I'm surprised she didn't come out reciting Shakespeare," said Hank, and he gave a loud hoot.

Sometimes you just have to go for it, my daughter told me. Well, maybe I should take her advice.

Around 11:30 on Monday morning, I call Iris's cell.

"Hello?" Her voice sounds annoyed. And there seems to be a rush of wind at her end, as if she's driving somewhere in a convertible.

"*Hello, Iris.*" I find myself yelling because of the wind noise. "*It's Jenkins.*"

"Oh, Jenkins," she says, loudly. "I can't talk right now. Let's meet Wednesday at six. The bar at Earls Polo Park?"

"Well—yes—"

"See you then."

Passing a Test

"Hey, Dad. Want to come for dinner tonight? Just vegetarian pizza, and then we thought we'd take you by the business we're close to taking over."

"Oh, Tracy … I can't. I—I have a date."

"You're seeing her again."

"Well, no. I'm going out for drinks with a woman I met at the Fosters'. A friend of Gwen."

"God, aren't you the gadabout."

"Just playing the field, passing the time, you know. Beats sitting at home moping."

"I guess."

"Can I have a raincheck? Maybe see you tomorrow?"

"I don't know. I think Clay's busy. But, Dad. You said you're going out for drinks. So *don't drive.*"

I park the car at Earls. I'm anxious to get my hand around a Corona. One of the things that bugs me about dating as an older man is, *your kids become your goddam parents.* Janie has Jason and I have Tracy, and, since talking to her, all I want to do is *rebel. Don't drive, my ass.*

The fact is, I had a manhattan before I left the house. Shortly after my little book *Never Too Early* came out, I was invited to teach an evening course in creative writing at the university. I got into the habit of having a manhattan before dinner on the nights I taught, telling Barb, "I need a drink to face these people." I had the idea that the liquor made me more scintillating in the classroom. Tonight, I don't have the supporting cast of Gwen, Charlie, Kathy and Hans to keep Iris entertained. But, as I step into Earls and see groups of sophisticated young men and women, I feel one manhattan isn't enough.

"Hi," says a young female host. "Going into the bar or ...?"

"Uh—meeting someone and then going into the bar. Okay if I wait here?"

"Sure."

The young people I see inside are dressed more casually than I expected. There are men in T-shirts, khaki shorts and flip-flops, women in tank tops, cut-off jeans and sandals. Because I had worn my favourite sport jacket on my ill-fated date with Janie, I went out and bought a new dark blue blazer that has a subtle yellow check in it, and I'm wearing that with a yellow shirt, matching tie and grey trousers. I felt good about the outfit when I left home, but now I feel overdressed.

In comes Iris. She's wearing a smashing scarlet outfit—a top with kind of a scoop neckline that shows a little more cleavage than before, and flared pants. She's carrying one of those handbags with a short strap that goes over one shoulder, the bag under the arm about breast-high. I remember reading that these kinds of bags are made from recycled automobile fenders. This one has a martini design with the word COSMOPOLITAN emblazoned across it. Iris is in high-heeled black shoes and she has one side of her hair pinned back to show off a zany earring that matches her pendant. Before she sees me, a female host effusively compliments her on the handbag, and I wonder what in hell I'm doing meeting this gorgeous woman for drinks. At least I no longer feel overdressed.

"Hi!" she says. "How are you *doing*?"

As she leans into me and touches cheeks with me, I say, "Great! I love your outfit—it really suits you." I don't tell her that scarlet is my favourite colour.

"Thank you," she says. "I like your shirt. Yellow goes well with your jacket."

Just like that, in two seconds, she makes me feel like the king of Earls, and all the jocks around us are mere plebes.

We go into the bar and sit on bar stools with backs at one of the high tables. She orders a crantini and I make an instant decision: instead of a Corona, I'll *really* rebel and have a manhattan, straight up.

"That was fun the other night at Gwen and Charlie's," I say.

"It *was*. Gwen's a terrific cook. I've been there before and every time it's something different and always scrumptious."

"Have you known Gwen long?"

"About three years. I think she told you we met at tennis—a group that plays every Tuesday afternoon."

"No work that day?"

"I usually work every Saturday, so I take Tuesday afternoons off."

Our drinks arrive.

"Here's to your book," I say.

"Cheers—yes."

"All ages, this tennis group you're in?"

"Well, I'm the youngest, by about ten years, I'd say."

"Ah—so you must win a lot."

"It's doubles—you get different partners. But no, some of the women are terrific. I like associating with people older than myself. I find I learn a lot—about all sorts of things."

Yes, and I'm the mentor du jour. I suppose we should get into the topic we're here to discuss. I think I can predict what she wants to write about: the new breed of women, so confident, so independent, so competent in so many ways, women who don't need to give birth to feel fulfilled. There are lots of books like that, but she'll put her own spin on hers, and anyway, she doesn't intend to have it published.

"What kind of book do you want to write?" I ask.

"Ah, you want to get right to it. No nonsense."

Although the room is full of young people, many of them good-looking men, I notice that at no time since we sat down has she looked around. She looks straight at me, taking her eyes off me only to look occasionally at her drink. She seems to have the confidence of someone who's used to being looked at without affecting any kind of pose. There is no doubt that she has the looks and the demeanour—to say nothing of the red clothes—to attract attention. It strikes me as curious that people used to refer to an attractive woman like her as a *looker* when surely such a woman is a *lookee*.

"I thought perhaps we didn't have much time," I say.

"I don't have anywhere else to go, do you?"

"No, I don't."

"You know, I should level with you. I don't have a college education. I never thought it was important—I just wanted to get out there and work after high school." She goes on to tell me about teaching herself a lot of things, like computer technology—she isn't afraid to take a computer apart to rescue the motherboard. "So do you think it's okay for somebody without a university background to try writing a book?"

"Lots of people have," I say. I tell her some of the benefits of *not* being influenced by professors—as long as you know the basics of grammar and have some familiarity with books through having read widely.

She orders another crantini. I, feeling a nudge from my responsible side, nurse my original manhattan. There's a lull. I think she might ask me about myself—my wife, perhaps, or my previous career, or my credentials. She doesn't. So I tell her what I've been thinking she might want to write about.

"The new woman?" she says. "No, far from it. I live that every day; I have no desire to write about it." She takes a sip of her new drink. A rosy hue appears on her neck and on the exposed skin beneath her pendant. "No, what I have in mind is quite personal. I haven't really talked about this with anyone before."

"I'm flattered." Gwen told me Iris was divorced. Perhaps she wants to write about that: what a hell her marriage was, how it fell apart, how difficult the divorce was, threats from her ex.

She says, "I was raised by my grandparents in Nova Scotia."

"You want to write about the effects of a broken home on—"

"No, no. My parents were killed in a car accident when I was little. I had some very happy times with my grandfather. I want to write about *that*. Being a little girl in Port Hawkesbury. My grandfather taught me how to row, how to catch white perch and steelhead trout, how to gut them. We'd have this boatload and we'd love to … But I don't want to write nostalgia, you know? I don't like to dwell on the past. What I want to do is a kids' book that shows the different kinds of things kids can do. It might be partly made-up—you know, fiction—but it'll be based on the fun times my grandfather and I had. If it's any good, maybe I could sell it in the shop."

She finishes her second drink.

"Sounds like you could have a lot of fun writing it," I say.

As inquisitive as I might be about her ex-husband, I'm grateful not to have to deal with him. "Say, since you said you're in no hurry, would you like to have dinner?"

"Jenkins, I'd *love* that. You mean here?"

"I don't know … maybe somewhere else? Rae and Jerry's is close by."

"I knew you were a meat-and-potatoes man."

"Well, I know you liked the ham at Gwen's, so you're not a vegetarian."

"But I'll clash with the red upholstery at Rae and Jerry's."

"You name a place then."

"Could we go somewhere Japanese? I'm dying for sashimi."

We both have sashimi platters—salmon, tuna, hamachi, hokkigai, tako—with side orders of kimchi and large bottles of Sapporo beer. I can't believe what I'm eating. I've never had anything resembling raw fish in my life before. Maybe the booze is helping me tolerate it, but I'm happy to try something different; just being with Iris seems to have put me in that frame of mind. She's so companionable, so much *with me*. And I'm *enjoying* the sashimi, though I stopped short of eating with chopsticks. The accommodating server supplied me with a knife and fork.

We drove to the Yugiro Japanese Restaurant in my car, leaving hers, which she said was thief-proof, in her spot at Polo Park. She said we could worry about it later.

"You passed a test tonight, you know," Iris says.

"I didn't know I was being tested, but I'm glad I passed."

"The last guy I dated—met him on the Internet—invited me to meet him at a bar after work. He was interesting, told me a bunch of things about computers I didn't know. After a few drinks, I gave him a big hint that I was pretty hungry—in fact, I was feeling faint. I finally said I was off to get something to eat, and he let me go! Didn't clue in that maybe we could have dinner together. Who knows—maybe he didn't *want* to have dinner with me. That was the last I saw of him."

"Well, as I say, I'm glad I passed."

"And I didn't have to give you a hint."

The Sapporo is going down well—each of us is into a second giant-size bottle—and I'm beginning to believe that I do have experience with children's literature. I spent many hours reading to Mason from her crib years on and, even after she could read herself, she liked me to read her books that had a vocabulary beyond hers. From the little Iris has told me, I figure she needs to find her niche somewhere between the Ramona Quimby books and *Anne of Green Gables*. I'm about to say this when Iris says:

"Do you like dogs, Jenkins?"

"Very much. I had a golden retriever in the 1990s. Called him Dave. He lived to be thirteen."

"That's the trouble, isn't it? You train them, they become wonderful companions, and too quickly they grow old. I had a chow chow called Ginger."

"I've heard chows are independent, sort of like cats that way."

"Yes, but that's what I liked about her. Such a personality! She'd tolerate my hugs most of the time. She could be a little prima donna, expect you to wait on her, but it was fascinating to see what interested her and what didn't. We were the best of buds. After she was gone, I thought I couldn't handle another—the sadness of watching her grow old and having her put down. That's one reason I went into a condo, so I wouldn't be tempted to get another dog."

"Were you with your husband when you had a house and Ginger?"

"Let's not go there. I just thought you might be a dog person."

"Have I passed another test?"

She laughs. It's nice to hear her laugh. She turned pensive when she talked about her dog, and I haven't helped her mood by mentioning the husband. I talk about Dave: how, on our nightly walk, he'd wait till we got to one particular park bench before he sat down and expected a cookie—the same park bench every time; how he'd know when it was Saturday, the day I sat in the living room to read—he'd go to the love seat before I did and get up on it and lie down and wait for me to join him, and he'd only go there on Saturdays; how he never barked unless I got him excited by playing with him. Iris counters with a story of her walking her chow chow, off the leash, along the Red River, Ginger taking off down the steep bank, Iris going after her, losing her footing and ending up with one leg in the river, sinking in the muck, having to grab hold of a branch to pull herself back, and all the while the dog standing, safe and dry on a little ledge, watching Iris with a look as if she thought her momma had gone nuts. We both laugh—more heartily now. We've veered away from her book and it doesn't seem to matter.

She's finished her dinner well before me, yet I barely noticed her eating. I'm struck by how much food she can consume and how quickly she can eat in such a—it's probably an archaic term—such a *ladylike* manner. She dabs at the corners of her mouth, breathes a sigh and says, "That sure hit the spot."

"Sorry I'm so slow."

"No, no, it's okay. You've been talking more than I have."

While I finish up, Iris asks our server a question or two. I hope we're going to linger over green tea or a liqueur.

"I'd like to get out of here, wouldn't you?" Iris says. "It's kind of stuffy—or maybe I need fresh air."

I'm enjoying the surroundings—subdued, quiet, the serving staff unobtrusive—and I thought we were having a good time. "All right," I say, "I'll get the bill."

"It's my treat," she says, as we both stand up.

My instinct is to object, to insist it's my duty as a man to pick up the tab, but I know that's a throwback to the old days, so all I say is "Why?"

"It was my idea to meet tonight and my idea to have sashimi, and you bought the drinks at Earls. Besides, I'm expecting you to help me."

Outside the restaurant, I say, "That was marvellous—you've conquered my fear of sushi or I should say, sashimi. Thank you."

"You're welcome. See, you need to try more things. I'll bet there are all kinds of taste sensations you've been missing."

I open the passenger door of my G6—an old courtesy that still seems to be acceptable—and she gets in. When I'm behind the wheel, I say, "Shall we go and fetch your car?"

"You know, my condo's only five minutes from here. Why don't we go there?"

She says this so naturally that I sense she wants to prolong the evening as much as I do. I'm grateful too that I won't have to drive far after all that beer. At the same time, I wonder if I am simply going to drop her off at her condo or … ? I feel a twinge of nervousness, what I used to feel on dates in my teens—wondering where the evening is headed and whether I'm going to be elated or devastated.

"Sounds good," I say, and I start the car.

"Could we put the windows down?" she says. "It's a gorgeous night."

I put all the windows down. She gives me directions and takes deep breaths of the air that blows in as we drive. I feel young again. I reach over and squeeze her hand. She looks at me and smiles. There's no need to say anything. She takes her hand away from mine and quickly opens her handbag and pulls out a tissue in time to catch a sneeze.

"Bless you," I say.

As we approach her condominium complex in South Tuxedo, she says, "Jenkins, instead of parking in Visitors', why don't you take my spot underground? Here's the key."

That answers one question—we're going in. I drive onto the downward ramp and insert the key and the garage door instantly opens. I drive down, feeling as if I might be descending into Hell—not the pain-and-suffering kind but maybe, just maybe, debauchery. Most of the tenants' cars are home for the night. Iris directs me to her space and I turn off the car.

"Windows," she says.

"Oh, yes." I hope she doesn't think I'm nervous. I probably *look* nervous. I turn on the electricity and put up the windows.

We both get out and I lock the car. Iris leads the way to an elevator. I can't think of a thing to say as we both watch the numbers illuminate on our way up to *4*. We step out into a vestibule, a seating area complete with two sofas and a table. On the table are a few magazines, three or four books and a low-lit lamp.

"Very nice," I say.

"The halls are a little stark," she says.

I follow her down the hall and, at the third door on the left, she unlocks the door and leans inside to turn on a light. She kicks off her heels and I take off my shoes, leaving them at the door. She scoops up a towel, which seems to be the only thing out of place.

"Have a look around," she says, turning on more lights.

The kitchen is small and immaculate. I go past that into a dining-living area furnished in a contemporary style and mostly black and white. On one wall is a framed painting of what seems to be a courtyard in some hot country—perhaps North African. I notice the initials I.B. in the lower right corner.

"You did this?" I say.

"It's from my blue period," she says, and she laughs.

"Iris, I'm astonished. This is *good*. Have you done much painting?"

"That's it. My one and only."

"Where is it?"

"Morocco, I think. I didn't go there. I copied it off somebody else's painting."

Beyond, by the windows, is another sitting area, with a built-in bar on the left and her computer and desk on the right. Adjacent to the dining room is a TV room and in the centre of one wall is a kind of picture window that has Venetian blinds. The blinds are open and I can see the bedroom through the window—and a king-size bed.

"Your place is lovely," I say, "and so nicely kept."

"Thanks. If you need a loo, there's one just there, and another at the back off the bedroom. I'm going to get more comfortable—why don't you?"

I look at her. I try to put a look on my face that doesn't reveal my shock. I think I know what she means, but I remember her saying at Gwen and Charlie's that she prefers sex in the morning. There is the possibility, though, that she doesn't mean that at all—and for some crazy reason I have this flashback to a night in the previous century when I was at Marcia's aunt's apartment and Marcia left the room and I thought *she* was *going to get more comfortable* and she didn't. Perhaps Iris really *is* going to get comfortable—put on sweats or something—and my jangled, liquor-laced imagination conjures up preposterous scenarios—Iris coming out in a filmy negligee (do women still wear negligees?); Iris dressed as some famous stripper like Gypsy Rose Lee; Iris in good old-fashioned pyjamas … but if she *does* want to fool around, shouldn't I be kissing her right about now? For God's sake, she probably expected me to take her into my arms as soon as we entered the apartment. Oh, I'm so out of touch with this sort of thing.

She turns from me and starts in the direction of that other bathroom.

"Iris?" I say.

She turns back and I put my arms around her and kiss her. She feels so soft and substantial and *perfect*. I open my mouth against hers—

"Mm—" she steps back "—sorry, I'm not big on wet kisses. Nothing against you—they just don't do it for me, all that exchange of saliva, to say nothing of the bacteria."

So much for the long-awaited return of The Kissing Bandit, I think, feeling like some sort of insensitive oaf. I say, "I'm sorry, I haven't—I didn't—"

"Don't worry about it. It's just me, okay? It's no biggy. Now, just give me a few minutes and I'll meet you in there." She gestures toward the bedroom.

"I thought you said you didn't … on a full stomach …"

She smiles. "I'm making an exception for you, okay?"

"I don't have a French—a condom—"

"It's okay! I'll take care of that. See you in a few minutes."

She kisses my cheek and walks around a corner to the bathroom I haven't seen. Her rebuff of my kiss seems to be only a slight glitch in what is rapidly becoming Jenkins's Most Amazing Adventure. I go into what I suppose she regards as the guest bathroom and I close the door.

To understand the extent of my excitement, my anxiety, my worry, you'd have to think back to—I don't know—maybe the time you took your driver's test. You've read the manual, you've had the lessons, you've become pretty good at backing your dad's car out of the driveway and parallel parking on vacant lots, but here you are, having to take a car through a variety of situations dictated by a stranger, getting tested on what exactly you know how to do. There is nothing like the *real thing*. All right, maybe that's not a good example, unless you think of Iris as both the car and the tester. All those adolescent dates flash past me as if I'm drowning—kissing Louise in the dark, feeling Trudy's bra cups, peeking at Shirley's big eye, necking with Alice and Dianne, holding Janie's hot body against mine as we dance, fondling Mary's plump bare breast with her parents in the next room, enduring endless double dates, indulging in petting and *heavy* petting in the Neck Room—the adolescent dates and all those years of marriage in no way prepared me for this night. Friends e-mailed me photos of gorgeous naked women with balloon boobs and clean-shaven pussies, and I've seen my share of those boring story-less porno flicks, and none of them could've prepared me for this night. And I've read innumerable books, from *Masters and Johnson on Sex and Human Loving* to *The Vagina Monologues,* and one that seems especially relevant to my situation, *Make Love, Not War: The Sexual Revolution: An Unfettered History,* by David Allyn, which reviews all the ways western society has changed, especially in regard to recreational sex, but this erudition did not prepare me for this night.

I take off my sport jacket. I wash my hands. I wish I was the kind of guy who could look at himself in the mirror and wink. I find myself avoiding my reflection, not because I'm ashamed of what I'm doing—not at all—but because I don't like the proof that I'm not young anymore. I wish, for Iris's sake, that I could take off my clothes and find Superman underneath. I wish I could yell *Shazam!* and bring down a lightning bolt that would change me into Captain Marvel, with a Marvelous repertoire of pleasure-making moves.

On a more realistic level, I wish that I could brush my

teeth—my breath is probably terrible after all the beer. I remember the mints I picked up at Earls. They're in my jacket pocket, each in a little package. Good! I unwrap two and put them in my mouth.

I untie my tie, undo the top button of my shirt and take off the tie. I undo my belt, unbutton and unzip my trousers, while my thoughts alternate between *This is ridiculous* and *This is amazing!* I step out of the trousers—oh, no! I forgot about my elastic support stockings. They are so comfortable, the way they let your legs breathe like a second epidermis, but I can't leave them on. It'd be like wearing an *I am an old man* sign. The problem is, I don't have the rubber gloves with me, the ones you're supposed to use to put the stockings on and take them off. They help you avoid a snag or a tear. Well, too bad. The less Iris knows about the stockings the better. I'm going to take them off as best I can, snag or no snag.

I need to go out of the bathroom and sit in a chair if I'm going to peel the stockings off effectively. But I can't risk having Iris see me. I don't want to sit on the toilet seat lid in case my weight cracks it. Best, I figure, to perch on the edge of the bathtub, though it's lower than a chair. With one leg crossed over the other, I feel precarious, as if I'm balancing—not something easily done after a few drinks. I try not to think how unlike Casanova I am as I pull off one sock and concentrate on peeling off one stocking and then, switching legs, manage to get the other sock and stocking off without slipping off the tub onto the floor. I give myself a *Way to go!* sign in the mirror and stand up and fold the stockings into one of the pockets of my sport jacket. I take off my Timex wrist watch and stash that in the pocket, too.

I undo my shirt, nervously fumbling with each button, quaking at the fact that I'm nudging closer and closer to the moment of truth. As I part the two halves of the shirt, I glance at the mirror and instinctively pull in my gut. I am going to have to remember to do that when I leave the bathroom. I turn from the mirror and take off the shirt and, for a moment, I wonder what the hell I'm doing here and what in blazes she sees in me. *Enough of that.* I take a deep breath, hold it, and look once more at myself, my chest extended as far as I can manage. *Go get 'em, tiger!* I tell myself.

But in boxer shorts?

To hell with it. As unmanly as they seem, I think I should be wearing something. I take another deep breath and go into the bedroom.

Iris is apparently still in the other bathroom. I sit on the bed, feeling my heart thumping away. I get up and turn out the lamp on the night table, figuring if we keep the light subdued, she might not notice my varicose veins and myriad other blemishes. The light in the hall should be all we need. Of course, then I won't be able to see *her* as clearly. Well, I reason, she'll likely find the softer light more conducive to whatever she has in mind.

I wonder if I should turn the bed down. At this stage, I'm pretty sure that we're going to get into bed. Since I'm nervous and want things to do anyway, I do turn the bed down, going around to the other side to make sure it's turned down equally on either side. I sit again, on the side facing her bathroom. Like Baby Bear's bed, this one feels *just right.*

I hear her door open. It sends a shiver right through me. Iris turns off the bathroom light and walks toward me at her normal pace, confident, un-shy.

She is naked.

"Hi there," she says.

"Hi," I say, in kind of a choked voice.

"Got the lights just about right, I see."

"Good."

There's a passage in Robert Olen Butler's novel, T*hey Whisper,* in which the narrator says he wished he could remember to ask a woman "to walk just a few steps away from me when she was naked and turn and let me take her nakedness in whole" but he never did. I wish Iris could've hesitated in her progress toward me and let me focus on the complete head-to-toe sight of her. As much as the two outfits I'd seen her in promised beauty, nothing could've prepared me for her in the nude. Unfortunately, the glimpse of her is over in two seconds, and she's beside me and saying in a soft voice:

"Move over a little and just lie back."

I'm grateful for direction—I have no idea how to begin. I lie back and she takes hold of my shorts and pulls them down and off.

"Hi there!" she says to my cock, which, thank goodness, is ignoring all my worries. She tosses my shorts across the room with a matador-like flourish.

She kneels beside me on the bed and magically produces a condom. She rolls it on and she follows her hand with her mouth, which feels warm and right, and she proceeds to do such lovely things that I can only moan. I close my eyes, but that's nuts, *I've got to see this,* and I open my eyes and see that what she's doing is hidden by her peekaboo bang, so I reach to pull aside the curtain of her hair and—

I poke her in the eye.

"Ow!"

"I'm sorry—god, how could I be so clumsy—oh, Iris, I'm sorry—"

"Ouch!"

"What a stupid—are you okay?"

"I think so. It was more the shock than anything."

"Let me see …"

"It's okay. Amazing how fast your eye can shut when it's being invaded." She's sitting on the bed now, her legs off the edge. "What were you doing, anyway?"

"I couldn't see your face. Your hair was in the way and I wanted so badly to see your face—I'm so sorry!"

"Listen, it's okay! Nothing to beat yourself up over."

We sit there for a minute or two, I feeling mortified, afraid to put my hand on her shoulder even in a comforting gesture. And, of course, I've wilted.

"I see *he*'s sorry, too," Iris says. "We can do something about that."

"No, no, it's all right. I'll go before I do any more damage."

"Don't be silly. Stay there."

Though I feel like a complete dolt, I stay on the bed till she returns from her bathroom. She has a narrow bottle in her hand and she sits beside me and takes off the cap. She pours some of what I assume is lubricant into her palm and puts the bottle down on the night table. She gently takes hold of my penis and spreads the oil over it.

"Come on," she says, "concentrate."

We both watch what she's doing with rapt expressions on our faces. I shouldn't be surprised at anything, but I'm astonished at how quickly that most unpredictable part of me responds.

"There we go," she says, wiping her hands on a tissue. "Should I get on top?"

"Yes, *please*," I say, now back into this as if there's never been a false move.

She gets up on her knees, straddling me, and she puts me into herself as if she's been doing such a thing for years, and I don't *care* if she's been doing such a thing for years because she's doing the same kinds of wonderful things that she was doing earlier with her mouth, kind of teasing me but titillating me too.

She moves up and down on me and says, "You can *touch* me, you know."

Of course! I think, and I take her breasts in my hands and play with them as if I'm an adolescent again.

And she says, "You can *move*, you know."

And, cursing myself, I do move, raising my hips to meet hers and dropping them down again and raising them again and I'm into the moment and I'm into the *zone* and she's saying, "Yes, yes," and I gloriously ejaculate.

She bends down to me and I hug her tight and, not knowing what in hell to say, I whisper, "*Thank you.*"

She coughs, ejecting me.

"Sorry!" she says. "Don't know where that came from."

"It's okay," I say, wanting to giggle with post-coital glee.

She lies down beside me. My heart is thumping audibly. We lie there for a while without speaking. My breathing and my heartbeat gradually become normal. Iris sits up to grab the sheet and pull it up over us. I wonder how this night, this absolutely fabulous *event*, could've possibly happened, and then I chastise myself for having such a thought. All I want to do is lie next to her. I move closer, so that our bodies touch from shoulder to ankle. I rest my head on her shoulder. We lie like that, I wanting never to get up again.

"Oh—'scuse me—" she breaks away from me and throws the sheet off. "Holy *crap!*"

"What's the matter?"

"A hot flash. They come out of nowhere. I swear I've got the world's longest-lasting menopause. Whew!"

"They come when you least expect them?"

"I often get them when I drink. I had one in the restaurant and that's why I had to get out of there. And I can get them from just being too warm. Like a minute ago."

"I thought we were nice and cozy, cuddling."

"Yah, you've got a portable furnace going there. It's okay, no offence. I've never been much of a cuddler, even before the menopause."

"Sorry—I thought we were enjoying, you know, the afterglow."

"Mmm."

We lie there for a few minutes. I reach and pull my side of the sheet up to my waist.

"I guess we'd better be going to pick up your car," I say.

"Aww, not now."

"When, then?"

"Why don't you stay over?"

What? And miss my nightly rituals? Not check my e-mail, not floss my teeth, not take my Baby Aspirin? Go to bed without my pyjamas? I say none of that. I'm aghast at her suggestion, but I don't have a plausible reason for leaving.

"Don't you have to work tomorrow?" I ask.

"Sure. You could drop me off. Best of all, I'll get my morning sex."

She gives me a wry smile, daring me to say *No* to that. Aside from my being unsure whether I can perform again that soon after being out of action for so long, I wonder if morning is a good time for *me*. Like most men, I've always thought lovemaking was the perfect end to an evening out. But the morning after? The pressure is definitely *on*.

"Does your sofa make into a bed?"

"What's wrong with this?"

"I'd sleep right *here*?"

"Big enough, isn't it?"

That isn't the point. Could I really sleep with someone who—let's face it—is *virtually* a *total stranger*? I say none of that.

"Hey, why not?" I say. "It'll be fun. Like I'm a kid again. Out on a sleepover."

"Oh, goodie," she says, clapping her hands as if she too is a kid again. "Do you want to watch some TV? Maybe we could find some news." She points to the flat-screen mounted just beyond the foot of the bed.

"Okay."

"Want anything to drink?"

"Some milk would be nice."

"And Kahlua?"

"Sure."

"Want me to see if I can find something you could wear to bed?"

"No—um—I'll probably just put on my shirt and shorts."

"Okay. So why don't you go and lose that *thing* and I'll go scare up some milk and Kahlua."

"Right."

She jumps out of bed as if she truly is excited that I'm staying over. I get up, pick up the shorts off the floor and go into the bathroom, where I've left my clothes strewn across the vanity. I take off the condom, flush it away, urinate, flush again, and give myself a sponge bath here and there with a wet cloth. I look at myself in the mirror. *You idiot. What are you moping for? You've just had sex with a gorgeous woman over twenty years younger than you, and there's going to be more in the morning. SMILE, for Christ's sake!* I smile. I take a towel and dance behind it as if I'm Salome with the last of her seven veils.

I put on my shorts, shake my shirt and put that on. Pretty crumby nightwear, but they'll have to do. This isn't exactly roughing it.

As I open the bathroom door, I'm singing an old Pepsi commercial, not knowing where the hell that came from.

"Good mood?" Iris says. She's coming from the kitchen with two glasses. She's wearing a thigh-length T-shirt with the Seven Dwarfs on the front.

"If I felt any better, I'd be dangerous."

"Excellent." She hands me a glass.

Mine is the spiked milk; hers is a large glass of cranberry juice. We clink glasses and sip. We arrange ourselves in the bed, I sitting up and she lying down with a couple of pillows raising her head.

"Oh, the clicker's on your side," she says.

I hand her the remote. "You know how it works. Find whatever tickles your fancy."

She flicks through the channels, watching CNN for two minutes, an old movie starring Charlton Heston for half a minute, one of the CSI programs for five or so.

"Oh, Iris," I say, "do you have an extra toothbrush and some toothpaste and some floss?"

"Toothpaste and floss for sure—I'll try and scare up a toothbrush. Do you want them now?"

"No, it's okay. I'll rough it tonight. But I'll need to brush my teeth first thing in the morning."

"I hear you."

She makes her way through channel after channel, show after show. I get interested in something and *click!* it's gone. I'm annoyed at first, but I never watch TV in bed, so I resign myself to her surfing. My mind drifts. This is the most activity—not to say *fun*—I've had in years. So *this* is dating in the twenty-first century! I'm in the *game!* At my age! By god, I'm proud of myself....

I must've dozed off. Not for long, maybe ten minutes. *Seinfeld* is on. George and Jerry and Kramer are in a restaurant arguing. There are some funny lines and I chuckle but there is no reaction from Iris. Yet the channel doesn't change. I look over at her. She's asleep. She quietly snores.

I marvel at how my fortunes have changed—from the Janie/Jason fiasco to reclining in this beautiful younger woman's bed. I study her clear face in repose and think how amazing it is that she trusts me enough to be able to fall asleep. I feel a warm glow inside.

So now I figure it's up to me to turn off the TV. I think I could gently take the "clicker" out of her hand—I'd know which is the Power button. I reach over.

Her hand is clamped onto the remote in a death grip. I try to wrest it away from her.

"I'm still watching this," she snaps, instantly awake and hanging on.

One click and *Seinfeld* is replaced by an old *Law and Order.*

"Sorry," I say.

Never Too Early

At three in the morning, with Iris sleeping soundly beside me, I lie wide awake, worrying. I've been lying here wide awake, worrying, since she turned off the TV some time around eleven.

For the first half hour or so, I assumed my usual nocturnal position, on my right side, with my legs together, the left one resting on the right, my hands tucked between my face and the pillow—the fetal position. I was turned away from Iris, which seems a bit rude, but she wanted to be on my left because it was closer to her bathroom and next to the phone. I listened to her breathing, her rhythmic snores, and thought I would drift off soon enough.

As I lay there in those first minutes, I tried to replay the whole evening in my mind. I tried to remember what Iris looked like when I first saw her come into Earls in the red outfit. I tried to recall exactly what she looked like in the nude, coming toward me out of her bathroom. I tried to recall exactly what her breasts looked like, but the image was fuzzy, the way television stations blur the faces of people who are only alleged to have done something wrong. I tried to recall exactly what her abdomen looked like—amazingly flat, I thought, with a trimmed triangle of black hair—but I wasn't sure what I saw—everything happened far too quickly. I thought how ridiculous it was to be trying to conjure up images of a body that was lying *right beside me,* and for the umpteenth time *I was blown away* by the stark reality of my being in Iris's bed. I thought, *Claude should see me now!*

After about half an hour, my right leg started to ache, having to support the weight of my left leg, and I shifted the left one forward.

Lying that way, I recalled her being on top of me and I tried to remember what she looked like as she coddled me and teased me. I couldn't get a clear picture of her face. Had I *looked* at her or had I closed my eyes and given myself to the *feel* of what she was doing? That line of thinking took me abruptly back to how we'd started out on the bed and my reaching to pull her hair aside and I was mortified all over again.

The big toe on my left foot ached. I turned the foot at an angle, causing a familiar ache to come to the tendon in the instep. I worried that I might have to stand up if the cramp got worse. I wished that I'd insisted on bedding down on one of her couches—or on going home. I toyed with the idea of writing Iris a note and sneaking out, thinking I could always come back early in the morning.

I gave myself hell for thinking I could leave. I turned onto my left side. For a while, I liked that position because I could see Iris there, sleeping, and I could marvel yet again at my being in bed with her—and we had *made love, she and I, in this very bed.*

This lovely thought didn't last long. I suddenly thought of

the other woman who'd fallen asleep beside me just days ago: Janie. In the front seat of my car. I felt guilty for abandoning her that night—virtually throwing her to the jackals, Jason and Krista. Couldn't I have done something more honourable? I felt promiscuous, having left poor Janie that way and now enjoying myself in another woman's bed. The wave of guilt was accompanied by a realization that my heart was thumping at an alarming rate.

Then I remembered that, whenever I lay on my left side after I'd been drinking, I'd hear my heart thumping, obviously working extra hard because of all the food and booze and activity. As slowly as I could, I turned back to my original position on my right side, but, by then, I was despairing about ever going to sleep. I heard noises in the building and had no idea what could be causing them and where they could be coming from. I remembered that we were surrounded by other apartments. I thought about all the people I didn't know who were so close to me right now. I thought how unfair it was that they were all sleeping and I wasn't. On the other hand, maybe I was surrounded by insomniacs. Maybe there was something about the air in the building that prevented you from sleeping. All right, then why was Iris sawing logs so peacefully?

I wondered how I could get up to go to the bathroom without disturbing Iris. I wondered why I hadn't had to go to the bathroom so far. Was it some internal problem? I always had to get up at least twice in the night, especially if I'd had anything to drink within seven hours of going to bed. Was I overheated? Had I been sweating the fluids out? Was it being with Iris that was causing my heart to beat faster and was that creating a change in my metabolism? Did all those romantic stories of women causing men's hearts to beat faster have some basis in scientific *fact*?

Such were the thoughts that kept me anxious and wide

awake. Fearing that I was never going to drift off made me more anxious—without a good night's sleep, how would I be able to perform in the morning? I tried to tell myself that one missed night of sleep wasn't going to impair me, but I didn't believe myself. My heart raced and my nerve ends jangled.

At one point, Iris turned over and one of her hands fell onto my arm. That sent a warm feeling through my entire body. It was as if she were subconsciously checking whether I was still there—her protector. She needed to be reassured and touching my arm reassured her. My skin, grateful to be contacted like this, felt as if it was glowing in the dark. The good feeling caused my penis to raise its head as if to say, *Is it time, coach?* I didn't want Iris to take her hand away, but she did, maybe ten minutes later.

Now it's after three and I think, What if tomorrow she expects *me* to give *her* oral sex? I've read in recent books and magazines that today's independent woman demands to be pleasured in this way, but I have no idea how or where to begin. Not that I haven't had some experience—well, a *little*, a miniscule amount, really, when I was drunk—but how could I know what *Iris* might expect? We would likely start out side by side; one thing is certain, I can't sit up, with my legs still parallel with hers, and lean over and dip my head down. I can't sit up and touch my toes in that position, never mind bend to the side and reach my face *down there*. The last time I had a physical checkup, my doctor asked me to do a sit-up and it took considerable effort to do one. I'd never try such a thing when I'm alone for fear that something might snap. But nobody, unless he's the most supple gymnast, can sit up with legs stretched in front of him and lean sideways and down the way I'd have to. There are, I figure, two ways I could do what she might expect me to do—probably more, but two for sure—and both require me to get up from the supine position. I could kneel at her side and bend down at an angle which would put my face upside down *vis à vis* her vagina, and she'd have to lift herself a little for me to get at her, and that would bring my eyes in close proximity with her anus, which I may not want to look at while I'm doing what I'm doing, and—perhaps more important—she might not want me looking at it so closely in any event. Furthermore, because of where the clitoris is situated, it's more difficult to approach at this angle. Of course, this is the only approach if you are attempting *soixante neuf.* In that configuration, I would have to either *a)* lie upside down beside her and twist at the waist so that the part of me she needs to reach is out in the open and accessible to her, while she also twists at the waist so that together we resemble a large cinnamon twist or a rope or a braid; *b)* straddle her with my knees on either side of her head, a posture that might be pretty claustrophobic for her; or *c)* lie upside down on top of her with little regard for her comfort. Another alternative would be for her to be on top for either *b* or *c*. None of these is especially appealing, so I hope I can avoid *soixante neuf.* The best way, it seems to me, is suggested in a silly joke about three chorus girls undressing. The first girl has the impression of a *Y* on her abdomen and she explains that her sweetheart is a Yale man who forgot to remove his belt. The second girl has an *H* on her abdomen and she explains that her sweetheart is a Harvard man who likewise forgot to remove his belt. The third girl's abdomen shows the impression of an *F.* The producer says, "I suppose your boyfriend goes to Fordham." The girl answers, "No, he's a fire chief. He just forgot to take off his hat." I would, then, in the manner of the fire chief, have to kneel at the foot of the bed below Iris, and it might be best to raise her by putting a pillow under her ass. All right, that's pretty logical, but what about all the effort oral sex would take?

It strikes me that, despite my not sleeping, my whiskers are growing, and Iris will not want my face coming in contact with her more sensitive parts if it's covered by stubble. Perhaps I can get up early and find a razor and some shaving cream—Iris must shave her armpits and her legs—and I can have a shave. Hell, I'll need a shower after the cold sweats I'm experiencing. So if I get up early—wait. What time are we supposed to get up? Iris didn't mention it. Yet she wants me to drive her to work. What time does she have to be there? How much time does she need for getting ready? What time do we have to get up in order for her to have time to fool around with me *and* get ready for work? Maybe she set her bedside clock. I didn't see her set her bedside clock, the clock that now reads *4:34.*

I lie there quaking. I've never felt so panic-stricken in my life. I should never have let her talk me into staying over.

And Iris sleeps on.

And thousands more thoughts career through my head and hundreds of aches and pains zigzag through my body, and I grimace and fight every impulse to lurch and leap up and cry out.

At 6:30, I'm exhausted and yet shaking with anxiety and I can't stand it anymore. I slide out of bed. Iris lies fast asleep looking beautifully free of tribulations.

I marvel again at having been invited into her bed.

If only I could've slept!

I walk carefully to the guest bathroom. Bending down, I look into the cupboard under the sink and see a new toothbrush still in its cellophane package and a new tube of toothpaste, but nothing to shave with. I pad into the other bathroom. There's an electric razor on the vanity; I don't want that—too noisy, and I've never used one in my life. Feeling as if I'm violating her privacy, I look through the batch of feminine products, in the medicine cabinet and in the cupboard, and I do find a razor—pink and delicate—and even a small container of shaving cream.

Back in the guest bathroom, I start the shower. The sound of it is loud, muffled somewhat by the fan that comes on with the light, but I reason that, if it wakes Iris, she'll quickly figure out what's going on.

By seven o'clock, I feel a little better—clean and clean-shaven, with breath smelling of spearmint. I go back to her bathroom, pick up the roll-on deodorant I saw earlier and apply it. When I return to the bedroom, Iris is still asleep.

Naked and feeling more than a little randy, I get into the bed. She's turned away from me and I lean over and whisper her name in her ear.

"Ooo," she murmurs, as if she's in the middle of a dream. She moves her head from side to side and snuggles back into her pillow.

"Iris," I whisper.

"What?" she says, without opening her eyes.

"I think it might be time to get up."

"What time is it?"

"Just after seven."

She rubs her eyes, opens them and turns to face me.

"What time did we go to bed?" she asks.

"It was about eleven when you went to sleep."

"Eight hours! I *never* sleep for eight hours in a row. Are you sure?"

"Positive."

"When I've been drinking, I usually have to get up to pee three or four times. Jenkins, that's the *best* sleep I've had in years! I can't believe it!"

"I watched you a little. You sure were sleeping soundly. I've already had a shower and a shave."

"You're kidding!" She feels my face. "What did you use?"

"I found a pink razor."

She chuckles. "You *showered*. And I didn't hear a thing. You must've thought I was *drugged*. How did *you* sleep?"

"All right," I lie. "Woke up a few times."

"I can't get over how I slept. It must be you. Your being here. What can I say?"

Her good feeling and her compliment stir me.

"But I sure have to pee now!" she says, tossing the covers aside. She jumps up, yawns and stretches. "Keep the bed warm—I'll be right back."

"Iris?"

"Yah?"

"I'm feeling sort of over-anxious—maybe I should put the condom on myself."

"Sure." She goes into her bathroom and I follow her. She takes a little square package from somewhere and tears it open. "Here it is—just like a little hat—this way up. I'll just be a minute."

I go back to the bedroom where the daylight is coming in around the blinds. Worried that, in my wired state, I might come prematurely, I take a deep breath and try to think of banal things—dish towels, dinner plates, Egg McMuffins—as I roll the condom on. I hear her flush the toilet and blow her nose and brush her teeth and, a few moments later, the bathroom door opens and she returns.

"Hi there!" she says.

She lies back on the bed and I kneel at her feet, facing her.

"You don't want me to go down on you?" she says.

"Too excited," I say, between deep breaths.

"I'll need a pillow," she says, and she grabs the one I used, and, as I think, *This is it!* I help arrange the pillow length-wise under her, which brings what is normally *down there* to a point *up here* within a foot of my face.

I bend to her, not really looking but sort of looking and I feel the soft hair against my lips—"C'mere," I hear her say, maybe because she senses my lack of expertise in these matters or maybe because she senses my urgency or maybe because she's anxious, too. She's reaching out to me so, feeling a peculiar kind of relief, I move up to her, supporting myself on my hands like a man doing push-ups, and I give myself to the forth and back motion that missionaries have practised for centuries, and she wraps her legs around me and matches her parries to my thrusts, and she cries out, "Don't stop! That's it! Don't stop!" as if she's cheering me on. "Oh, that's so *good*! Oh, yes, right *there*! *Yessss!*" So tuned is she into what's going on in my body, she arches *her* body, pushing herself against me, driving me deeper, at the instant that I so joyously come.

I drop to my elbows, panting, and she hugs me, and all I can think to say, innocuous as it sounds, is, "I love you, Iris."

"I'm glad," she says.

I kiss her briefly on the lips and on the ear and on the neck.

"Oh, that tickles!" she says, kind of shrugging me away.

I move over and together we pull the pillow out from under her and I collapse beside her. I've used every ounce of energy I had left. I know it's stupid to feel anything but elated after what we've just done, but I feel confused.

I say, "You do like me, don't you?"

"Jenkins. You wouldn't be here if I didn't."

"Will I be able to see you again?"

"Of course! Are you trying to spoil what we just had?"

"No!"

"It sounds like you are."

"It's just that—when two people like each other—"

"Wait! Stop right there. You're beginning to freak me out here. I *had* a long-term relationship; I'm not looking for another one. I don't dwell on the past, and I sure am not planning for the future. It's the *here and now* that counts with me. Don't you think that's the best way to look at things?"

"I admit I'm old-fashioned ... and I could try looking at things that way."

"Good. So did we have fun or what?"

"It's been fabulous."

"And I can't believe how well I slept!"

"I'm really glad about that."

"Okay, I'm going to hit the shower. We've got about an hour—do you want to make us some breakfast?"

"I make a mean poached egg."

"Terrific! You'll find what you need in the fridge."

"One egg or two?"

"Two would be great."

She jumps up and heads into the bathroom, and again I forget to tell her to stand right there for a minute so that I can feast my eyes on her bare bosom, her flat abdomen, the fluid lines of her curves and contours. I lie there, fighting disappointment. It's natural, isn't it, to want to plan another date with somebody you like?

If I'd give my head a shake, though, I'd appreciate having fun without commitment. Isn't that what I should want?

Enough of this mournfulness, I tell myself, and I get up.

I'm saddened by the sight of yesterday's clothes, strewn across the guest bathroom vanity. I should've put them on hangers. I flush away the condom and put on everything but my stockings and my jacket. I look and feel shabby. I take my jacket to the closet beside the front door and hang it there.

Best to tackle breakfast—that might improve my mood. I go into the kitchen and find eggs and whole-wheat bread and margarine and a large frying pan. I run water into the pan and put it on one of the range elements and set the heat at *10*, just under *Hi*.

I can't hear the shower and I think she must be out of it. "Can I start them now?" I call.

She appears in the kitchen doorway, naked except for a

towel wrapped like a turban around her head, and a pink bra she's in the process of putting on.

"Wow, Mr. Executive Chef," she says. "Sure, go ahead."

I look at her. "Iris, you have a beautiful body."

"I'm glad you think so."

She hasn't yet fastened the bra and I pull it down.

"I haven't given these enough attention," I say. I take a breast in each hand and I bend to kiss one nipple and then the other. "See you, gals. Have a nice day."

"You're funny," she says, laughing, as she fits the bra into place again.

I watch her as she goes back down the hall. I still find it hard to believe that we've spent the night together.

I set the dining-room table and pour two glasses of cranberry juice. I sprinkle salt in the panful of water. I put four slices of bread in the toaster. I crack the eggs, one at a time, against the side of the pan and drop their innards into the water with a minimum of spill.

While the eggs cook and the bread toasts, I pour myself a glass of water and drink it as I look around. There are no pictures on the fridge and no sign of a calendar. I'm glad I don't have to see "Jenkins" written in the Wednesday square and something like "Eddie Vanderbilt III" in Thursday.

I take down two dinner plates from the cupboard. I butter the toast and set two slices on each plate. I place an egg on each slice—the two I give her are classic in shape.

"Ready!" I call, as I carry the two plates to the dining room.

She appears in a form-fitting blue floral top and hip-hugging deep blue slacks. Her hair is sprayed into a tousled look.

"This looks delicious, Jenkins," she says, sitting down.

"I couldn't find any coffee."

"I never touch the stuff. Makes me hyper. Sorry, you'd probably like some."

I sit opposite her. "I don't need it. This'll do just fine."

"Looks great. Some mornings, I get by on a mandarin orange. This is a treat."

We eat. I love the domesticity of this scene. I wonder if Iris has a camera, one we could set up to take a picture of the two of us at the table. Her cell phone is likely one that takes pictures—but that is the last thing she'd want. If you live for the moment, you don't reminisce.

"Do you have any travel plans in the next little while?" she asks.

"No. I have invitations to visit friends but nothing concrete yet."

"You should go. What's keeping you here?"

"Nothing, really."

"You know where I'd like to go again sometime? Disney World."

"I'm surprised. I would've thought you'd want to go somewhere more exotic."

"I know. People think it's an odd choice, but that's just me. I'd like to see what new rides they have and just hang out on a few of them."

I tell her I liked Epcot Center when I was there years ago. She tells me about the rides in the West Edmonton Mall. It seems weird to be sitting in her condo eating a breakfast I cooked an hour after we made love and talking about amusement parks.

And then it's time to leave. We stack the dishes in her dishwasher and put things away and every minute I want to stop her in her tracks and hold her but I know she doesn't want me to. At last, at the door, after I've put on my shoes, I do take her into my arms. I want to say I'll cherish this date forever but of course I don't say that.

"This has been marvellous," I say.

"It has been fun." She slips out of my grasp. "Come on. I don't want to be late."

I pull up to the Polo Park entrance she says is closest to The Lucky Elephant.

"I had a terrific time, Jenkins," she says, leaning over to kiss my cheek. "And thanks for breakfast."

"Thank you for dinner. And Iris, do start making notes."

"Notes?"

"For your book."

"Right! Jenkins, promise me you won't get all hung up, okay? Don't get into your head about us."

"I promise."

"Good. I'll give you a call. I won't say when, but I *will*."

She gets out of the car. I watch her go; she looks magnificent. I hope and hope and *hope* that she'll turn to look back at me. There are people headed for the same entrance and I worry that I won't be able to see her if she does turn. She reaches the door and I think she's already forgotten me. I see the door open and she lets a woman precede her into the mall and, at the last possible second, I see her turn and wave.

A Winter Night Long Ago

There is nothing worse than driving home in the morning after you've been awake for more than twenty-four hours. It's Thursday, I think, and everybody is going to work, well rested, ready to give 'em hell. Driving south on Route 90 away from the city toward suburbia, I experience a peculiar mix of feelings. I shake with fatigue but also elation. I despair of being old yet I haven't felt so *young* in years. I want to go over and over every minute with Iris and yet she encouraged me to believe that the experience itself—not the reliving of it—is all that matters. To dwell on this might plunge me into a gloomy void, something similar I suppose to the downer after a drug-induced high. It's difficult for me to concentrate on driving and I feel some relief when I see my house ahead of me on the bend of the bay.

The relief lasts about two seconds. My neighbour Hildy is outside in her front yard, a few feet away from my driveway. She stops what she's doing—pulling weeds or something—and watches my car approach. I'm going to be forced to speak with her. Feeling instantly more weary, I stop the car within a few feet of the garage and get out.

"Jenkins, there you are!" Hildy says, levelling an inquisitive stare at me. "We were worried. Are you all right?"

I'm sure I look awful. I'm too tired to come up with a brilliant story about where I've been, yet it seems like a bad time to tell the truth. I'm not even sure what the truth is. And even if I were sure, how would I describe it to Hildy? Dear, plump, curly-headed, heart-always-in-the-right-place Hildy?

"I'm—uh—fine," I say, trying to be vague. "Why?"

"You know how early Mark gets up. He noticed there was no car in your garage."

Ah, yes—they can see through the window on their side.

"I wondered if you'd had a chest pain or something in the night. You wouldn't drive yourself to the hospital, would you, Jenkins? You'd call us, wouldn't you? You know you can call us at any time."

"Yes, I know that, Hildy. I would certainly call you."

She keeps staring at me. The puzzled look on her face is asking the next question: *If you weren't at the hospital, where were you?*

"I was at a friend's," I say. "Had one too many drinks and didn't think I should drive … you know."

"Mark *said* that might be the case." One of her eyebrows shoots up. I swear she's thinking, *Here I've been worried sick about you and you've been out screwing around.* "I was pretty concerned. Glad you're home."

"Thanks, Hildy."

I turn to open the garage door. It feels ridiculously heavy. By the time I've driven into the garage and come out, Hildy is gone. She's likely inside calling Mark: *You were right, Mark. Jenkins had himself a one-night stand. The nerve of some people!*

What I notice as soon as I enter my house is an appalling stillness. It doesn't feel like the comfortable sanctuary it usually is. And, if facing Hildy was difficult, facing Barb is worse. I skulk past the dining room and head straight upstairs.

I'm desperate to shed my clothes, but, once I'm out of my sport jacket, I flop into my La-Z-Boy and lie back and stare. I think about Iris, the drug I was high on. I fix on the moments we had—in the bar, in the restaurant, in her bed. My god, I'm already reminiscing. Yes, here I am, wanting to hold onto the memory. Meanwhile, she'll go on to new experiences, enjoy them and never cling to a recollection of any one of them. As far as I know, she has no desire to repeat an experience, and the very idea of my wanting to see her again seems to her to be possessive.

If it's good for me to look at life the way she does, it's going to take a radical change. I am the product of a generation that got to know a partner sexually through incremental steps. To have the whole enchilada in one grand feast is mind-boggling.

... But it was *fun*, wasn't it? The whole fifteen hours with her was incredible, wasn't it? That gorgeous body of hers, so much younger than mine, so fit, so *female*! Beside me, over me, under me! Even the goddam tug-of-war over the TV remote seems exotic!

I get up from the chair and jauntily go down to the dining room.

"I suppose you know what I've been up to," I say to Barb. "I'm telling you, it was pretty wild and crazy. Can you believe, I didn't even have any pyjamas with me? I didn't even *floss*? I know, it's pretty hard to believe. Why didn't you and I ever do anything crazy like that?"

But we *did* do something crazy like that, something that wasn't recorded in any of the photo albums we religiously kept.

It was back in the mid-1970s—a February, I think. I'd been away on a leave of absence at Toronto's York University, working on my post-graduate degree. Barb regularly wrote to me, keeping me posted on how the kids were doing, how she was coping with the winter, the usual stuff of letters between spouses. We'd lived with her mother while I was launching my career in education, but, at the time I'm speaking of, we'd had our own place for a few years and, while I was away, Barb had the full responsibility of kids, house and yard. Her latest letter that February sounded an alarm:

> *... We are all a little ratty today. Brian is bored and Tracy can't find some stupid little shoe for the doll she was playing with. I'll survive I guess. I only wish I had some excitement to look forward to tonight.*
>
> *Jenkins, I have an uncontrollable urge for excitement at night and if I know I'm going out for some fun, I'm terrific all day. Gloria and Zack took me to the Montcalm last night for a few beers. Twice inside of ½ hour, two guys tried to join us when they realized I was alone. It gave my ego a boost I guess although I guess this will annoy you to hear it. I'm really scared, Jenkins, as I seem to have a fire inside me, a fire for wild, devilish fun. What am I going to do? I never drink more than 2 beers as you know how I am after just one! I love to be in a crowd all the time and I love compliments. I'm trying so hard to figure out what's wrong, Jenkins, we must talk about it more. I love these kids more than you'll ever know and I could never sacrifice their happiness for mine. I*

like my house, the car, and my daily obligations, but I still seem to have a big cavern in my life.

Sorry to have thrown this at you. I feel better just writing out my problems.

Well, I must close now and do some ironing. The new washing machine works great.

I'm dieting like mad and I guess that's why I feel so low.

I plan to go over to Gloria's next week and Patsy's as well, and before that you know there's the bonspiel in Pine Falls. Mom will be staying with the kids.

God, Jenkins, sometimes I feel I can't stand the sight of you, and then suddenly I can't live without you. WHAT IS WRONG?

I phoned home as soon as I received this, but by then Barb had gone to the four-day curling competition. I talked to Mrs. Mason, didn't mention Barb's letter—just told her I was going to catch a plane in a day or so and surprise both the kids and Barb.

It happened that I managed to book a flight that got me into Winnipeg on Friday afternoon. The bonspiel wasn't due to wind up until Saturday. Those were the days before cell phones, and I thought I'd wait until Barb made her nightly call to check on how her mother was doing with the kids.

The call came around nine o'clock.

"Jenkins!" Barb cried. "What are *you* doing there?"

"A little surprise," I said.

"Jenkins, you weren't supposed to be—oh, God, you didn't come because of what I ..."

"It was time I took a break."

"Jenkins … Jenkins, listen. We're out of the bonspiel. We lost tonight. Val wants us to drown our sorrows here but … Jenkins, could you come and get me?"

"Tonight?"

"Would you?"

"Your mother's gone home … maybe I could get her back or—I'll think of something."

"Oh, *thank you*!" She gave me instructions on how to find the arena and said she'd watch for me at the front door.

I made a call to our regular babysitter, sixteen-year-old Debra across the street, and was lucky to find her willing to come over. That saved me bothering Mrs. Mason. I explained to Debra and her parents how late I might be.

I started out around 9:30 in our Dodge station wagon, figuring it'd take about two hours to reach Pine Falls, a paper-mill town north of the city. It was a cold night. At least a foot of snow blanketed the countryside, but luckily it wasn't snowing that night and Highway 59 was mostly clear.

By then, Barb and I had been married for over fifteen years. Maybe it was good for a couple married that long to be apart for a few weeks, because I was anxious to see her. In other words, I wasn't going out there only because of her letter or because she wanted me to. The drive seemed long and the night bleak, but good old anticipation carried me.

The road from 59 into the town of Pine Falls—number 11—wasn't as clear or as easy to manage, so I slowed down. I had to watch out for wildlife and I had to be careful passing other vehicles. There was no moon and, except for a few lighted houses, both sides of the road were dark, and I focused on the path laid down by my headlights.

When I found the arena, there were still some people around—in fact, Val, Barb's skip, was waiting with her inside the front door. Because of Val's presence, our greeting was conservative—a quick kiss.

"That was awfully good of you to drive out," Val said. "Wilf wouldn't have done it, that's for sure!"

I felt the cold crisp air in the minute it took me to throw Barb's sports bag and broom into the back of the wagon. Barb jumped into the passenger side. Maybe she'd had more than one or two beers—I could sense something about her, something more than her gratefulness. Or maybe it was my excited view of her.

"Jenkins," she said, as we started back the same long dark way I'd come. "I can't believe you're here! Did it cost you a pretty penny to get a flight on that short notice? I'll bet it did."

"I can't wait to get you home."

We drove along, I trying to concentrate on the road. We were both quiet for a few miles, maybe because we were both pent up, or maybe because it was winter and our surroundings were anything but hospitable.

"Jenkins?" said Barb, in kind of a breathless voice.

"Yes?"

"Do we have to go all the way home?"

"What do you mean?"

"Couldn't we pull over and …"

"Sure we could!"

"Oh, God, really? Do you think—"

"Well, not here. Wait till we get to 59. We'll pull off on the—you know, the road to Patricia Beach, or something."

"We could go to Mother's cottage."

"A bit out of our way. And the road might not be plowed."

"And we don't have a key."

"Right!"

I drove on, now far too excited to be driving. I felt as if I was on a *date*. That was it. It felt *just* like a date. A date without restrictions—except maybe those imposed by the Highway Traffic Act.

We reached 59, turned south, and looked for a side road.

The one we picked was plowed, and the surface under the snow cover was gravel. The road dropped off on either side; there wasn't much of a shoulder and there was a danger of sliding down into the ditch. About half a mile in from 59, I pulled over as best I could and stopped and put the gear into Park and left the engine running.

"What if someone comes along?" I said.

"Who'd come by here at this time of night in the middle of winter?"

"I don't know—cops, a farmer on his way home, teenagers ..."

"We'll tell them we're married."

"I don't *feel* married."

"Neither do I!" She got up on her knees and gave me a deep, thorough kiss, the kind we hadn't indulged ourselves in for years. She unzipped her jacket and I went in under her sweater with both hands and undid her bra. "Oh! Your hands are cold!"

"Sorry—I need to warm them."

"On *me*?" She shuddered. "It's okay, leave them there."

I thought I noticed something in front of the car—it startled me.

"Look, a deer!" I said.

Barb turned to look. "Aww ... so pretty!"

The deer ran into the woods.

"What if a bear comes along?" I said.

"It wouldn't come close, would it?"

"I don't know."

"Your hands are warm now. Oh, that's nice." She kissed my face. "How are we going to do this?"

"I'll have to get out from under this steering wheel."

"And I'll get on top."

All this was said with gasping voices and me checking the road ahead and Barb checking the road behind, though the windows were fogging up. The threat of somebody coming along made this caper even more thrilling than it already was. Barb sat back on the seat to push off her boots and to wriggle out of her pants and her panties. With her jacket and sweater and the unfastened bra still on, she backed herself up against the door and the glove compartment to give me room to move to the passenger seat. I wondered how in blazes teenagers executed this—did they always move into the back seat?—maybe they were just younger and more flexible.

"My bum's getting cold!" Barb said.

I sort of leaned my shoulders against the seat and raised my hips and unzipped and pushed my trousers and shorts down and at last she arranged herself above me, one knee on either side of me, and she lowered herself onto me—"Oooooo," she breathed—and I warmed her buttocks with hands that now were hot.

"Oh, God!" She stopped moving. She was looking past me through the rear window. "Someone's coming!"

She didn't mean me, though that was close to being the case.

"Wait … It's all right," she said. "They turned off."

"Thank God," I whispered, as she resumed what she'd been doing.

She got into it with a kind of abandon I'd seldom seen before.

Maybe the stars were aligned a certain way that night—who knows why these things happen when they do? It was one of those perfect times.

We hugged in utter joy.

After a bit of housekeeping with facial tissues, we got back into our clothes. I realized we'd risk going into the ditch if we tried to turn around right there, so I drove up the road for a couple of miles till I came to a cross-road. Taking it carefully, we got back to Highway 59.

We giggled all the way home like two mischievous kids who'd gotten away with something.

Did we ever do anything like that again? Something kooky and different and outrageous? We must've.

Or did we, like most people, get too caught up in our proper lives? Too caught up in our roles as mother and part-time nurse and father and school principal? Taking ourselves too seriously to do something together just for the sheer fun of it?

Well, we could cherish that night. It went down in our history as the one and only time we did it in a car.

Back to Betty

The expected call comes from Tracy.

"So how was this one?"

"Iris is very nice. We had a good time."

"You drank, didn't you? I bet you drank and drove."

"It wasn't just drinks. We had dinner, too."

"Well!"

"She's thinking of writing a book. She wanted my opinion."

"So that was it? Drinks and dinner?"

I think of the times Barb tried to interrogate Tracy in this way and Tracy deferred to her health teacher's advice: *Your sexuality is yours. It's a private matter. As long as you are taking all precautions, there is no need to talk about it.*

"I took her home. That's about it, Trace."

"I have a feeling you're not telling me everything—but Dad, listen, we've decided not to buy that business. At least not right now. Our banker said the numbers didn't add up."

"So there is merit in being cautious."

"I guess."

And Patsy.

"Jenkins, what went wrong?"

"What do you mean?" I know *exactly* what she means. I've nearly forgotten Janie. That evening seems months ago.

"I talked to Janie this morning and she sounded *awful*. The last thing she wanted to talk about was her date with you."

"I met her son when I picked her up and we had dinner at The Keg. I think she enjoyed the meal. We compared notes on kids—that's about it."

"How did she look?"

"Good. She's put on weight—but so have we all."

"Jenkins, I don't mean to pry. You know I like you both—I've kept in touch with both of you all these years. It's just that she sounded angry—or upset—can you think of why that might be? Did you see any sign of it?"

"I'm not trying to be mysterious, Patsy. I know you care. Give her some time and I'm sure—if there is anything—she'll tell you about it."

And Gwen.

"Jenkins, dear, I want to apologize."

"Whatever for?"

"I know Iris can be aggressive, and I knew she'd like you. I thought we could have a nice dinner party, just a group of friends—I didn't think she'd go after you."

"Gwen, I enjoyed meeting her. If she likes me and she went after me, I'm flattered. We had a nice time. She's a fine lady."

"Are you sure you're not mad at me?"

"Positive."

"Barb's probably up there shooting *daggers* down at me."

And a telemarketer.

"This is Karen, and this is the third time we've tried to contact you to tell you you are paying too much in monthly charges on your credit card ..."

And Charlie.

"Jenkins, you missed a great day of golf."

"I let Hal know I wouldn't be there."

"You missed my birdie on nine."

"Sorry, Charlie."

"We're at the club as I speak, celebrating."

"Good for you."

"Jenkins, I know why you missed this afternoon. You spent last night with a certain young chick."

I don't answer.

"All I can say, Jenkins, is: you horny old devil, you. I'm going to take you out for a nice leisurely beer at the King's Head and you're going to give me a blow-by-blow description—if you'll pardon the pun."

"Charlie, congratulations on your birdie. I have another call coming in."

It's Brian.

"Dad, Tracy tells me you've been dating."

"Word does get around."

"Two dates with two different women."

"Yup."

"You *are* awful."

"Thanks, you old *loafah.*"

"She said one was an old girlfriend? And the other was a younger woman?"

"Yup."

"How young?"

"About the same age as your Naomi, I think."

"Dad, way to go!"

No call from Iris.

As the days pass, I feel the way teenaged girls used to feel, waiting for a call, getting more and more paranoid when it doesn't come. I think of going by her shop at Polo Park but then she'd accuse me of stalking her like that guy the night of Gwen's party. I think of calling *her*, but I'm pretty sure she doesn't want me to—she distinctly said she'd call me. She said, "I don't know when but I *will*." She emphasized *will.* And here am I, the elderly fellow who should've put this stuff behind him eons ago, *getting into my head about her* the way she told me not to. I picture her in a bar with some guy who knows something about filmmaking and she's telling him how much she'd like to make a movie. *"Just for myself, you understand."* I picture her sitting up at the bar, asking the male bartender to show her how to make a Copenhagen or an Iberian or a Dizzy Lizzy. Or she's in a restaurant—not Japanese; maybe Russian now—and she's talking the chef into going home with her to whomp up a pot of borscht. I imagine her with all kinds of people, mostly young and good-looking, laughing over drinks, over dinner, over some electronic game. They're all laughing at what she's telling them; not laughing at me, though—she's forgotten me and moved on.

As September comes, I immerse myself in golf. My game is getting worse and I want to improve before winter. I go to a driving range and shoot two buckets of balls. I spray the first few all over but gradually adjust my swing and start hitting them straight, 200 yards more or less down the middle. As soon as I get home, I jot down the things I think I did: *Left foot a little forward; feet closer together, short backswing; good follow-through, turning trouser fly toward green.* I spend that evening reviewing some tips in recent golf magazines.

The next day, after a good sleep, I head out to Victoria Beach with Clay and Charlie and Charlie's son-in-law Buzz. On the first hole, Buzz hits one about 250 yards down the middle. Clay puts one near the mound where the green used to be before this was turned into a 400-yard hole. Charlie sends his ball toward the bushes on the right, but it hits a tree and bounces into the middle of the fairway.

I go up last. I never felt better prepared. The weather is just right. I take out a new ball and a new tee. I pull the moose-head cover off my handsome driver. I take a practice swing. Ahh, just the way my dad taught me: smooth, not too hard, let the club head do the work.

I step up to the ball. *Remember to shift weight and turn the hips so that your fly faces the hole. Easy does it.* I swing.

The ball squirts off to the left about twenty feet and lands behind a bush.

I'm almost as far from the hole as I was to start with. I have to take a stroke to move the ball to a playable lie. Charlie is doing his best not to laugh. I pretend to be unruffled.

I muff my next shot. I understand what professional athletes mean when they say their confidence is shattered. In a few minutes, Tiger Woods has become Tigger.

Two more erratic shots. Is there no end to this masochism?

About a hundred yards out from the green, I think, *To hell with it!* and I give a nine-iron my all.

The ball soars in a wonderful rainbow-like arc. It comes down and bites into the green about two feet from the pin and rolls oh so close.

Do I wonder where that shot came from?

No.

That shot is the real me.

I have at least *three* more shots like that in the round, and they are enough to put me in a good mood.

Heading back to Winnipeg, we stop at the Half Moon for double-dogs, and I am still feeling pretty good at home that evening when my doorbell rings. I think it's likely a canvasser, somebody looking for a donation to a charity, and I think, *If it is, I'll give.*

I'm shocked by who it is.

"Liz!"

"Hello, Jenkins."

She stands there in a fuchsia-coloured summer dress, looking uneasy. There's no sign of brochures or receipt books, but I say, "Are—are you canvassing for something?"

"No, no." She seems nervous. "I didn't want to phone … I wanted to speak with you in person." She looks around. A car goes by. "Could I come in?"

"Oh, sorry, yes, of course."

She steps inside.

"Do you want to sit down?"

"No, no. I won't stay. I just wanted to apologize to you, Jenkins. I treated you badly. And well, maybe you haven't heard. Darcy has gone back to Amy."

"Oh. No, I hadn't heard."

"A few weeks ago. I realize now how stupid I was to listen to him. And I'm trying to get things back together. I'm hoping you'll forgive me. And I'm wondering if you'll accept an invitation to dinner at my place. Maybe this Saturday night?"

"Oh, Liz, I don't—"

"That's another thing. I'm not Liz anymore. Liz was a tramp. I'm back to being Betty."

"I—I appreciate your apologizing … Liz—I mean, Betty—could I let you know? Could I maybe call you tomorrow?"

"Sure. I know this is all pretty sudden. Look, you think about it, okay? And call me. I'd really like to make it up to you, Jenkins." Her hand is on the door handle. "Let's not wait till New Year's Eve to see each other again."

Wouldn't you know that half an hour later, as I battle with myself over what to think about Betty, the telephone rings.

"Hi, how're you doin'?"

"Iris! Long time no hear."

"I'm so sorry. I've been up to my ears. I had to miss two weeks of tennis, and when I squeezed it in this week, I saw Gwen and she asked me how you were and I thought, Holy crap! I told you I'd call you and I haven't called you. I gave Gwen some vague answer—I never talk about my private life."

"But you told her I stayed over that night."

"No, I didn't. I called her to thank her for introducing me to you—I should never have done that because she badgered me about details and I gave her absolutely none … except I let it slip that you make a great poached egg."

"That'll do it."

"I'm sorry if I caused you any embarrassment."

"Not at all." By now I'm reliving *that night* and wishing I'd slammed the door on Betty the way Charlie always did on me. "There were times when I wanted to broadcast to the world how much fun I had that night."

"We *did* have fun."

"I know they say you can never duplicate a perfect evening, but I sure would like to try for a close second. Is there any possibility …?"

"Good question. Work has been hell—all the fall stuff—our accountant is getting on our case—we have a staff problem that won't go away—and I've got a cold I can't shake—and hot flashes that're my own private global warming. And then there's my sister. She's been freaking me out—just a second, I've got a cough coming on." She must have put her hand over the phone because the cough is muffled. "You still there?"

"Yes. I think you mentioned your sister before. Does she live here?"

"And two cousins. God, don't get me started on *them*. They think *I'm* screwed up! My partner here at the store, Margot, was off for a week and that was … shall we say *different*? But I got through it. Now she's saying I should take some time off, but I can't. God, I wish I could, though. I'm so worn out, it's all I can do to drag myself to work in the morning and drag myself home to bed. And then I don't sleep."

I resist saying, *You need to sleep with me! Remember how well you slept with me?* The cynical side of me thinks she's putting up a thick smokescreen to keep me away.

"I'm sorry you're so busy and you feel so lousy," I say. "That's a horrible combination. But thank you for taking the time to call—it's really good to hear from you."

"I *like* talking with you, Jenkins. And we will get together again—when the worst is over. Just please don't pressure me to say when that might be."

"Don't worry. I won't."

"Thanks, Jenkins. You're being very good about—" She coughs again.

"Do look after yourself, Iris. And whenever you're ready, we'll have a nice dinner somewhere."

"I'd like that. Bye, Jenkins."

As night falls, I miss her and tell myself there's a spark there, it isn't just the sex. In the middle of the night, I wake and think about how empty my life is and I hear noises I'm sure must be home invaders. In the morning, I wake up thinking how pathetic I am to wait around for somebody like Iris.

And after breakfast, I phone Betty and accept her invitation to dinner.

It dawns on me as I walk up Betty's steps that Darcy Jephson has been living in the house since I was here last. I worry about imagining him in every room and I wish I'd never agreed to this dinner. But when Betty answers the door wearing an apron over her denim shirt and slacks, I think how pleasant she looks and at least I'm going to have a dinner that I don't have to cook myself.

"Hello!" she says, and she chuckles. "How *are* you, Jenkins?"

I hand her the bottle I've brought in its liquor-store brown bag. "Bouchard's Beaujolais. I hope it works with …"

"Thank you! It will, it will. I've made a meat lasagna."

Her apron is white with a pattern of drawings printed in shades of Delft Blue. There's a grazing cow, a windmill, a boy and girl kissing, tulips, a boy skating.

I say, "Dutch motifs, aren't they?"

"Yes—friends in the Netherlands sent it last Christmas

with a matching oven mitt and pot holders. I think they think I'm a cook or something. Jenkins, come in."

"Thanks." The living room is pretty much the way I remembered it, except for a painting I'd never seen before. Perhaps it was a gift from Darcy. "Good likeness of Elvis."

Betty laughs. "That's Paul Lemoyne, a sculptor. It's a print of a painting by a Frenchman named Ingres."

So I suppose Darcy is a goddam connoisseur. "Sorry—the sideburns—the nose ..."

"Yes—I see what you mean—but Ingres, the painter, died in 1867." She laughs again. "He's considered one of the French Romantics. Well known today for his nudes. Could I get you a beer? Or a mixed drink? Maybe you'd like to mix one yourself."

"Sure." I want something strong. "What do you have?"

"Come into the kitchen and have a look."

"The lasagna smells terrific," I say as I follow her.

"Thank you. It should be ready in about half an hour, if that's okay." She opens a closet door.

What I see is a garbage can with one of those dome tops and a flap you push open to deposit waste inside. Wedged in beside it are a vacuum cleaner, a broom and a mop. Above these are shelves that hold packaged light bulbs, cleaning solvent, an opened six-pack of Bud Light, a carton of twelve cans of ginger ale, and a two-litre bottle of root beer. There is an assortment of cleaning rags alongside an opened box of heavy-duty garbage bags.

I say, "Is the liquor ...?"

"Oh, sorry, that's the mix." She opens a cupboard above the kitchen counter. "There's some—oh, that's sherry—I know I have—what's that?"

"Dark rum."

"Yes—do you like it?"

"Do you have Diet Coke or Diet Pepsi?"

"Oh, that's what I meant to stop at the drugstore for! I knew there was something else."

"It's okay.... Oh, it looks like you have some Johnny Walker Red Label."

"What's that?"

"Scotch."

"Where did *that* come from?"

"It'll do fine. Do you have any club soda?"

"Uh—no."

I take the bottle down from the shelf. It's about a third full. *Probably goddam Darcy's leftover.* "I'll have water with it. Where are the glasses?"

"Right here."

Betty opens another cupboard. There are water tumblers and juice glasses. I find one highball glass and ignore the chip in it.

"Ice?" I say, feeling as if making a drink has become one of life's most laborious tasks.

"That I have," says Betty, opening the freezer above the fridge. "Do you see it in there? The open bag behind the frozen peas."

I do see it, between the frozen vegetable mix and the ice cream. I reach in and feel ice—a boulder-sized chunk that must be several cubes stuck together. I pull it out and we both laugh.

"I'm not very well prepared, am I?" she says, suddenly turning red. "I'm sorry. I've been a bit out of sorts—but I do have a nice meal—I just have to make sure I serve it at the right time."

Running hot water over the chunk and using a spoon to chip away, I create two drink-size pieces. "What are you going to drink?"

She checks the oven. "I'll just have—I don't know—one of those ginger ales."

I mix my own drink and pour a can of ginger ale into a tumbler. "Should I maybe open the wine? Let it breathe, as they say?"

"Good idea," Betty says, beginning to assemble a bowl of salad.

"Um … do you have a corkscrew?"

The lasagna is so delicious that I have a second helping. The wine is good despite the little pieces of cork floating in it. Betty couldn't find the corkscrew—a Swiss army knife that used to belong to one of her husbands. I used a paring knife to dig the cork out but fragments fell into the bottle. Betty did come up with wine glasses—champagne flutes, to be accurate—and we made a little game out of using dessert spoons to snag the cork bits.

We talk about cooking—how lazy you can become when cooking only for yourself. I play down the number of times a week I fry steak or eat Chunky Soup. Betty begins to make a reference to Darcy's culinary skills, catches herself, blows her nose, jumps up, tosses off the apron and suggests we move to the sofa.

We sit down with our wine and a minute later she sets her glass down on a table and takes mine and sets it down too. Just as I'm thinking about how I can politely leave, she leans into me and presses her mouth against mine. I've been thinking way too much about Darcy, even imagining him behind a curtain snickering at everything we say. Now I find it difficult to resist this woman's unbuttoning of my shirt and running one warm hand over my bare chest. There is no interrupting phone call this time. She's on her knees now, leaning over me, kissing me hungrily, and I'm caressing her behind.

I don't know if it's my relatively recent experience with

Iris or my contempt for the way Betty treated me back in February, but I feel a crazy confidence even though I think I'm taking advantage of a needy woman. Somehow, it seems perverse to be enjoying her active mouth, her fingers tweaking my nipples, the unflinching response of her flesh to my hands. And I sense that she's every bit as well equipped for where this seems to be heading as Iris was.

"Betty," I whisper, as she licks the curve of my jaw.

"Oh, Jenkins, Jenkins," she breathes.

"Do you want to have sex?"

She barely hesitates, her hand inside my shirt moving from my chest hair to my bare shoulder, as she says, "Oh, Jenkins, of course I do."

I undo a couple of her buttons. "Right here," I whisper, "or do you want to move to a bed?"

"Oh, Jenkins," she says, staying close to me, "not tonight. I can't. Not tonight."

I'm surprised, confused, and yet glad in a weird way, and I pull her shirt up and unbutton it all the way and she grabs hold of my head with both hands and straddles me and pushes herself against me as she says into my ear, "I'm just not ready yet, okay?" as everything about her cries out, *I'm ready! I'm ready!* and then she breaks from me and flops back on the sofa and says, "We need a little time—well, *I* need some time," and she covers her face. Minutes later, she says, "I promise you: When I'm ready, you'll be the first to know."

Twilight

October comes and I've heard nothing further from Iris. I hoped for at least a report on her health. I would've been grateful for a quick call like "Jenkins, I can't talk right now but I just thought I'd say *Hi*." I become resigned to never hearing from her again and I try to convince myself that it's all for the best. From the little she's said, her family sounds as complex as Janie's. And Iris is at the peak of her working years, whereas I'm long past mine—I have no interest in what it takes to keep a business like hers functioning. And that one night—was it really that much fun? What about all those sleepless hours while she was totally out of it? And perhaps most trying is her dilettante nature; the only spot where our interests intersect—a liking for books—is minor at best, nothing on which to base a friendship or—dare I say it?—a love affair.

I've heard nothing further from Betty, either. In the sober light of the morning after my dinner at her place, I saw her as unstable, maybe even deranged, or—just as bad—having a difficult time accepting Darcy's defection. I'm already planning my excuses for turning down an invitation to Bea Branwell's next New Year's Eve party.

And so I gradually readjust to my solitary widower's life, and one Tuesday morning, just after Thanksgiving, I go to my local Safeway to pick up some apples, some skim milk, a frozen spinach pizza and some medium cheddar cheese. I seldom see anyone I know at Safeway, but on this morning I hear my name.

"Jenkins?"

Behind one of the new small-sized black carts in the aisle I'm passing stands Maude Sanderson, my neighbour at Victoria Beach. She is the widow of Alec, who died some four years ago. We partied together many times over many summers; Barb and I went to Florida with them for a few winter vacations. The Sandersons were part of the group that used to organize beach celebrations whenever somebody's kid was getting married. Maude and Alec hosted the bash put on for Tracy and Clay way back in 1993, the same weekend Barb's mother died. Maude, my age or a year or so older, looks good—trim, with her white hair shaped in a flattering way. I stop to speak with her.

"Jenkins, how *are* you?" she says, with a look of concern, as if she might've heard I have a dreadful disease.

"I'm fine, Maude." I glance at her cart, in which the prominent item is an upside-down box of Post Spoon-sized Shredded Wheat. "Do you know, I read that it's common these days for people who want to let others know they're single and available to walk supermarket aisles with their shredded wheat inverted like that? They call them cereal daters."

"Oh, Jenkins, you just made that up."

"No, no, I read it somewhere just recently."

She laughs. "Well, I *am* single and available, aren't I? I just never think of it that way."

"What are you doing in this part of town?"

"My optometrist is out this way. I was just there and I thought I'd drop in here for a few things."

"Well, whether you're advertising for companionship or not, how would you like to go for coffee after you're finished here?"

"Oh! You know, I think I'd like that, Jenkins. Where would you like to go?"

"Bread and Circuses? Over on Corydon at Lilac?"

"Yes, I know it. Meet you there in half an hour." She chuckles and turns the shredded wheat right-side up.

My sudden invitation is not intended as a way of getting over Iris—not entirely, anyway. Maude is a good-looking woman and, now that I'm into this dating thing, I kind of like it. And I think Maude will be relaxing in her way, unlike Betty or Iris or Janie.

Once we're at Bread and Circuses, settled at a window table with our large medium-roasts and our date cookies, Maude says:

"Are you coping all right, Jenkins? I know it must be difficult for a man, what with the cooking, the dishes, the laundry, on top of all the yard work. You're still in your house, aren't you?"

"I am, but so are you."

"Yes, but you know, I had an agent in just this week. I think the time has come to put it on the market. You don't think the time will come, but it does, you know. It does."

"I'm sure you're right."

"Do you do your own cleaning?"

"I have an excellent couple of women come in once a month. I asked one of them what was the best way to clean my sweaters and she took them home and washed them for me. So I'm pretty spoiled."

"You haven't been down to the lake much this year, have you?"

"No, but Tracy and Clay have been down a lot." We are at that stage of succession. The Masons passed the place on to Barb and me, and it was a great place for the kids to go in summer when they were growing up. Now the next generation is gradually taking over.

"I know how it must be for you. Seeing Barb everywhere she used to be—getting dinner ready in the kitchen, reading the paper over coffee on your deck. It's not easy, I know. Even with our kids there so much, I'll still walk into the tool shed and expect to see Alec, working on something or sneaking a bottle of beer." She laughs. "He used to like sneaking his bottle of beer, didn't he?"

I had no idea Alec liked to do that, but I say, "Yes."

"I saw Tracy there on Thanksgiving and she said they were closing up, but she said you like to go out a week later for one last check around. Are you going this weekend?"

"Sunday, yes. If there's something you'd like me to get from your place …"

"Oh, that's very kind of you, but I want to go out—it's something Alec and I always did after Thanksgiving—it's so peaceful when everyone else has packed up for the season."

"Then why don't we go together? I'll drive. Save on gas and all that."

"Oh, Jenkins, would you? I'd be happy to pack a lunch and we could have sort of a nice little picnic—outside if it's nice out, inside if it isn't. Does that appeal to you?"

At this moment, having Maude Sanderson accompany me to the beach on Sunday afternoon seems like a splendid idea.

In stylish prescription sunglasses, a hip-length black leather jacket, a white scarf and black slacks, Maude Sanderson sits beside me as I drive my Pontiac G6 to Victoria Beach. The day is sunny and cold, meaning we'll likely have to eat the lunch indoors. What Maude prepared sits in a large red cooler on the back seat. As we drive along, she looks out at the bushes and trees and says:

"I used to like the autumn colours. Such a variety of yellows and reds. But look—most of the leaves are on the ground now and the branches are bare. A reminder of the brevity of life. Did you know that Jackie Mortimer went into the hospital this week?"

"No! Not Jackie! She's been the dynamo in our group for so long ..."

"They saw something on an x-ray and when they went in they found a lot more .... And I'm sure you knew Alf Gorman's back on chemo."

"I didn't."

"He was such a big man—he's half the size now. Poor Alf."

Maude continues to give me updates on the beach people who are ill or recently deceased and I realize how out of touch I've become. Much as I appreciate the information, I hate to dwell on it and, when she gets to some names I barely know, my mind wanders and, at the cut-off to Patricia Beach, I recall once again the winter night when Barb and I parked. It seems important to think about some life-affirming event.

Magically, at that moment, Maude says, "Remember when a gang of us went skinny-dipping after the Adult Dance?"

I'm not sure how Maude moved from death and dying to skinny-dipping, but there, that's another wild and crazy thing we did!

"Wasn't that fun?" I say. "Do you remember what year it was?"

"No, but we were a lot younger and easier to look at."

"We'd all had lots to drink. It was oppressively hot that night, especially in the Club House. After the dance, we all went out on the beach—I think we were going to walk home along the sand instead of the road because it was cooler by the water."

"And can you believe it, Jenkins, we took our outer clothing off and went into the water in our *underwear*."

"And when we got in so far, we took off our underwear and waved it in the air as if we were completely liberated."

"Or completely insane!"

I remember Barb staying close to me, jumping into my arms, and how easy it was, with the buoyancy of the water, to carry her with her legs around my waist, and I remember the lusty sensation of feeling our nether nakedness juxtaposed underwater with oblivious friends all around us bantering with each other.

"It was incredibly dark that night," I say. "No moon, no stars. It was hard to see anything in any detail."

"Most of the men moved closer to Vicky, hoping to get a look at her, because she had the biggest bosom."

"Poor Vicky," I say. She's another who's gone from our midst.

And just like that, we're back to the dead and the dying.

There's really nothing to do in the cottage. Tracy and Clay followed all the procedures for turning off the water and locking up the bikes and cleaning out the freezer and the fridge and covering the furniture and leaving nothing of value visible. I look into the little back room I slept in before Barb and I were married—it's now a storage area. I stare with awe at the narrow cot—now loaded with boxes of odds and ends—and wonder how two of us were able to lie on it that night Barb sneaked in to see me. I smile at the innocence of it all; at the time, I considered it one of the most sexy events of my young life.

I move one or two things, throw some ancient Pringles into the garbage, tuck in the duvet on my bed to keep spiders out. I look out the master bedroom window at the lake, remembering Barb's walks up the path to Scott Point. I remember all the times we took the kids down to the beach. How fleeting those childhood years were! My thoughts go further back, to our dating days and our walks hand-in-hand along the sand to Government Pier. I recall one blustery grey day when the cold lake water lapped over the pier and Barb wasn't dressed warmly enough and I took her into my jacket the way I used to do when we wanted to be close.

At one o'clock, I go outside, across the lawn to the path, and I enter the Sanderson yard through the front gate. I walk up the front steps, across the deck and into the screened porch. Maude has the sliding main door partially open but I tap anyway.

"Come in, come in!" she says, playing the jolly host. "Jenkins, I meant to tell you, since the water's off, please feel free to use our outhouse. I don't want you going into the bushes." She laughs.

"Thank you, Maude. I hate to admit it but I've already used it—Alec gave us permission twenty years ago."

"Then you noticed we still have the Charles-and-Diana tea towel mounted on the wall. Despite what happened to them, I've always thought it gives the place a little class." She snickers. "Oh, Jenkins, look what I found."

She holds up the *TRACY AND CLAY* banner I made for the party back in 1993.

"You've kept it in good shape," I say. "I thought *we* had it."

"I did, too! And there it was in the back of a closet. Whatever happened to the *Congratulations* part?"

"Well, you may remember I did a *Congratulations* LOUISE AND JEFF banner for our very first pre-wedding party. Because it took me two whole days to draw, and everybody loved it, Barb had me cut the names off and re-use *Congratulations* each time we put on another party. So we still have it, but it's wrinkled and tattered now, much like me."

"Nonsense! You've looked the same for twenty years."

"I'll take that as a compliment—and since we're handing out compliments, I must say, Maude, you look ravishing today."

"Oh, Jenkins, you must be going blind. Now, everything is on the table. These are tuna sandwiches, those are ham and tomato. Pickles, carrots, cheddar, celery. Oh, and apples and bananas. I have a thermos of coffee, but would you like to start with a beer?"

"Maude, this is magnificent! Yes, I will have a beer—but only one. I'll have a coffee chaser."

"All right. Now, please sit down and help yourself."

As we eat our delicious lunch, Maude reminisces about the pre-wedding party she and Alec had for Tracy and Clay. "Bea and Donald's son-in-law—what was his name—Sean brought that lovely baron of beef. And remember Matt and Letitia played guitars? And here none of us knew Barb's mother was dead in your cottage. She'd played bridge with us only three weeks before! She could still bid and go into club convention at ninety-five. What a neat old lady! And poor Barb knowing before she came over that Mrs. Mason was dead and not letting it spoil Tracy's party. I remember when the party was over going to your place and seeing Mrs. Mason lying there so peacefully. Tracy and Barb and I had a good old cry."

"It was a strange day, all right. I'd driven to Winnipeg in the morning and picked Barb's mom up from the home and she talked the whole way out here."

"And now poor Barb is gone, too."

We're silent for a few moments.

Maude says, "Do you think Barb and Alec have gotten together up there, Jenkins?"

"Quite possibly, Maude, but they have an awful lot of others to choose from."

"Do you ever wonder why things happen the way they do?"

"Of course. We all do, don't we?"

"I mean, who would have thought, five years ago, that Barb and Alec would be gone and you and I would be left."

"No one can predict these things."

"Do you think it happened for a reason? Do you think the Good Lord is trying to tell us something?"

"Like what?"

"Oh … I don't know."

"I think the Good Lord knows you make delicious sandwiches and He knew I'd be hungry at one o'clock today."

"Now you're making fun of me."

"I don't mean to. I just know I used to read a lot into things but maybe it's best to take things at face value, not try to second-guess, just enjoy what we have."

"Maybe."

"Someone once said, 'You know you've reached maturity when you realize you can't do a damn thing about anything.'"

"I'm not sure that's a healthy way to look at life, Jenkins."

I think I can hear an edge creeping into my voice, and maybe that's due to disappointment over Iris, and I'm a fool for giving *her* any thought at all. I'm trying to ignore Maude's none-too-subtle overtures. Yet what would be wrong with giving in to them? Here is a pleasant woman who is healthy, capable, attractive, and who doesn't mind spending time with me. Except for our respective kids, we are both pretty much alone in the world, and wouldn't it be marvellously convenient if each of us took on the care of the other? As we have today—I providing her transportation, she providing my lunch? Or is she a trifle too morbid?

Maude talks about some of Alec's possessions; she likes to dispose of a few items every time she comes to the lake, or at least take them into the city. There are books she's picked out, and I'm free to go through them before she gives them away and pick any I want.

"That was a fantastic lunch, Maude, thank you," I say, standing up and carrying my dishes into the kitchen. "I'm going to help you clean up."

"No, no, Jenkins, you take a look at the books—I'd appreciate that more. They're over there on the sofas."

They are war histories, military biographies, books on wildlife. I've seen most of them before on previous visits. I have little interest in them, but I can't reject them all and hurt Maude's feelings.

"Okay, I've picked three. Do you want me to take the rest to the car?"

"Oh, would you, Jenkins? There's a dear."

On the way home, Maude says, "You know, Jenkins, I sometimes think Barb and Alec were the lucky ones."

"How so?"

"They had someone who loved them to the very end."

"You have your son. My son's in Toronto, but I have Tracy here."

"It's not the same, though, is it? I was by Alec's side nearly every minute of every day. In the hospital, they wheeled in a cot for me and I stayed with him even at night."

"That was wonderful of you. I went home every night—the nurses recommended it. They thought I'd sleep better without the commotion."

"Do you know what Alec wanted two days before he went back into the hospital for the last time?"

"What?"

"He wanted to have sex."

"Really?"

"And I obliged him the best I could."

"That was nice of you."

"You see what I mean when I say he was the lucky one?"

She talks about some of our friends who were "lucky" because they died before their spouses. I don't exactly see things that way, but I don't argue. We're approaching the city, following the perimeter highway to Route 90, when she says:

"Are you going somewhere warm this winter, Jenkins?"

"I hadn't really thought about it. I don't mind winters here as much as some people. I did used to like the trips Barb and I took to Arizona—something nice about golfing in January."

"You should rent a place in Mesa. This year you can get some wonderful deals with the financial situation the way it is down there. I'm going down next month, renting a place in Leisure World. Who knows, I might put my house up for sale while I'm away."

As we drive, I wonder if she's hinting that I could go down there and stay with her. She doesn't come right out and say it.

"We don't have a lot of time left," she says. "We need to go gracefully into our twilight years."

We drive along without speaking, both staring ahead as if we're visualizing our twilight years. It seems sensible for someone like me to spend those years with someone like her. And yet …

We pull up to her house in River Heights. We both sit for a minute, as if we're mesmerized by our visions.

"I'll carry those books inside for you," I say at last.

"Oh, thank you, Jenkins."

The house is a two-storey stone structure with mock balconies outside each of three upstairs windows. Maude carries her cooler up the front steps and unlocks the front door. I make four trips inside with piles of books. The house interior, which I've seen at social functions over the years, is tastefully furnished, but it now seems tomb-like, everything lying in state.

"I'll be leaving now, Maude," I call from the door. "Thank you for the wonderful lunch."

She comes to me from some other room. "Oh, Jenkins, the lunch was nothing. Thank you for the drive and the lovely companionship." She looks at me in kind of a shy way. "May I kiss you?"

We both blush. She reaches one hand around the back of my neck and gently pulls me close. Her lips are soft. It's the kind of sweet kiss I craved when I was in my teens, as sweet as Barbara's on our first date those zillions of years ago.

Space Mountain Sideshow

I enter my house and pause in the dining room.

"Maude thinks you were lucky," I say to Barb. "How about that? It's an interesting way to look at …" I don't finish the sentence.

I go into the living room and sit there for a while. My house is smaller than Maude's but no less unanimated.

Eventually, I go upstairs and turn on my computer. I scan the list of items in my Inbox and write a message to my travel agent. It's Sunday and she won't answer until Monday, but that's fine. She likes to be called LA—after her initials, not the city—but I always call her LAX—not after the airport but as a little joke—she's the *opposite of lax* and has been my travel agent for more than thirty years.

I do a lot of stewing, wondering if I might be off my rocker.

In the morning, about half an hour after the travel agency opens, I check my e-mail. There's a message from LAX:

Mr. Jenkins, are you NUTS?

But she attaches the flight information I need. I send her an answer telling her I'll confirm arrangements within an hour or two if possible.

I'm jittery when I make the phone call and deflated when I hear the recorded voice: "Hi there. Sorry I missed your call, but I'll get back to you just as soon as I can."

I leave a brief message, not giving any details, just saying it's urgent. I spend the next hour or more in total agitation, walking back and forth and up and down in my house. Twice I check my phone to make sure I'm getting a dial tone. It's after 11:30 when the phone rings.

"Hello?"

"Jenkins, what's up?"

"Do you still want to go to Disney World?"

"Yeah, sure—"

"Would you go with me? My treat?"

"When?"

"Tomorrow?"

"Jenkins, you know I can't just leave here like that."

"You said your partner told you to get out of there for a while—you deserved a break."

"That was weeks ago."

"We're not talking a long while. Five days tops. You skip tennis tomorrow and we take off."

"It's tempting ..."

"Would you ask Margot?"

"Hey, you know, it's crazy enough to make sense. She's out right now—back after lunch. I'll talk to her. I can't promise anything."

"Try to get back to me soon, okay? I have to confirm the bookings."

"You have bookings?"

"I have a great travel agent."

I think I'm going to have to suffer through more hours of stewing but she calls me twenty minutes later.

"I couldn't wait for her—I called her cell. She said, '*Go for it*!' So I've got a helluva lot to do to get ready, but I'm calling your bluff."

"That's fabulous!"

"Jenkins. I can't believe you."

"I can't believe me either. Hey, we'll have fun. I haven't been there in years."

"Listen, I've been making notes."

"What?"

"Notes? For the book? And I wrote a couple of sample chapters. I've made a copy of everything for you. You can read it on the plane."

We say we'll talk on the phone later, about how we'll get to the airport and what time, and she assures me that she has an up-to-date passport. When I get off the phone, I pump my fist: *Yes*!

I run downstairs to fetch my suitcase, not feeling any of the pains that usually plague my feet and my knees. I phone LAX instead of e-mailing her and she assures me that I am nuts but our tickets would be waiting for us at the check-in counter. She booked the nicest hotel in Disney World and she tells me not to bother renting a car because I won't use it. I change two appointments, cancel the newspaper and leave a message for Hildy to take in the mail.

Okay, I've opted for a wild and crazy trip instead of resigning myself to my twilight years—is that so bad? Maybe Iris will get fed up with me after five days, and *then* I can worry about twilight. God, five mornings with Iris are better than a winter in Tahiti! So what if I don't sleep? All right, I know twilight is coming, but *not yet*.

I spend an hour picking out and rejecting clothes—what does a guy like me *wear* in Disney World? I think for a minute about Disney World—up to now I've thought only about Iris—my friends like Claude and Gillian would not be caught dead in Disney World. Well, as a matter of fact, I *like* Disney World, God damn it! And I'm going to have fun there.

I have a shower to calm myself down. Putting off the clothing selection, I go through my shaving kit, making sure I have all the vital things, like little blue pills and deodorant and blood pressure pills and razors and shaving cream and dental floss and—where's that nice cologne I used to have?

I hear a car door slam. I look through the bedroom window: Tracy and Mason. *Shit!* Have I forgotten another commitment? Am I supposed to take Mason to gym and keep her here till the morning?

I'm still naked from the shower—barely dry—and I toss on my old dressing gown. I go to the top of the stairs.

The door opens.

Oh, no, I think, feeling like an irresponsible teenager, *how the hell am I going to explain Disney World?*

~

Hey, Mum & Dad!

I'm writing this on Iris's iPhone! Cool! Iris & I had a game of air hockey on it! Can I get one? Maybe for Xmas?

Mum, Iris has these killer designs on her fingernails. Witches, cats, bats, ghosts. In black and orange for Halloween!

She's writing this story. About a girl. She let me read some of it to see what I thought. It's fun!

Thanks for letting me come here. Awesome, having my own room!

Did most of Epcot yesterday. Papa freaked on the trip to Mars.

Iris and I are waiting in line for Space Mountain. Did Papa tell U she was a gymnast once? Artistic, not rhythmic. She did a hand-stand right here while we're waiting! The people in the line cheered. Another woman did a cartwheel. So of course I had to do an aerial.

Poor Papa missed it all. He's back at the hotel having a snooze.

Mum, Iris rocks!

Luv U!

Mason.

Acknowledgements

Many thanks to Wayne Tefs, whose editorial suggestions freed the narrative from shackles I had imposed. I'm also grateful to Heidi Harms for her astute copy-editing. And thank you to the staff at Turnstone Press for magically turning my manuscript into a Turnstone book.

Small sections of *Dating* appeared in much different form in the following: "Retrieving," a short story originally published in the anthology *Beyond Borders* (Turnstone Press and New Rivers Press, 1992), and republished in *North Dakota Quarterly* (Fall 1992) and in the collection *Accountable Advances* (Turnstone Press, 1994); "Confession (September, 1960)," a short story in *Windsor Review* (Spring 2004); "Tracy and Clay," a short story in the anthology *A/Cross Sections* (Manitoba Writers' Guild, 2007); "Experiencing the joys of not skiing," a feature article in the *Winnipeg Free Press* (November 3, 1996); and "Why golfers golf," a feature article in the *Winnipeg Free Press* (August 10, 1997).